*TO THE WORLD,
THEY WERE THE GLITTERATI....*

SERENA—The world's most glamorous model. Her fabulous features reflected every fantasy. Would anyone ever look beyond her pretty face to the woman within?

MALLINI—The world's greatest photographer, a temperamental genius tormented by jealousy and unfulfilled desires.

MARVENA—Mallini's devoted wife. She would do anything to make her husband happy—even if it meant sharing him.

GORDON—The brilliant designer. He created the world's most expensive jewelry, but he expected anyone who wore it to pay a high price.

HELEN—The powerful head of the world's top modeling agency. She could see through anyone, except the person who mattered most.

*BUT THEIR PRIVATE LIVES WERE
TARNISHED BY THEIR
SECRET OBSESSIONS!*

THE
GLITTERATI

Charlotte Payne

A DELL BOOK

Published by
Dell Publishing Co., Inc.
1 Dag Hammarskjold Plaza
New York, New York 10017

Dell ® TM 681510, Dell Publishing Co., Inc.

ISBN: 0-440-13067-0

Reprinted by arrangement with
William Morrow and Company, Inc.
Printed in the United States of America
First Dell printing—July 1981

To
Jean Patchett Auer

PART 1

ONE

The small shiny-clean brass plate on the door was inscribed with a single name, "Mallini," etched in block letters. The door was set in the brick façade of the four-storied, double-width town house, to the right of the large sliding garage doors. It was finished with black lacquer, as shiny as the nameplate.

The thick wooden stable doors of what had once been the carriage house took up the major portion of the ground-floor front wall. At one time the floor had been used for housing horses and carriages.

The carriage house and stables and sleeping quarters on the ground floor had been converted into a reception area, shooting galleries and dressing rooms. On the first floor there was a ballroom-size salon where the Mallinis did their considerable entertaining. Also on the first floor were an anteroom, a supper room, a kitchen and pantry. The Mallinis—Antonio Mallini and his wife, Countess Marvena Florenzo—lived on the third and fourth floors. Marvena sometimes but seldom used one of the galleries on the ground floor. She had an attic studio with skylights, north and south, and a darkroom. Marvena specialized in nude male studies.

Mallini and Marvena were not idle people. By nine o'clock in the morning Marvena was in her studio and Mallini was on the ground floor either photographing or developing or discussing future sittings with clients. Mallini did not go to clients. They came to him.

Antonio Mallini was one of the most famous photographers of high fashion and beauty, not just in New York City, but in every fashion center on the globe. Mallini was innovative, and he was creative. He was one of the first to use the human body as if it had movable parts. Until Mallini, it had been nothing less than sacrilege for a model's knee to disturb the line of a skirt. Mallini had models not only thrust their knees into the skirts, but at such an exaggerated angle as to look distorted. Commercial clients drew back in horror, and fashion editors were leery—until Sybil Singlehurst, the editor-in-chief of *Milady*, the leading American fashion magazine, featured his brilliant new concepts.

Mallini had it made absolutely. Neither his enemies nor his rivals could topple him. But on this particular morning he was close to the point of bringing about his own downfall.

Mallini was too agitated to settle down. There were a number of things he should be doing. He should be setting up, testing his lighting for the sitting coming up. He should be taking the jewelry that was to be photographed that morning out of the safe. He should be checking the fashions that the jewelry would be worn with. He was doing none of that. For the dozenth time he went to the darkroom.

"Things coming along, Carmine?"

Carmine, Mallini's chief assistant, didn't turn his head from his work. He wondered if Mallini realized how many times he had asked him that that morning.

"Almost finished with this batch," he said. "Better knock before you come in next time. We're about to start a new one."

Mallini hovered in front of the line of negatives clipped on a wire to dry for a minute and then turned and went out. Carmine shook his head in resignation at his two helpers and made sure the door was tightly closed. It was going to be a bad day.

Mallini started toward the rear shooting gallery, changed his mind, turned around and walked back across the front gallery and into the reception room. He had no business there, but he'd gone in there that morning as many times as he'd gone into the darkroom.

Miss Olsen, the receptionist, tensed every time he came in her view. She tried to pretend she wasn't watching him. But she saw every detail—how much brighter and more black and darting his eyes were than usual, how he kept blinking them and tightening his lips and clenching his hands. He was so hunched within himself that he seemed even smaller than he really was. She would have sworn that he was sweating, from fear.

"Everything lined up?"

"Yes, Mr. Mallini." She quaked when she said it. She didn't want to set him off, and one wrong glance could do it.

Mallini walked over to the elevator. Miss Olsen stole a look at him. Her heartbeat quickened at the sight of his small dark figure, his tumbling short black curls. Silly as it was, considering the difference between Mr. Mallini and her, she had to lower her eyes when he flashed his quick smile that showed his small, white, perfect teeth. She knew he didn't realize the effect of that smile.

Miss Olsen wished that the countess would come down. Mr. Mallini's wife was the only person who could soothe him when he was upset.

Mallini was abjectedly miserable, and Miss Olsen was right, he was afraid. He was afraid he might be losing Gordon. Gordon had never given him as bad a night as he had given him the night before, and he had —

given him some bad nights. Usually he made up to Mallini before they parted, but last night he hadn't.

Mallini was totally in love with Gordon, totally committed to him. He knew that Gordon didn't feel the same commitment. But he knew that Gordon liked him, knew, in fact—or, until the night before, had thought he knew—that Gordon wouldn't give him up for anything. But Gordon took great pleasure in teasing him and taunting him and torturing him. Mallini cringed, remembering one of Gordon's remarks the night before. "My God, Tonio, I think your little dingledangle's shrunk. I wonder if Dr. Nash could do something for you with silicone." And he'd laughed.

Mallini knew that it amused Gordon to keep him uncertain, on the edge of hysteria and subservient. He also knew that, even if he didn't like him, he would still keep up their association. He wanted the access Mallini had to each season's fresh crop of females.

Gordon had been frank to point out that Mallini had an open field to draw from between the models that he worked with and the society matrons and debutante daughters he photographed, whose husbands and fathers were willing to pay the $30,000 fee demanded by the great Mallini for a sitting that lasted two hours —not to mention the titled European puddle hoppers who thought it the height of *ton* to get laid by somebody whose name was always turning up in the columns of *Women's Wear Daily*. Gordon laughed at himself and belittled himself as quickly as he laughed at and belittled others, and he was laughing at himself with that remark about *Women's Wear Daily*. He did a perfect imitation, dipping a shoulder, flicking a limp wrist, eyebrows raised and eyelids lowered, the picture of female ennui: "It's the only paper I ever pick up, dahling. I have it sent to me wherever I am."

It had been a difficult evening from the moment Mallini arrived at Gordon's place. For the most part,

Gordon had been withdrawn and silent. He made it obvious that he was only putting up with Mallini's presence. Mallini was more miserable with every moment that passed, and he was devastated by the way the evening ended. "Don't sniff around me, little she-dog," Gordon had said, making what he said worse by using his term of affection for Mallini. "Set up my water pipe, and then leave me."

TWO

Serena felt her smile stretching as she stretched her limbs, arms high above her head, hands making fists. Her long, lacquered nails bit into the skin of her palms, and she opened her hands wide, stretching them, too. She loved the feeling of extending herself like a cat to the limit of the elasticity of her body.

She looked down onto the street below, only the gauzy window curtain shielding her naked body, wondering idly which of the taxis might be the one that would pick up Stephen and take him to the airport to catch the plane for Boston.

Poor Stephen. He hadn't wanted to go, but she had finally gotten rid of him. He thought she was going to live with him in Cambridge while he finished his last year at Harvard. Had she ever really planned to do that? She brought her arms down and drew her shoulders up, thrusting her buttocks out in a deep arch, stretching her back. At any rate, the pretense that she was serious had given her a reason for leaving school and coming to New York.

She turned and looked around the comfortable room. She was going to have to find a cheaper place than the Carlyle, now that she was going to be in New York for a while, maybe forever. She had a little more than $3,000 with her. She had had to clean out her savings account and checking account in Atlanta and use her school cash—which was supposed to have gone into an account at the school—in order to get that much together. She had a trust fund from her Grand-father Carr, but her father managed it, and would un-til she was twenty-one. Her father certainly wouldn't let her use it to finance a stay in New York.

But she was going to worry about all that later. The first thing she had to do was get on with the business of becoming a model. That was her new plan.

Serena douched and had a warm, satisfying bubble bath. She dressed and went out, bought the latest copies of *Milady, Vogue* and *Harper's Bazaar,* brought them back to the room, and called room service and ordered coffee. She turned the pages of the magazines, looking at the names of the photographers the photographs were credited to—only those in the middle sections of the magazines. She knew, from things she'd heard her mother say, that the middle section was what was called the editorial section and that the photographs in that section were far more important than the rest of the photographs in the magazine, which were paid ads, "commercial" photographs. Any dress designer or Seventh Avenue wholesaler or cos-metics company or whatever that could pay the tab could have an ad in the magazine. Space in the edi-torial section was not to be had at all except at the discretion and choice of the editors of the magazine. The pictures in the editorial section were the maga-zine's "statement," the editors' endorsement from among the newest offerings in dress design, makeup, airstyling and all the perimeter things, such as diet and skin care, of what they deemed would combine to assure a woman that she was the latest word in fashion. Editorial work for the fashion magazines was the prestige work for models. Their commercial work was their bread-and-butter work.

Serena recognized very few of the names of the photographers that the pictures were credited to, and most of those she did recognize she was familiar with only because she had seen them in credit lines before.

But there was one whose name was almost a household word—Antonio Mallini. It was a name as well known as Avedon's or Scavullo's.

Serena Carr had had the best of everything all her life. She had seldom ridden in a public taxi or on a commercial airline. Her father had his own fleet of planes as well as cars. She had had her path smoothed in front of her by servants and retainers every day of her life from the moment she stepped out of her bed in the morning until she returned to it at night. Her past life hadn't taught her how to start anywhere except at the top—in this case, Antonio Mallini.

Serena looked up Antonio Mallini's address in the telephone directory. She brushed her teeth and brushed her hair and looked herself over in the full-length mirror on the bathroom door. She made a face at herself and turned away from the mirror. What did she think she was qualified to criticize or change? She didn't know what a model-in-the-raw would be expected to look like.

She left the hotel and started walking to Mallini's East Sixty-ninth Street studio, watching the numbers until she came to the street address listed in the telephone directory.

Serena looked at the façade of the big barn of a building, wondering if she could possibly have made a mistake. She pushed the bell that was discreetly inset at the side of the black-lacquered door and waited. She expected a buzzer to sound, releasing the lock, but instead, the door was opened.

A small, dark-eyed, nervous-looking man stood in the doorway, looking up at Serena. She recognized him from pictures she had seen of him as Mallini.

A plump gray-haired woman came hurrying to the small foyer.

"Oh, Mr. Mallini, you shouldn't trouble yourself answering the door!" The woman looked at Serena with some exasperation. "Yes . . . ?"

Serena looked from the man to the woman. Were they going to keep her standing in the door? "May I help you . . . ?" the woman asked. The man was simply staring up at her still, his face changing as he stared. The lowering black frown left it. His eyes opened wide. His eyebrows lifted. His mouth opened slightly.

Mallini, looking at Serena, felt as if he were seeing, conjured up before him, the answer to his prayers. He knew what she had come there for, but he didn't look for model material in her; he could make a model out of a broomstick if it were worth his time and trouble. What failings he couldn't correct on the person he could correct with the camera or in the darkroom. His interest in the girl was for quite another reason. He had never needed somebody as badly as he needed her.

"Come in," he said. "Come in, Miss . . . ?"

"I'm Serena Carr."

Even the accent and intonation were perfect! Well bred, a little aloof. A delightful, childlike smile lit up Mallini's whole face. Serena thought he looked as though a light had been turned on inside his head.

"Come in," he said again.

Mallini turned and walked from the foyer into the reception room. Serena followed him. Miss Olsen hustled along beside them as if she were trying to get between them.

"Are you from one of the agencies?" she asked Serena nervously. "I wasn't expecting anybody from any of the agencies. You don't have an appointment. Mr. Mallini doesn't see drop-ins."

In her discomfort, Miss Olsen had forgotten entirely that it was Mallini who had asked Serena to come in. She scurried to her desk and to the chair behind it. "I'll have to get some information from you. . . ."

"Never mind, Miss Olsen," Mallini said. He continued past the reception desk toward the galleries to the rear. "Cancel me for the morning," he said.

Miss Olson's mouth flew open. "But, Mr. Mallini,

Miss Singlehurst herself is coming for the sitting this morning. The photographs today are for the center spread."

"Push the sitting down until the afternoon. Tell Singlehurst I'm busy working on a surprise for her."

Miss Olsen stared after his disappearing back in utter dismay. She didn't want to make the call to Sybil Singlehurst. She was as much intimidated by the editor-in-chief of *Milady* as everybody else was. She picked up the telephone gingerly, as if it were the instrument itself she was afraid of.

Mallini hadn't broken his step, and Serena still followed him. He called out for Carmine and his other two assistants. The set must be made ready, the darkroom cleared for work. He wanted every plate developed as it came out of the camera, and the rolls of film as well.

The vast high-ceilinged spaces of the studio had held an almost funereal silence—Mallini's soft-soled slippers had made no sounds of walking on the concrete floors, and no sounds ever came from the darkroom when it was closed for developing. Now the place was full of sound and activity. Fresh white paper of almost cardboard thickness was rolled down like a window shade from the twelve-foot-long rod bracketed eight feet high on one wall. It was rolled down to the floor and out on the floor for a length of eight feet. Lights were placed around the edges of it, switched on, switched off, moved an inch or two, moved a foot or two, switched on again, switched off again, some moved again. A large camera on a tripod was placed at the edge of the white paper on the floor, dead center. A small handheld camera and plates for the large camera were placed on the shelflike sheet of metal that braced the legs of the tripod. A bench of natural straw with curved sidearms of the same natural straw was placed in the center of the white paper.

Everything was done at Mallini's order, from in

back of the large camera, now and then from a study of the set in the small camera. Sometimes he dashed about, making adjustments himself.

Serena stood off to one side, watching. When she and Mallini had left the reception room and entered the gallery, Mallini had stopped and turned to Serena. "You came because you want to be a model?" he asked simply.

"Yes." Serena wasn't able to answer him with as much confidence as she would have liked. Everything around her—the people, their attitudes, the place, the business of the place—was as alien to her as if the door that had closed behind her had whizzed her to another planet.

Mallini put his hand on her arm in a reassuring gesture. "We'll make some test shots," he said. "Have you ever posed before?"

"I've had my picture made."

"Not modeling?"

"No."

"Good. I won't have to unteach you anything."

Mallini looked foreign-born to Serena. She had expected that he would speak with a foreign accent. He spoke Italian to Carmine and the other assistants, but he spoke English to Serena in a low, rather husky voice without a trace of accent.

While Serena was standing about, a woman of about thirty, very chic, very businesslike, came in. "I'm Margo, Mallini's stylist," the woman said to Serena. "The dressing room is this way." She walked on, and Serena, glad for something to do besides stand about, followed her.

Margo opened a door in the wall opposite the set, reached in and snapped on the lights. There was such a glare of light after the dimness of the gallery that it took Serena a moment to adjust her eyes to it.

The dressing room was an oblong space with closets at each end. Both long walls were mirrored. Along the length of one wall there was a dressing table with four small benches pushed beneath it. There were hand mirrors and magnifying mirrors and combs and brushes, all spotlessly clean, on the dressing table, and a double row of all kinds of makeup and applicators and cleansing creams. Serena had never seen such a variety of makeup.

Margo took a number of things out of one of the closets, costumes for various times of the day—suits and blouses, evening gowns, hostess gowns and at-home pajamas, trousers with matching jackets and capes—and hung them on brackets set into the mirrored wall opposite the dressing table. She checked them all for wrinkles and hang marks. Apparently they passed her scrutiny, for she left them and went to a bureau set inside the closet at the other end of the room and took gloves and scarves and bags from the drawers and arranged them on top of the bureau. From the same closet she took shoes and boots and placed each pair under the costume it was meant for.

"Aren't you going to do your makeup?" she asked, finally taking some notice of Serena.

Mallini came in just then.

"Miss Carr is here for test shots," he said. He took Serena by her arms and stood her in front of him and looked at her from arms' length.

Margo turned an unbelieving look on him. "Test shots . . . ? You mean she's not booked? I assumed she was booked for the sitting."

Margo had never known Mallini to do test shots. Test shots were done by photographers just starting out, who did them free for the experience, or by photographers who were established but not kept busy —or were on the way down—who did them for a nominal fee. Antonio Mallini doing test shots . . . ?

Mallini didn't answer Margo. He was looking at Serena from all angles—back, front and both sides. Serena had never felt so ill at ease. Finally, he settled his attention on her face. "Do you know how to put on makeup?" he asked.

Serena was wearing only a light lipstick. "I don't use much," she said.

Mallini smiled. "Do you mind?"

"Mind . . . ?"

"I want to put some makeup on you."

"No, I don't mind."

Mallini pulled out one of the low benches near the center of the dressing table, and Serena sat down. He studied her face in the mirror. Margo brought a small huck towel folded lengthwise to a width of about three inches and bound Serena's hair back from her face with it, the edge of the fold following her hairline, leaving her full face exposed.

Mallini tested makeup colors on the back of his hand, cleaned them off and tested others, all the while studying Serena's face in the mirror. He worked quietly and intently while he studied her and the colors. Then, having made his selections, he became animated. "Look at the skin, Margo!"

"Divine," Margo said calmly.

"No base! No powder! Nothing! I want the clear skin tones!" He picked up a small container of amber-colored eye shadow and a small brush. "Close your eyes, please." Serena closed her eyes while he applied the eye shadow. When he finished, he toyed discontentedly with three eyebrow pencils in shades of brown that he had selected, but he couldn't make up his mind about them; none of them really pleased him. "Not brown," he said to himself. "Brown's not right." Finally, he penciled her eyebrows lightly with a regular lead writing pencil. Then he lined her eyelids, upper and lower, with black liquid liner and brushed black mascara on her eyelashes. He danced about so much while he was working on her face that Serena was sure he was going to smear everything. But he didn't.

Serena couldn't believe what she was seeing in the

mirror. With the severe towel framing her head, and her eyes made up, her face looked unfamiliar and exotic. She lowered her eyelids, looking out from under them at herself in the mirror to see the effect. Mallini laughed delightedly. The girl had the right instincts.

"Fantastic eyes! Fantastic! Great space! The space between the brows and lashes is great! Look how much space, Margo!"

"Divine," Margo said.

Mallini outlined Serena's lips with a crayon wax pencil the color of burnt sienna and then, with a tiny sable brush, applied a lipstick of the same color but lighter in tone. All the while he worked he was alternately leaning toward Serena and peering hard at her, his nose not five inches from hers, and rearing back on his heels at such an extreme angle to get a longer view that he seemed in danger of falling on his back.

"Fantastic!" he kept repeating. "Fantastic! The face is pure Botticelli! Isn't the face pure Botticelli, Margo?"

"Divine," Margo said.

Margo was Main Line Philadelphia, and "divine" was her word for everything that wasn't "rubbish," but it wouldn't have mattered if she had been repeating "fiddlesticks" because Mallini wasn't listening to what she said, and she knew it.

"I want the daytime things first," Mallini said to Margo. "First the Geoffrey Beene tweed." He turned his head over his shoulder toward the door and called out, "Carmine! I want brown velvet! The darkest brown! A strip across the back! I'm going to do beige tweed on natural straw on brown velvet on stark white!"

He picked up a hairbrush, removed the huck towel from Serena's head and started brushing her hair, which was cut in lengths, the longest part at the back well below her shoulders. He stopped brushing abruptly and gaped with wide-flared eyes and open mouth at the hair on Serena's head and then at its reflection in the mirror as if that were the first time he'd seen the hair that he'd been brushing or even seen that it was hair. He looked surprised and then dumbfounded, and then a seething flush of anger suffused his face. He grabbed her hair in both hands—one still clutching the brush—gathered it at the nape of her neck and then threw it out over her shoulders. He grabbed it together again and pulled it back from her face. Then he dropped it out of his hands as if it were too hot to hold and threw the brush on the dressing table. His anger turned to black despair. It filled his face, his whole body; he sagged with it. "It's not going to come up," he said.

Serena was first shocked and then bewildered by the precipitous change in Mallini. He'd been ecstatic about her just seconds before, and now he was thoroughly irritated with her, even contemptuous of her. And why her hair had brought about the change in him she couldn't imagine. Her hair was one thing she had never had to worry about. It was thick, had good body and was always lustrous and shining. It wasn't curly, but there was a soft upward turn at the ends so that her face and throat were framed by wayward swirls. It was the color of wheat.

"It's not going to do what?" she asked Mallini.

"It's not going to come up!" Mallini screeched, his voice at the opposite end of the scale from its former huskiness. He turned sharply from Serena to Margo, as if he couldn't expect Serena to have enough sense to understand, but Margo would. "It's not going to come up!" he screeched at Margo. "The lights will kill it! The velvet will kill it! It has no color! It has no life!"

Margo shrugged.

Serena thought that would be the end of that; her modeling career was over right there. She felt a terrible sinking disappointment. She expected Mallini to tell her to go home and forget it.

But Mallini picked up the hairbrush again and turned to her, brandishing it as if it were a weapon. She thought for a minute he was going to strike her with it. "It's ruined!" he shrieked. "Whoever put that dye on it killed it!"

His tone of voice made his words an accusation. Serena got indignant then because the accusation wasn't fair. "My hair isn't dyed," she said. "This is its natural color."

Mallini glared at her, his whole body bristling with unbridled fury. "Natural color isn't color!" He spit the words out. "Natural color is *shades* of color!"

"My hair has been this color ever since I was born," Serena said. That wasn't quite true, but it was near enough to the truth for her to say it without feeling she was lying. It had been lighter until she was about seven. Then it had darkened to the color it was now.

"Shall I put the clothes back in the closet?" Margo asked.

"No!" Mallini shouted. "The Beene tweed!" He threw the hairbrush wildly. It smashed to the floor and skidded to a stop in the far corner. "I'll start with the tweed!" He wheeled around, his face set and limbs rigid, and disappeared through the door as if gusted out on a whirlwind.

Margo closed the door. "You'll have to get out of your things," she said to Serena.

Serena let out a long-held breath as she got up from the bench. "Is he always like that?" she asked.

Margo smiled. It was the first time Serena had seen any expression at all on her face. "Always," she said.

"It doesn't seem to get to you," Serena said. "I don't know how you can stand it."

"If I let it get to me," Margo said, "I'd have ulcers on my ulcers."

"Is it just ranting that doesn't mean anything, like his bark is worse than his bite?"

"No, my dear, and don't ever make the mistake of

thinking it is. And take my advice, and start as of now
not letting his tantrums get to you. If you let them
get to you, you'll start trying to second-guess him about
what might bring one on. There's no way on earth of
second-guessing him. There's no pattern in his be-
havior except that you can expect a tantrum at any
time, for any reason . . . or none."

"Does he act like that in front of everybody?"

"If something happens that puts him in a rage. He
plays no favorites."

"And everyone puts up with it?"

Margo smiled again. "He's Mallini," she said.

Margo got Serena into the Geoffrey Beene tweed
and accessorized it—except for jewelry. The blouse of
the suit was of creamy white-beige silk foulard. The
fabric of the suit itself was of a deep thickness, made
more textured by the heavy nubs of the tweed. There
was a leather-colored suede vest under the unbuttoned
jacket. The vest was a little too loose. Margo pinned
it in at the back. Otherwise, the outfit might have been
made for Serena. "Thank God you've got good shoulders," Margo said.

"What can we do about my hair?" Serena asked.

"Not a thing!" Margo said emphatically. "The last
thing in this world I'd touch is your hair. Sometimes
Mallini likes it if someone tries to help solve a problem, and sometimes he doesn't. I've learned not to
take chances. Anyway, I wouldn't know anything to do
except cover it up. It looks perfectly fine to me. Don't
worry about it. Mallini will figure something out.
He'll put the wind machine on it or something."

"Is it always going to be a problem for me, if I *do*
get started as a model . . . my hair?"

"Why would it be a problem? Do you know how
many hair colorists there are in New York City?"

"I don't want to have my hair dyed."

"You don't have to have it dyed. Have it streaked."

* * *

The jewelry that was to be photographed was in ornate black and gold boxes. It had been brought from the safe and placed on a baize-covered table near the set. The initials GK, in embellished gold, were centered on top of each oblong, square or oval box. The boxes were black velour. The gold trim looked to Serena to be real gold leaf.

When Margo brought Serena out to the set, Mallini opened all the boxes. After some deliberation, he chose a two-inch-wide heavy gold bracelet set with huge uncut amber stones. He put it on Serena's right wrist, studied the effect, left it on her wrist. He took a knuckle-length, inch-high, free-form hammered gold ring from its satin bed in its box and put it on her finger, shook his head quickly and took it off. He was as impersonal toward Serena as if she were a department store mannequin.

Mallini studied the various articles of jewelry, trying to see them with Gordon's eyes. What would Gordon choose to go with the bracelet? He didn't want to make a mistake. Gordon's taste was so definite. He decided to photograph each piece separately, give each its own singular, undiminished importance. Gordon surely couldn't find any objection to that.

Mallini was everywhere—on the set with Serena, tilting her chin, angling her head to get the best shot of her throat, lifting a shoulder, lowering a shoulder, darting to the lights, strengthening this one, lessening that one, clicking them off, clicking them on, moving them; demanding constant change in the lighting, depending on the way Serena moved, the way the lights hit the planes of the jewelry, the planes of her face and her arms and hands—all the while running back and forth to and from the camera and singing out instructions to Carmine and the other assistants. Serena had never seen anyone move so fast and seemingly in all directions at once. He was laughing out with pleasure one moment, shouting impatient instructions the next and so sunk in concentration the next that he didn't hear people when they spoke to him. When he looked in the camera, he was so concentrated that it seemed he might assume liquid form and flow through it as if it were a funnel.

Not a word was said about Serena's hair during the entire sitting, throughout all the changes of costume and jewelry, all the changes of background and props, all the changes in the lighting. Sometimes Mallini pulled it tightly back from her face; sometimes he had the wind machine blow it; sometimes he brushed it down full front to the camera while her face was in profile. Anyone who hadn't seen his temper fit would have thought he was entranced with Serena's hair.

Even Serena could hardly believe that Mallini's rage had happened. He was as exuberant and extravagant in his praise of her as he had been angry and despairing before. She had never known anyone in her life who acted, and spoke, with such utter lack of all reserve. "Exquisite!" "Marvelous!" "Too marvelous! Too marvelous!" "Perfect! perfect! perfect! Don't move! Don't breathe!" He would forget himself and speak to Carmine in English and to Serena in Italian. "She can't make a wrong move," he said to Carmine. "Every move she makes works. It's the jewelry I have to watch . . . to get the best angle on the jewelry."

Serena was more puzzled than anything else when she heard him say that. It seemed to her that she wasn't doing any moving, that every change in her position was one he made for her. He even told her when to raise her eyebrows. But he was obviously pleased, and that was what counted, she guessed.

Mallini was, in fact, too happy to try to hide his excitement. He was more excited about Serena in the camera than he had been with Serena in the flesh. Singlehurst would adore her! But what was really im-

portant to him—what made all the difference to him—
was the fact that Serena would be a magnificent show-
case for Gordon's jewelry. Gordon's clunky jewelry, his
newest "overstatement," would become the height of
chic if for no other reason than the fact that Gordon
Knightsplit had designed it. Serena Carr's long-col-
umned, elegant throat, her narrow, bony wrists, her
long, tapering fingers with their long, strong nails and
her not overfull bosom were perfect for it. Her high,
chiseled forehead, the prominent cheekbones with the
hollows beneath, the straight aristocratic nose and
strong jawline, softened by her slightly petulant
mouth, combined to form the perfect face for it. The
class that oozed out of her every pore showed clearly
in the camera. And class was of extreme importance,
for Gordon was a self-confessed snob. He was the only
person Mallini knew who was eligible to succeed Noel
Coward.

The test shots were finally finished. Serena, more
exhausted than she had ever been in her life, was in
the dressing room with Margo having a lunch of deli
sandwiches and coffee.

"I don't know how I can be so tired," Serena said.
"I'm too tired to eat."

"You'd better eat," Margo said. "If you don't, you
won't be able to get through the afternoon."

"Aren't models coming to do the real photographs?
From things you've said, I gathered they were."

"Oh, yes, the models booked will be coming. But so
will Sybil Singlehurst, and if my guess is right, Mallini
will want her to see you in action."

"Who is Sybil Singlehurst?"

"She's the honcho at *Milady*. There's no one like
her. You'll see what I mean when you meet her."

THREE

"Ms. Olsen!"

Miss Olsen's hands shook on the phone.

"This is Sybil Singlehurst!"

It was only a voice on the phone, Miss Olsen told herself. A voice couldn't come out of the phone and hit her.

"Did you want to speak to Mr. Mallini, Miss Singlehurst?" she asked weakly. "I'll see if Mr. Mallini—"

"No! I don't want to speak to Mr. Mallini! I want you to give Mr. Mallini a message! Tell him that I will not be at the sitting this afternoon! Tell him he's to go ahead with the *minor* pieces of Mr. Knightsplit's collection . . . the *minor* pieces! I will be at the studio tomorrow morning at nine o'clock sharp . . . *nine o'clock* . . . to do the *important* pieces! Thank you!" She cut the connection.

Miss Olsen's hands were wet when she hung up the phone. She pulled a Kleenex from the box on her desk and dried her palms. She'd known that call was coming. She'd known she wouldn't get by with leaving a message with Miss Singlehurst's secretary. She'd known Miss Singlehurst wasn't going to like having her arrival at the studio put off until the afternoon, surprise or no surprise. Miss Singlehurst wasn't at anybody's beck and call, and she wasn't about to let anybody think for a moment that she was. That was what all that *minor* pieces and *important* pieces was about.

Now Miss Olsen dreaded seeing Mr. Mallini. He wasn't going to like Miss Singlehurst's message any more than she had liked his.

Mallini was in the darkroom with Carmine. When the black-and-whites were developed, he selected three of them and sent them by messenger to Gordon. With the photographs he sent a note: "These are nothing compared to the flesh-and-blood original! Dinner at seven. My place or yours?"

Gordon returned the note by the same messenger who had brought it, but he didn't return the photographs. Under the words Mallini had written—Mallini's script small and precise, Gordon's sprawling, with flourishes—were the words "Dinner at eight. My place."

The sun came out on Mallini's world. Quivers of pleasure ran through him. He read the words over and over as if it were a love letter. He could feel Gordon's down-filled kidskin mattress on his bare flesh. He shivered and tensed as if already feeling the coming on of an orgasm. Gordon wouldn't be withdrawn and bored tonight.

Miss Olsen pushed her work aside and sat idle, nursing a pet that she felt she was entitled to. Mr. Mallini knew that Miss Singlehurst attended sittings only for the center spread of the editorial section of *Milady*. And not always those. It depended on the importance she was giving the spread in a particular issue. Sittings, for the most part, were handled by the editors of *Milady*, not by the editor-in-chief. Miss Singlehurst's attendance at a sitting wasn't to be taken lightly, and Mr. Mallini knew it. But when he got in one of his moods, you could be Sybil Singlehurst or you could be the lowest man on the totem pole—he did what he pleased. He ought to have some consideration for other people. Look at the condition he had put her in by the way he'd been acting up. She was getting one of her nervous headaches.

She'd put off telling him until she had to, she decided.

But Mallini was on top of the world. He smiled that quick smile that made her knees go weak. "Good show, Olsen!" he said. "Good show!"

Miss Olsen went back to her desk, trembling with relief. She took back every bad thought she'd had about him earlier.

FOUR

Mallini's two booked models were Zoe Bergson and
Shari Holliday. They both arrived made up and ready
to work. Serena had seen them often in magazines
and on television commercials.

The women were as opposite as two people could
be. Shari Holliday was a tall, willowy honey-blonde
with long hair and a casually pretty face. She had a
girl-next-door, tomboyish look. The down-to-earth girl-
next-door was Mallini's latest radicalism. Shari Holliday was the first of a new breed, and she was great.

Zoe Bergson didn't fit into any category. She had a
long skinniness, not fluid like Shari's, but all angles.
She had short, black, tossed hair and flashing, snapping violet eyes framed in heavy black lashes and
deeply arched pencil-thin eyebrows. She had a short,
snippy nose and a red slash of a mouth. Her movements were either short and jerky or sweeping. She
didn't do anything in halfway measures. Her personality matched her looks. It was as vital as her violet
eyes.

The same clothes that Serena had been photographed in that morning were used that afternoon.
Shari treated the clothes and the jewelry with great
respect and care, taking off her shoes or boots before
stepping into dress or skirt or trousers, and tying a
scarf over her face and head so not to get makeup on
the things that had to go over her head. Zoe shrugged
and twisted herself into them. She never covered her

face. She tossed the jewelry around as if she were playing ball with it.

"Doesn't she know that jewelry's real?" Serena asked Margo at one point.

"She knows," Margo said.

When Shari was on the set, she was an earnest and conscientious worker. Zoe's attitude seemed to be catch-me-if-you-can. Mallini put up with it. In fact, he seemed to enjoy it.

Mallini never had to instruct Zoe or Shari. That morning he had been forever tilting Serena's head, tilting her chin, tilting her shoulder, pushing her elbow closer to her body, bending her wrist. Working with Zoe and Shari, he would simply call out, "Less elbow"; "I don't want to see the underside of your chin"; "Give me a three-quarter . . . that's too much"; "You love it. Show me you love it"; "You don't know you're wearing it"; "Give it some movement. Don't let it lie there dead." It might have been a foreign language to Serena, but the models knew exactly what he meant.

They were always in movement except for the split second when Mallini clicked the camera.

"How do they know when he's going to take the picture?" Serena asked Margo.

"It's something you learn," Margo said. "When you've worked long enough with a photographer, you know when you're giving him what he wants."

"How long is long enough?"

"Not long. A few sittings. Sometimes not more than one. A photographer's not going to waste his time with a model he can't work with."

"Then when does a model get the chance to learn how to model?"

"I don't think modeling is something that can be learned. I think either it's in you or it isn't."

"What they're doing out there now certainly wasn't in me this morning."

"You weren't all that bad."

"I sat there just like a clod! He had to put me in every position he photographed!"

Serena spoke with such emphatic self-reproach that Margo laughed. "That was your first time in front of the camera," she said. "But I might as well warn you, if he keeps on having to pose you, it'll soon be 'Bye-bye, Serena.' "

When the sitting was over and Shari left, Zoe lingered a moment. "See you tomorrow?" she asked Serena.

"I don't know."

"She'll be here," Margo said. "Mallini told me to put her down."

"Oh, God! Another lamb to the slaughter!" Zoe said, laughing. She turned to leave. "See you then," she said to Serena, and left in a rush, singing out over her shoulder toward the darkroom, her voice trailing an echo behind her, "Tally-ho, Mallini-o!"

Mallini had asked Serena not to leave until he had a chance to speak to her. After Zoe had gone, he came from the darkroom to the dressing room where Serena was waiting.

"I'd like you to meet the designer of the jewelry we're photographing," he said, "and him to meet you. Are you free for dinner tonight?"

Serena didn't know what to answer. She hadn't expected this. But she wasn't about to spoil her chances with Mallini. He wasn't asking her for a date anyway. This was business.

"I don't have a date for dinner," she said.

"Good," Mallini said. "Great! Where do you live?"

She told him where she was staying.

"I'll pick you up at seven-thirty."

He went back to the darkroom.

FIVE

The Villa Florenzo outside Rome—January 1943

The child bolted upright in her bed, eyes wild with fear. They were there! The ones her mother and father wouldn't talk about when they thought she could hear. The blackshirts! Marvena didn't know whether she sensed them or heard them, but she knew they were in the house. She scrambled out of bed and ran in the dark down the long hall to her mother and father's room. The carved bronze handle of the door was high for her, but she reached it and pulled on it with all her weight until the lock released and the door opened. She almost fell in her haste to get inside the room.

"Mama! Papa!"

They were already out of their bed, running toward the door. They had heard what she had heard, too. Her mother fell on her knees beside her and clutched her tightly in her arms. Her father continued toward the door.

"No, Vittorio! Don't go down to them!" She reached one arm toward him, still kneeling on the floor, holding Marvena. "Lock the door! We'll barricade the room! You can't fight them! You have no gun!"

"It may not be blackshirts."

"No one else would dare break in! Please, Vittorio! I beg you!"

"Mother. . . ."

"She can't hear them! They won't bother an old woman!"

Count Vittorio Florenzo was a monarchist, implacably opposed to the dictatorship of Il Duce. He had no political power, but the words of a Florenzo still carried weight with the scattered, mostly impoverished aristocracy. He was outspoken in his criticism of the regime and the German alliance, and the underground papers quoted him.

The retaliation he long expected had started. First the servants. They had been conscripted into the army or forced to take jobs that would contribute to the war effort. Some had fled the villa in fear of their lives. The only ones left were too old or too ill to be of use to Mussolini. Next, his properties had been confiscated, also declared necessary for the war effort. He was allowed to live in the villa, but he was a prisoner within his own walls. He had no say in the management of his fields, his orchards, his vineyards. The villa and every building on his lands had been searched, and all weapons removed, including the crested dueling pistols that hadn't been fired for generations. His cherished hunting guns and rifles had been taken. He could not shoot a pigeon or a hare for food. Even the long-rusted, long-out-of-use shotguns put out of the way in a stroage shed had been taken.

His passport, his wife's and his mother's had been taken from them. His attempt to smuggle his wife and child and old mother out of the country had come near to resulting in death for them.

"Vittorio! I beg you! Don't leave us!"

"I must, Clarissima. . . ." He was the one they were after. If he gave himself up to them, there was a chance they would spare the others.

"Please, Papa!" Marvena broke into crying, like her mother holding out one arm toward her father, the other tight around her mother's neck.

The noise of the intruders was louder now. The trampling of their boots could be heard on the carpeted stairs.

"Barricade the door, Vittorio!"

Marvena was convulsed with fear. Her wide, frightened eyes followed her father's every move as he closed and locked the door and then struggled with a heavy armoire to shove it in front of it. All the while she could hear the blackshirts. They were in the long hall now. They were opening doors and slamming them again, calling out to each other that no one was there. They were getting closer. Marvena clung to her mother. She was no longer crying. She was silenced by fear. Her father came to them and knelt beside them and put his arms around both of them.

The blackshirts were at the door. The handle was rattled and then rattled again.

"Open up!"

The harsh order came from behind the door. Marvena's father's arms tightened.

"Open up, or we break it down!"

Marvena loosened one arm from around her mother's neck and flung it around her father's, hanging on as hard as she could. Her head was turned back, eyes on the armoire in front of the door.

"Don't cry. Don't say a word," her mother whispered against her ear. "It will be all right. They will go away when they find they can't get in."

Heavy boots kicked at the door. Some of the men beyond it laughed; some cursed.

Suddenly a shot exploded. One of the doors of the armoire, shattered by the exploding shell, hung awry, some pieces of it falling to the floor. Marvena couldn't keep a keening wail from rising from her. She buried her face on her mother's neck, biting her own arm to try to keep the sound from coming out of her. Her mother took her by the waist and pulled her out of her father's arms and pushed her away from them.

"Get under the bed!" she whispered. "Get under the bed! No matter what happens, stay there! Stay under the bed, Marvena! Go now!" She pushed Marvena toward the bed.

Marvena whimpered. She was too afraid to move. "Mama. . . ."

"Get under the bed!" Her mother pushed her so hard that she knocked her down.

Marvena crawled under the bed, for the first time in her life afraid not to obey her mother. She held her whimpers back, but tears slid out of her eyes. She didn't know what she had done to make her mother mad at her.

Another gunshot exploded, and a loud crashing followed it. Marvena tried to turn around so she could see. She was hampered by the low bottom of the bed. When she could finally see through the fringed edge of the bedcover that fell to the floor, black-booted men were climbing over the overturned armoire. She could see her mother and father still kneeling on the floor, holding each other. Again the gun blasted, so near this time that it hurt her ears and set them ringing. For a second or two she didn't realize that her father's head had blown apart. Then she saw his blood splattered on her mother's face and on her white nightrobe. Her mother screamed. Before she could scream again, the men were on her. One stuffed a yellow scarf in her mouth. One pried her arms loose from the faceless corpse she still held. One grabbed her under the arms. They dragged her backward. The corpse swayed on its knees and then fell over, in the direction of the bed. The bloody mass that had been her father's face almost touched the fringe that hid Marvena.

A faintness came over Marvena. She tried to hold it back, tried to crawl out to where the men were holding her mother on the floor. They were holding her by the arms and the legs, cursing at her struggles, laughing, breathing hard. One straddled her and yanked at her nightrobe until he got it up to her neck; then he flopped himself heavily down on her.

Marvena couldn't breathe. Her arms and legs wouldn't move. She had to get to her mother, but she couldn't. She felt the faintness coming again, and this time she couldn't hold it back. It overcame her.

SIX

New York City, 1956

"This is the twentieth century, Papa! It's not a hundred years ago!" Antonio's face was white with rage . . . and shame.

The senior Mallini looked from his son to the woman and back again to his son. There was shame in his face also—shame for his son, not for himself. For himself, he felt disappointment and soul-withering outrage. The son he had spawned was not a man. He hadn't been able to perform with the woman.

"He's young yet," the woman said. "He's not yet sixteen."

"He's old enough! And God knows you're old enough to teach him!"

"You had no right to set this up!" Antonio screeched. "You had no right to do this to me! When I'm ready for a woman, I'll find the one I want for myself!"

"I had my first woman when I was *fourteen!* And from then on every time I could plant my stick I planted it! *That's* a *man's* way!"

"He's small for his age," the woman said. "He's late developing in his growth. Maybe he's late developing his manhood."

"Shut up! Get out! Whore! Take the money you didn't earn, and get out!"

"It was a whore you hired; it was a whore you got!"

the insulted woman shouted, enraged. She snatched the money he thrust at her and stuffed it in her purse. "You could have picked a kid off the street for a couple of bucks and saved yourself some money, for all the good you got out of it!" She gestured toward Antonio with her thumb, her face a sneer, taking her anger out on Antonio. "You can give up on him, *Papa!* If I couldn't make him get it up, no woman can! You haven't got a man here! You've got a man *lover!*"

Antonio started dating girls and making a show of it. He avoided any close friendship with a boy. He lived every day of his life in misery. He was afraid the whore was right. If she were, he would never regain his place in his father's respect, and he wanted that above all things. He tried to make himself have a man's feelings about girls. He looked at naked pictures of them. They sickened him. The thought of kissing them, putting his hands on their breasts, feeling their naked bodies against his sickened him. Every night, when he went to bed, he swelled and ached. He was afraid to masturbate. It might make him less a man than he already was. Many times he awakened in the night to find the sheet wet with his ejaculation. He hadn't been dreaming about girls. At first, there was no one in his dreams. And then one night he dreamed of the boy he had played tennis with that day. He woke up drenched in semen and sweat. He knew then that it was all over for him. He was what the whore had said he was.

But he didn't have to live the part, he told himself. He swore to himself he never would. That was all he could do to make up to his father for having failed him in the thing that was more important to him than anything else. His father was of the old school. A man had to be a *man*.

Antonio lived in the prison of a shadowy world of

pretense. He continued to date girls, but none of his liaisons lasted long. The girls broke them off. They wanted kisses and petting. Some wanted sex. When they found they weren't going to get any of that from him, they dropped him. Each time he was dropped, it was another proof of his inadequacy, another shame tallied on his record of failure.

A more humiliating proof was the fact that boys like himself made overtures to him. They recognized him as one of them. He steered clear of them, and normal boys steered clear of him. He was lonely and miserable. As he got older, the loneliness and misery became more bitter, the silent censure of his father more unbearable.

By the time Antonio graduated from Columbia University, where he had gotten a liberal arts degree, he was a passionate photographer, having found company in a camera that he couldn't find in people. With a camera slung over his neck he was less lonely. He asked his father for the money to go to Europe. He needed to broaden his scope in photography, to learn European styles and techniques. He would manage to earn his keep somehow.

His father gave him not only the fare but enough to subsist on. He seemed relieved that Antonio wanted to go. Antonio's mother broke into sobs when she was told. It was the first time she had let either one of them see that she knew how bad things were between them. "We have the daughters, Anna," her husband said. "We still have the daughters." He might as well have said, *I never had a son,* for that was what Antonio heard.

Antonio got nowhere with portraiture. He tried human interest and news photography. He was better at that. He sold a few of his photographs to papers and magazines. He thought for a while of going into it full time, free lance, but it wasn't truly satisfying work. The emphasis was on the human-interest aspect or the event, not on excellence of photography. He left Paris and traveled in England and on the Continent, doing landscapes and seascapes. He tried industrial photography. None of them gave him a real feeling of fulfillment, and little of accomplishment, although he was, by that time, a good technician. He realized that he wanted to work with human subjects, but not in portraiture.

In London he applied for work at the studio of Gerald Symonds, a fashion photographer, and Symonds took him on as his assistant.

Antonio knew from the beginning that Gerald was a homosexual. But he told himself that he couldn't avoid homosexuals all his life, especially if he wanted to go into fashion photography. If he kept himself reserved, kept the relationship on a purely impersonal level, Gerald would understand that he did not want to be approached. He would respect that, or he should. At any rate, Antonio told himself, he wouldn't make an approach that he knew would not be welcome.

For eight months things went well. Antonio was the best assistant Gerald had ever had. His proficiency in the darkroom outdistanced his own. True to his word, he let Antonio photograph the fashions when time permitted.

Gerald came up behind Antonio and put his arm over his shoulder. Antonio was studying some photographs that he had done on his own.

"Very good," Gerald said. "Bloody good! You've got the touch, Antonio. I could put these off to *Femme* as being mine." He grasped Antonio's shoulder tighter. "What do you say?"

Antonio didn't want his work put off as someone else's. He wanted credit for it. When he hesitated about answering, Gerald realized what the problem was. "You're right, you're right," he said, squeezing

Antonio's shoulder even harder. "They'll see these as *Mallini's.*"

When *Femme* accepted the photographs for publication, Gerald invited Antonio to his flat for dinner in celebration of his breakthrough. "You'll be rivaling me soon," he said. "You'll be leaving me and taking some of my business with you. Let's celebrate while we're still on terms." He said it in a light tone, but there was an edge in his voice.

Antonio didn't hear it. His head was full of visions of himself opening magazines and seeing photographs credited to him. Pride rose in him. He wasn't accustomed to feeling proud, and he thought he was being immodest, even brazen. He tried to hide it. He smiled shyly at Gerald. "It's not so much," he said. "Two pictures. . . ."

"Full-page color! Both of them! First pop out of the camera and into the magazine! Are we going to celebrate?"

Antonio didn't want to go to Gerald's flat. That was the personal kind of thing that he had been avoiding. But Gerald had given him his opportunity. He couldn't be ungrateful. "I'd love to celebrate," he said. "Thanks for inviting me."

"Just us," Gerald said.

Antonio was uneasy, but he chided himself for being. Gerald didn't have in mind what he was afraid he did. He didn't need him as a lover. He was well supplied with lovers. They were always drifting into the studio.

The uneasiness didn't leave him. He was in a bad state of nerves by the time he got to Gerald's flat.

"My God, what's this?" Gerald exclaimed, laughing. "You're white to the gills! Is this what success does to you? You need a drink!" He slapped him on the back, still laughing, and drew him into the room.

Gerald gave Antonio a stiff gin, warm. "To Mallini!" he said, lifting his own glass. "To the future

Great Mallini!" He downed his drink in one long swallow. Antonio felt compelled to do the same. He was almost overcome by a strange light-headedness. He had arrived physically and mentally depleted. The warm gin almost finished him off.

"Now see what I've got for us!" Gerald said. He unlocked a small antique tea chest on the table beside him and took out a joint and lit it. "The best," he said. "I get it straight from Turkey." He puffed away for a moment and then handed the joint to Antonio and got up and got them both another drink.

"I don't think I can handle another," Antonio said.

"Of course you can."

Antonio woke up the next morning in Gerald's bed. He couldn't remember much about the evening—the events: dinner, the music they had listened to, the dances that Gerald had taught him. He couldn't remember going to bed. He couldn't remember resisting Gerald. But he could remember what had happened after they were in bed, what he had felt. Everything that he had bottled up inside himself for years had been given release. Gerald had wooed him, caressed him, murmured love to him, explored his body, kissed him, taken him, made him come time after rapturous time.

On first awaking Antonio was in a state of euphoria. He reached his hand across the bed for Gerald, but Gerald wasn't there. He sat up and looked around for a clock. It was almost ten. Broad daylight was streaming through the windows. The sounds on the street outside were the sounds of normal people and normal traffic going about the normal things of every day. Horns sounded. Tires screeched. An occasional word floated up, laughter, admonishments to children in the little park in the square that Gerald's apartment house faced on.

Where he was, and why he was there, juxtaposed

to the sounds of normal life beyond where he was, struck Antonio like a blow. What he had sworn since he was fifteen would never happen had happened. And he had awakened happy that it had.

Antonio wanted to crawl back under the covers and disappear from the world. He didn't know what he should do. Did Gerald expect him to come to the studio as if nothing had happened? Of course he did. As far as Gerald was concerned, nothing earthshaking had happened.

But something earthshaking and unendurable had happened to Antonio. He had thought once before, because of a dream, that his last hope for himself was gone. Now he knew it with deadly certainty. He felt his father's eyes on him. Thousands of pairs of them floated about in the air of the room, piercing him like knives, seeing his shame, condemning him and renouncing him. He was no son of his.

Antonio didn't go to Gerald's studio. He didn't stay in London for his moment of triumph—when the issue of *Femme* that included his photographs would be on all the stands. He went to his own flat and packed his things and went to Victoria Station and booked himself on the boat train to Paris.

Mallini, as Antonio now thought of himself—Gerald had called him Mallini from the time his pictures had been accepted by *Femme*—couldn't find a place that gave him any comfort. He believed now that Gerald had seduced him because he really did believe that Mallini would be competition for him. The edge that had been in Gerald's voice when he had said that he would leave him and take some of his business with him echoed in his head. He hadn't heard it then, but he heard it now. Gerald had wanted ascendancy over him. He was convinced of that. Gerald was a good photographer, but Mallini was better. He knew he was. Gerald had known it, too. It wasn't Mallini he

had seduced. It was his competition. That truth gave
Mallini almost as much bitterness as the fact that he
had failed his father.

But underneath, the little seed of pride was still
there. His work had been good.

Mallini traveled south through France, not staying
long anywhere. He found himself in northern Italy,
his father's homeland. A sense of destination came to
him. He went south to Rome.

He took a room in a small *albergo* near the Piazza
Navona. For days he walked the streets of the city
from early morning until nightfall. He carried a small
camera with him, but he did little photography. He
got up very early in the morning, packed a lunch and
took a bus in one direction or another from the city.
He would get off some distance away and walk the
countryside.

Mallini walked out of a wood and found himself
in a park that was part of a large estate. He could see
the villa in the distance. It was a *palazzo*. It looked as
old as the rocky hills he had just left, but it was cared
for. There was a look of peace about it, and he kept
walking toward it. He came to the edge of the park
and found that he was still a distance from the villa,
orchards and gardens between. He stopped.

It was awhile before he realized that he was not
alone. A girl was sitting at an easel among the trees
in the orchard nearest him. She was not painting.
Her hand was arrested, the brush a few inches from
the canvas on which she was working. She was watching him. Mallini was startled at first, and then he felt
embarrassed. He realized that he was trespassing. He
walked a little way out of the park toward the girl.

"Are you lost?" Her voice was low, but it reached
him.

"Not really," he said, continuing toward her. She
belonged to the scene—a girl seated at an easel among

the trees of an orchard, a peaceful, mellow villa in the distance beyond her. "I wasn't looking for any place in particular." He wanted to photograph what he saw. He wondered how to ask her.

"The villa isn't open to tourists." She spoke the same Italian he had learned from his parents.

"I'm a photographer."

"I'm sorry. We don't allow photographs inside the grounds. If you want to photograph, you can take pictures from the tour bus. It stops on the road by the gate. We can't prevent that."

He knew she was asking him to leave, but somehow the place, the peace that he had disturbed, made him feel compelled to explain himself. "I'm not a tourist," he said. "I can understand your wanting to keep the curious out. I was photographing in the hills. I didn't realize I was on private property until I came out of the woods."

The girl relaxed somewhat. "Oh. Then you *were* lost."

"I guess I was."

"You speak with an accent . . . American?"

"Yes."

"Making a pilgrimage to the *old country*, I suppose." Some of her former stiffness had returned. "Many American Italians have been doing that, I'm told, ever since the war. Are you afraid another would destroy the *homeland* completely?"

Mallini didn't think he deserved what she said or the sarcastic tone in which she said it. "Your villa . . . I suppose it's yours . . . ?"

"It's mine."

"It doesn't seem to have been touched by the war."

"The Villa Florenzo was *useful* during the war." There was hard, ingrained bitterness in the word she stressed.

Mallini was immediately contrite. "It's a long time since the war," he said gently.

"For you perhaps."

Mallini wanted to get off the subject. The girl's eyes had dimmed. She didn't look like a girl now.

He could see that, even sitting, she was short. She looked small-boned under the coverall smock she was wearing, but she wasn't. The bones of her wrists were sturdy. She had thick reddish blond hair. Her eyes were green, deep-set but wide, her mouth full, her nose patrician. She was not a beauty, but she gave the illusion of beauty . . . or she could. At the moment she looked like a peasant. He wished she would laugh; he wished frankness would come into her eyes. She looked the way he so often felt. There was a sadness in her as great as the sadness in him. Had she failed herself, he wondered, or had someone failed her?

"Do you mind if I look at what you're painting?"

The girl shrugged and leaned back to give him a full view. The painting was of one particular tree in the orchard against the background of those behind it. It wasn't good, but it almost was.

"I can never get the perspective," the girl said.

"You have an eye, though. The composition is perfect for what you're trying to do."

"Do you think so?"

Mallini wasn't sure, but he thought a little light had come into her eyes.

"I know so. Wait, I'll show you." He focused the camera on the scene she was painting. He held the camera in the exact position and moved his head away. "Look in the camera. Isn't that what you want to paint?"

She looked in the camera, then looked at him. "That's exactly what I want! That's amazing!" She held up her brush. "But this is not a camera," she said. She sounded resigned.

Mallini smiled. "Perhaps it should be. Maybe you're in the wrong medium. You can see what you want, but you can't transpose it to the canvas."

"A camera would be difficult for me. To get the film. . . . Everything would have to go into town for developing. No. . . ."

A heavyset man in work clothes came into view, walking hurriedly toward them through the near garden.

"It's all right, Luigi," the girl called out. "I'm all right."

The man stopped.

"I'm all right," the girl called out again.

The man hesitated, looking at Mallini; then he turned and walked away, soon lost from sight among the trees.

"My cousin," the girl said. "He manages the estate now."

"Now . . . ?"

The eyes looked lost again. Mallini wished he hadn't asked. "I'm sorry, I haven't introduced myself," he said. "I'm Antonio Mallini." When she didn't tell him who she was, he went on. "I'm from New York. I've been in Europe for almost two years now learning all I can about this"—he indicated the camera—"so I can set myself up in my own studio when I get back."

Her only reply was a nod.

"Won't you tell me your name?"

"This is the Villa Florenzo," she said, as if that should make everything clear to him.

Mallini watched her, waiting. She realized the name didn't mean anything to him.

"I'm Marvena Florenzo," she said. "I'm the only one left. The man who was here is not a Florenzo. He is a cousin on my mother's side."

Somewhere behind those words lay her sadness, Mallini knew.

"Look," he said, smiling, changing the subject again, "now that I know you, I can invite you to share my lunch." He took the knapsack from his shoulder. "I have fruit and cheese, bread and wine."

"A picnic," she said.

"Yes. Let's have a picnic."

"There's an old tree with roots. . . ." Marvena got up from her folding chair and led him into the park and to the tree.

They sat on the exposed roots and ate Mallini's picnic lunch. They talked very little. They were comfortable with each other. Neither knew why.

When they had finished, Marvena said, "Show me some more scenes in the camera, please."

Late in the afternoon, when Mallini said that he had better be getting back to Rome, Marvena asked, "Do you come this way often? Will you be coming tomorrow?"

"Yes, I'll come," Mallini said. He had a thought that pleased him. He knew her interest was in the camera. "I have another small camera," he said. "I'll bring it. You can practice taking pictures with it."

"I'd like to do that," she said. Her eyes were grave, but he thought he saw a faint eagerness in them.

For almost three months Mallini returned to the Villa Florenzo every day. He brought Marvena film and took it back to town to have it developed and then took the developed pictures to her. She was bad on focus, on getting the right slant of light, on everything except composition. Gradually she began to get better on the mechanical aspects of working the camera. When a photograph showed improvement she would laugh—not a full laugh, but one that showed that if she could forget her sadness, she could abandon herself to laughter.

One afternoon in late summer, when Mallini was ready to leave, Marvena said, "If no one's waiting for you . . . Can you stay? We could have dinner in the garden. It's nice in the evening in the garden."

"No one's waiting for me."

"Luigi can drive you back to Rome later."

After dinner, when they were finishing the bottle of wine, Marvena said, "Why did you go away from home . . . from your family . . . for two years?"

"To learn more about photography. To practice it."

"You could have done that at home."

Mallini's intuition told him that she didn't want to hear about him as much as she wanted to talk about herself. "Why do you stay here at the villa all the time?" he asked. "Why do you keep yourself so secluded? Why won't you even come into Rome for dinner with me?"

"Oh, not because of you! Not because . . ."

"Why?"

"I . . . I'm not like other people."

"Who told you that?" Mallini immediately suspected the cousin Luigi. The cousin had convinced her she was crazy. He was after the estate. "There's nothing wrong with you!"

"I don't like to be with people. I'm not comfortable. You're the first person I've met since . . . since . . ."

He thought she was going to mention a breakdown. "You're as sane as I am!"

"It hasn't to do with sanity. It's . . . I don't want to make myself available. I don't want to meet people . . . men. I should marry, you see. My cousin worries about that. He says . . . It doesn't matter. But he worries, and I can't tell him how it is with me. He wouldn't understand, even though he knows about—" She stopped.

"Knows about what, Marvena?" Mallini asked softly.

Marvena looked at him a long time, her eyes searching his, her wish to speak evident, the difficulty of speaking also evident. She was wondering how he would receive what she had to say.

"Knows about what, Marvena?" Mallini repeated, his voice even softer, encouraging.

Marvena turned as if in a trance and lifted a hand

toward a window on the second floor of the villa. "Do you see that window? That's the room where it happened. . . ."

The fever that Marvena had suffered had blanked her mind of everything in her past existence except the night the blackshirts came. She came out of the fever remembering that in vivid detail. It remained as vivid to her all her life as it had been then. Slowly, with many stops and hesitations, but with determination and courage, she told it all to Mallini. "I couldn't help her," she whispered when she finished. "I couldn't do anything to help my mother."

Mallini listened horror-struck. The atrocities of the Second World War had never been more to him than chapters in a history book. He couldn't remember the war; it was over before he started to school.

". . . They let my grandmother and me stay here. I suppose they had no choice. I was ill with a fever they thought would kill me. It wasn't killing me. When I would come to myself enough to start remembering, I would bring the fever back. Did you know you can do that? You can. I did it. I was trying to die, I think. But I didn't. The fever left me with a paralysis of the nerves. It was more than two years before I was well enough to learn to walk again. The war was over by then. . . . My grandmother was deaf, but otherwise, she was a very strong woman. She hounded the authorities until she got the estate returned to her. Then she put my cousin Luigi's father in charge of it and took me to Switzerland. I was educated there. My grandmother was sometimes there with me and sometimes here at the villa. When I was fourteen, she became so crippled with arthritis that she couldn't come to be with me anymore. I was very lonely. I didn't have friends because I didn't trust anybody. I was afraid of everybody. I thought everybody blamed me for what had happened. I blamed myself. I didn't think I was worthy of friends. For a while I even thought my grandmother didn't come to Switzerland to be near me anymore because she blamed me. . . ."

"Marvena. . . ."

"I know what you're going to say . . . that I was only a child. I was. I know that. But I was the one who was there. I was the *only* one who was there, the only one who could have helped her . . . my mother, it was already too late to help my father by the time I saw what had happened to him. . . ."

"Marvena—"

"Please let me finish. If I don't tell it now, I'm afraid I never will. . . . My grandmother wrote me a letter, or had it written for her. She said that I must learn to live with other people, that she wouldn't always be here. She thought, you see, that she was nearer to her death than she was. She told me I must find my own way out of the psychological trap I was in—those were her words. I had made myself a prison, she said. It was a hard letter. It almost killed me. But it made me try. I quit painting so much. I had been spending all my free time from classes painting. I wasn't any good at it, but it absorbed me, and it gave me an excuse for not mixing. Now I tried. I went to the school parties and dances. I found that I liked dancing. The girls danced together when there were no boys. That led to pairing off . . . I thought for friendship . . . maybe it *was* only that sometimes . . . but more often it was for sex. I tried it with several of the girls. I tried sex with boys. I tried, I really tried, but sex with anybody, in any form, was repugnant to me. I went to a psychiatrist—you can see I really tried—he said that the trauma I had gone through, seeing what happened to my mother, had given me a block against sex. He worked with me for four years. In the end he had to admit that he had failed. I would always be asexual, he said. So then. . . . Well, I was relieved. That was the only feeling I had. I didn't have to try anymore. He explained to me, and finally made me understand, that there was nothing mentally or physically or morally wrong with me. Something that I had no control over had happened to me, and the result was that I was asexual. What is supposed to happen to girls in their early teens didn't happen to me. The physical manifestations of change, yes, but not . . . You understand?"

"Yes, I understand."

"While I was still at school, my cousin Luigi's father died. That death didn't affect me. I'd hardly known him. My grandmother was too ill to attend my graduation. She died a few months after I returned to the villa. I was by myself then because I knew Luigi even less than I'd known his father. Then . . . Well, so here I am. I have the Florenzo title, the Florenzo estates . . . and my painting. I've never felt lonely, except for my grandmother. I've never felt sorry for myself. I wanted things the way they were. But now. . . ." She paused and then looked at Mallini. "Do you believe in kindred souls?"

Mallini's astonishment showed in his eyes. "Those very words were in my mind. *Kindred souls,* I was thinking, *Marvena and I are kindred souls.*"

"You're an outsider, too," Marvena said. "I knew it from the beginning, I think."

Marvena reached over and put her hand on Mallini's. Mallini didn't feel the impulse to draw his away. It was the first time a girl had touched him that he didn't. But Marvena wasn't like other girls.

"I've come to terms with myself," she said. "I don't think you have. You will be miserable until you do. You're unhappy. I've known that from the beginning, too."

"I know myself now," Mallini said. "At least that."

"You have to be able to live with yourself."

Mallini looked up at the sky. The night was waning. The bottle of wine was empty. How long had they been talking? He should leave now. Marvena had purged herself. She had talked it all out. He should leave. But he didn't want to leave. He wanted to talk now. It was like a compulsion. Here was someone who would understand. "I find it hard to live with myself," he said, "because I wish things were different. Not for my sake, but for my father's."

"It's yourself you have to think about, your life."

"I failed him. I'm his only son, and I failed him. . . . We were so close, my father and I. There was never anything I couldn't tell him, never a problem that I couldn't go to him with. He took them all over and handled them. There wasn't anything that he couldn't make right. Until . . ." He found he couldn't go on.

"Yes, Antonio . . . ? Until . . . ?"

Mallini took a deep breath. She had trusted him enough to tell her story to him. Where was his trust? "When I was fifteen . . . because he thought it was his duty as a father to his son . . . it's old-fashioned thinking, but my father is old-fashioned . . . he arranged a—a meeting for me with a woman. I didn't know what was going on. He took me to a place in New Jersey, drove me over there one night. A motel . . . it was a motel. He left me there with a woman . . . a whore. I . . ."

He told her the whole story, the whore, Gerald Symonds.

"You were destined to come here, Antonio. It was destined."

They were silent for a while. Then Mallini said, "I want the normal things. I want a normal life. I don't mean children. I know I'll never have children, but I want a woman in my home. Maybe that sounds foolish, things considered, but there are times when a man like me needs a woman, a wife, for the sake of normality, for the sake of his friends and family who live normal lives. It may be a false front, but it's a necessary one for the sake of the comfort of the people around him. I have a mother and father. I have four sisters. Two have married since I left home. The other two will marry. They will have families. I don't want to be cut off from them entirely. I want . . ."

"You can have what you want, Antonio."

He shook his head.

"We like each other," Marvena said. "We respect each other. We amuse each other. Most important of all, we know each other. You know my whole story. I know yours. . . ."

Mallini stared at her. He couldn't believe what she was saying, what it implied.

"You're thinking about going back to New York, aren't you, Antonio? You have been for the last week. I could feel it."

Mallini nodded.

"That's why I thought we had better talk tonight. I was afraid you would leave suddenly, leave a letter for me, or call me from the airport when you were ready to catch your plane."

"I wouldn't have done that. I would have said good-bye to you."

"I didn't want to take the chance." She had been very somber. Now she laughed softly. "I didn't want to lose my teacher. I haven't learned all I need to know about photography yet."

Mallini stared at her. "Would you really marry me, Marvena?"

The teasing laughter left her face. "I would have a life if I married you," she said, her eyes earnest on his. "I would be safe from others who want me or want the Florenzo inheritance. I would have contentment. You've brought me the only contentment I've known, Antonio."

"You may change, Marvena. The time may come when you will want a normal marriage, a normal sexual relationship."

"The time will *not* come."

Mallini stood up suddenly and walked around the table several times. His body made a slight shadow on the ground, but his eyes were shining, his white teeth sparkling as he smiled, almost laughing. "I'm just realizing what we're talking about, Marvena! It's just hitting me!"

Marvena looked up at him. Her eyes were so full of life he could see their green color even in the pale light. She was smiling the openhearted, abandoned smile he had wanted to see her smile the first day he met her.

"We'll do it!" Mallini said. "We'll do it! We'll get married! Then, when I go home . . ."

Marvena laughed. It was the first time he had ever heard her really laugh. "When *we* go home," she said.

Mallini rushed around to his chair and sat down, leaning eagerly across the table toward Marvena. "We'll set up a studio! Mallini and Mallini! We'll . . ."

"The studio will be *Mallini*," Marvena said, leaning across toward Antonio, her eyes as bright and eager as his. "It has a greater importance . . . *Mallini* . . . one word. I see it on a small brass plaque on a great shiny black door. . . ."

"You're right! Of course, you're right!"

The studio on East Sixty-ninth Street was grossly ostentatious at first, considering Mallini's position among the ranks of photographers. But his genius was there, and Sybil Singlehurst saw it in the pictures in his portfolio when he finally got to her to show them to her. He had refused to show his work to an editor. Why show them to somebody who didn't have the final word? he had reasoned. He waited until the editor-in-chief was willing to give him a few moments.

The first things he did for Singlehurst were black-and-whites for the shopping column, illustations for articles, small color shots for back pages. But then he began getting assignments for quarter pages in color, half pages, full pages, and finally a center spread.

SEVEN.

Gordon Knightsplit's apartment was not a Manhattan apartment decorated in the Japanese style. It was a Japanese house, with Western adaptations, which might have been picked up intact from its garden setting in Osaka and placed on the ninth floor of the apartment house on Park Avenue where he lived.

The servants were Japanese—the butler, the houseboy, the male cook and the two maids. When Gordon entertained at dinner, the two maids dressed in the traditional costume and makeup of the geisha and attended the guests on arrival.

A number of Japanese customs were observed at Gordon's establishment, one in particular. Visitors were permitted to come into the entrance hall of the apartment wearing their shoes, but before they entered the foyer, which was covered with tatami—two-inch-thick mats with a straw core and a woven straw finish—they had to submit to having their shoes removed by the maids-turned-geisha and replaced by slippers. Gordon had more in mind than keeping the tatami on his floors free from street dirt and germs. He subscribed to a theory of his own that once a woman's shoes were off, she was halfway undressed, or felt that she was. It was the beginning of her capitulation, the small submission that would lead to the ultimate one, the first abandonment of her protective covering. Everything that Gordon did or said was calculated to bring about an anticipated result. He didn't waste his time doing things that were casual, or incidental, or necessary simply to the moment.

Gordon sauntered about the apartment while he waited for Mallini and the girl he was bringing. He always did that when someone new was going to see the place, trying to see it with their eyes. He wanted it to be as perfect for them as it was for him. He was proud of it and happy in it. Everything around him was a reminder of the two years he had spent at the University of Tokyo that had changed his personal life and shaped his professional life. He had left England for Japan believing himself a confirmed homosexual. He had left Japan for America committed to a life of bisexual pleasure. He thought often of Ono-san, who had served him in Tokyo.

Gordon opened the door of the small house he had rented near the university to see a diminutive kimono-clad girl standing before him.

The girl's arms were crossed in front of her, her hands hidden in the sleeves of her kimono. She bowed. "I'm Ono-san," she said, in a musical, almost inaudible voice, halting over the words because of her difficulty with spoken English—she was better at reading it. "The employment office sent me."

"I ordered a houseboy."

The girl bowed again but said nothing.

"They made a mistake sending you. I asked for a houseboy."

"Ono good cook, fast cleaning house, understand English."

"I don't want a woman living in the house!"

"Ono keep out of way. You not see Ono."

Gordon didn't know what to do. His digs were a mess. He'd had to eat every meal out. And he had to be at the university in half an hour. He couldn't take the time to go downtown to the employment office on

the Ginza and again go through the hassle of trying
to make them understand what he wanted. He stepped
back from the door. She could come in for one day
and clean up the place. He'd get somebody who spoke
Japanese to go to the employment office with him the
next day or the first day he had the time again. His
schedule at the university didn't leave him much free
time.

When he arrived home that night, the house was
in perfect order; his dirty laundry had been washed
and ironed; there was food in the kitchen prepared
for cooking. Ono was nowhere around.

Gordon went to the sliding door of the servant's
room and rapped on it. "Ono-san!"

Ono came out. She had one of his shirts in one hand,
a needle and thread in the other. She bowed. "Button
loose," she said. "What time Mr. Gordon want dinner?"

Gordon let out an impatient breath. He thought
he'd made it clear that she was to be gone by the time
he got home.

"Thirty minutes!" he said, and strode off to the
bathroom to bathe and change. How the bloody hell
was he going to get rid of her?

When he came to the main room thirty minutes
later, the table had been set up, a hibachi beside it.

All through the meal—every bite of it delicious—
Ono was no more than a presence when she was cooking on the hibachi or serving him or pouring sake for
him. She could have been male or female, or neither.

By the time Gordon finished dinner he was feeling
less uncomfortable with the girl. "How did you buy
the food? Where did you get the money?"

Ono dipped her head. A little smile that she was
trying to hide showed on her face.

"Buy on credit," she said. "Everybody glad to give
Englishman credit."

Well, at least she was resourceful.

When Gordon went to his bedroom, his bed—the futon—had been laid out, the books that he had dumped everywhere were stacked on the side of the writing table, his notebooks and writing pads were in the center of it, a lamp beside it was lit. Everything he needed was at hand for studying. He sat down and went to work. If Ono made any noise cleaning up the dinner things, he didn't hear it. The following morning he said nothing to her about leaving. He didn't want to go back to living in the shambles he'd been living in, and it would be at least a week before he could get back to the employment office. He wasn't going to trust a telephone call. He was going to interview on the spot and pick out the boy he wanted.

The course that Gordon was finding the hardest was the one he needed to learn the soonest—the Japanese language. It irritated him that he was having such difficulty with it. He had had no trouble with French or German or Italian. He had always thought of himself as something of a linguist. One night in frustration he threw his notebook down in disgust and got up and paced the floor. Ono came quietly into his room. He didn't know she was there until she spoke. "Ono help," she said.

"Nobody could help me with this bloody stuff!"

Ono picked up the notebook and compared what he had translated with the Japanese text. "Not all wrong," she said, "only some wrong." She explained how the last sentence he had been working on translated. When she explained it, he understood it. The professor had not been able to get across to him.

Every night after that Ono worked with him for several hours. He began making real progress. His confidence in his ability to master languages was restored. He became eager to write the language in its own characters. Ono taught him a few of the simpler ones and suggested that he sign up for a course in calligraphy. He had the perfect feel for it, she insisted. He started a course and found that he had a second cause to be grateful to Ono. He had come to the University of Tokyo to complete his studies in architecture, but after he took up calligraphy, he realized that design on the small scale was his forte. He also realized that his affinity was for the beautiful things of the earth— the precious metals and precious and semiprecious stones.

"Jewelry is the answer, Ono-san. I'm going to try my hand at designing jewelry."

Gordon had developed the habit of gripping the back of his neck as he studied. It ached all the time because it was forever bent over a desk. After one particularly grueling session Ono, standing behind his chair as she always did, moved his hand and started massaging his tense muscles. Gordon's first impulse was to pull away, but the soft probings of her fingers were already easing the strain in his neck. He relaxed in his chair and let her go ahead. By the time she stopped all the strain was gone, the ache was gone and Gordon was half asleep. "Bed now," Ono said, and Gordon got up and stumbled over to the futon. He got the first good night's sleep since he'd enrolled at the university. He lived under such pressure from his overloaded schedule that he went to bed only to turn and twist until it was time to get up.

The next time Ono massaged him she extended the massage to his shoulders. The next time she suggested that he lie on the futon so she could give him a full massage. He didn't have to get out of his clothes. By this time he was changing to a comfortable kimono when he came home in the late afternoon.

Gordon hadn't made a connection since he had come to Tokyo. He was picking his way carefully, finding the lay of the land. He'd had a few close calls at Oxford. He didn't want to get into any trouble here.

He hated jerking off. It offended his dignity, but he had had to resort to it on several occasions.

He expected that he would have to overcome a feeling of repugnance when Ono touched the more intimate parts of his body; he did not expect to become aroused. No woman had ever aroused him. His indoctrination into sex had been by a boy four years older than he when he was thirteen. He'd never had sex except with boys and men. He had been convinced since his first experience that sex, for him, was strictly a one-way street.

Ono's hands were light but firm as they kneaded his resistant muscles, traveling from his shoulders to the small of his back. When she had worked some time there, she got up from the side of the futon, went to its foot, knelt down and started massaging his feet and ankles.

When she started working up his legs, Gordon felt a stirring in his groin. His body stiffened involuntarily. Ono moved her hands back down to his lower legs and ankles. Gordon forced himself to relax. When her hands started moving back up his legs, he was able to force himself to stay relaxed, until they were on his thighs. He stiffened again when he felt his penis begin to enlarge. Suddenly he was seeing Ono's face behind his tightly closed eyelids. Somehow the image of her dainty, exotic face and the feel of her hands blended to give him the sensation he was feeling, to start the rousing of an urgent need in him.

Gordon's whole body was wet with perspiration. A hard ache was growing in his stomach. He was scared to try to take a woman. But the ache in him was becoming intolerable, and the fear in him did not make his penis go limp; it was becoming more engorged with his every breath and every movement of Ono's hands on him. "Turn out the lights," he muttered.

Ono, silent as always, turned out the lamps, came back to his futon and lay down beside him. She started

again to massage him, with one hand, on his buttocks.
She slid her other hand under him and took hold of
his penis. "On top of me," she said, "lie on top of
me." She held his penis while he moved on top of her
and then put it in the warmth between her legs. Gordon moved without knowing he was going to, thrusting himself fully into her. Once the thrust was made
he couldn't stop. When she started moving with him,
the sensation that her movements produced in him
made him abandon all restraint. He rammed himself
into her again and again, trying to drive himself ever
farther into the clinging warmth of her, irresistibly
impelled by the mounting urgency of his body. Suddenly she cried out and flung her legs around him.
Her warm, wet inner muscles tightened in spasms on
him. A feeling that overwhelmed him flooded over
him. He cried out, as she had, when the feeling exploded throughout him and he felt the release of his
ejaculation.

For several weeks Ono always had to make the approach, but one nght, in the middle of a study session,
Gordon turned from his books and pulled her to him.
He held her for a moment, then got up, picked her
up in his arms and carried her to the futon. After that
she always waited for him to make the overture, and
on the nights he was home he never failed to make it.

When she was confident that her position with him
was secure, Ono confessed to him that she had tricked
him.

"I was the one who sent me to you."

Gordon thought she'd gotten her English mixed up.
But she meant what she'd said.

"I worked in the employment office. I saw you when
you came in. I was supposed to give the boy they chose
for you his card to come here. But I didn't. I came
myself."

"I didn't see you there."

"I was behind the partition."

"You gave up an office job to work in somebody's house?"

"To work for you."

Gordon teased her. "You decided then and there that this was how this was going to work out?" They were in bed. They had just made love, and Gordon was still holding her.

"If I could make it. I was with an American once for a few months. He was older, not beautiful like Gordon-san, but he made the Japanese boys I knew seem like . . . like *boys*. When I saw you . . ."

"You set a trap."

"I set a trap." She laughed softly and flicked her tongue against his throat and into his ear. She knew how to make him want her again.

Ono was with Gordon all the time he was in Tokyo except for the last three months. She had to return home. Her father was ill of a debilitating disease of the nerves, and there was no one else to tend him. Although she wept, Ono accepted the fact that she had to leave Gordon with stoicism. Gordon was inconsolable at first. Ono had become a talisman. His whole life had changed because of her. He bought her a necklace of the finest jade and had the most perfect pearl he could find set in a ring for her. He wanted to give her money, assure her future security, but she would not accept it. She put him off when he asked her exactly when she would have to leave. One late afternoon, when he came home from the university, she wasn't there. All her things were gone. Gordon walked through the empty rooms with a terrible sense of loss. He couldn't get out of his mind a picture of Ono quietly getting her things together, quietly tidying up the house, hurrying so that she could leave before he came home, to try to make the parting easier for him.

Gordon missed Ono, but he had not been faithful

to her. He had had affairs with several of his fellow
students, male and female, and with the wife of an
American businessman. After Ono left, he sought out
one or the other of them every night to fill the empty
time that had been Ono's. He was soon over his depression. He was caught up in the details of winding
up his stay in Tokyo and preparing for his trip to
America. He was not going back to London. The op-
portunities for success in his field would be greater
in New York City, he felt.

Gordon had no real problems establishing himself
among the ne plus ultra of the New York fashion
world. He had a greater flair for design in jewelry
than anyone who had come along in a decade. He was
taken up by Sybil Singlehurst when he gave her a
private showing of his first collection. It was Sybil
who introduced him to Antonio Mallini.

He was sought after by the party givers. He was rich,
and he was English, titled English. He didn't use the
title, but he didn't hide the fact that there was one.
With all those credentials he was sought after. Gordon
had a strong appeal to women—he was tall and languid, with a predatory look in his bony features. He
was, by any standard, a handsome man. He was often
told that he resembled Laurence Harvey. The compliment might have pleased some, but it did not please
Gordon. Gordon preferred to be regarded as unique
in every way.

EIGHT

When Mallini called for Serena, he was wearing skin-tight black denim slacks and an open-fronted white shirt with an accordion-pleated stand-up collar.

Serena was a little startled by the sight of him; he was dismayed by the sight of her. She was wearing a simple black silk taffeta suit, which she had chosen because it would be appropriate for any place from "21" to P. J. Clarke's.

Mallini's disappointment in the way Serina looked showed clearly on his face. He started fidgeting and made no move to leave the hotel. "Have you something more comfortable?" he finally asked. He was fairly dancing around Serena in his distress. "We'll be dining at home with Gordon. I should have mentioned . . ."

"No problem," Serena said.

She left him in the lobby while she went upstairs to change. When she came down, she was wearing a clinging, long-sleeved, ankle-length oatmeal linen knit, ruffled at the wrists, the plunging V neck and the hemline. Relief washed over Mallini's face.

"That's more in your style," he said. "The other was—"

"Too conservative," Serena said dryly.

"It didn't—"

"Do anything for me."

Mallini smiled apologetically.

"No problem," Serena repeated.

Mallini took her arm and hugged it happily. Thank God she was flexible. She'd looked as unapproachable as a nun in the black.

Gordon met Serena and Mallini in the *zashiki,* or principal room, when they were ushered in by the butler. He was dressed in a kimono and wore tabis on his sock-clad feet. Serena was relieved to see that he wore a shirt and tie and trousers under the kimono. Mallini was surprised to see that he had anything at all under it.

"Mallini, old thing! Come in! Come in!"

Mallini presented Serena as if producing a prize from clouds of cotton fleece and then stood back, beaming, his eyes on Gordon.

Gordon bowed once, low, and then bowed again, even lower. "Miss Carr," he said, "Serena Carr. Very pretty. . . . Very pretty. . . ." He could have meant the compliment for Serena or for her name. "May I call you Serena?"

"Please do"

Mallini composed himself to conform his mood to Gordon's. Serena was going to get the low-key approach. Everything low-key. Everything underplayed. Gordon never made a mistake. He'd read Serena Carr right. She wasn't one you gave the rush act.

There were no awkward first moments after the introduction. Gordon was an accomplished and easy host, and Serena was enchanted with the place. She felt that she had entered a fairyland and said so. Gordon was delighted. He showed her over the whole apartment, omitting nothing, not even the bathrooms, complete with small wooden buckets beside low wooden benches and tiled sunken tubs. No Japanese, Gordon explained, would soap and scrub himself in his bathwater. He sat on the bench and washed himself with water from the bucket before entering the tub.

When they finished the tour of the apartment, they returned to the *zashiki*. A low table had been set up in the center of the room over a recess in the floor. The table was square. On the floor on three sides were *zabuton*, which were the cushions they would sit on. Mallini took his place on a cushion and put his feet in the recess, to illustrate to Serena how it was done. Gordon helped her take her place, then seated himself on his cushion in one fluid downward movement of his body.

"As I imagine you know," he said to Serena, "the Japanese would not normally sit so. They would sit on bent legs. The only time the Japanese put their feet in the *horigatatsu* is when the weather is cold and there is a charcoal brazier in it for warmth. However, my American friends . . ." He smiled, indicating their feet in the recess.

Suddenly, appearing noiselessly from nowhere, one of the geishas was on her knees beside Serena, bowing repeatedly and proffering a small container shaped like a fat bud vase. The other geisha was on her knees beside Gordon, going through the same motions.

"She is offering you sake," Gordon said. "She can't pour unless you give her permission. You must pick up your cup to let her know you accept." He picked up a tiny, deep bowl before him on the table. Serena picked up the one before her, and the geisha, giggling and ducking her head and murmuring something in Japanese, poured a white liquid into it. "She is thanking you for accepting," Gordon said. "Now you accept her thanks by drinking the sake." Serena sipped the liquid. The taste didn't surprise her as much as the fact that it had been heated.

"What is it?" she asked.

"It's a wine made from rice," Gordon said. "Do you like it?"

"I think so."

Business was not discussed throughout dinner. Gordon made light conversation or explained the various dishes to Serena and how they should be eaten.

"Where do you do your designing?" Serena asked Gordon finally. "I didn't see a workroom."

"Oh, not at home! Never! I have a workshop tucked away at the rear of my atelier," Gordon answered, and went on to something else, but not in a way to make Serena feel rebuffed. "Ah," he said, his attention diverted by the arrival of the geishas with another dish. "Now this, you may have to cultivate a taste for." It was raw fish—*sashimi*—and seaweed.

The serving geishas knelt and rose with perfect ease. Serena noticed the daintiness of their hands, the painstakingly contrived arrangement of their hair (like that of Madame Butterfly) the ornate design in the fabric of their kimonos, the complicated bindings of their *obis*. The disturbing thing about them was their masklike faces. The powder was chalk white, with a texture like lacquer that had hardened and been dusted over. The stark black lines about the eyes and the brilliant red lip rouge accentuated the masklike effect. The faces looked as though they would crack if they moved, yet the geishas smiled and giggled and chattered away with no damage done.

If geishas really did go to bed with men as part of their night's work, Serena thought, the men must spend a good two hours cooling their heels. It would take that long for the geishas to get their clothes off and their faces cleaned up and their hair combed out.

Dinner over, Gordon rose and helped Serena to her feet. He led the way to another room. Three low cushioned chairs were grouped around a low table. Against one wall sat an elaborately carved wooden railing which enclosed a huge pillow the size of a mattress. It was encased in a quilted silk comforter embroidered with brilliantly colored peacocks in all stages of preening and mating. Serena remembered that Gordon had called the room a sitting room. It was beginning to look more like a bedroom to her.

Serena had decided before they even sat down for dinner that there was more to the relationship between the two men than that of photographer and client. Not from any indications that Gordon gave, but from the way Mallini had changed from the moment Gordon met them when they arrived. He hadn't been the great Mallini anymore. He had become an eager-to-please little boy. Gordon treated Mallini as if he were amused by him.

Mallini excused himself, and Gordon seated Serena at the low table. The chairs were sideways to the table; one had to recline in them. When Mallini returned, Serena found out the reason for the arrangement. He had a hookah, a water pipe, which he put on the table before taking his seat.

Gordon took a long, appreciative pull at the pipe and passed it to Serena.

"What is it?" It could be opium for all she knew.

"Hashish."

"No, thanks," she said, and handed the pipe back. "Good stuff is wasted on me. I don't smoke, so I can't really inhale it. I don't get anything out of it."

Gordon smiled indulgently and passed the pipe to Mallini.

"How long have you been in New York?" he asked Serena.

"I came Friday."

"First time here?"

"No. I've been here several times with my father and mother."

"You're southern, I gather, from your accent."

"Atlanta."

"Charming. I like the South. How old are you?"

"Twenty-one," Serena lied.

Gordon drew out a lazy smile. "You have the sophistication for it," he said, "in looks anyway. . . . But we're not twenty-one, are we, Serena?"

His attitude irritated her. She wouldn't back down to the solid truth, which was that she would be twenty her next birthday. "I will be," she said.

Gordon laughed.

Serena was more irritated than ever with him, and she was as irritated with Mallini as she was with Gordon. Mallini was trying to hide it, but he was watching her every minute, like a cat watching a prey. What was going on here? If they thought they were going to have a cozy threesome on that peacock-covered mattress, they had another think coming.

"Gordon liked your pictures . . . the way you photograph," Mallini said. His voice was encouraging, a little ingratiating. Serena's suspicions were more than just suspicions now.

"When did he see photographs of me?" If he had seen and approved photographs of her, this little dinner-for-three ploy was just exactly what she thought it was.

"I don't go about things blind, my dear Serena," Gordon said calmly before Mallini could answer. "I saw them soon after they were done. Tonio sent them over to me. After all, if he hadn't, and Singlehurst had been on hand for the sitting this afternoon"—he smiled at Mallini—"I know she wasn't, old man. She called me and blasted off." He turned his smile on Serena. "As I was saying, if Singlehurst had been on hand, and if she had liked you, there would have been pitcures in *Milady* of a model, unapproved by me, wearing my little creations. We couldn't have that, could we?"

Serena looked at Mallini. "You sent pictures of me to him, and he said, 'Okay, bring her on'?"

Gordon laughed outright.

"Maybe we are twenty-one, Serena," he said.

Mallini had turned pale.

"If this is the couch routine, forget it!" Serena said.

"I like you, Serena," Gordon said. "Why don't we send Tonio along home?"

"I said forget it!" Serena snapped.

Mallini was more than pale now. His face was white. He looked cold, but he was perspiring. His black eyes were very bright.

"Don't get such a scare on, Mallini, old thing," Gordon said. "Serena and I will be friends in the long run. We'll all be friends in the long run."

Gordon was more amused than rebuffed. He liked the chase, and he seldom had opportunity for it. Most hopefuls were all too willing to fall on their backs in the direction of any body-length space at the flick of his finger. Mallini had brought him a rare one this time.

"Perhaps you should take our Serena home now, Tonio," he said. He rose to his feet and helped Serena up. He held her arm a full moment longer than he needed to, his eyes on hers. He released her arm, but his eyes stayed on her, full of meaning.

"You don't hold it against a man for liking what he sees when he looks at you, do you?"

He sounded as if he were paying her the sincerest of compliments.

Serena was furious with herself because she hadn't handled the situation better.

She made her voice unconcerned. "Of course not," she said.

"Good. Because I'm going to go on liking it."

Serena knew he was telling her that he expected some evening in the future to have a different ending. She'd be ready for him the next time, and she'd handle it better. In the meantime, she'd be a fool to offend him; he might refuse to let Mallini use her in the photographs the next day.

She smiled at him. "I've loved being here," she said. "It's like leaving the world behind to come into your apartment."

While Serena was helped into her shoes by one of the geishas, Gordon drew Mallini aside.

"Why don't you come back after you've dropped our little pigeon home?" he said. "The pipe is barely tasted. . . ."

Mallini's very soul had turned cold toward Serena. Now he overflowed with goodwill toward her. She hadn't ruined him forever with Gordon. Because of her, Gordon was inviting him back. He knew Gordon had the kidskin mattress in mind as much as he did the unfinished pipe.

NINE

"So this is the surprise."

The voice was strident, the eyes hard, the attitude uncompromising. Sybil Singlehurst didn't sound as if she found anything pleasing in the surprise.

"This is Serena Carr," Mallini said enthusiastically. "She photographs like a dream. Gordon thinks she's perfect for his things."

Sybil Singlehurst might have heard him, or might not have, for all the notice she took of what he said.

"Come here where I can look at you, miss," she said to Serena.

Serena stiffened at hearing herself addressed as "miss." The woman was being deliberately rude. She walked—stiffly and awkwardly, she felt—to stand in front of Sybil Singlehurst. She tried to keep her face pleasant or at least blank, although she was seething inside. The older woman's attitude had manipulated her into giving the worst possible first impression of· herself.

Sybil Singlehurst was short and thin, sphinx-eyed, hawk-nosed, thin-lipped and big-toothed. It was impossible to guess what color her hair once was. It was reddish black now, white around the hairline. Obviously that was the way she liked it. Her face was lined; her hands were like claws, her fingernails as long as a mandarin's. She looked like the dragon that legend had named her.

Sybil Singlehurst did not examine Serena in the im-

personal way Mallini had. Her examination was totally personal. Her eyes widened and narrowed as they
traveled over Serena and back to her face. Serena felt
that she was trying to see inside her to see what made
her tick.

"We'll see," she said dryly to Mallini, dismissing
Serena by simply taking her attention from her.

There were six people in and out of the dressing
room. There was another model, Khalie King, and
there was Karen Vogel, who had come from *Milady*
to style—and to fetch and carry—for Sybil Singlehurst.

Khalie King was a classic beauty in the tradition of
the models of the forties. She was older. She was a
survivor, or returnee, from the forties and was in her
forties herself—fifties, some said. She wasn't active in
the business anymore. She was married to Alfred Finn,
a sometime *Milady* photographer who was as famous
for his still lifes as he was for his work in fashion. The
Finns were close to Singlehurst, and Khalie, from time
to time, if the photographs were important enough,
could be prevailed upon to appear at a studio for an
hour or so. She was Singlehurst's own little surprise.

"Miss Singlehurst will want Khalie on the set first,"
Karen Vogel said bossily. "Let Khalie have a middle
bench at the dressing table!"

Zoe and Shari Holliday were seated on the center
benches. Shari started to get up. Khalie put her hand
lightly on her shoulder and sat down on the end bench
next to her. She smiled. "This will be fine," she said.

Khalie King was the most beautiful person Serena
had ever seen. She moved as if she weren't in this
world. She was ethereal in her beauty and in her movements. She seemed to drift, not walk. Her hair was
light blond and of a baby's silkiness. It was pulled
softly back from her face and arranged in a twist that
extended to the crown of her head. The hairdo emphasized the remarkable length of her neck. Her eyes

were pale blue, rather deep-set and clear. Her forehead
was high, also emphasized by the hairdo. Her mouth
was narrow but soft, her chin slightly pointed. Her
nose was the most striking feature of her face. It was
high-boned, long and pointed. On any other face it
would have been too prominent. Her skin was pale
and translucent. She was not as tall as the other models
and was thinner than any of them—but it was not a
bony thinness; it was more an otherworldly transpar-
ency of person. She was too beautiful to be real, at
least to Serena's eyes.

Karen Vogel, from *Milady*, was short, brown-haired,
ordinary in looks, and she just missed being plump.
She was sublimely superior, very much aware of her
position on the staff of *Milady* and of her close connection with Sybil Singlehurst. With Singlehurst she
was darting-eyed and hyper and nervously anxious to
please. Serena thought she must surely collapse from
sheer nervous exhaustion when she closed her own
door behind her after work. She had a pushy determination that never let up; she forged straight ahead,
her eyes focused on her goal. It was clear that she
would slim down, chic up and eventually become a
full editor of *Milady*.

"Khalie King is the model Singlehurst took to Paris
for *Milady* when she went over to photograph the first
collections after World War Two in 1947," Shari said.
"Can you believe that someone who looks like her
was working that far back?"

"She's indestructible," Margo said. "She'll look just
the way she does now until the day she dies."

"God, the tales I've heard about that little ex-
cursion!" Zoe said. "Can you imagine"—she turned to
Serena—"drooping boobs like Singlehurst must have
playing peekaboo from behind forty strands of pearls?"

"What?"

"That's what Singlehurst wore for blouses . . . so

the story goes," Zoe said. "Forty strands of pearls. Runs like ladders in her stockings and forty strands of pearls. That's Singlehurst chic!"

"She wore stockings with runs in them on purpose?"

"Not just runs! Ladders! They went all around her legs."

"It's true," Margo said. "I've seen pictures."

"But why?"

"Because she wouldn't wear any stockings but silk ones, and you couldn't get silk stockings. All the silk had been used during the war to make parachutes. The runs proved her stockings were silk."

"She doesn't look to me like somebody who has to prove anything," Serena said.

"She was proving she could wear runs and still set the fashion. Don't think everybody didn't take up wearing runs. They even made runs on purpose in their nylons."

"That's ridiculous."

"Not as ridiculous as trying to buck Singlehurst on a trend."

"Was everyone else wearing forty strands of pearls, too?"

"That wasn't a trend she was setting," Margo said. "That was a Singlehurst exclusive. Nobody touch."

"Black broadcloth Jacques Fath suits and peekaboo pearls for blouses!" Zoe said.

"And not costume jewelry pearls either, I'll bet," Margo said. "Cultured pearls."

"That's where you'd be wrong," Zoe said. "Not cultured. Real. Every beady-bead on every string. Natural pearls. Straight out of the oyster's belly from a grain of sand he got stuck in him screwing around on the ocean floor. No artificial insemination brought about a single bead on Sybil's forty strands of pearls."

"God, she must have been wearing a fortune around her neck!"

"And down her front."

"Maybe they were on loan."

"That could be. What better advertising? But I wouldn't be a bit surprised if the pearls were an out-right gift."

It was getting on toward noon when Mallini sent word that Serena was to be dressed in the black crepe Galanos. Serena felt goose bumps come out on her skin. Oh, God, she thought, every goose bump on her would show. The evening gown was practically back-less and frontless.

She'd have given anything not to have to dress and go out on the set. She felt like a waterlogged hunk of wood. Every ounce of her confidence had been sapped, first by the encounter with Singlehurst and then by the long wait.

Serena gave herself a mental jacking up. If she were going to play with grown-ups, she told herself, she'd have to act like one. If she were going to be a ninny, she might as well pack up her things and go back to school.

When she walked out on the set, Singlehurst took one look at her and said to Karen, "That Galanos is for Khalie." To Serena, she said, "Don't wrinkle it when you get out of it." She stood up. "We'll break for lunch now," she said to Mallini. She turned her back and walked out of the gallery, pausing at the door just long enough for Khalie King to catch up with her. The two left together.

Serena was almost paralyzed with humiliation. It was all she could do to walk back to the dressing room. Zoe was standing in the door. "That bitch!" she said, following Serena inside. "God, she can be a bitch!"

"Don't worry," Margo said to Serena. "Mallini will pay you an hourly rate for the time you've been here."

Serena stood like a stone while Karen got her out of the Galanos.

"Mallini should know by now," Karen said, "that Miss Singlehurst always prefers Khalie for the blacks."

She checked the dress, as if to see whether Serena had done it damage, hung it back on its hanger and hurried busily out of the dressing room. She had to rush over to *Milady* during the lunch break to get something that Sybil Singlehurst had forgotten.

Mallini came to the dressing room door. "Okay, girls . . . break," he said. He looked straight at Serena. "Everybody back by one, please, or order lunch here if you want. Miss Olsen will take care of it for you."

"I need some fresh air!" Zoe said, leaving no doubt as to what she meant. "Come on, Serena. I know a little bistro on Third that's quick."

After Serena and Zoe were seated at a tiny checkered-clothed table in the tiny restaurant, Zoe said, "Don't let that bitch scare you off. The only way she knows how to handle people is to intimidate them."

"Well, she's intimidated me!"

"You let her find that out, and you can forget it as far as *Milady* is concerned."

"You know, Zoe, it could be that she just doesn't think I'm right for *Milady*."

"If she didn't think you had possibilities, you'd have been *out* of Mallini's before she'd been two minutes *in* Mallini's. She's throwing her weight around. Right now she's throwing it at you. I don't know what set her off, but she's really got it in for you."

"She didn't like it because Mallini pushed her sitting down yesterday to make test shots of me."

"That figures. That would do it."

Zoe's deep violet eyes widened at the thought and then narrowed. "Do you know what that bitch is capable of doing if she's after Mallini's hide? She's not beyond going through this whole goddamn center spread and then scrapping every single shot! She's done it before. She doesn't let anybody get any wrong

ideas about who stands where in this business. If she
has to take Mallini's time, and mine and yours and
Shari's, and even Khalie's, to photograph this whole
goddamn center spread and then scrap what we've
done and take the jewelry to somebody besides Mallini
to photograph, just to prove that hers is the last say-so,
she will!"

"You've got to be kidding."

"I'm *not* kidding!"

"But if that's what she's doing, she's wasting her
own time as well as everyone else's."

"It's never a waste of Sybil's time, to her way of
thinking, to remind everybody just where the power
lies."

"That's some kind of power to have," Serena said.
"Is it the same with the editors-in-chief of the other
fashion magazines?"

"No. There's only one Singlehurst. Thank God."

They were silent for a moment. Then Serena said,
"It must be nice to be up there where she is. I wish I
knew how she got there. I'd go the same route myself."

"She got there the same way every woman gets to
the top—through the crotch!"

Serena's eyebrows lifted. "I'd think she'd shrivel a
man, not make him tight in his pants. You're not
serious, are you?"

Zoe let out an angry gust of breath. "No, I'm not
serious. I'm just being as bitchy as she can be," she
said. "Singlehurst got where she is because she's got
more fashion sense in her little fingernail than anybody else has got in her whole body. She's eons ahead
of everybody, and she's not afraid to go out on a limb.
I wouldn't sell her short on the sex bit either."

Serena studied Zoe for a moment. Then she said, "I
think she fascinates you."

"The devil his due . . ." Zoe muttered.

Their food was served. They ate quickly, in silence.
When the table had been cleared and coffee brought,

Serena said, "I really don't want to go back to the studio."

Zoe's eyes zeroed in so hard on hers that Serena felt they were nailing her to her seat.

"It's very important to you to be a model, isn't it?" she asked.

"Yes."

"Why? I don't think it's the money. Personal reasons? The glamorous life?"

"Personal reasons."

"Then go back to the studio; give it a good try. A word of advice. The only way to get on with Singlehurst is to stand up to her."

In late afternoon, after Khalie King had left and after Serena had again been ignored for hours, Karen said to her, "Miss Singlehurst wants you in the mauve Theroudopolos." She took a sheer wool hostess gown from its hanger.

"I hate purple," Serena said. "I don't want to wear that."

"What?" Karen looked at her as if she didn't believe her ears.

"I said I hate purple. I don't want to wear that."

Karen looked at Margo. Her look said, *What's the matter with her? Is she crazy?* She said, "This is what Miss Singlehurst wants her to wear."

Margo shrugged.

"I'm not going to wear it," Serena said.

"If your objection to it is that it's purple," Karen said, her expression and her tone of voice lofty, "that's hardly a *valid* objection. The gown is mauve." She forced a smile. "You wouldn't want me to go out and tell Miss Singlehurst . . ."

"That's the least good-looking outfit of the lot," Serena said. "If she wants somebody to wear it, she can wear it herself."

"What's the holdup? What's going on in here?"

The voice electrified everybody. Sybil Singlehurst stood in the doorway.

"She won't put on the dress," Karen said, her face suddenly flushed, her anxious eyes flashing back and forth between Serena and her boss.

"If I put on purple, I'm going to *look* like I'm wearing purple," Serena said. "I hate purple."

Singlehurst looked Serena up and down, and she took her time doing it. "I suppose you like black," she said.

"Yes, I like black. I like the black dress I had on before."

Singlehurst's slitted eyes stayed on Serena a full minute. Then, "I'll see what she can do with the Galanos," she said to Karen. Her eyes were still on Serena as she spoke. They were as hard as steel.

Singlehurst did not thaw during the shooting of the black Galanos. She watched with a cold, critical, unrelenting eye. Serena stood there like a stick of wood. Then she began to move. She stayed centered to the lens of the camera as if that focus were home to her. She lifted the hem of the skirt as if to climb a step. She threw a heel out backward as if abandoned to the Charleston. She flirted and coquetted with the lens as if it were the man in her life. All the while she felt Sybil Singlehurst's critical eye. The more she felt the eye, the more self-assertion rose in her. She *knew* that what she was doing was right. The gown was severe. It couldn't be carried off except by a woman who was absolutely sure of herself, so sure that she could be completely uninhibited and still retain the sophistication the gown demanded.

Nothing she did brought a look of approval to Sybil Singlehurst's face. At first, Serena had hoped to please her. Now she didn't try. She was furious enough to become defiant. She twisted her body to give back view from the waist down, profile of the upper body, face

to the camera, eyebrows arched, lids lowered, eyes
sultry, disdaining to look full in the camera. She gave
back views and profiles as well as full front, always in
motion, arms sometimes extended, sometimes straight
at her sides, sometimes holding the skirt pulled to the
back or folded over on itself in the front. She twirled
around so that the skirt wrapped itself around her
legs or lifted halfway up her calves. The more furious
she became with Singlehurst, the higher her eyebrows
arched and her eyelids lowered, the more haughty the
sultry eyes that she kept always just off camera.

Sybil raised her own eyebrows, made her attitude of
unacceptance even more unbending, finally looked
totally disinterested in what Serena was doing. She
liked what she was getting, and she knew that she was
getting it by goading Serena into anger. The girl's
anger gave her a look of marvelous hauteur. There
was something of petulance in it. It was feminine, it
was regal and it was sexy.
    When she was satisfied that she had exactly what
she wanted, she dismissed Serena from the set with a
negligent wave of her hand.

It was almost nine o'clock. Serena was the only
model still at the studio. She was dead tired, but she
was too hyped up to know that she was. She felt as if
she could go on forever. She was back in the Geoffrey
Beene tweed. The brown velvet was again across the
background. The Beene was the fourth outfit she had
been photographed in since the Galanos.
    Mallini had gotten all the shots he wanted. Serena
got up to leave the set.
    "I'd like to do something if you're not too tired,
Serena," Mallini said.
    "I'm not too tired."
    "Do we have more of the brown velvet?" he asked
Carmine.

"Yes. There's more."

"Take the strip down, and put it up again, but on the vertical. Give the other piece to me."

"What do you have in mind?" Singlehurst asked.

Mallini paused. "The cover," he said.

"The cover has been decided on!"

"Just let me set this up. If you don't like it when you see it in the camera, we'll forget it."

Singlehurst looked as if she were going to say no. But she compressed her lips impatiently and said, "I'll look at it."

Mallini took the velvet from Carmine and went with Serena to the dressing room. When they came out again, Serena was wrapped in the velvet, the long end of it over one shoulder like a toga.

Mallini took a heavy gold carved neckplate from its box and fastened it around Serena's throat. "I've been waiting for the right chance to use this," he said. "It's Gordon's favorite piece from this collection, and nothing has been right for it."

He had Carmine remove the straw bench that had been returned to the set for the Geoffrey Beene and stood Serena against the velvet on the background. He had all the lights turned off except those that lit her face and throat. Then he asked Singlehurst to look in the camera.

Singlehurst took her time at the camera; then she walked around in back of it for a minute or two and came back and looked again.

"Take the photograph," she said.

The photograph that had been scheduled for the cover of the December issue of *Milady* was replaced by Mallini's photograph of Serena. It was a full-face head shot. Her hair had been pulled back so that only wayward tendrils showed about her face and throat. Her face and the carved gold neckplate and the suggestion of one bare shoulder were in relief against the rich brown velvet; she seemed to be emerging from the folds of it.

It was Serena Carr's debut as a model, right at the top.

TEN

"Let's talk secrets," Zoe said to Serena after they were seated at the counter and had ordered coffee. They had met for breakfast at a corner drugstore on Madison Avenue before going to Models, Incorporated.

"Talk secrets?"

She waited, but Zoe didn't continue. Finally, Serena prodded, "So?"

Zoe smiled softly, her eyes staring far away. "I was just thinking."

"About . . . ?"

"About Tim . . . Tim and me. . . ."

Serena kept her eyes on Zoe.

"Don't look shocked," Zoe said. "Tim and I didn't invent anything new."

"It's just that everything you read about Helen and Tim O'Neil refers to them as Helenandtimo'neil . . . one word, one person."

"What do you expect? Helen has a good PR man," Zoe said bitterly. "But all that oneness is a lot of crap. This isn't the first time Tim has taken a walk."

"You've got yourself into something you're finding hard to handle?" Serena asked.

Zoe looked at her. Her violet eyes, usually so bright, were dull. "That's right." The words came slowly as if she didn't want to hear herself admit it.

"If I can do anything to help. . . ."

"You can't do anything," Zoe said, "except listen.

You're the first person I've ever felt I could talk to about it. I mean, you've got a problem. I've got a problem." She smiled thinly, tried to make what she said a joke. "Let's share. I'll take half of yours if you'll take half of mine."

"I don't have a problem anymore," Serena said. "I left it behind when I came to New York."

Zoe shook her head. "No way," she said positively.

"I'm serious. It was time for me to cut out, and I did."

Zoe looked at her steadily for a moment. "I have the feeling that your folks don't know about that little development."

"They know I'm not at school. I wrote them before I left."

"That you were coming up here to try modeling?"

"I didn't tell them what I was going to do. I just told them I was going to take a year and get my head straight. To tell the truth, I wasn't thinking of modeling when I came. I came to meet somebody here and go to live with him in Cambridge, but I changed my mind."

"Felt trapped once you'd committed yourself?"

"Perfect description."

"Count yourself lucky you didn't get in any deeper. Is that where your folks think you are . . . Cambridge?"

"I'm sure it is."

"Will they sit still for your living with a guy?"

"That doesn't make any difference now since I'm not going to."

"What's the 'time to cut out' bit? Bored with school?"

"I didn't like the school."

"That particular school or school period?"

Serena made a wry face. "I guess it was *anything* period. I hadn't been happy at home before I went away to school the first year. You know that old worn-out thing about mother-daughter rivalry?" She poked herself in the chest. "Right here. The prime example."

"Rivalry in general or for something specific?"

"In general, I guess. Well, not really. Oh, I don't know. . . ." Serena twisted about as if she couldn't get comfortable on the stool. She was getting into something she didn't want to think about, but she went on, opening old sores. "Do you know what it feels like to be always and forever second best?" she asked.

"I've been learning a lot about that lately," Zoe said.

"Then you know what it's like. Do what I did, and cut out."

"Can't." Zoe shook her head. "No can do. . . . Who were you second best to? Brothers and sisters?"

"I don't have any."

"Who then?"

"Oh . . ." Serena started, and then stopped.

"Come on. You can't let it traumatize you for life," Zoe said. "Tell me about it."

"Some other time maybe," Serena said. "I don't want to talk about it now. I want to feel up this morning. That old stuff is down like you wouldn't believe down." She looked at her watch. "Hadn't we better get over to Models, Incorporated?"

"No rush. My first booking isn't until ten, and Tim isn't there this morning. Just Helen and her henchman."

"Her what?"

"Arthur Hamlisch, the financial brain. Helen masterminds the talent; Hamlisch masterminds the money."

"What does that leave for Tim O'Neil to do?"

Zoe's face hardened. "Tim is the PR man I mentioned. He's the smiling face, the solid front Models, Inc., puts on for the world to see. Damn bastard's good at it, too!"

"Why did you call Arthur Hamlisch Helen's henchman?"

"Because that's what he is. He thinks he's the be-all,
end-all. He's an asshole in my book."

"Should I mark him down as one in mine?" Serena
asked. "What does he do that makes him an asshole
. . . try to make it with the models?"

"Oh, God, no! He's a priss-ass where the models are
concerned."

"Maybe that's your real problem."

"I don't want Arthur Hamlisch!"

"He's obviously getting to you about something."

Zoe dug in her purse for a cigarette and lit it. "He's
trying to break up Tim and me," she said, exhaling a
stream of smoke, angry eyes on the burning end of the
cigarette.

"I don't see that it's any of his business . . . Tim
and you."

"Try telling him that!" Zoe jerked an ashtray on
the counter nearer her and ground out the cigarette
she'd just lit. All the frustration and angry hurt she
felt showed in the jabbing mangling of the cigarette.
Serena had a sinking feeling that Zoe knew she wasn't
going to come out on top.

"What do you have in mind for Tim and you?" she
asked. "Marriage?"

"Of course."

"Is that what he wants?"

"Of course."

"Then why is he dragging his feet?"

"Oh. . . ." Zoe hitched her shoulders up and dropped
them again. "He wants to do it the way it'll be easiest
on Helen. Between the way she grabs on, and the
agency, and the way she keeps getting herself pregnant
when she knows she can't carry. . . ."

"She can't have children?"

"She's had more miscarriages than I can count! But
she keeps getting herself pregnant. It's one of her ways
of hanging onto Tim. The way she's got it worked,

that marriage might as well be put together with cement."

"If that's the case, it seems to me you'd be better off to forget Tim O'Neil."

"I told you, I can't. And he's close now to making the break. He swore to me last night he was going to tell Helen about us this weekend."

"How many times has he sworn to you before he was going to make the break?"

"I told you, Serena, it's hard for him. He doesn't want to hurt anybody."

"He's hurting you." Serena gave Zoe a long look. "You'd be out at Models, Inc., if Tim O'Neil told Helen O'Neil he was leaving her for you. You know that, don't you?"

Zoe threw back her head and laughed. Several heads turned to look in their direction. "Could I care? Christ, Serena! Could I care?"

Serena stood up. "Let's get over there," she said. "Let's get me in Models, Incorporated, first, and then I'll help you get yourself kicked out."

ELEVEN

Zoe walked along beside Serena as tense as a wire coiled to spring. Serena knew that except for her Zoe wouldn't be going to the agency that morning. She had told her that she took all her bookings over the phone, always from one of the booking girls, never from Helen. The only reason she was going now was to introduce Serena to Helen O'Neil.

Serena would have liked to tell Zoe how much she appreciated what she was doing for her, but it was obvious that Zoe didn't want to hear about that or about anything else. This was a new Zoe who could be as emphatically off as she could be emphatically on. And now she was off, sunk in a glum, withdrawn silence.

Zoe knew that Serena was puzzled by her silence and withdrawal, but there wasn't anything she could do about it. Her fits of depression were not long-lasting, but they controlled her when they were on. Letting loose her frustrations about Tim hadn't helped her. The opposite; it had brought back the old frustrations about her father that she'd lived with so many years.

Zoe had been seven the first time her father had spread his hands over her naked chest, his hands so large that his fingers curved around her sides and almost touched at the center of her back.

He'd brought his fingers back and had laid both hands side by side on her chest. He'd spread his forefingers in a V, and when he'd closed them again, he'd had between them and the middle finger of each hand the pink spots that she had on each side of her chest.

"Do you know what these will be?" he asked, smiling down at her with his teasing look on his face. "First they will be little acorns, and then they will be big walnuts, and then"—he'd leaned over and licked first one and then the other with his wet, soft tongue—"then"—he'd bitten each of the little pinched-up pink spots, making them red, almost hurting Zoe—"then they'll be big, so big they'll fill up my hands." He'd looked at her again. He wasn't smiling anymore or teasing. His lips were tight and drawn back, and he was breathing between his teeth. "I'll be proud of you then. You want to make me proud of you, don't you?"

It had taken years for Zoe to have even acorns. She was almost beginning to despair of ever making her father proud of her. It wasn't until she was eleven.

He'd started spending more time with her at nights then. He'd sit on the side of her bed and pull up her nightgown.

"See? Wasn't I right? I don't have to pinch them up anymore."

He'd play his hands over them, tickling her in a way that wasn't really tickling, that felt better than tickling. He'd lean over her and put his mouth on her, take one side of her in his mouth and then the other side. He'd bite her pink points. They were bigger now, and pinker—*nipples* he called them.

"Does that hurt a little? Do you like it when I hurt you a little? I wouldn't really hurt you. You know I wouldn't really hurt you, don't you?"

Zoe would giggle. It tickled. It didn't hurt. Well, maybe it did hurt a little. But she liked it.

One night when she was thirteen, when she'd grown big enough to start hoping she really might fill up his hands if she kept on growing, he was different from all the other nights when he played with her. He made her take her nightgown off, not just pull it up, and he looked at her nakedness a long time. He looked at her, and then he put his hands on her. He rubbed one hand over her breasts—they were big enough to be breasts by then—squeezing them and pinching the nipples, and he ran the fingers of his other hand through the hair that was growing at the bottom of her stomach, tangling his fingers in it and pulling it so much it hurt.

A funny not-seeing look came into his eyes, and he was breathing hard with his mouth open. He reached over and turned out the lamp on the night table beside her bed. The only light in the room was the nightlight. He leaned over her—he was sitting on the side of her bed as he always did—and put the flats of his hands around one of her breasts and pushed it up as high as he could and came down on it with his mouth wide as if he'd take every bit of it in his mouth if he could. He started biting on it and licking it and nursing it as if he were starved and were eating it. He sucked it into his mouth so hard when he nursed it that Zoe almost cried out from the pain.

He was hurting her worse than he ever had, but she didn't want him to stop. She wished he had four hands and two mouths so he could be doing the same thing to both her breasts.

He put one hand between her legs and pushed them apart. And then he touched her on a place that made her yelp. Not from pain. The feeling was sharp, but it wasn't pain.

"Ahh! Ahh! Ahh!"

"Shhh!" her father said. He put one hand over her mouth. "Shhh!"

He kept his hand over her mouth, and with the other hand he got his trousers off. He climbed up on the bed over her and straddled her, one knee on the bed on either side of her. She wasn't afraid at first, but then she saw the big thing between his legs pointed straight at her, and she got scared as she'd never been scared before.

"I'm not going to hurt you," her father said. "I'm not going to hurt you. You be quiet." He was breathing so hard she could feel the gusts of his breaths hitting her face and spilling down on her still-wet breasts. "Be quiet."

He lowered himself down on her and put his big thing between her legs. He started pushing it at her. After a while he was hurting her, really hurting her. She couldn't scream out or tell him because his hand was still over her mouth, pushing her head back hard into the pillow. She tore at his hand. He was suffocating her. Tears were welling up in her eyes and running back down her throat and strangling her. She pushed frantically against his face and tried to bring her knees up between them, but his body was too close on hers, and she couldn't. He acted as if he'd gone crazy. He acted as if he didn't know she was pushing at him and trying to get him off of her. He didn't pay any attention to anything except what he was doing.

Suddenly he drew a little away from her, and then he lunged his big hard thing between her legs with such force that it went into her body. She had never felt such pain. She felt as if she had been split wide open. Everything went black. Her hands fell away from him, and her body went limp. But she could still feel the tearing, ripping pain. He hadn't stopped pushing his thing into her. He was pushing it in harder and faster and deeper.

She couldn't stand anymore. She wished the blackness would overtake her completely. She tried to faint.

And then she began to feel something besides the pain. She felt it stronger every time he drove himself into her. At first it was just a tiny pinpoint of feeling where he had touched her and made her yelp. Then it began to spread and grow stronger. It didn't make the pain go away, but it made her want him to push himself even farther into her. She tried to push herself up against him, tried to turn herself up to him so he could go in farther. He wasn't doing it fast enough, and she tried to make him do it faster.

The feeling had drawn her up so tight she thought it was going to make her explode, and she wished it would. She threw her arms around his shoulders and threw her legs over his back. She locked herself around him as tightly as if she were in a convulsion. Everything in her squeezed as hard as it could on the part of him that was inside her. That was the only place in her body that she could feel, and she felt it tighten in a spasm and explode. Wave after wave of feeling broke loose over her whole body. Her whole body jerked with each wave. She felt something hot come out of him and fill up in her, and the waves of feeling started up even stronger.

He slumped down on her as if all the breath and strength had gone out of him. His hand relaxed and flopped away from her face.

The waves of feeling grew less strong and slowed down and stopped, and she felt him shriveling up inside her and sliding out of her. Disappointment in herself was like a sharp knife cutting through her. It was worse than the pain that was coming back. She started to cry, hot tears of disappointment running out of the sides of her eyes and down into her hair on the pillow. "I didn't do it right," she sobbed. "What did I do wrong that made you stop?"

"You didn't do anything wrong, baby," her father said. He was crying. She saw the tears on his face. He moved off her and got up from the bed, not looking at her. "Don't cry. You didn't do anything wrong."

Zoe couldn't count the number of men she'd slept with. She couldn't even remember the names of a lot of them. But none of them had ever taken her to the hellgate-raising heights that her father had.

She hated her father's guts. And she hated herself for the nights from the time she was thirteen until she was seventeen, when her mother took night-duty nursing, that she had lain in her bed, panting and squirming and sweating, until he came and got on her bed over her and chewed on her nipples until he got his thing up and got it into her and they pounded their bodies together until both of them exploded with the waves of feeling that had a stronger hold on them than any drug could ever have had.

When he died, she thought she'd go crazy. She went from man to man like the nymphomaniac she was afraid she was. But—until Tim—no matter how often she had sex, her insides had gnawed and twisted and convulsed with the ache of wanting him. Every night, unable to sleep, she'd finally pushed herself up from her damp pillow and sheets and flung herself out of her bed and paced the floor, sweating from every pore, every tender, bruised nerve end raging for release.

It wasn't that sex with Tim was so great. Maybe she had changed, grown out of the old feeling for her father. She didn't know. But whatever had brought it about, her deliverance had come when her affair with Tim started. And she was afraid to give him up.

"We're here," Serena said. She had to repeat it and catch hold of Zoe's arm and stop her. "Isn't this the number you told me?"

Zoe looked up at the stone and concrete of the building, at the number carved in the stone over the entrance. Tim's wife was up there in that building, solid and secure in her position, solid and secure in her possession of Tim. . . .

That brought Zoe out of her trancelike reverie. She squared her bony, elegant shoulders and tossed her head; her pencil-thin eyebrows rose in peaks; her violet eyes became alert and alive. "Open sesame!" she ordered, and marched through the revolving doors.

TWELVE

Models, Incorporated, owned by Helen and Tim O'Neil, was the top model agency in New York and, by that token, the top agency in the world. Ten floors above the revolving doors, Helen O'Neil was interviewing applicants.

"My God, you're as big as a horse!"

Helen didn't subdue her voice. The words exploded out of her.

The disappointed girl was unable to keep her disappointment from showing.

"Lose twenty pounds and come back," Helen said.

The girl, taking no hope from that, turned to leave.

"Wait a minute! Wait a minute!" Helen sat up in her chair. "Where are you going to lose that twenty pounds?"

The disappointed hopeful turned back. "I don't know," she stammered, puzzled that Helen O'Neil was interested enough to care. "What do you mean, where? I'll go on a diet, I guess."

"Go to Gounovsky!"

Helen scribbled an address on a note pad—in a hurry; she did everything in a hurry.

"Here! Go here!" She ripped the page from the note pad and thrust it toward the girl. "Tell Gounovsky I sent you!" Without a pause . . . "Where are you staying?"

The girl reached for the piece of paper. "At the Summit on—"

"That's no good!" Helen interrupted. "That won't do! My God, the Summit!" She snorted in disgust. "Pack your stuff, and get out of there! Go to the Barbizon! I'll call them and tell them to give you a room!"

The girl watched the woman across the desk with wary amazement. She had been warned that Helen O'Neil could be an ogress or a godmother. She was getting both barrels. Helen O'Neil's light brown eyes had become sharply alive, animated as if by anger. Her short brown hair was tousled and unkempt from the vigorous bobbing of her head for emphasis. Her short, blunt nose seemed to be quivering. Her small but large-boned body seemed to be moving in all its joints even though she was seated. She was fairly bristling in every nerve of her body. People said of Helen O'Neil that she treated every word she uttered as if it were of cataclysmic importance, that she acted as if she were about to take on the world at Napoleon's side every time she prepared to launch a new model on a career, and in fact, Helen attached as much importance to her conquests as Napoleon had to his. Her grandiose attitude might be put down by some, but her position at the top couldn't be.

"Get moved first," Helen ordered, "and then go to Gounovsky. Report back to me when you've lost five pounds, and if it isn't by the end of the week, don't bother."

The girl stared at Helen. Helen O'Neil was telling her that if she wanted to lose five pounds in a few days badly enough, she could do it. A ripple of pride went through her. She tried to stand taller than her five-foot-eight frame, to minimize the heft of her 130 pounds. She determined in that moment to lose 20 pounds, and maybe more, even if it meant living on nothing but black coffee. If Barbara Hutton could do it, she could.

Helen O'Neil hadn't smiled at the girl once, but the

girl left her presence knowing that Helen O'Neil was on her side. If she would do her best for Helen O'Neil, Helen O'Neil would do her best for her.

The next applicant was less lucky. She had possibilities, but she wasn't up to the mark for Models, Incorporated.

"Go to Wilhelmina," Helen told her. "I'm not the last word. Get somebody else's opinion. You're not right for us, but . . ."

Her tone of voice said that the girl could get on the modeling ladder but that she would never get to the top rungs of it.

The next applicant had no luck at all.

"Go back home," Helen said. "The kindest thing I can say to you is to forget it. You might wind up working in New York, but you wouldn't be modeling."

Everyone always knew exactly where they stood with Helen O'Neil.

Serena's preconceived notion of what Models, Incorporated, would be like might have been born in the 1930s in a Hollywood set designer's head. She had pictured offices in the grand manner with much wide space, deep carpeting, many gilded mirrors, lavish flower arrangements, inviting sofas and chairs and an overall air of luxury and glamour. She had expected to see several of the famous models—whom she would recognize from pictures—all dressed in the height of chic, their every movement and stance as languorous and seductive, or as vital and full of life, as their pictures in magazines and their commercials on television. She had expected an atmosphere of hush, of quiet dignity. What she found looked to her uninitiated eye like total chaos.

Models overran the small reception room. They were dressed in everything from ankle-length cotton skirts and high boots to threadbare, thin-seated jeans and ratty fur jackets so ancient they had rusted. They stood in slouches or leaned on the walls or sprawled on benches or squatted on the floor.

The harried receptionist was trying to handle a continuously ringing telephone, a continuously flashing intercom system and the continuous flow of people through the room. She apparently was the conduit for the internal traffic as well as that from outside—except for the models, whose chatterings and moving about added to the atmosphere of clutter and confusion but whose presence she hadn't the time even to acknowledge. The models obviously used the reception room as a lounge.

Before Serena could take it all in, a woman about five feet six, shorter than any of the models, came into the room. She stopped just inside the door. Even standing still, she didn't look still. Everything inside her continued in high gear.

The phone kept ringing and the intercom kept flashing and the receptionist kept trying to answer both at the same time, but the models quieted, breaking off their chattering in mid-sentence and even midword. Serena knew without being told that the woman was Helen O'Neil.

"Serena Carr," the woman said. Her voice was deep-throated or hoarse, but it was piercing at the same time. She didn't speak unnecessarily loud, but she would have been heard over even more noise than there was.

The models, who up to now had paid scant attention to Serena, all looked at her with interest.

"Oh, God!" Zoe flung up a hand. "I might have known! Here I come ready to spring my big coup, and you already know about her!"

There was no response from Helen O'Neil except the amused look she gave Zoe. It was an open, level look that clearly said that whatever she cared to know she knew.

"She's got more spies than the CIA," Zoe said to Serena.

A sudden and unexpected smile twinkled on Helen's face. It was more than a smile because it changed her whole face, gave her an elfin, infinitely younger look. She was in her late thirties. When she smiled, she looked like a teenager. Her eyes crinkled almost closed; dimples showed in her cheeks; her mouth opened, showing her teeth as if she were laughing rather than smiling. "That's one of the nicer things they say about me," she said to Serena.

The models around the room came out of their locked-in silence and laughed or giggled. It was obvious that in Helen's roost everyone followed Helen's lead—except for a bearded man who had come to stand in the door behind Helen. He was not smiling.

"You have a ten o'clock with Asha Coleman," Helen said to Zoe.

"Christ! I know my bookings!"

"You were late for your last booking with her. You'd better get over there. I don't want her calling up here again, chewing *me* out because *you're* late." Helen was still smiling, but her eyes had sharpened. She meant what she said.

"Okay! Okay! Can it! I'm going!"

"I've booked you tomorrow for a go-see for Eye-Wonder," Helen said. "I had to make it for nine o'clock. That was the only free time you had this week. Don't be late, and don't be bleary-eyed."

Zoe's head flew up. Her eyes flashed with anger. "A *go-see!*"

"A go-see," Helen said firmly and with finality. She turned to Serena. "Come with me, Serena," she said.

"*Shit!*" Zoe exploded.

"Nine o'clock at Farkus," Helen said, not turning

her head back to look at Zoe. "Be wearing Eye-Wonder when you get there."

Zoe let out an exasperated breath and flapped both arms down against her sides. She compressed her lips and shook her head in a slow, angry jerk in the direction of Helen's uncommunicating back. Then she turned in a huff and stamped out, muttering about "goddamn go-sees."

The man in the door stood aside to let Helen and Serena pass, his eyes on Zoe all the while. He watched her until the outer door closed behind her. Zoe hadn't glanced in his direction once, but she had been aware that he was there.

Helen led Serena through a room about four times the size of the reception room. It was not as crowded with people, but it was even more chaotic. Serena had only a blurred impression of what she passed. Every counter top and desk top was cluttered—to a depth of a foot in places—with sheafs of filled-out forms and scrawled memo pads and typed file cards, magazines, tear sheets, newspapers and portfolios, date pads and calendars. The walls were hung with posters, notices, framed photographs of models, covers of models torn from magazines and discount-house advertisements. There didn't seem to be any order in any of it. There was a counter almost the whole length of one wall at which half a dozen girls sat answering telephones. On the wall they faced were sliding panels, which they pushed back and forth so they could pull out long horizontal cards as they talked on the telephones. The cards were hung in overlapping tiers on the panels. "The models' booking charts," Helen said briefly, indicating the panels.

On the other side of the room there were several desks, a girl at each desk talking on one or more telephones at once, consulting clipboards and making notes on lined yellow pads. They didn't finish their business on the phones as quickly as the girls at the counter. She heard one girl say, "This will knock you out of all other detergents. I want you to know that before you take it. . . . No, it doesn't conflict with soap. They know about your Ivory commercial."

Helen indicated the desks along the wall. "Television bookings," she said.

Before they were out of the room, one of the girls answering telephones at the long counter on the wall called out, "Helen! Lugano Studio is on the phone. Isolda Mellors didn't show this morning."

Helen whirled around. "Again!"

"She was due at nine. It's almost ten. They want to know who you can get over there in a hurry." She was holding the telephone to her ear, her hand over the mouthpiece, listening while she was talking. "They want somebody like Shari Holliday or—"

"Are they crazy? Shari's booked solid for—"

"Hold it! Isolda just walked in."

Helen rushed over and snatched the phone from the girl's hand.

"Put Isolda on!" She tapped her foot angrily while she waited. "Isolda! When you finish your bookings today, come over here! I want to talk to you!" She slammed the phone down. "It's that Rod Ingram!" she snapped. "Ever since she started seeing him, there's been nothing but trouble! It's going to stop, or she'll find herself with a one-way ticket back to Sweden! Musicians! They're the worst kind you can get yourself mixed up with! Boozing all night! Drugs! . . ." She was fuming when she got back to where she'd left Serena.

She hadn't got the best start in the world with Helen O'Neil, Serena thought. First, someone who was having an affair with her husband had introduced her to her, and now someone she never even heard of before had made her as mad as a hornet.

Helen led the way through a door at the far end

of the big room and closed it behind them. They went down a short, narrow corridor and into another room. When Helen closed the door to that room, none of the noise they had left behind could be heard. Helen seated herself behind a large desk and motioned Serena to a chair in front of it.

"Why did you go to a photographer before you got yourself signed up with an agency?" Helen asked without any preliminaries. "That's putting the cart before the horse."

"How did you know who I was?" Serena countered.

"I make it my business to know what goes on in this business," Helen said.

Serena decided then and there that she didn't like the flat-out way Helen O'Neil had of putting things. She also decided that Helen O'Neil was trying to put her down. Helen continued. "The fact that you lucked into being photographed for *Milady* before you'd unpacked your suitcases doesn't mean you've got it made. It may be months before *Milady* uses you again . . . if they *do* use you again."

"There's other work, isn't there?" Serena was on the defensive, and didn't like it, and didn't know why she should be.

"Oh, there's plenty of work."

"Well . . . ?"

"For models. And you're not a model yet. There's plenty of work, and there are at least a dozen models available for every piece of it, who are capable of doing it. If you get to be a model, and if you want part of the available work, you'll have to grub for it, just like the rest. You'll have to go after it. It's not coming to you."

Serena was getting angrier. Why did Helen O'Neil keep putting her down? Who the hell did she think she was? If she'd heard the way Mallini had raved over her, she'd be singing a different tune, Serena told herself.

"I think Mallini will use me again before *months*," she said.

Helen laughed. "And invite you to Gordon's for dinner again before *months?*" She stopped laughing. "Let me clue you in about Mallini and—"

"I got the picture when I was at Gordon Knightsplit's for dinner," Serena interrupted.

Helen's eyes narrowed. "I hope you got the whole picture."

"I got it. Gordon Knightsplit is about as subtle as a sledgehammer."

"First time I've heard that. I thought he was Mr. Smooth. He's got a near-perfect track record."

"He didn't score with me!"

Helen gave a "so what" shrug, and Serena wished she hadn't blurted out her answer so fast. She'd sounded like a prig.

"I've always liked Gordon," Helen said. "He's good company."

"He's very good company and a great host," Serena said. "I was having a great time until he started coming on."

Helen didn't seem to be listening to her. She wasn't. "Tell you something, Serena," she said. "You'll have to develop a tougher hide than you've got if you want to get ahead in the modeling business."

"My hide's tough enough."

"Is it? Twice, in the five minutes we've been talking, you've let something I said get to you. But if you say you're tough, I'll take your word for it. I'll lay it out to you like it is. . . . Modeling is a trade. It's not a profession. A profession—like law or medicine—is something you can be taught. The only way to learn a trade is by doing it—like an automobile mechanic. You're going to have to learn your trade, and a few sessions in front of a camera with a photographer fawning all over you and going spastic as if he's having an orgasm every time he clicks the camera won't teach it to you. Success in this business doesn't come that quickly or that easily, not if you want to be something more than a flash in the pan. You've got the physical requirements, but that's all you've got. You haven't got the basic skills, and you're not going to learn them in studios like Mallini's, where everything is done for you. You learn them in one-man studios like Stegler's or Mano's, where you do your own makeup and your own hair, where you provide your own costume jewelry and accessories and sometimes even style yourself with a halfway assist from the photographer. . . . Do you think you could handle that after two days spent with Mallini?"

"No. Of course, I couldn't."

"That's what I meant when I said you'd put the cart before the horse. You'd be a lot better equipped for modeling right now if you'd spent those two days with Stegler instead of with Mallini."

"I must have gotten something out of it. I'm not altogether stupid."

"You got a view from the top, and that's not the best idea either. Most studios, after Mallini's, are going to be a comedown for you."

"That's the kind you would have sent me to first, I suppose."

"Damn right. Because that's the kind you're going to spend the major portion of your time in, if you work it right. And for the reason I mentioned before . . . learning your trade. Out of every hundred studios in New York, there's maybe one like Mallini's. The rest grade down to the one-man studios. How many would you feel confiident to walk into?"

"I wouldn't feel confident with anybody at this point except Mallini."

"I think I'm beginning to get through to you."

"You've been getting through to me from the beginning, but I've already spent the two days with Mallini. I can't do anything about that now."

"That's right. That's something we'll have to live with."

Serena hesitated before she could make herself ask, "Does that mean you think I'm good enough for Models, Incorporated?"

"If I didn't, I'd be wasting my time, and I don't have time to waste. I told you you have the physical requirements." She pursed her lips and studied Serena. "I can turn that little head start with *Milady* to advantage," she said. She cocked her head to one side and then to the other, still studying Serena, concentrating on her eyes. "I'm going to send you on the go-see for Eye-Wonder," she said.

"The one Zoe's going on?"

Helen nodded.

Serena didn't want to be in competition with Zoe for a job. "I don't have any pictures to show them," she said. "Mallini's going to give me some, but he hasn't yet."

"They don't want to see pictures. They'll do some shots of you. They always take shots of the models they might use to show the client. If nothing else, you'll get some good eye shots out of it for your portfolio."

"But if Zoe's going. . . ."

"Zoe and a hundred others. I'm sending six from here, not including you and Zoe. Some of the other agencies will send droves, but I don't flood a go-see. I don't send anybody that I haven't culled for the job myself."

"I don't want to compete with Zoe. What if I got the job?"

"What if Zoe gets it?"

"But she had the go-see first."

Helen gave her a long look. "I'll tell you what," she said. "You let me handle my end of this thing, and I'll let you handle yours. Who goes on a go-see is my end of it."

Helen stood up. "I'll show you around," she said, "introduce you to the booking girls and the rest of the staff."

The last person Helen introduced Serena to was Arthur Hamlisch. She flung open his door without knocking and popped her head inside the room, thrusting out her rear end and bending around the door frame at a forty-five-degree angle. "How about taking two gals to lunch?" she sang out. She sounded as if she were yodeling across a mountain pass instead of speaking to somebody across a room.

Arthur Hamlisch snapped off the dictaphone he'd been using. "Can't," he said. "I'm giving Hopworth my monthly blast about the stock portfolio. I'm going to have a sandwich at the desk." He stood up and came around the desk, his hand stuck out toward Serena. "Arthur Hamlisch," he said.

His handshake exactly described the man, Serena thought. Every grain of skin in his hand, and every ounce of grip, spelled M-A-L-E. He held her hand in his just as long as the handshake required, and no longer. The expression in his eyes was receptive, but no more than that. His manner was affable and friendly, but only to a degree.

It was impossible to guess how old he was. He could be anywhere from thirty to forty. He was taller than Serena's five eight, but not by much. He was compactly built, obviously in excellent physical shape. He had black gray-peppered hair and a full beard, bright brown eyes, a strong, straight nose and a wide, not overfull mouth. His open-collared skin-tight shirt stretched over a massive chest. His slim-legged pants were unbelted. His jacket was collarless, lapelless and buttonless. His clothes had to be custom-designed to his order. They wouldn't be found on any rack in any department store or boutique.

Arthur Hamlisch held his dynamic sexuality under

control. He made Serena think of a stalking lion. He would make contact—and it would be violent contact —when he chose. Until he spotted the prey he wanted, no one—no matter how attractive—could tempt him. Zoe had said he played it strictly hands-off where models were concerned. Serena wondered what kind of women he *did* come on with.

THIRTEEN

By the end of the week Serena was signed up with Models, Incorporated, and had moved into an apartment on East Sixty-first Street. Zoe had helped her find the apartment and get settled into it. Zoe and Serena had become as close as sisters (which neither had ever had). They spent all their time together except for the times when Tim was free to see Zoe and except for the times when Stephen came for the weekend. The two couples never double-dated.

Helen was in Rome on one of her scouting expeditions for promising talent. She wasn't expected back until Monday night. All of Zoe's evenings were taken up with Tim, and the weekend as well. Serena found herself with time on her hands. She could spend just so much time practicing putting on makeup and practicing poses and facial expressions in front of her mirror.

Stephen called every night, but he came into her mind when he said hello and went out of it when he said his reluctant good-bye. Her aloneness made her think of home. Scenes from her life at home drifted through her mind as if viewed in a kaleidoscope.

"Leave the room, Serena!"

Her mother always looked taller to Serena when she was angry. She towered over her now. Her head seemed to rise right up to the ceiling.

"Mind your mother," her daddy said. "Go to your

room. Tell Nurse to put you to bed. I'll come up later and read to you."

Serena left, knowing the quarrel would start as soon as she closed the door behind her. Quarrels always started between her mother and daddy when her mother ordered her to leave the room.

Her nurse, Lorrie, loomed up in front of her from out of nowhere. She always did, times like this.

"What's the matter with you now?" Lorrie said. "Look at you! Face all pruned up ready to cry!"

She picked Serena up and cradled her to her broad, soft bosom. "What they done to my baby this time?" She started up the stairs to the second floor, going slowly, taking each step with both feet before going on to the next. She was too heavy to move fast.

Lorrie was as big as the side of the house, Serena's mother said, and as slow as Christmas. She said it right to Lorrie's face, but Lorrie didn't pay any attention to her. She wasn't afraid of her. Serena had asked Lorrie once why she wasn't afraid of her mother when she got mad.

"Many times as I turned her up and spanked her when she was little like you, you think I'm gone be scared of her now?" Lorrie had answered, her eyes sparking fire at the very thought. Lorrie had been her mother's nurse when she was little.

Wells Carr was born to money and had made millions in his own right. He was the senior partner of Carr International, the brokerage firm he had inherited from his father. He was a commodities broker, one of the most powerful in the world, a controller of national and international markets, a world-wide manipulator of grain, produce and cotton futures. He was a successful man—except with his wife.

Wells was medium in height, medium in build and medium in coloring. He had a pleasant, open face, candid in expression. He was not given to brooding, but he was sometimes sad. His light brown hair was beginning to show gray at the temples. His light brown eyes looked out mildly on the world no matter what he was feeling. He had a trim figure, kept in shape by swimming and golf. He looked like what he was—a well-turned-out, well-mannered, well-educated Atlanta businessman.

Eleanor Carr—Ellie—was from a background equal to that of her husband—old money and good family. Like Wells, she had grown up in Atlanta.

Ellie was five feet eight to her husband's five feet ten and liked to wear three-inch heels to make herself taller. She had been beautiful all her life, a standout in any gathering. She had long, graceful legs, thin flanks, a narrow waist and full breasts. She had glossy blond hair, which was long or short, casual or contrived, depending on the fashion. Her hair, makeup, clothes, even her nail lacquer were always up to the minute—matching the prevailing fashion in New York and Paris. One of Ellie's constant complaints was that new trends were slow in getting to Atlanta.

Ellie had cat-green eyes and a nervous disposition. Her total concentration was centered in herself.

She was bored, bored, bored! She wanted great things, explosive things, to happen to her. She rebelled against what she considered the dullness of her life, rich as it was, traveled as it was. Her rebellions were confined within the home and her personal life. But they were not harmless.

"Why do you keep promising the child something you know she's not going to have, Wells?"

Ellie did not try to keep her voice down. When she was angry, she didn't care who heard what she had to say.

"Because it's something she should have, Ellie,"

Wells said quietly. "She's lonesome. She needs a play-
mate. You weren't brought up as an only child. You
don't know how lonely it can be. I do."

"I ruined my figure to have one child for you! I'll
not ruin it again to give you another! None of your
whining, and none of *hers*, will make me!"

This was not the first quarrel on the subject, and it
had come about the way such quarrels usually came
about. Wells had asked Serena what she would like to
have for her birthday. Her answer had been what it
always was: "A baby sister."

"Wells!" Ellie said warningly.

Wells ignored her. "Your mother and I will have to
see what we can do about that," he said to Serena. "It's
too late to get it here in time for your birthday. How
about Christmas?"

Serena began to feel excited inside. Her friend Lacey
Blair had just had a baby sister. She had taken Serena
into the nursery to see it. Lacey had touched the baby,
but she wouldn't let Serena. Serena's fingers had actually tingled at the tips, she had wanted so badly to
touch the baby.

"I told you, Wells!"

Serena knew how mad her mother was getting, but
her daddy didn't seem to. He went right on talking
about the baby. He was making Serena feel nervous.
She wished she hadn't said she wanted a baby sister.

"We don't always know what we'll get when we
order a baby," her daddy said. "What if it should turn
out to be a baby brother?"

Serena sidled up to his chair. She spoke very softly,
not daring to look at her mother.

"Will it play with me if it's a baby brother?" she
asked her daddy.

"Of course, it will play with you."

"Then it's all right if it's a baby brother," Serena
whispered, making what she said a secret between herself and her daddy.

Her mother stood up, towering over her.
"Leave the room, Serena!"

Serena couldn't remember having spent much time
with her mother when she was little. She bored her
mother, and she was humiliatingly aware that she did.
The first time she could remember her mother acting
glad about having her along was the time when she
was six and her mother decided to take her on a trip.

Ellie was excited about the proposed trip with
Serena. Wells was not.

"I don't understand this sudden change of plans,"
he said. "I need you with me in Amsterdam, Ellie. I
have to do a good deal of entertaining while I'm
there."

"I hate Amsterdam!" Ellie flared out at him. "You
know I can't stand it! It's nothing but filthy canals and
filthy odors and filthy drug addicts that you can't walk
down a street or through a square without stumbling
over! I'll meet you later in London."

"It's in Amsterdam that I'll need you with me, Ellie," Wells said doggedly.

"Well, make up your mind you aren't going to have
me with you in Amsterdam! I promised Serena I'd
take her on a trip, just the two of us. I promised to
show her the Florida Keys."

"The Keys? . . . You've always claimed you hated
Florida. If you want Serena with you, we'll take her
with us to Europe. I hadn't mentioned taking her because you've always refused."

"We wouldn't have any time to spend with her.
You'd be at business all day, and I'd be busy all day
getting ready to entertain at night. Stop arguing with
me about it, Wells! I'm not going to Amsterdam with
you!"

Ellie didn't want one of the Carr International
planes to fly her and Serena to Florida.

"I'm going to drive."

"Drive?" Wells was astounded. "Don't be ridiculous, Ellie. What kind of trip would that be for Serena? Two days driving there and two days driving back."

"I can show her things of interest as we drive along. That's the best way to see a country, to drive through it."

"I don't know what's come over you, Ellie, but whatever it is, I don't like it. This whim of yours to go to Florida . . . this business of driving . . . these are not things you—"

"Shut up and leave me alone about it! You'll spoil the trip for Serena with your eternal nagging! When are you leaving for Amsterdam? I wish to hell you'd already left!"

After Wells left, there was not a trace of anger in Ellie. Everything made her laugh, even things that would normally have irritated her—the bikinis she had ordered that arrived in the wrong colors, the Joy perfume bottle that wouldn't open, the butler's complaints about the housekeeper. Ellie waved all the anoyances off gaily and went ahead with her preparations for her trip with Serena. "We'll take lots of trips," she said, "if we have fun on this one. Wouldn't you like that? We'll take lots more, just the two of us."

Serena thought her whole life had changed and was going to be different from then on. Her mother liked her now. From now on her mother would be always laughing, always gay and happy because of looking forward to trips with her—just the two of them.

They left in midafternoon two days after Wells had flown to Amsterdam, the first stop on his European trip. Ellie talked and chatted and laughed and teased all the way out of town, dodging in and out of traffic, ignoring caution lights and stop signs, driving with the top of the XKE down, her blond hair flying in the wind. Serena was in seventh heaven.

"I don't think we'll drive all the way to Lake Sinclair today," Ellie said after they were on the broad superhighway. "We'll stop for the night at Locust Grove. How would you like that?"

Serena was disappointed. "You mean we're not going to the lake? I thought we were going out on the lake."

"We can do that tomorrow. The lake isn't going anywhere."

When they were at dinner that night in Locust Grove, at a table for four—which Ellie had selected in preference to the table for two which the headwaiter had first shown them to—a man came into the restaurant and came over to their table, a look of great surprise on his face.

"If it isn't Ellie Carr!" he exclaimed. "What on earth brings you to Locust Grove?"

Ellie's face flushed. A bright smile came over it. She got the same look of surprise on her face that the man had on his.

"Sonny Thatcher!" she exclaimed. (Serena thought her voice sounded like the man's, the same way her face looked like his.) "I could ask you the same thing! You're the last person I would have expected to see in this corner of the earth! What are you doing here?"

"Right now I'm being real lonesome. I was about to have dinner by myself. I don't suppose you'd take pity on me and let me join you?"

"Of course we would. We wouldn't want you to be lonesome." She beamed gaily at Serena. "Would we, Serena? . . . This is my daughter, Serena," she added, her head already turned away from Serena again and back to the man.

The man patted Serena on the head, at the same time pulling out the chair between her and her mother and sitting down. That pat on the head was the last of his attention that Serena got all through dinner. Every now and then her mother would include her in something she said. "Isn't that true, Serena?" "Don't we, Serena?" She never waited for Serena's answers.

Ellie had taken a suite of rooms—two bedrooms with a parlor between. Sonny Thatcher went to the hotel with her and Serena after dinner and up to the suite. Ellie took Serena to her bedroom and drew a bath for her while she undressed and brushed her teeth. Then she found a program on television for her and tucked her in bed after she came out of the bathroom in her nightgown. She told Serena she'd be in later to turn off the television, for Serena to go to sleep as soon as she could so she'd be fresh for all the driving they had to do the next day. Then she went back to the parlor.

The next morning the television set was off and Ellie's bedroom door was locked when Serena went to tell her that it was after nine o'clock and she'd better hurry if they were going to get an early start.

Serena stood staring at the doorknob she was twisting, or trying to twist. Every now and then she looked at the door itself. She kept hoping that it wasn't really locked and the knob would turn fully and the door would open. She was afraid to knock. She wasn't allowed to knock on her mother and daddy's bedroom door at home because if her mother were sleeping, it would disturb her. But she could always just open that door. It was never locked.

"Ooh! Ooh! Ooh!" Serena heard. She caught her breath. Was her mother hurting? "Ooh, that's so good!" she heard. "Ooh, that's so good!" Serena let out her breath. Her mother wasn't hurting, but whom was she talking to?

Serena backed off from the door a little, leaned over and looked through the keyhole. At first she couldn't see anything, and she thought the key must be in the keyhole. She looked with one eye and then the other and kept changing positions and finally she realized that she was seeing into the room but that it was dim and shadowy because the shades were down and the light couldn't come in. When her eyes got used to the dim light, she made out the bed, and then she saw her mother.

Her mother was naked, sitting up in the bed on her spread knees, facing the head of the bed. She had her hands down in front of her and was pushing herself up and down. What in the world was she doing?

Then Serena saw what looked like hands sliding up her mother's legs and to her waist. She thought she saw arms. She couldn't see the rest of anybody because the covers were piled up on the bed. She couldn't see all of her mother. She couldn't see her feet.

Serena would have given anything if daylight had come into the room and she could see better. If that was somebody's hands and arms, her mother had to be sitting on them, and her hands were on them, on their stomach, not on the bed.

Her mother started pushing herself up and down faster and faster. "Ooh! Ooh! Ooh!" She flung her face straight up to the ceiling. " Oooooh!" She fell down flat on the bed or on somebody, if that was somebody she was sitting on. "Ooh, so good! Ooh, so good!"

Serena jumped back from the door, ran as fast as she could back to her room, scrambled back up in the bed and pulled the covers up over her head. She was shaking all over. She hadn't seen anything, she told herself. She hadn't seen anything! People didn't act like that! She didn't know why it scared her so to think that they might. Anyway, she knew they didn't. Not unless they were crazy. And her mother wasn't crazy! She wouldn't do something crazy like that!

Serena huddled under the covers, hugging herself with her arms around herself. The next thing she knew her mother was waking her up.

"Oh, my, what a sleepyhead!" her mother said. But she wasn't scolding. She was laughing, teasing Serena. "Jump out of bed now, and I'll help you get dressed."

After Serena was dressed, she said, "Run down to

the dining room, and get a table for us while I get dressed. I won't be but a minute."

She was a lot longer than a minute, and when she came into the dining room, Sonny Thatcher was with her. "Look who I met in the lobby!" she called out gaily to Serena.

During breakfast Ellie said to Serena, "Mr. Thatcher is going to drive with us to Florida. Won't that be fun?"

"We don't have room for him in the car," Serena said.

Ellie laughed. "We'll *make* room!"

Serena didn't want Mr. Thatcher to come with them to Flordia. She didn't like him. Her mother ignored her when he was around. "You said it was going to be just the two of us," she said.

"Well, it *was* until we ran into Mr. Thatcher. It'll be a lot more fun with him. He has a lovely big boat. He's going to take us deep-sea fishing. You'll love deep-sea fishing. We just never could get Daddy interested in boats and fishing, could we?"

Serena couldn't remember that they had ever tried to get her daddy interested in boats and fishing. She was disappointed at the way the trip was turning out. She pouted all the way to Florida, but her mother and Mr. Thatcher were too busy talking to each other and laughing to notice.

Serena took a number of trips with her mother. She came to dread them. There was always a man. At first it was always Sonny Thatcher, but then he didn't come along anymore, and there was a succession of strangers.

When the first of the strangers turned up, Serena's mother told her that the man who was going on the trip with them was a doctor, that she had a chronic illness, that it was nothing that was going to kill her but that it required periodic treatment. She said that if Serena's daddy knew about it, he would worry, so both of them must be very careful not to breathe a word about the doctor to him.

Every time they took a trip a different "doctor" went with them.

Serena was a long time figuring out that the men were not doctors. If they were, all their treatments were such that they had to be administered to her mother after Serena had gone to bed in her room, which was always at least a parlor removed from her mother's.

When Serena finally figured this out, she also figured out that her mother was using her to cover up what she was doing that was wrong. She didn't know what the wrongdoing was, but she knew that it was something her mother had to hide from her daddy and that she figured he wouldn't suspect her of wrongdoing when she had Serena with her. That was the only reason she took her along on the trips. She certainly didn't take her along for her company because she spent very little time with her. Serena spent most of her time while she and her mother were away with baby-sitters, in swimming pools and at the movies. At night she watched television alone in her room.

Serena had a strong reaction to what she had figured out. She violently resented the fact that her mother had, for years, duped her into helping her hide dirty secrets from her daddy. The next time Ellie planned a trip "just for the two of us" Serena got sick. She got sick every time after that until her mother finally got the message.

Ellie reverted to her old attitude toward Serena. She no longer laughed with her and teased her. She no longer showed worry and concern over her stomachaches and dizzy spells. She threw up her hands in disgust and said Lorrie could carry on over Serena if she wanted to but there wasn't a thing in the world wrong with her except that she wanted her way and would go to any lengths to get it.

Not having Serena's company didn't stop her from going on her trips. She went alone.

Serena welcomed the times when her mother was away because her father spent a lot of time with her then. He was home every night for dinner except for the rare occasions when he couldn't get out of a business dinner. On weekends they swam together and rode together, and sometimes she walked around with his foursome when he played golf. "This is my best girl," he would tell his friends. Serena would be embarrassed and shy, but she'd be proud, too. She would stand straight-backed and proud even when she ducked her head so his friends wouldn't see that she was blushing.

One day, when they were alone in the car leaving the country club, she screwed up her courage and brought up the subject. "Why do you tell people I'm your best girl?"

"Because you are. You're my best girl, my best friend, my best pal, my best everything."

It took more courage to ask what she asked next. "You mean when Mother's not home to be all those things? When she's home, she is?"

Her daddy took awhile to answer her. His face went blank, but there was a hurt look about it. Serena wished she hadn't asked him any questions. She hadn't meant to hurt his feelings.

"You're my best girl all the time," he said finally. "All the time."

It became the case that even when her mother was home, Serena and her daddy were two together and her mother one alone—but she and her daddy were the castoffs. A sadness that had been in him since she could remember grew more pronounced, and Serena knew that it was because of the way her mother treated him. She tried to make up to him for it. She tried to give him enough love to make up for the love her mother didn't give him. And she made up her mind that she would never love a man the way her father loved her mother—enough to let him make every minute of her life a misery. She doubted that she'd ever love one at all.

When Serena was twelve, Ellie had her portrait done —hers, not Serena's. Ellie's portrait had been done before. In the music room there was an exquisite water-color of her, serene, softly pensive, ethereal in its beauty. It was done in muted pastels. It gave the appearance of protecting its subject with a shield of gossamer. There was another painting of her that hung in the dining room. It was done in oil. In that one she looked beautiful, of course, but also proud, a little condescending, a trifle disdainful. Serena thought the one in the dining room was a truer likeness of her mother than the one in the music room.

The artist who did Ellie's portrait when Serena was twelve was Toby Heller. He wasn't a famous portraitist or even a recognized one. He was a commercial artist. He had been hired by the architectural firm of Haddon, Haddon & Hill to make renderings of their proposed buildings. He was not a draftsman. He painted in watercolor on line—not glorified exactly, but certainly not unflattering pictures of what the proposed buildings of HH&H would look like when they were finished. He had been hired at a large yearly retainer to come to Atlanta from New York, where he had been employed by another architectural firm, Arden & Graustark, a sometime associate of HH&H. Cummings Haddon, president of HH&H, liked Toby Heller's work and had no compunction about offering him enough money to make it worth his while to leave Arden & Graustark and come south. Cummings Haddon had reason later to regret that he had ever laid eyes on Toby Heller and his seductive watercolors on line.

Toby Heller was offbeat. He had a dark-haired,

long-haired, languid, loose-jointed look about him. All
his bones seemed in danger of disconnecting at the
joints. He looked like a puppet strung on strings that
extended from the top of his head down through his
trunk and limbs and held him together. His eyes, when
not veiled, were piercing and intense and hypnotic. A
long, hard look from him had the effect of a physical
blow. He was thin and a little hungry-looking. His
hair was never quite combed; his clothes were never
quite fresh. His attitude about himself and everybody
else was a negligent "so what?"

Women found Toby Heller irresistible. They
thought that the veil he kept over his eyes most of the
time hid a hunger for love and mothering. They
thought that he had been deprived in childhood and
was still suffering from deprivation. They all wanted
to supply the lack.

Pet Haddon, Cummings Haddon's wife, was the first
woman of importance in Atlanta to get to know Toby.
Cummings invited Toby for dinner the first time he
came, and Pet invited him every time he came after
that. Sometimes there was a dinner partner for him,
but mostly he was an extra man. Pet displayed him to
her friends as if he were a personal accomplishment—
her latest crusade. When she decided to sponsor him—
to promote him as a portraitist—Cummings fumed,
and Toby smiled tiredly and shrugged.

"I know you could paint from life," Pet encouraged.
"There's so much life in your watercolors."

"He hasn't got the time," Cummings said.

"Of course, he has the time! Every man I know has
a hobby. You have time for golf, don't you?"

"It might be interesting to try something in twilight," Toby said. "You have long twilights here, I've
noticed. Something in the garden perhaps . . . against
the eastern sky . . . reflected light. . . ."

"Perfect!" Pet enthused. "But in the greenhouse!
There's the most fantastic light in the greenhouse late

in the day! It just seems to hold the light forever! Come with me to the greenhouse now. I'll show you what I mean."

Toby painted Pet's portrait in the greenhouse. It was an idealized, romanticized likeness of a very glowing woman. Pet's friends were agog over it.

"I don't want to pay a compliment backwards, honey," Jane Lanaway said, "but it makes you look so *young!*"

"Radiant!" another friend said. "That's the word for the way you look in your picture, Pet. Just radiant!"

"That painting doesn't belong anywhere but in your bedroom," another said. "Look at the look in your eyes. If I were you, I'd put it on the wall where Cummings would see it when he goes to bed every night. If the way you look in that picture won't turn him on, nothing will."

"What were you looking at, Pet?" Ellie asked. "Or thinking about? That's a bedroom look if I ever saw one."

Pet smiled. A dreaminess came over her for a moment, but she snapped herself out of her reverie and became alert and very businesslike.

"He won't be doing any more portraits in the greenhouse," she said. "The light in there wasn't as consistent as we had thought it would be. You all know how many sittings it took for him to finish this painting of me. He's going to work on the terrace and in the garden from now on." She looked around at her friends seated at the two bridge tables—it was her turn to host their weekly bridge session. "I set the price myself. I had to talk him into this, remember. He didn't really want to do it. Three thousand dollars. . . ."

Groans and protests rose from the women.

"Allan would think I was out of my mind! Why, no one ever heard of Toby Heller!"

"Jim would tell me to go soak my head!"

"Three thousand dollars isn't much," Pet said, "not when you consider what he turns out. I wouldn't think of letting him do anybody for less." She looked around the room, skimming her friends' faces with bright, encouraging eyes. "Who wants to be first?"

"What was that you said about his painting out in your garden?" Jane Lanaway asked. "You mean we have to come over here?"

"Yes! Of course!" Pet's answer was a little too quick, a little too snappish. She caught herself and laughed. "My garden is going to be his studio. The only other place where he could paint you would be in his office. You don't want to go there, do you?"

The other ladies who had Toby Heller do their portraits went for cocktail-hour sittings in Pet's garden. Pet was present throughout the sittings. She didn't trust Toby, and she didn't trust her friends. But she was willing to share Toby with her best friend—Ellie Carr. Ellie had her portrait done at home—in the small sitting room off her bedroom where the light of the setting sun "just seemed to gather."

"You're the best-looking woman I've seen since I left New York," Toby said to Ellie during the first sitting. "That's the kind of town where you belong. Why'd you let yourself get stuck down here in Atlanta?"

Ellie had two reactions to that. Her civic pride was insulted. She might rail against Atlanta or listen to another Atlantan rail against it, but that was a privilege reserved for the city's natives. Outsiders had better show Atlanta the respect it was due.

On the other hand, her vanity was flattered.

"If you were in New York, you could be a model," Toby went on, his eyes raking Ellie up and down. "You've got everything it takes."

Ellie had two reactions to that also. She was flattered, but she thought he was talking about models who posed in the nude for students in art classes—he looked as if he were seeing her naked body through her clothes.

"Hardly my idea of the good life," she said, "sitting in the buff and freezing my ass for a bunch of greentails to gawk at and pretend they were trying to draw."

"I'm not talking about that kind of modeling. I'm talking about fashion modeling. Photography for the magazines. I worked with fashion models when I was free-lancing. I sketched for all the big dress designers."

Ellie came suddenly and singingly alive in every nerve in her body. A fashion model! For photography! She could be a fashion model! Have her picture in all the magazines!

No wonder she'd become more discontented with every day of her life, she told herself. Look what she'd been missing out on. She'd always known she was missing out on something. Now she knew what it was.

An outrushing surge of feeling for Toby Heller came over her. Until now she had viewed him as simply another conquest—a slightly disturbing and unpredictable one, but a conquest. Now she saw him as much more than that. Beneath his arrogance he was a sensitive and understanding man. He only seemed standoffish because he was discriminating. When a woman deserved his appreciation, she got it.

The muscles in Ellie's lower abdomen tightened, and the familiar ache began. She looked at Toby Heller and let a slow smile glide over her mouth.

"But if I weren't stuck down here in Atlanta," she said, her words as slow as her smile, "you wouldn't be doing my portrait right this minute, would you?" She lowered her eyelids and let her eyes move down his body. "Do you wish I weren't stuck down here in Atlanta?"

She stopped her eyes at his crotch. The bulge inside his pants grew as she looked at it and pushed against the fabric of his pants. When she looked back up at

Toby Heller, the smile was gone from her face. Her lips were wet and parted. Stark wanting was in her eyes. Toby Heller's dark eyes veiled. They never left Ellie's as he deliberatly let the brush he was holding slide from his fingers and drop to the floor and deliberately moved toward her.

Ellie began to refer to Atlanta as "Hicksville, USA" and to spend a lot of her time absorbed in fashion magazines. She studied the posturing and poses of the models in the magazines and adopted many of them. Her thoughts were filled with visions of herself posing in front of cameras and turning page after page in *Milady* and *Vogue* and *Harper's Bazaar* and seeing herself on all of them. Her life seemed duller to her than it ever had before.

When she first mentioned to Wells what Toby had said, she made her manner casual and offhand and spoke in a smiling, rather self-deprecatory way, as if she were just quoting Toby and didn't take what he'd said seriously for a moment. But that changed—probably because she got no reaction whatever from Wells —and she began to make pointed remarks about being tied down in nowheresville by marriage and motherhood.

"You're hardly tied down, Ellie," Wells said. He was referring to her frequent trips.

Ellie gave him an exasperated look. "I'm not too old, you know, to have a career!"

Wells's eyebrows lifted slightly. "You're thirty-five," he said flatly.

Ellie was furious. Rage boiled in her. Wells's goddamned complacency drove her up the wall! The goddamned blinders he wore kept him from seeing anything but what he wanted to see! And all he wanted to see in her was a thirty-five-year-old woman! Keeper of his house and mother of his child and ornament on his arm when he needed her there for business! He didn't see in her any of the things that Toby Heller saw!

"I don't *look* thirty-five! No one has ever guessed my age to be over twenty-eight, and most don't even guess that high! Besides, it's not age that counts. It's the look!"

"No one has ever questioned your looks, Ellie," Wells said. "Certainly I haven't."

"You don't even know what I'm talking about! *Looks!*" she scoffed. "I didn't say *looks!*" She knew the difference between "looks" and "the look." Toby had taught her.

Ellie bristled under Wells's seeming unconcern for all that she had missed and bridled under Toby's continued flattery. She wished that something would happen at HH&H and Toby would go back to New York. She had made up her mind that if he should, she would go, too, at least for a trip. But Toby stayed on in Atlanta—for a time.

Wells's attitude dampened Ellie's confidence in her ability to make a great career for herself. If he had been enthusiastic or even worried that she might try for one, her confidence would have zoomed right up to the sky—and her ambitions probably would have stopped right there. But he made her doubt herself by the way he just simply didn't take seriously anything she said or the threats she implied. Her resentment toward him and the life that she felt he had locked her into became greater than ever. She blamed him for everything, including the fact that she had married him, although at the time she had been as eager for their marriage as he. She felt that the only person in the world who understood her was Toby Heller.

And Toby Heller was turning out to be not the man she had thought he was.

Toby still flattered her and commiserated with her over the fact that she was "buried" in Atlanta, but he

was a man of odd sexual habits, and she was finding
them harder and harder to go along with. His latest
thing was to pull out before he came and jump off
the bed and come on Ellie's priceless antique Venetian
standing mirror, watching the spew and splash and
downward roll of his ejaculation on the glass. Ellie's
part was to hold onto his upper legs while he grasped
himself with both hands and squared off at the mirror.
If he were a split second late jumping off or she were a
split second late grabbing his legs and joining him to
watch, his pleasure was spoiled. "Now!" he would
screech when he pulled out, his voice high-pitched and
frenzied. "Hurry, goddammit!" He'd be off the bed
and at the mirror.

"I'm coming!" Ellie would scramble hurriedly to sit
on the side of the bed and grab his legs and stare at
the mirror with him. "Go ahead! Go ahead!" she'd
encourage. "I'm watching!" If his pleasure wasn't all
he wanted it to be—or if he failed to come at all, as had
happened—he would refuse to finish Ellie afterward.
Their lovemaking was at the point where she was getting very little from it and he was daily more addicted
to it. He demanded more and more meetings with her.

There was a mean streak in Toby that showed itself
when he was denied what he wanted. And there was a
rashness in him that was dangerous. He was reckless
in the extreme. He didn't give a damn if he were
found out, and he gave less of a damn if she were. The
danger grew with every meeting.

In the end Toby was found out, but Ellie wasn't. Pet
Haddon got the brunt of it.

Toby hadn't neglected Pet. Cummings Haddon arrived home unexpectedly in the middle of the afternoon one day when Toby was supposed to be at a
building site making line sketches and found his wife
fully dressed but Toby in shirttailed modesty, his trousers down around his ankles and Pet hastily getting to
her feet from the floor in front of him.

Cummings Haddon hadn't hit a man since he had broken his best friend's jaw in a sparring match at Georgia Tech when he was nineteen. It was twenty years later, but he hadn't forgotten a thing he'd learned from his boxing coach. He'd have broken every bone in Toby Heller's body if Toby had stayed conscious and on his feet long enough for him to do it, but Toby was knocked out by the first blow Cummings landed.

When Toby came to, he was in the end seat of a coach car on a train bound for New York, dumped there by Cummings Haddon's chauffeur.

The ensuing scandal rocked Atlanta society, although the details were not known beyond the fact that Cummings Haddon had surprised his wife in a compromising position with the fellow he'd hired out from under the nose of an associate in New York. Ellie thought she knew the details, but later, when she wanted to laugh with Pet about Toby's little sexual quirk, she found out that Pet didn't know what she was talking about until she explained it fully. Pet wasn't willing to explain fully her experience with Toby.

Ellie and Pet were lazing away an afternoon at poolside on the deck of a ship when the conversation took place. The natural solution to the problem of the scandal had been resorted to. Pet flew to San Francisco and sailed on a three months' cruise around the world. Ellie went with her. Two months later, in June, when school was out and Serena was free to go, Wells and Serena and Cummings flew to Capetown to meet the ship and join Pet and Ellie for the rest of the cruise. When they all came home again, the scandal had blown over. Pet did the natural thing. She lifted her head and went about her usual pre-scandal activities as if no breath of anything untoward had ever touched her.

If Ellie had continued regrets about the great modeling career that she had missed out on, she didn't mention them. Wells took no notice of that fact, but Serena did. For a while she made a point of taking an interest in the fashion magazines that still arrived in the mail. She was trying to spark a response in Ellie, but Ellie made just as much a point of not rising to the bait, and Serena finally gave up. But she didn't forget. For months her mother had made her father's life a hell over something that she now wanted just to turn her back on blithely. Turn her back or not, in Serena's mind it was another score to be settled.

Serena had an extended gawky period—from eight to thirteen. Fourteen wasn't very promising, but by the time she was fifteen she showed every indication of rivaling her mother in looks.

Ellie's attitude toward Serena changed. She didn't like having a teenage daughter. Serena was living proof of Ellie's age. She also didn't like having a daughter who drew as many eyes as she did. She became wary of Serena, and watchful.

Her attitude toward Wells also changed. She hadn't minded his absorption in Serena when Serena was a child—had been glad of it because of the freedom it gave her—but it was a different thing now that Serena was a young lady on the fringe of womanhood. In subtle ways, Ellie began to vie with Serena for Wells's attention.

Wells responded eagerly and thankfully to every smallest indication of feeling for him on Ellie's part. He had been in love with her—enslaved by her—since he was in high school. From the time he had become aware of girls as the female opposite of male, he had been alternately elevated to bliss and thrown into abysses of despair by Eleanor Carr, née Buckalew. The happiest day of his life had been the day he married her. The unhappiest day of his life was the day he found out that she didn't love him.

By the time Ellie began to show some interest in him as a man again he had put up with ten years of unfaithfulness on her part without ever once having been unfaithful to her. He had had a sustaining faith all through the bad years that Ellie would not leave him. That is, she wouldn't unless he forced a show-down. He had always felt that if he gave her enough time and a free enough rein, she would eventually set-tle down to a normal life with him and be a constant and faithful wife to him. It seemed now that his sus-taining trust was going to prove itself justified.

Serena was not unaware of what was going on. She watched every move in the game like a contender gird-ing himself to take on the winner. She saw clearly her father's reception of her mother's renewed—or pre-tended—interest in him.

Serena was jealous and hurt. She felt set aside. She didn't come first with her father anymore. Her mother did, and she didn't deserve to. Serena's abiding hope was that her mother would do something that would once and for all prove that she didn't—something that her father couldn't close his eyes to, the way he'd closed his eyes to everything up to now.

The one aspect of the thing that Serena didn't know was why her mother had changed. She didn't realize that her mother was jealous of her. It would never in the world have occurred to her that her beautiful and brilliant mother could be jealous of anybody, espe-cially her. When her mother smiled and stroked her hair and said, "Yes, in a few years I'll look positively plain beside her," when people complimented her on how pretty Serena was growing up to be, Serena thought she was joking or making fun of her. She'd heard her mother call her father dull once. "How can you be so dull? There's not the least bit of life in you! You're not bad-looking . . . or you wouldn't be if you had a little personality! But you're dull! Just dull! And you're making Serena just like you!" Serena thought that was her mother's for-all-time opinion of her.

Wells and Serena both had birthdays in September—Wells's on the fourth and Serena's on the sixth.

The year when Serena was sixteen and Wells forty, Ellie gave a joint birthday party for them on September 5. She had planned it as a really grand affair. All the family was there—Ellie's mother and father, her brother, Jeffrey Junior, and his wife and their two teenage boys, her sister, Barbara Buckalew Lawson, and her husband, William, and their three subteen girls. Wells's father had been dead for years, but his mother was there. Wells didn't have any brothers or sisters. The immediate family was small, numbering only fifteen, but they all lived in or close to Atlanta. In addition to the family, 270 guests were invited.

It was still warm enough for the party to be held in the garden. Two large tents were set up and tables arranged and places set for 285. It would be a seated dinner. A platform was built for dancing. Two bands were engaged to provide the music for dancing and two strolling violinists to entertain the diners.

Ellie was absolutely stunning in a flame-colored chiffon Elizabeth Arden that she had flown to New York to buy. Serena was "sweet" in a pale blue gown that Ellie had selected for her and finally convinced her to wear. Serena thought it was more suitable for a twelve-year-old. Besides, she looked completely faded out in it, especially when she was next to Ellie.

There was much talk at the party, especially among the members of the family, about the fact that the school year coming would be Serena's last year in school in Atlanta.

"You'll love Fox Hill," Grandmother Buckalew said to Serena. "Of course, it's not the school it was when I went there—no schools nowadays are what they used to be—but Fox Hill has held to tradition more than most."

The last thing Serena wanted to do was leave home. As far as she was concerned, battle lines had been drawn between herself and her mother—with her father the prize—and she couldn't win the battle in absentia.

"I don't think I'm going to Fox Hill," she said. "I've been thinking about going somewhere closer to home."

Grandmother Buckalew was appalled. "The Buckalew women and the Carr women have always gone to Fox Hill," she said.

"Where did you have in mind to go if not to Fox Hill?" Serena's Aunt Barbara asked.

"I might decide on Randolph-Macon," Serena said, "or Spelman."

Grandmother Buckalew was horrified. "I'd like to hear what your mother and father have to say about that!"

Wells had come up to the group. He put his arm around Serena's waist. "She'll go to Fox Hill, just like her mother," he said.

"I don't want to go as far away from home as Virginia," Serena said.

"Far from home!" Grandmother Buckalew sniffed. "Virginia far from home? Wait until it's time for your year of schooling in France. Then you can talk about far from home!"

"Virginia is farther than I want to go," Serena said stubbornly.

"You're certainly not like most young girls today," Grandmother Carr said. "Most of them . . . boys, too . . . can't wait to get as far away from home as they can."

"The way Serena feels speaks well for Ellie and me, wouldn't you say?" Wells asked proudly. "Our little bird isn't eager to fly the nest."

"If I go to Spelman, I can be a day student and live at home," Serena said. She was encouraged by what her father had just said, in spite of what he'd said earlier about Fox Hill. She was hoping he would say he wanted her to go to Spelman so she could live at home.

But he didn't.

"A year from now, when it's time for you to enroll, you won't want to go to Spelman any more than your mother and I want you to," he said complacently.

Serena had a sudden thought that made her feel as if someone had punched her in the stomach. He didn't want her at home! He wanted her to go to Fox Hill so he could be alone at home with her mother! He *couldn't wait* for her to be gone!

At that moment, on cue, the two bands started playing the "Anniversary Waltz."

"Excuse me," Wells said, turning to leave, looking about. "I must find Ellie."

He wasn't even going to dance the birthday dance with her! He was going to dance it with her mother! He didn't even notice when she ran from the group. He was too busy looking for his *Ellie!*

Serena had never been so hurt. Nor so angry.

She'd show him! She'd pay him in the same coin her mother had!

Tears were running down her face. She brushed them away, furious with herself for crying, and looked around for her target—Nicky Weems. Nicky Weems had the worst reputation of any boy she knew. She hoped every word she'd ever heard about him was true—and she was about to find out!

She didn't have to go looking for him. She practically stumbled over him and Jimmy Brandon in the bushes behind one of the bandstands. They were hiding there smoking—and what they were smoking wasn't cigarettes. They were sharing a joint.

"Miss Sweet Sixteen herself," Nicky said, getting to his feet. He took a deliberate drag on the joint. "Looking for me?" he asked, holding the smoke in, getting every gram of charge from it.

Serena gritted her teeth. He had the most overbearing ego of anybody she knew. She couldn't stand him.

"Hi, Serena," Jimmy said, on his feet, dusting off the seat of his pants, a little embarrassed. "Great party!"

Nicky offered the joint to Serena. "Want to turn on?" Serena took the joint. "Get lost, Jimmy-boy," Nicky said.

Jimmy laughed uneasily and looked at Serena. She pretended to be absorbed in the byplay with Nicky and the joint and ignored him. He took the hint and walked away.

"I've been looking everywhere for you," Nicky said. "Where've you been?"

Serena recognized the obvious lie, but she smiled at him as if loving every word. "Family conclave," she said.

"Ugh."

"Ugh is right."

"I've got a stash of these," Nicky said, taking the short butt from her and dropping it to the ground and crushing it under his foot. "Want to dance, or want to see where I've got my stash?"

He moved so close to her she thought he meant to knock her off-balance. He put both arms around her, put his face on her hair and breathed heavily into it. He didn't waste any time, Serena thought.

"I take back the question," he said. "Why should I share you?"

He nuzzled her hair breathily and pushed his body against hers. She could feel a hardness against her abdomen—he was making sure that she did.

"You don't want me to share you, do you?" He made

his voice as husky as he could. She knew he was doing the heavy sex bit. Well, that was what she had come looking for, wasn't it?

"Where've you got your stash?" she asked.

Nicky took her hand and pulled her after him toward the gazebo some distance away. Serena became acutely conscious of the blaring music, the voices and laughter, the lantern light all around her. She felt that it was all a backdrop and that she was exposed to every eye against that backdrop. But the feeling went away as they left the party noises behind them and moved from light to shadow.

The lanterns in the gazebo had been turned off—by Nicky, no doubt. She probably wasn't the first girl he'd taken there that night.

"I always knew you weren't really Miss Touch-Me-Not," Nicky said. He pulled her down on the wooden bench that circled the inside wall of the gazebo. He hadn't even kissed her yet when his hands started exploring. That was fine with Serena. She didn't want him to kiss her. She didn't want him to take forever either. She wanted him to get on with it and get it over with.

Serena was a virgin, but she knew all the details of the sex act. Her introduction to that knowledge had been one of the most nauseating experiences of her life. All the stories she had heard, all the tales she had listened to, had featured her mother (in her mind) in the leading role. She couldn't think of sex without connecting it with her mother. That's what she'd been meeting men for on all those trips she used to take. Well, Serena told herself, she was about to find out what all the hullabaloo was about!

Nicky's hands were all over her, on top of her dress so far, squeezing her breasts and trying to get between her legs. The curving wooden bench didn't suit him. He slid off it onto the floor and pulled her down with him. He was breathing as if he'd just run the four-minute mile. He jerked her dress up, thrust his hand under it and pulled her pantyhose down around her knees. Then he unzipped his pants. He acted as if he were about to wet them. He pushed his fist up between her legs, thumb extended, and jabbed it at the soft flesh. It rammed through her maidenhead like a knife slash, and Serena almost screamed out from the pain. She twisted away from him. "What are you doing? You're hurting me!"

"I'm giving you what you want," Nicky muttered, hardly able to talk. "What they all want." He pulled her back roughly and sprawled on top of her, his hand between their bodies, trying to take his penis out and get it in position. His body was already making thrusting motions. When he finally got his penis out, it was hitting her everywhere but where he wanted it to. It was as hot as a fired rifle on her bare thighs and stomach. The feel of it made Serena sick to her stomach.

"I thought you knew how to do this," she gritted out between clenched teeth.

"Be still!" Nicky hissed. "Keep still!"

"I'm not moving! How can I move with you on top of me? Hurry up, can't you?"

All of a sudden Nicky froze. A cigarette lighter had been lit, and flickering patches of light loomed large and then small in the darkness. Serena looked up and straight into her father's face, illuminated by the cigarette lighter he held.

Serena didn't know what her own face looked like, but she knew that she would never forget the sight of her father's. There was no expression at all on it. It looked as if it had turned to stone.

Nicky jumped up off Serena, somehow got his penis back inside his clothes and got his pants zipped by the time he was standing up. Serena threw her skirt down to cover her legs and got up off the floor, clumsy and stumbling because she was hobbled by the pantyhose that were still down around her knees. She turned her back, pulled up her skirt and pulled them up. Not a word had been spoken so far.

Nicky turned to face Serena's father, brushing back his hair with his hands, trying for bravado. "I didn't have to talk her into—"

"Get out!" Wells said. "Get out!"

Serena couldn't look at her father. She could feel no sense of triumph, no sense of victory, no satisfaction of revenge. All she could feel was disgust, and that was for Nicky Weems. She looked down at his pants. There wasn't any sign of the big macho man now. His thing had shriveled to nothing. He was as scared as he could be. And he must feel like fifteen kinds of fool. He hadn't come close to being able to do it. His reputation was all just bragging on his part with nothing to back it up. She wasn't the least surprised when he left without looking at her. She wouldn't want to look at somebody either if she'd just made a fool of herself in front of them.

"Your mother has been wondering where you were, Serena," Wells said. His voice was as stony as his face.

Whatever Serena had expected from her father, it hadn't been that. The words "your mother" brought back all the feelings she had had when she had gone looking for Nicky Weems. She had heard those two words a thousand times a day lately. Her father carried them in front of him like a shield.

She stared straight at him. "It ought not to be hard for her to guess where I'd be," she said. "I'm where she'd be if she had the chance."

Wells's slap struck Serena across the face before she saw it coming. The force of it knocked her halfway around. When she turned back to him, his face was as white and stark as a death's head. His voice was a strained whisper. "Apologize!" he croaked.

Serena pulled herself up to her full height. The skin of her cheek stung and throbbed. Tears stood in her eyes. She forced herself to look straight at him again. "To you," she said. "Not to her." She expected him to strike her again, but he didn't.

"Go into the house," he said. "Go to your room. I'll give your excuses to your mother's guests." His voice was as cold as ice. Each word was like a drop of ice-cold water down Serena's back. She walked past him and out of the gazebo.

Serena didn't see her mother until the next morning. Ellie was as cold as Wells had been, but for a different reason.

"You weren't sick last night!" she said. "You were up to your old tricks! You're just as willful as you always were! Playing sick when things don't go exactly to suit you! You'd have spoiled my beautiful party if your father hadn't gotten you inside before you made a scene in front of everybody . . . fainting or whatever worse than that you could have thought up to do!"

Serena's father never mentioned to her what had happened in the gazebo. Perhaps if he had, she would have felt guilt or at least repentance. As it was, she felt nothing—except the disgust she still had for Nicky Weems.

And she felt a deep hurt. She had to recognize that she had always been second best to her father. She had thought all that time that she was first, but she had never been more than second best. When he had told his friends, "This is my best girl," he had been lying. He hadn't meant it any more than he had meant it when he had told her that she was his best everything. She would never have had a minute of his time if he could have had that minute with her mother instead. She didn't come first with anybody, never had.

Serena had no choice but to go along with her parents' preparations for entering her at Fox Hill. Grandmother Buckalew and Grandmother Carr had a lot to say about everything. Serena felt that she was being suffocated by *family.*

The family was discussing which of the tea services she should take to Fox Hill—Grandmother Carr's or Grandmother Buckalew's.

"Let's just buy one for me and stop all this arguing," Serena said.

"One doesn't *buy* a tea service, child," Grandmother Carr said. "A tea service is something one comes in to."

"Somewhere back there somebody had to buy one!" Serena exploded.

A stunned and outraged silence fell over the room. Four pairs of eyes clamped on Serena, all cold and disapproving, as united by their common censure as if they had been welded together. *You'd think I'd slapped her face,* Serena thought.

"Apologize to your grandmother, Serena," Wells said.

"I apologize for my temper, not for what I said."

The lift to Grandmother Buckalew's eyebrows took on a permanent look. "She wouldn't have that willfulness if she'd had the experience of boarding school, as she *should* have had," she said. "The military drill there would have taken it out of her. It's none too soon that she's going to Fox Hill."

Serena hated everything about Fox Hill. The students were treated like infants.

She loathed the school itself and all that was part of it—the lovely old English Tudor buildings, the gravel drives and boxwood walks, the formal gardens that flanked it and the tended parks that spread around it, the swans that floated majestically on the artificial lake. All that gave it its gracious stability were the very things she hated. She felt trapped in its antiquity. And it was going to be a waste of her time. Whatever she was going to do with her life would not be helped by Fox Hill. Most Fox Hill graduates went straight into marriage and set about the business of bearing girl babies that they could, in turn, send to Fox Hill. Marriage was the last thing Serena had in mind. She didn't know what she wanted, but she knew it wasn't marriage. Vassar was a school she would have chosen, or Sarah Lawrence.

The only thing that made Fox Hill something Serena could swallow was her roommate, Bug-Bug Neilly. Bug-Bug, with her unmanageable red hair, her unabashedly flat-chested shape, her abrupt way of moving and loud way of speaking, the liberal sprinkling of "cunt" and "fuck" and "screw" and "shit" in her conversation, was everything that Serena had never expected to find at Fox Hill. And Bug-Bug felt the same way about the school she did. They were friends from the moment they met. Bug-Bug—her name was Eugenia—was from Boston. "That accounts for that stupid nickname," Serena said. "I never in my life met anybody from Boston or Philadelphia who didn't have a stupid nickname."

Bug-Bug was always in trouble with the dorm mother or the dean. She racked up more demerits than anybody in the school. Her worst crime was habitual lateness. Non-attendance was her second worst. Her most disruptive was parking her Fiat wherever she wanted to step out of it, including squarely in the middle of the gravel drive in front of the dorm and blocking traffic to the buildings on the circled drive beyond it. Just after Thanksgiving her car was impounded for the remainder of the term. It made no difference to Bug-Bug. She and Serena did everything together anyway. They used Serena's car.

The accident happened just before the start of Christmas vacation. Serena and Bug-Bug were driving on dirt roads and country lanes, looking for holly and mistletoe. They were on the committee to decorate the

gym for the annual Christmas party. Neither was the
least interested in decorating the gym, and neither was
particularly artistic in that direction. Gathering the
red-berried and white-berried greenery was their part.
They were going to dump the mass of it that they
gathered in the middle of the gym floor and call that
their contribution.

They were having a grand time. They chose the
scroungiest-looking limbs and most listless, dried-up-
looking berries they could find and laughed hilariously
at the thought of the looks on the faces of the rest of
the committee members when they found the dismal
stuff they had to work with.

They were driving at a fast clip with the top down,
shivering in the sharp, damp cold that came with late
afternoon. Bug-Bug was sitting on the top of the back
of the bucket seat on the passenger side, her hand
shading her eyes, Indian fashion, scanning the woods
for limp and drooping holly and mistletoe. It wasn't
easy to find—the fucking stuff was in season, as Bug-
Bug said. Pretending they were on a boat, "Ten
o'clock!" she would yell out when she saw something
that looked bedraggled enough, or "Three o'clock!"
or whatever. Serena would slow down, look in the
direction Bug-Bug had called and, if the holly or
mistletoe looked promising—or unpromising—enough,
would stop the car, and they would get out, chop off
limbs and load them into the open back of the car.

It was getting almost too late to distinguish color. It
was only a little after five, but a haze had settled over
the countryside along with the growing twilight.

"Twelve o'clock!" Bug-Bug yelled, screeching with
laughter, joking.

Serena, who should have been onto Bug-Bug's sense
of humor, was caught off guard and stared straight
ahead at the ribbon of dirt road in front of her, eyes
alert for mistletoe or holly. Bug-Bug howled with even
louder laughter, and Serena caught on. "You fool!"

She turned her head to give Bug-Bug an exasperated look and flicked her finger at her. When she looked back in front of her, there was no road. It had curved away from the straight path of the car, and they were headed over a steep embankment. The last sound Serena heard was Bug-Bug's terrified, spine-wrenching scream.

Few cars traveled the back roads of that Virginia countryside. The wreck wasn't discovered until well after dark when a hunter walking out of the woods with his dog saw the overturned car in the beam of light from his flashlight.

Contrary to what might have been expected, Bug-Bug was pinned beneath the car, and Serena had been thrown clear. Serena, except for having been unconscious for some time, was unhurt. Bug-Bug was alive, but barely. Her chest was crushed. Both her arms were broken. She had massive internal injuries.

Serena was released from the hospital after twenty-four hours. Bug-Bug was in intensive care.

Mr. and Mrs. Neilly were summoned from Boston. Bug-Bug's brother, Stephen, came from Cambridge. He was in school at Harvard. Ellie and Wells came up from Atlanta.

The strain of waiting was intolerable. They weren't waiting for Bug-Bug to rally. They knew she was going to die. The doctors said that they were doing everything they could, but that it was out of their hands, that it wasn't what they were doing that was keeping her alive but some will to live within herself.

"She doesn't want to die," Serena said over and over to Stephen. "She's trying so hard to stay alive. She doesn't want to die."

Stephen would never answer her. He would look at her and shake his head. Serena thought he was motioning her to be quiet because it was painful to him to hear her say that.

They wouldn't let Serena go inside Bug-Bug's cubicle, but she got a glimpse of her once through the door when Mr. and Mrs. Neilly went in. All she saw was Bug-Bug's red hair and the forest of tubes that punctured every natural opening of her body and those that the doctors had made in it.

"I didn't get to see her face," Serena said to Stephen when the door closed. "They didn't even give me time to see her face."

Ellie and Wells tried to get Serena to leave the hospital, but she wouldn't. All of them, the six—Mr. and Mrs. Neilly and Ellie and Wells and Serena and Stephen—stayed at the hospital almost every hour of the three days that Bug-Bug lived. They'd been given one of the doctors' offices as a waiting room. A couple of cots had been set up in it. Mr. and Mrs. Neilly and Ellie and Wells sat together, or stood or paced together, on one side of the room. Stephen stayed with Serena on the other. Serena could hardly bear to let her eyes meet those of anybody except Stephen.

After the interminable waiting was over, both sets of parents were adamant that Serena not go to Boston to attend the funeral. By that time Serena was numb to feeling. When Stephen told her the decision, she showed no reaction. "It's not Bug-Bug they're going to bury," she said. "I saw inside the casket. That wasn't Bug-Bug."

Bug-Bug's body was at the funeral home. Mr. and Mrs. Neilly and Ellie and Wells were together at the Colonial Inn. Wells was making arrangements for a Carr International plane to fly the Neillys and the body to Boston. Stephen took Serena to a motel next to a roadhouse, where he bought a bottle of scotch. He poured her a double and put a little water from the tap in it and sat down beside her on the bed. "Bug would have laid it on you sooner or later," he said.

"What are you talking about?"

"She always told me everything. I was the only one she could be open with."

"What are you talking about?"

"Didn't you ever guess the truth about her?"

"What truth? What are you talking about?"

"My little sister liked girls."

"You're lying!"

Stephen looked at her and didn't answer.

"You're lying! I'd have known it!"

Stephen shrugged. "You were about to find out."

Serena could feel the scotch making hot inroads into her stomach. She could feel it undoing her. "How can you talk about her that way and her dead?"

"I'm trying to tell you you did her a favor. She's better off."

"She's dead!" Serena screamed. "Don't you care? Doesn't that mean anything to you? She's *dead!*"

"It means a lot to me," Stephen said. "*She* meant a lot to me."

"She meant so much to you you're glad she's dead!"

"That's right," Stephen said. His voice was hard. There was anger in it, a deep-seated, hard, cold, long-held anger. "What chance would she have had for any kind of normal life? She had as much right to that chance as anybody else, but she never had it."

Serena jerked herself up from the bed and glared down at him. "You sound like she was some kind of freak! Some kind of cripple!"

"She was. In the eyes of the world, she was. And she wasn't cut out for it. She couldn't have fought it. She'd have killed herself sooner or later. She tried twice."

Serena's skin tightened on her body. Icy needles of gooseflesh prickled in sharp stabs over every inch of her flesh. Her mind didn't want to believe him, but her very body told her that every word he said was true.

"Your mother and father thought I was like her, didn't they? That was why they gave me the cold shoulder, wasn't it? . . . Don't tell me they didn't!"

she shouted when she thought he was going to deny that they had.

"I won't say they didn't. I'd say you're probably right."

Serena backed off from him. "You think so, too, don't you?"

"No, I don't think so. I know better. I told you, she told me everything." He got up, took Serena's glass and poured another drink for each of them. "She was working on you," he said. "She hated herself for doing it, but she couldn't help herself. She was going to head you down the same road she was headed down."

Serena started trembling and couldn't stop. "I'd have known it if she'd been"—she almost strangled on the words—"working on me. I'd have known what she was doing. She never gave me the least indication . . . the least reason to think . . ." She flung her arms out suddenly. She was shaking so hard the glass fell from her fingers. "I don't know why I'm listening to all this! I don't know why you're saying it!"

Stephen took a letter from the inside pocket of his jacket and held it out toward Serena. "Read it," he said.

Serena stared at the letter. She started to reach for it and then pulled her hand back. Stephen kept holding it out toward her, but she wouldn't take it.

Stephen unfolded the letter and started reading it aloud. Serena didn't hear all of it, or all of it didn't register.

"So sweet . . ." she heard. "I didn't know the meaning of sweet until I met her. She's going to be the best ever. I'm going to be her slave, her little dog. She's going to command me, and I'm going to do anything she wants. She doesn't know it—that's one of the things that's so sweet about her—but it's in her nature to give orders. She's every inch an empress. She can be imperious, my lady can. She's going to make me cringe, and I'm going to love every minute of it. Oh, my sweet Serena! It won't be long now!"

Stephen stopped. When he started again to read aloud, he emphasized each word.

"Why doesn't something happen to stop me? Why can't I stop myself? Is this going to go on and on and on and *on* the rest of my rotten life?"

"She was in love with you," Stephen said. He tore the letter into small pieces, dropped them into the metal wastebasket and set the pieces on fire.

Ellie and Wells took Serena to Prague for Christmas. The snow-covered city, the peaked roofs and dormers, the steeples and the gingerbread balconies resembled something out of *Grimm's Fairy Tales*. The place seemed as unreal to her as her own life, as out of kilter with the world as she was. But when she left it, she left unreality behind her. She tucked her time with Bug-Bug into a small pocket in the fabric of her life and sewed up the opening of the pocket. What it had done to her, though, had left a deep and enduring mark. What little trust she had in people was no longer there. When she returned to school and Stephen called and wanted to come down for the weekend, she told hm sure, fine, she'd love to see him.

"You really got to me, Serena. My God, I had no idea how hard I was hit until I had been away from you for a while."

"Sure," Serena said. "Sure."

"I mean it!"

"You mean you want what you want regardless of what anybody else wants and regardless of the consequences. It's a trait that runs in your family."

A red flush of anger darkened Stephen's face. "If that's what you think, you could have told me not to come," he said.

"You'd have come anyway," Serena said.

"That's right. I would have," Stephen said. His mood made an abrupt switch. His eyebrows went up. He grinned a lopsided leer at her. "I've got this itch, see, that I can't reach to scratch." He covered his crotch with his hand. "Right here."

"Very funny," Serena said. For the first time his resemblance to Bug-Bug struck her. He had the same lanky build. His hair was red, but darker than Bug-Bug's had been. His features were bony. His eyes were the same amber-flecked green.

Stephen took his hand off his crotch and moved toward her. "You know what your trouble is? You're still a virgin, and you're afraid someone will find out."

"I'm still a virgin, and I don't care who finds out."

He put his arm around her. When she tried to wriggle free, he held her tighter. He grinned down at her. "Let me find out," he said.

"Go to hell."

He laughed and started undoing the buttons of her blouse, still holding her with one arm tight around her waist. She tried to twist away from him. "If you want your clothes torn off so you can call it rape, that's all right with me," he said.

"Gross," Serena said. "That's really gross."

"I knew you'd come around." He leaned down and kissed her, then lifted his head and looked at her. His eyes were soft beneath the feverishness that was in them. He shook his head as if in wonder. "I'm really speared," he said. He kissed her again. "You like what's happening," he said against her ear. "Admit it."

"Take your clammy hands off me. I can get out of my clothes myself."

"Good. When you get out of yours, get me out of mine."

Serena couldn't remember later just how they got out of their clothes. She was caught up in the same fever he was caught up in. She remembered a tangle of arms and hands getting in each other's way, and she remembered them stumbling around with legs and ankles hampered by their dropped clothes. She remembered being naked on the bed with him and the searing flash of pain when he entered her. He had been very gentle at first, very cautious. "I love you, Serena. I swear I do." He had kissed her mouth, her breasts, closed her eyes with his kisses. "I'm trying not to hurry. I'm trying." He had moved his hand softly over her stomach, her abdomen, her inner thighs.

Serena felt herself beginning to sweat, heard her shortened breaths hissing in and out of her parted lips, knew she was panting. She felt a tickling drop of wetness roll down between her legs. "Now!" she whispered urgently. "Now!" Stephen braced himself over her and lowered himself until he was on her. She felt his penis when it touched her, felt its first tentative probings and then felt the searing flash of pain. He had made full entry with one forcing thrust. She wanted to cry out, wanted to push him away from her. But she lay still, bit her lips to keep from crying out and tightened every muscle in her body against the pain of each thrust he made. She felt nothing except the pain. She wasn't wet anymore. She was as dry as a bone. His penis felt like dry rough leather chafing against her tender membranous skin. She didn't know, when he climaxed, that was what was happening. All she felt was a more forceful thrust and a sharper, harder pain. But when he withdrew, the semen that he had expelled inside her seeped out and slid over her chafed raw flesh like a soothing balm. Little shivering thrills raced through her body. She wondered if that was an orgasm.

Stephen lay beside her on the bed, spent, but not relaxed, pulled away from her even though his body was touching hers.

"Why did you lie to me?" he asked after a while, his voice angry, accusing.

Serena had expected gentleness, gratitude, tenderness, soft caresses, whispers of love—anything except sullen anger. She got angry in return. "Why did you turn into an animal? You nearly killed me!"

"You got what you asked for. You tried to play me for a fool."

"If you know what you're talking about, it's more than I do."

"You can't lie about whether you're a virgin. You ought to have sense enough to know that."

Serena leaned up on her elbow and put her face directly over his so that he had to look at her. "What makes somebody a virgin or not?"

"Whether they've been fucked, for Christ's sake. What kind of kindergarten is this?"

"Is that why you went at me like a bull elephant? Because you thought I wasn't?"

"Can it! You're not going to make me the heavy!"

"Look, Stephen, I don't have a maidenhead, or hymen, or whatever you want to call it, because a jerk that I decided to find out about sex with when I was sixteen jammed his thumb up me. And that's all he jammed up me. If that's what you call being fucked, you *belong* in kindergarten where sex is concerned."

Stephen's expression changed. A different kind of anger came into it. "Is that true, Serena? You swear that's true?"

"No, it's just a lie I made up. I thought it was a sweet little story you'd like to hear." To Serena's total surprise tears came into her eyes. Before she could stop herself from doing it, she was crying. She hadn't shed a tear when that stupid fiasco had happened. Why the hell was she crying about it now?

Stephen put his arms around her and pulled her down and held her against him. "Don't cry, Serena. I can't stand for you to cry. Please don't."

"I'm not crying about *him!*"

He clutched her tighter to him. "Don't cry because

of me!" He sounded ready to panic. "My God, Serena, the last thing I ever want to do is make you cry! I'm sorry I said what I did." He tried to lift her face so he could look at her, but she wouldn't let him. "Do you hear me, Serena? Stop crying, and listen to me. I said I'm sorry I said that." He kissed her hair, talking against it. "Don't cry. Please don't cry. I'm sorry." He ran his hand over her back and pulled her body full length against his. He was hard again. He wet his finger with saliva and put his hand between her legs and moved his finger about until he found her clitoris. A sharp thrill like nothing she'd ever felt before went through Serena. Her legs opened involuntarily, and she turned on her back. Stephen rolled over with her, his finger still working like a feather over her clitoris. Serena wanted him. She didn't care how much it hurt. She wanted him inside her.

"If I don't touch you here when I'm inside you, tell me," Stephen said. "I don't want to hurt you this time."

"You won't hurt me!" She arched her body against his. "You won't hurt me!"

Stephen flew down to be with Serena every weekend, except for the weekends they met in Washington. He spent the most part of the following summer either in Atlanta or traveling to wherever the Carrs happened to be. Before Serena's second school year was over he asked her to marry him.

The mention of marriage was like cold water thrown over Serena. She liked Stephen more than she had ever thought she would like anybody, and she liked sex with him more than she liked him, but marriage was as far from her mind as it had ever been. She told him all that, laid it on him the way it was. He didn't believe her or pretended that he didn't. He wanted what *he* wanted, and that was to marry her. She made up a lie and dumped it on him. She told him she was going to spend the summer in Hawaii on an archaeological dig.

"Christ, Serena! Is that the farthest place you could think of to go?"

"Exactly the reason I chose it. For a while it was a toss-up between that dig and one in Mexico."

"I can find my way to Hawaii."

"You'll do yourself a favor to give me some breathing space."

"What are the guarantees if I do? Will you marry me when you come back?"

"I don't know whether I'll marry you, but you can count on this much: I'm not going to grind out another year at Fox Hill. If I don't marry you, I'll come live with you in Cambridge."

That didn't satisfy Stephen. "I don't trust you away from me all summer. You like sex too much."

"Maybe I just like your brand."

"I don't want you shopping around to find out whether that's true."

"You'll have to take your chances."

"What are you trying to do to me? You don't give a damn about me, do you? You just goddamn well don't give a damn!"

"You can give a damn about somebody without turning yourself over to him body and soul. I don't intend to turn myself over to *anybody, ever!*"

"I'm not asking that."

"That's what you want whether that's what you're asking or not."

"What's changed you? What's put you off me? What have I done?"

"I haven't changed."

"You've been different toward me ever since I asked you to marry me."

"Then quit asking me."

Stephen went into a sulk. "I'm coming out to Hawaii. You can't expect me to go the whole summer

without seeing you. I'm coming out there at least
once."

"That may be once too often."

"I'll have to take my chances on that, too."

As it happened, Stephen didn't come to Hawaii. He
broke his leg in a water-skiing accident in the Gulf of
Aqaba, where he'd gone to watch the tryout for the up-
coming Olympics. He hobbled around on crutches the
rest of the summer and was still walking with a cane
when it was time to go back to Harvard. He didn't
see Serena again until she left Fox Hill that fall and
met him in New York, en route, he thought, to live
with him in Cambridge.

PART 2

FOURTEEN

Serena looked at her schedule for the week. She was booked all day Monday at J. Blanchard's. Tuesday was tough—four bookings: Jay Sloame, Alan Blumenthal, Winthrop Studio and Stegler—a half hour between bookings, and she'd be crisscrossing the city. Wednesday morning fittings at *Milady*. That afternoon and all day Thursday shootings for *Milady* at Yuri Aleijinski's. All day Friday on the beach at Westhampton with Mallini to shoot an ad for Gordon Knightsplit.

She didn't look forward to Tuesday, and she didn't look forward to Friday. Tuesday would wear her out, and Friday she would be sparring all day with Gordon. Would he ever get the message and give up?

The days with Aleijinski would be fun. She liked Yuri. He was completely crazy; every shot he made was crazy. He tried to make the models look like lesbians. He loved extremes, and he loved shockers. If he could get by with it, he'd have one bare breast hanging out in every shot, especially if he were shooting furs. He also liked to expose an inside thigh, just barely missing showing the crotch. He wouldn't have any trouble getting that kind of stuff approved by the French magazines, but America wasn't ready for it.

"Here's Speed Queen!" Tim, the stylist, called out to the photographer when he saw Serena get off the elevator. He stood grinning, watching her come into the studio. "Hi, Moondrops," he greeted her. "Gorgeous as ever!"

They adored her at J. Blanchard's department store. What they adored—and Serena knew it—was the fact that she could do more outfits in a given time than any of the other models they used. She was an easy fit because her shoulders were broad and she was long-waisted and long-legged. She arrived ready to work—makeup on and wearing the right undergarments: bra that could be made strapless and pantyhose that could be stripped off because she wore bikini pants under them. She hadn't joined the group that went braless and pantsless—not for reasons of modesty but because you weren't as ready for work. It was easier to get out of something than to dig around in your bag to find it and then put it on.

J. Blanchard's was one of Serena's steady clients. Working there was a hassle, not only because of the whirlwind rush once she was there but also because of the time it took to get to the store from her apartment and back to her apartment. The store was in Newark. She had to take a taxi from her apartment to Penn Station, take the train from there to Newark, and take a taxi—if she could get one—from the station in Newark to the store. If there was no taxi available, she walked the six long blocks.

She was booked there all day every Monday. If she cancelled for any reason, she was expected to make up the cancellation during the week, and if she couldn't during the week, then on Saturday or Sunday. There was a steady flow of work out of the studio. All of J. Blanchard's photography was done at the store, whether it was for newspaper ads, leaflets to be enclosed in monthly statements to charge customers, seasonal catalogs, holiday brochures or full-page color ads for national magazines. It was a heavy load, and cancellations were not allowed to hold it up. Blanchard's was

Newark's largest department store. The only other stores that matched it for photographic output were Macy's—which also did in-store photography—and maybe Bloomingdale's.

The studio was on the seventh floor, the top floor. It was a huge warehouse-looking area of open space broken up by partitions. Two sets were used—one for full-figure photographs, one for close-ups of hats, jewelry, etc. The cameras were always at the ready, the angles never changed and the lights seldom.

The work was assembly-line work. It was out of your clothes into one of their outfits, run in front of the camera, strike a pose, click-click, strike another pose, click-click—six or eight poses in quick succession, and back into the dressing room and out of that outfit and into another. Serena had once done eight outfits in a little more than an hour. That was when she was dubbed Speed Queen.

Sometimes they worked on the roof on white sheets spread out instead of paper, held down against the gusts of wind by broken pieces of brick and other roof-top debris. It was no relief to work on the sooty roof. It just meant faster running back and forth to and from the dressing room. That the photographer got any dignity into the photographs they did there was proof positive of his ability with the camera. The pictures were good. There was life in them, animation—or maybe it was frenzy, Serena sometimes thought.

There was one photographer who worked all the sets. He'd been with the store since the studio had been set up. It was his only account, and he made enough from it to own racehorses and have his own silks. He looked like a racetrack tout more than a horse owner. He was pencil-skinny, had a pencil-line mustache and wore a small-brimmed felt or straw hat, according to the season. He looked as if he belonged anywhere else other than behind a camera. Serena had been com-

pletely put off by him when she first met him. She was
sure her first day with him would be her last. No way
was she going to like the man.

But she did like him. His attitude toward the work
was the same as hers. He was there to do the shot at
hand and get on to the next one, and so was she. They
worked well together. He almost never had to do re-
takes of the merchandise he photographed on her. The
main reason for that was that neither one of them had
any illusions about what was expected. There was a
certain look J. Blanchard's wanted, and they used a
photographer and booked models who could get it.
They didn't want variety or innovations or strivings toward the aesthetic. They wanted a technician at the
camera and clotheshorses who fitted their size tens
without too much pinning. You recognized the job for
what it was and gave your best to do it, or you didn't
work for J. Blanchard's. It was not a place for a beginning model to learn. If Serena hadn't had solid
training at the one-man studios Helen had pushed on
her when she first started, she never would have made
the grade at J. Blanchard's. She learned more and
more surely every day that passed that Helen O'Neil
knew her business.

Serena had learned early on that studios had personalities. It wasn't atmosphere; it was personality. It
was made up of the attitudes of the people who worked
at the studio and the physical layout of the studio itself. There were studios you horsed around in, some
you prima donnaed in, some you relaxed in, some you
floated around on a cloud of elegance in and some you
kept to yourself in and got your work done without the
waste of a second of time. J. Blanchard's was the last.
Serena always left there exhausted and feeling as
grimy as the dusty studio floor and the soot-caked roof.
But she also left knowing she'd done the job expected
of her and done it well. It wasn't exactly an ego trip,

working for the store, but it wasn't *not* one either. She preferred a day at J. Blanchard's to some of the other days she had.

Still half asleep and wanting to go back to sleep, Serena played a game with herself. She'd look at the clock, and it would say ten minutes of seven instead of ten after, she pretended. No, she'd look at the clock calendar and see that it was Wednesday instead of Tuesday. Either way she could sleep a little longer. She tried to slip into a dream in which someone—not Stephen, someone more like Arthur Hamlisch—was looking intently into her eyes in the middle of a roomful of fractured lights and pulsing music and gyrating people. "Let's get out of here," he was about to say. "Let's go to my place." The alarm went off. It was ten minutes after seven. And it was Tuesday.

Serena hauled herself out of bed, showered, got herself dressed, had grapefruit and black coffee, put on her makeup, checked her tote bag to make sure the things she might need were in it—makeup in several shades, extra false eyelashes, nail lacquer, hair pieces, plain black pumps with heels (she was wearing flats), costume jewelry (some of the smaller studios expected that to be a staple)—threw on a raccoon coat that struck her at the ankles and ran down the three flights of stairs and onto the street.

She wasted precious time trying to get a taxi and finally walked the block and a half across to Lexington and took the downtown bus. She should have taken the subway. She was ten minutes late.

"Sorry, Jay," she said. "Couldn't get a taxi. . . ." She was out of breath from walking at a run from the bus stop.

"Take your time, take your time," Jay said. "So you'll stay over fifteen minutes."

Jay's wife, Harriet, came out of the dressing room.

She was the twitchiest person Serena had ever met.
When Serena first started working there, Harriet made
her nervous.

"You're late," Harriet said, looking at her watch and
then looking at it again. Serena was sure she had said
to Jay every minute on the minute since nine o'clock
that Serena was late.

Serena hurried toward the dressing room. "Want
some coffee?" Jay called after her.

"We're fifteen minutes late already . . ." Harriet
said to Jay, almost trodding on Serena's heels into the
dressing room.

"No, thanks!" Serena called out to Jay. She was
getting out of her things.

"You're wearing flats," Harriet said. "Why do all
you models have to wear flats? Did you bring shoes?
We're doing a dressy suit. Didn't your agency tell you?
You can't wear those flats. . . ."

Serena took the pumps out of her tote bag and put
them on.

"What costume jewelry did you bring? Did your
agency tell you to bring costume jewelry? I told
them . . ."

Serena put the costume jewelry case on the dressing
table and unzipped the cover and laid it back flat so
Harriet could see all that was in it. She could have had
the contents of a whole counter from Kenneth Lane
with her, and Harriet would have been dubious about
every piece.

Serena tossed a brush through her hair and put on
the earrings and bracelets Harriet had finally, reluc-
tantly selected.

"You've got circles," Harriet said. "Can't you cover
up those circles?"

Serena patted some base under her eyes and blended
it. She didn't have circles. The overhead lights in the
dressing room would make a baby six months old look
as if it had circles. But it was easier to go along with

Harriet. She got into the suit, Harriet practically holding her breath as she helped her, afraid she'd get a single wrinkle in it.

It was a pleasure to walk into Alan Blumenthal's studio on Central Park South. It was a beautiful studio on a high floor with floor-to-ceiling windows opening to the north on Central Park. The view of the park was magnificent. The studio was hung with fringed velvet drapes and furnished with antiques. A liveried butler answered the door chime, and a uniformed maid was always visible in the background. The stylist dressed in the traditional black of a Paris *vendeuse*.

Blumenthal was a man of enormous pretensions. He was American, but he spoke French even to people who didn't speak or understand it. He was rich, and he was not professional about his work. There was no such thing as his taking a "bread-and-butter" client. And there was no such thing as his photographing something that didn't come up to his standards. He had once snatched a hat he thought atrocious off Serena's head and thrown it at the designer.

He was an excellent photographer for the kind of work he did. He loved all things elegant, and elegance was the hallmark of his photographs. The models who worked for him were treated like visiting royalty. Not because Blumenthal had all that much respect for them but because he was a snob. His pretensions had practical results. The models photographed as though they were royalty.

Today Serena was to be photographed in a floppy-brimmed garden-party hat of yellow straw and horse-hair. Dozens of yellow roses—$400 worth—were on hand, some in vases, some still glistening wetly in green wax paper. Blumenthal often used flowers for props, and they were never artificial, nor were fresh ones skimped on.

The booking was scheduled from ten-thirty to

twelve-thirty. There was plenty of time to be relaxed. Blumenthal joined the hairdresser and the makeup artist in the dressing room with Serena. (There were always a hairdresser and makeup artist on hand for a Blumenthal photograph.) The butler served coffee. The assistants were arranging the set. Blumenthal didn't have to run back and forth to oversee their work. They had been fully instructed in what he wanted. Blumenthal was free to play the gracious host.

The designer arrived at eleven-thirty to put the hat on Serena and to watch the photography. Everything went as smoothly as if the cogs had been oiled with butter. Serena felt—and looked—pampered, elevated, catered to, and deserving of all of it. The designer loved the splendor of the set. He had been a little worried about yellow on yellow. But he had worried needlessly. It was perfection. Blumenthal worked with an air of supreme assurance. What he saw in the camera was grandeur. That was what he wanted. Grandeur.

It was a comedown, after having been at Blumenthal's, to stop at a drugstore and grab a sandwich at the counter, but Serena was pushing the clock to take even that much time for lunch in the thirty minutes she had to get from Central Park South to Tudor City, where her next booking was. She was doing a location shot in the little garden there. The dressing room would be the mirror in her tote bag.

When she arrived, the photographer from Winthrop Studio was already there. So were the art director and the stylist from the ad agency and the other model who had been booked. It was to be a double—raincoats.

Serena was surprised when she saw that Isolda Mellors was the other girl booked for the double. Isolda was a good two inches shorter than she. She was one of the few girls under five seven and a half or eight who had been able to make it as high-fashion models. Five eight and up were the norm. Helen O'Neil had picked up Isolda on one of her trips to Europe to look for talent. She always kept an eye out for Scandinavians. They had a sultry sexiness that seemed at odds with their pale-skinned, blond-haired looks—a Sophia Loren sexiness that was not surprising in the girls from southern Europe. The difficulty with the Scandinavians was to keep them thin. They were usually big-boned and inclined to weight. But Helen knew how to handle that. Isolda was small-boned and petite, but within the shortness of her frame she was long-waisted and long-legged. When photographed alone, she looked much taller than she was. She was so good that a number of the top designers had sample copies made scaled to her size. Helen O'Neil had known what she was doing.

Serena sighed. It was going to be a difficult session. To have her and Isolda in a double was bad booking on the part of somebody. Height was something that should be checked out when a double or triple was booked. It was an easy enough thing to do. The head sheets that were sent out monthly by the modeling agencies gave the models' vital statistics: height, dress size, shoe size, color of hair, color of eyes (bust, waist and hip measurements depending on the agency—Models, Incorporated, didn't include them) and whatever the model specialized in, if anything—hands, excellent legs, etc.

It hadn't been checked out in this case, and Serena knew that she was the one who was going to be put to the most trouble because of the blunder. A tall person could make herself look shorter, but a short person couldn't make herself look taller, not when both were being shot full length.

"Hi, Isolda."

"Hi, Serena." Isolda came over to her. She was already in one of the raincoats. "They gave me the belted one. I hope you don't mind. That tent thing was practically down around my ankles."

"I don't mind," Serena said.

Isolda turned her back to the others. "Somebody goofed on this one," she said in a low voice.

"Maybe one of the new girls at the agency took the booking."

"The manufacturer is my bet. A fat, cigar-smoking big-shot guy who never saw either one of us except in pictures. 'I want those two,' he said, and who's going to argue with a fat, cigar-smoking—"

"Ready, girls?" the photographer called.

Serena went through all sorts of contortions, bending in exaggerated poses away from Isolda, leaning over to whisper to her, standing gatelegged (legs widespread and toes out). Everything she did was necessarily unnatural and contrived, but it had to look natural and not contrived.

They went through four rolls of film before the art director decided to call it a day.

Serena leaned back against the seat of the taxi, neck, arms and legs limp, and tried to relax all the muscles of her body. The raincoat session had undone all the good the Blumenthal sitting had done. And the Stegler session coming up was going to be a bad one. She felt it in her bones. Stegler wasn't accustomed to working on location, and this was a location shot—at Grant's Tomb. Well, it would take the full thirty minutes to get there. She would make the most of it.

When the taxi pulled up, she couldn't believe what she was seeing. Three other models were there, one girl and two male models. A foursome, on location, for Stegler!

It was worse than she had thought it would be. It was windy. That made Stegler nervous. The sunlight was thin. That made him nervous because he couldn't get the light he needed from the reflector. His permit for shooting there was for only an hour and a half. He couldn't run overtime even if all the models could stay. That made him really nervous.

They were shooting a new line of unisex boots. Anything unisex wouldn't have been Stegler's cup of tea, and a fad like unisex boots had to be totally out of his universe.

The boots were of stiff leather and had to be forced on. They were tight and unwieldy. They were not only uncomfortable but unattractive. Serena and the other models tossed cracks back and forth, trying to get in as far-out a mood as the boots demanded. The cracks were not all flattering to the merchandise.

Stegler, who wasn't pleasant at best, was in a snarly mood by the time Serena arrived. Before the first shot was made, he was spitting out what he had to say between clenched teeth, his brow like a thundercloud with rage and frustration.

A crowd of urchins who had ganged up to watch didn't help. The longer they stood around, the bolder they became with their remarks. "Oh, Lord, I'm tired," Serena said at one point when she and the other models had been holding one awkward position for what seemed like a year while Stegler took exposure after exposure.

"Ain't dat jes' too bad?" a little boy of about seven jeered. He made a swaggering imitation of her pose, his grinning face a picture of impish devilment. He pronounced the last word "b-e-e-u-ud," drawing it out, his bright brown eyes looking up at Serena, saucy and daring. She had to smile.

She didn't smile when one of the older boys sidled up to her. "Ya wanta fuck?" he said, leering, and turned and ran, hooting and calling out to his chums who raced after him, "D'ja hear what I said to her? D'ja hear?"

At five o'clock Stegler had to quit. The whole shooting had been a waste of time. It would have to be re-shot in the studio. Serena couldn't very well refuse to take the booking if he wanted to use her on the reshot, but she sincerely hoped that if he tried to book her, the time would already be taken up on her chart.

FIFTEEN

"Are you sure this thing can take off?" Serena asked. She was squeezed with Gordon on the back seat of the seaplane looking out at the bucking gray-black water of the East River. "What's making that water act up?"

Gordon laughed. "Don't worry, baby." He freed his arm from between them and put it over her shoulders.

Mallini, squeezed between them and the cockpit, holding his favorite camera cradled in his arms, laughed with Gordon as if on cue. "It's okay," he said. "Don't worry."

"I take off from here at least once a day," the pilot said over his shoulder. "No problem. Nothing to be scared of."

"I'm not scared," Serena said. "I just wonder how you do it. Wouldn't it be easier on smooth water?"

"Nope," the pilot said. "The rougher the better. Don't often get it this good."

"I'll take your word for it, but before you get this thing revved up, one more question. What are you going to do about that bridge?"

The pilot grinned. "You watch."

Serena had never been up in a seaplane. She wasn't prepared for the grinding, earsplitting noise of the engine or the seemingly overwhelming resistance of the water. The plane didn't lift up from the water like a helicopter from its pad; it plowed through the bucking waves. And the Manhattan Bridge loomed just ahead of them. She squinched her eyes tight shut and literally

held her breath when she felt the plane clear the water.
When she opened them, the bridge was behind them.
The pilot had gone under it! She shivered. "Pretty
neat," she said. Gordon laughed again and tightened
his arm around her.

There wasn't enough room for Serena to move away
from Gordon, and she didn't want to get into a bad
scene with him before the day even started. She
leaned forward as if to get a better view of what was
below. Her position put Gordon's arm in an awkward
position, but he left it where it was and gripped her
shoulder with his hand.

Serena had learned that the way to handle Gordon
was simply not to be alone with him.

But she liked Gordon. She liked everything about
him except the way he liked her. He was doing them
both out of a friendship because of his preoccupation
with sex. Too bad she hadn't gone to bed with him
the first night she met him. If she had, they'd be good
friends now.

Well, she hadn't, and now sex was a duel between
them. One of them was going to lose, and it was going
to be Gordon. When it happened, there would be fireworks. All she could do was keep her own temper in
hand and put off the fireworks as long as possible.

The plane landed in the bay at Westhampton. A car
met them at the dock and drove them to a house on
Dune Road that belonged to a friend of Gordon's.
The friend wasn't there—it was too early in the season
for the house to be open—but the caretaker had a
roaring fire going in the huge glass-fronted room that
faced on the ocean. Gordon's friend had wanted them
to feel welcome and comfortable in the house although
they were going to work on the beach.

Serena dressed in one of the bedrooms. They were
doing a full-page color ad of Gordon's gold mesh girdle

which he called Chastity. The ad would appear in *Esquire, Playboy* and *Penthouse*. The girdle had been designed with a male market in mind. Serena was to wear a white chiffon gown with a matching white chiffon cape, no jewelry, and she was to be barefoot. After she came out of the bedroom in the gown and cape, Gordon adjusted the girdle around her waist and started fastening it.

"Lovers and husbands who buy this little trinket get a free course on how to get their ladies out of it," he said.

"And the ladies?" Serena asked.

"Top secret from the ladies."

"I can see why you named it Chastity," Mallini said.

The girdle extended in a point at center front that reached almost to the crotch.

"Are you sure I can sit without stabbing myself?" Serena wasn't at all sure she could.

"The mesh will move with you," Gordon said. "I tried the girdle first in solid metal, but there wasn't enough give. It wouldn't follow the line of the body movement. That's why I changed to mesh."

"The band that frames it is solid metal!" Serena said.

Gordon patted the point of the girdle. "That's not what I have in mind for Serena," he said.

When they got to the steps down to the beach from the lawn, Gordon said, "I'll carry you. The sand is wet down near the water. It will be the devil to get off if it gets on your feet or the dress." He swung her up in his arms. Before he started off with her, he gave her a mock-worried look. "You okay? Stabbed anywhere?"

A white palomino was to be used in the shot. Its trainer was pacing it slowly up and down the beach. When he saw them coming, he turned the horse and brought it to them. Gordon lifted Serena to its back.

"I'll walk her a bit with you up," the trainer said.

"She's used to people riding bareback, but she's not used to people sitting sideways. You sure you'll be all right?"

"I'm as sure of me as you are of her, I guess," Serena said. "I'm not used to riding sideways either."

It was easier than she had thought it would be. The trainer walked the horse and then circled it around him on a long lead rope, first at a trot and then at a canter. Serena learned that the trick to keeping a seat was to roll back on her buttocks and relax and just go with the horse. When the trainer was satisfied that she wasn't going to come off, he changed the rope for reins and gave them to her.

It was a blustery, windy day, but not too cold. Serena's spirits suddenly were as bouncy as the wind. She had always loved the feel of a horse under her, and now, when she was on the prancing horse, under bright blue sky and brilliant sun, beside the crashing waves, with the sharp salt smell of the biting wind in her nostrils, every nerve in her body tingled with ultimate vitality.

The others were in as abandoned a mood as Serena, all responding to the glorious day. Mallini was ecstatic. He wanted a wild, free, body-to-the-wind feeling. And he was getting it. Serena's long, loose hair, the gathers of the cape and the folds of the gown streamed and billowed with the wind. The hemline of the gown lifted away from her legs, sometimes at mid-calf and sometimes at mid-thigh. The horse behaved beautifully. Mallini got shots at the trot, the canter, the full gallop. Serena even coaxed her to rear.

"Get that, Tonio!" Gordon shouted. "Get that! Do that again, Serena-baby!"

"I got it!" Mallini shouted back. "God, what a shot! Pure sex!"

"Get it again! Make her rear again, Serena! Push your foot up under her like you did before!"

The horse didn't like the shouting. She would come up on her hind legs, but she kept tossing her head.

Gordon was so excited he was fairly chortling. "My God, if that horse were a bull, I'd call that piece Europa!"

"Or Rape!" Mallini was as beside himself as Gordon. "It's the bare feet and legs! I told you this picture screamed for bare feet and legs! You'll double the circulation of those mags with this one!"

Mallini was clicking away like crazy. Gordon was pounding him on the back.

"The horse's muzzle was almost in Serena's snatch when she turned her head! Did you get that? And Serena's foot up under her belly! God, I hope you can't tell she's a mare in the picture! Christ! What a shot that is if you got it!"

"I got it! I got it!"

A movement on the part of the trainer caught Serena's eye. She turned her head and stared. She couldn't believe what she was seeing. He'd run behind some reeds on the dune and was jerking off!

Serena slid off the horse. She walked over and handed the reins to Gordon. "I don't think I can top that last shot," she said. "I'm quitting while I'm ahead." She started walking toward the house. She didn't know whether to laugh or throw up. She felt like doing both. My God! A barefooted woman on a horse a turn-on! That was a new one on her.

She went straight to the bedroom, forgetting that Gordon would have to unfasten the girdle. By the time she remembered, he was in the bedroom with her, the door closed after him. He walked up behind her as if to undo the girdle, but he didn't even pretend to touch it. He slid his arms around her and leaned down and took the lobe of her ear between his teeth. He wasn't biting hard enough to hurt her, but he was biting hard enough that Serena was afraid to try to jerk her head away. She wriggled a little. "Come on, Gordon," she said. "Get me out of this chastity belt. It may not be lethal, but it's not the most comfortable thing in the world either."

Gordon's arm tightened. He pulled her body close to his and slid his hands down below the girdle and pressed her closer to him, at the same time pushing himself against her. He was hard.

"You're going to make marks on my ear, Gordon. . . ." She moved slightly, hoping he would think she meant to pull her ear free if he didn't let it go. Whatever he thought, he didn't let go. He tightened his teeth. He was hurting her now. If he bit any harder, he would draw blood.

Serena made herself relax. She made herself speak lightly. "There's this odd thing about me," she said. "My ears are not one of my erogenous zones. Sorry 'bout that." It would have been a lie if she had said it to others, but it wasn't a lie to Gordon. His hands slid down and caressed her thighs. Every time they made the upward stroke, they brought the dress up with them. What the hell was going on? Did he have in mind to take her from the back? Standing up? And if so, just where?

"Look, Gordon, old chum," Serena said, "I don't like your hot breath down my neck. I don't like your hot hands up my legs. I like that ear of mine a lot, but you unclamp your teeth from it this minute, or you're going to owe a plastic surgeon whatever it costs to have it put back together after I jerk it out of your mouth. I'm not going to be blackmailed into having sex with you!"

Gordon unclamped his teeth from her earlobe, but he kept his mouth on her ear, darting his tongue in and out of it. Serena ducked her head and bent away from him and pulled at his arms, trying to break his hold on her.

"You got me this way, Serena-baby," Gordon muttered. His tongue was as thick as if he were drunk. "You got me in this shape." He thrust his hard penis against her. "It's up to you to get me out of it."

"You got yourself in the shape you're in! If you're in such bad shape you can't stand it, go fuck the horse! That's what set you off!"

Gordon let go of her so fast she almost lost her balance. She didn't know what he was going to do. She wouldn't have been surprised if he had hit her.

Nothing could have surprised her more than what he did. He threw back his head and laughed. Then he started unfastening the girdle.

"Serena," he said, still chuckling, "you may drive me straight out of my tree, but you will never bore me." He finished unfastening the girdle and tossed it on the bed. He kissed her lightly on her hair. "You and I are not finished," he said. "Sorry 'bout that." He went out of the room still chuckling.

SIXTEEN

Hamlisch had asked Serena to stop by his office for a drink after she finished her last booking.

"I went over the year-end figures yesterday," Hamlisch said after he had mixed their drinks and sat down with Serena on the large leather sofa opposite his desk. "I wanted to congratulate you. You came near topping a hundred thousand dollars for your first year's work."

"Thanks for the congrats," Serena said without much enthusiasm. She didn't feel much enthusiasm. She didn't feel any. "Did you latch onto the fact that I worked my ass off to do it? I mean, you didn't see any weeks booked out for vacation on my charts if you looked them over."

"That's the price you have to pay if you want to do editorial for the fashion magazines and make a pile, too. Actually, you've got a good balance between editorial and commercial work now. You started out doing mostly editorial. Now it's about half and half. That's what I'd try to keep it at if I were you."

"I don't see that I have any control over that. It's first come, first served, isn't it? Whoever calls first to book the time gets it."

"There are ways . . . and ways," Hamlisch said. "Talk it over with Helen."

Serena gave him the "I know" look she'd so often seen Helen give somebody. "I have the feeling you've already talked it over with Helen," she said.

"I have," Hamlisch said, not the least disconcerted, "and she agrees with me. But the decision is yours. You're the one out in the studios. You've been modeling long enough now to know the grooves you fit, where you're happy working and where you're not. There are some girls who can't take the rat race of commercial work. Janice Conlan, for instance. She only wants to do editorial work, and to hell with the money."

Serena shook her head. "That's bad business. She'll kill herself at the magazines if she's always on tap."

"That's right. She'll be overexposed. Her bookings will drop off, and the commercial people she's snubbing now aren't going to pick her up later when she needs them."

Serena shrugged. "She's over twenty-one, isn't she? Over twenty-five, in fact."

"Oh, yes, she's old enough to know what she's doing."

Serena shrugged again. "Well . . . ?"

"I'm just getting your views. Your rate is going up as of the first of next month. Not your editorial rate, of course. We have no control over that. I want you to be aware that with your higher commercial rate, you can top a hundred thousand dollars this coming year and go well over it if you work it right."

Serena was thoughtful. She wondered whether to tell Hamlisch now that Eye-Wonder wanted to talk contract to her. They wanted her under exclusive contract for a year for their television commercials and print ads, wanted to give her a big buildup, tout her as the Eye-Wonder Wonder Girl. She had been thinking that she wouldn't tell anybody until she made up her mind—which actually was pretty well made up.

"Eye-Wonder was my biggest money account this past year," she said, bringing them into the conversation through the back door.

"That's right. It was all those thousand-dollar days for Eye-Wonder that put your earnings up so high."

"And the residuals."

"Yes. The really big money is in television. But you don't want to overexpose yourself there either."

"The daily rate for television commercials will go up, too, I guess," Serena said, still playing games.

Hamlisch looked at her steadily. "Yes," he said. "We'd set a rate of fifteen hundred a day or make the daily rate negotiable." His eyes stayed on her.

Hell, he already knew Eye-Wonder had approached her. She could tell by the way he was looking at her. "They've spoken to me about a contract," she said.

"I know they have." Hamlisch smiled. "There aren't any secrets in this business," he said. Then: "What are your feelings about it?"

"I wouldn't mind a contract, but I'm not sure that's the one I want."

"You didn't in any way commit yourself?"

"No."

"That's good. I was afraid you might have. There aren't that many contracts around. The girls tend to jump at the first one offered."

"If my name is going to be linked to a brand, I want it to be a top brand."

Hamlisch smiled again. His eyebrows went up a little. "A businesswoman, are you?"

Serena thought he was being patronizing. "Why put your goods in a hardware store when you could put them in Hammacher Schlemmer?"

Hamlisch's smile widened to a grin. "You're right to hold out for one of the really big cosmetics houses. Incidentally, how did Zoe feel about it when you got Eye-Wonder? She was up for it, too, as I recall. You two are good friends, aren't you?"

Something in Serena was alerted. Something about Hamlisch had changed with the mention of Zoe. He had tried to sound casual and noncommittal. Maybe he had tried too hard. But a difference was there, and Serena sensed it.

"Zoe couldn't care less," she said. "She doesn't need Eye-Wonder. She pushed me as hard as Helen did to go on that first go-see."

"It's true she doesn't lack for work," Hamlisch said easily. Too easily, Serena thought. He was leading up to something. "But she's also a good friend."

"She's my *best* friend."

Hamlisch's face became serious. He watched Serena gravely for a moment. Then: "Do you want to do her a favor?"

Serena knew now what he had been leading up to. She knew what was coming. "I'd do any favor in the world for her, provided *Zoe* was the one who wanted the favor."

"Zoe doesn't always know what's good for her."

"And *you* do," Serena said.

"In this case, I do."

Serena wasn't going to discuss Zoe with Arthur Hamlisch. She put her drink down on the coffee table and stood up. "Well, I have to go. Got a date. Thanks for the drink."

Hamlisch stayed seated where he was, looking up at Serena. "Won't you even talk about it?"

Serena didn't answer.

"She's headed for a fall, Serena."

Those were the exact words that had come to Serena's mind about Zoe and Tim O'Neil. She couldn't keep her expression from changing a little, but she tried not to let Hamlisch see that she knew what he was talking about. She wasn't going even to acknowledge that there was anything between Zoe and Tim O'Neil if she could help it.

Hamlisch stood up. "Tim's not going to leave Helen," he said. "Zoe is going to tumble down the mountain."

So much for not acknowledging it, Serena thought. "When she does," she said, "*if* she does, I'll be around to pick up the pieces." And then, because she was so sure she had hit on the truth, she added, "Unless you want to pick them up."

Hamlisch looked away from Serena, but not before she had seen a vulnerability in his eyes. "I'd rather see her not to get hurt in the first place," he said.

He'd rather not see Zoe with Tim, Serena thought. She was right. Hamlisch was in love with Zoe.

She couldn't see what was on his face now. He had bent down to put his glass down. Why was she being so hard on the guy? she wondered. If he were in love with Zoe—and he was—was that something to fault him for? Of course, it wasn't. What she blamed him for was for not going after Zoe, declaring himself to her, taking her away from Tim. Zoe and Hamlisch would make a perfect team. She wondered why that hadn't occurred to her before. She began to feel a little better about Zoe. Maybe that was how it would turn out, she told herself—Zoe and Hamlisch.

Hamlisch straightened up. His eyes didn't say anything or try to hide anything. "If you change your mind," he said, "I'll always be ready to talk."

Serena felt a strange little sense of loss. She didn't answer Hamlisch. She smiled at him and kissed him on the cheek and left.

Walking home, Serena thought about that sense of loss. She began to realize why she had felt it. Men weren't first in her life, and though sex was important and necessary, they never would be. She wasn't meant to be part of a team; she was meant to be alone. She was the one who would tumble down the mountain, if it were ever any other way.

SEVENTEEN

Zoe was waiting for Serena in the little vestibule of the converted brownstone where she lived. They climbed the three flights to Serena's apartment.

Magazines were lying around. Serena's picture was on the cover of several of them. She had often tried to picture her mother's reaction, her father arriving home with a magazine held up in his hand, calling out to her mother, "Ellie! Did you see this, Ellie? Did you see Serena's picture on the cover of the new *Milady?*" But she couldn't picture that. What she could see was her father trying to hide the magazines from her mother. She could see him putting the magazines aside if Ellie found them and changing the subject.

"If your face were any longer, you could root snakes out from under rugs with your chin," Zoe said. "What's got you so low?"

"Oh, I don't know. This so-called *business* we're in gets me that way sometimes."

"What are you, crazy? Look at all your covers. Look where you sit in the business. Not only are you booked three months ahead, but you've got a list of photographers a page long hoping for cancellations. I saw it the other day. You've got as many secondaries as I have."

"What's so great about that? So a girl's got a face that photographs and a shape they can hang clothes on. What does that make her?"

"It makes her somebody who doesn't have nine-to-five facing her five days a week for the rest of her life, for one thing. Come on, Serena. At least in this business your time's your own."

"I don't know how the hell you can say that. I feel like I'm in prison. Twenty-four hours a day that goddamn agency has to know where I am, so they can get in touch with me if they need to. You call that your time being your own?"

Zoe blew out a breath and fanned her face with slow, wilted-finger movements. "This girl is really set off," she said. "Let us not discuss 'this business.' Let us have a little drinkie."

Serena fixed Perrier and lime for both of them. That was Zoe's idea of a drink. "What are you doing tonight?" she asked. She knew Zoe wasn't seeing Tim because he was out of town.

"I'm going to a do at Regine's with Oscar Woolmer and some of his hangers-on. I'm the dragon lady who keeps the groupies at bay. You . . . ?"

"Something or other at Alice Tully with Danny Shriver. Maybe we'll see you later at Regine's."

They sat in a heavy silence. Serena was pretty sure Zoe had come because she wanted to talk about something, probably some new problem with Tim, probably the fact that he had left that morning without having settled anything with Helen. She knew Zoe was hesitating to bring it up because of the low mood she was in. She felt she owed it to Zoe to lift herself out of the mood so Zoe would feel free to talk, but the revelation about herself that had come to her while she was walking home from her meeting with Hamlisch wasn't fully clarified in her mind yet, and she didn't want to squash it back. What she wanted to do was sink down in a tubful of hot, bubbly water, assimilate it and come to terms with it. Hamlisch's feelings for Zoe were also on her mind. If the time ever came when she thought it would do any good, she was going to tell Zoe. But the time wasn't now, much as she wished it were.

"What are you going to do when you quit this racket . . . or it quits you?" she asked.

"Raise a bunch of Tim's kids," Zoe said.

Serena knew she had opened the door wide for that. "That's about all modeling prepares you for," she said, "getting married and raising a bunch of kids."

Zoe gave her a "what's so bad about that?" look.

"I'm serious," Serena said doggedly. "What does a girl get out of modeling? It doesn't train you for anything. I want to *do* something with my life. After it's all over, I don't want to just have *been* here."

"You know what's wrong with you? You're having a reaction. You think you got to the top too fast, that it was too easy, that you didn't have to work hard enough to get there. But that's the way it happens. A model either makes it or doesn't. Zoom, she's there, or ploomp, she never gets there or gets only halfway there. A model who's going to make it makes it right off. She goes from high to higher. If she wants her modeling time to be a 'career,' she rations her time. She doesn't do all editorial. She—"

"I heard all that from Hamlisch today."

"There's always Stephen. Marry Stephen and raise kids." Zoe grinned. "Yours and Stephen's can play with mine and Tim's."

"Marriage is the last thing I want!"

Zoe's mood changed. All the lightness left it. "Problems," she said. "Is there anyone in this fucking world who doesn't have problems?" She stared moodily into her glass, swirling the contents in agitated half circles. She came out with what was on her mind, what had brought her to Serena's apartment. "Isolda killed herself," she said.

Shock almost blanked Serena's mind. "What?"

"Isolda Mellors jumped out of a tree and killed herself."

"You can't mean that!"

"I wish I didn't."

"Jumped out of a tree? . . . When? . . . Where? . . . I worked with her—when was it? Last week! Was it last week? Yes, last week. What are you saying, jumped out of a tree? No one would jump out of a tree to kill herself!" Serena's words came out in a jumble. She hardly knew what she was saying.

"*She* did."

"But that wouldn't kill you!"

"It killed her."

It was too crazy for Serena to be able to believe. "It would have been in the papers," she said. "I didn't see anything about it in the papers."

"No, and you won't if Tim and Rod Ingram's manager can keep it out."

The very fact that Zoe was speaking without any emotion in her voice showed how deeply she was upset about what she was telling Serena.

"What's Tim got to do with it?" Serena asked.

Zoe didn't look at her. She was still swirling the dregs of her drink. "That's where he went this morning. Up to New Hampshire, where it happened."

"I wondered why you were so mysterious about where he was going."

"He didn't want me to say anything. Still doesn't. So I'm only telling you about it. Besides, I didn't know any more this morning when I talked to you than where he was going and why. I didn't have any details until he called me after I got home from work this afternoon."

"What did he say when he called you? Why did she do it? Why a tree? Why a crazy thing like jumping out of a tree?"

"The way Tim patched the story together, Isolda went up to New Hampshire for the weekend with Rod Ingram. She's been with him for a while now, you know. He's got a house up there. What she didn't know was that he's also got a live-in boyfriend—artist or would-be artist—who was supposed to clear out before the weekend. But he didn't; the boyfriend didn't. He was there when they got there."

"Did Isolda know about the boyfriend before?"

"I told you she didn't. Tim said he was pretty sure she didn't."

"Well, my God, she didn't have to kill herself over it! Why couldn't she just have bowed out if she didn't like what she found when she got there? My God, to kill herself over . . ."

"Who knows why she took it the way she did and did what she did? Anyway, Isolda and Rod Ingram and his boyfriend—Chris is his name—the three of them were there all weekend. What went on is anybody's guess. Monday morning, yesterday, Isolda called the agency to tell them to cancel her bookings, said she was staying over till today. Early this morning Rod Ingram's manager called Helen and told her Isolda was dead, had killed herself. That Ingram bastard didn't know what to do with the body. He didn't want to get stuck with the body!"

"It was this morning she killed herself?"

"Yesterday. The police had Isolda at the morgue by the time the guy called. Tim said Rod Ingram claims he doesn't know exactly when she did it. He said she disappeared around noon yesterday. According to him, they spent all afternoon looking for her, he and his boyfriend, Chris. It was night before they found her. She was lying on the ground by a tree. It had some boards nailed onto the trunk for steps. Some kids used to have a tree house up in it." Zoe paused, staring into the glass she was holding. "No telling how long Isolda sat up in that tree, thinking about what she was going to do. . . ."

"She must have been on something to do as crazy a thing as that. She *had* to have been."

"That's what Tim said."

"She was so beautiful," Serena said. "And always so sweet. And thoughtful. . . . She just wasn't the kind to commit suicide, Zoe. I don't believe she committed suicide."

"It was suicide. She left a note."

"Oh, God. . . ."

"The note said she was going to jump off the highest place she could find. And she turned up at the bottom of a tree with a broken neck. That adds up to suicide."

"Are they going to do an autopsy?"

"They've already done one. Broken neck."

EIGHTEEN

"Where the hell's the goddamn car?"

It was getting dark, and a stiff, cold wind was blowing. It had caused them a rough landing in the small plane Rod had chartered to bring them there.

"There goes the plane," Isolda said. The small plane was taking off for the return flight to New York. "If the car's not here, we don't have any way of getting anywhere." She looked around the small airport perched on the flat crest of a hill. There was nothing else in sight, only more hills and deep woods. "Maybe we could call into town for a taxi."

"The goddamn car was supposed to be here!"

"But it isn't." She put her hand on his arm. "Let's not let it spoil our weekend, Rod. Let's go inside and see if we can call a taxi."

"Fucking bastard!"

"Who?"

He jerked his arm away and headed for the wooden building that housed the office and the small waiting room. She followed after him, running to keep up.

"Any way I can get a taxi out here?" he demanded of the man in the office.

The man looked up. It was clear in his face that he didn't like what he'd heard and didn't like what he saw. Then he looked at the girl. She looked anxious, worried. She smiled, timidly, he thought; she looked as if she were apologizing for the other's rudeness.

"No taxis would come out here now. Where do you want to go?"

"I've got a place on the other side of town."

The man looked at the girl again. If he hadn't felt sorry for her, he'd have let the guy find a way out of there the best way he could.

"I'm closing up," he said. "I'll take you. I go that way."

The man from the airport let them off at the dirt road that led from the highway to the house. You couldn't even see the house from there. He'd wanted to take them all the way—it was fully dark now, no lights anywhere—but the guy had insisted on getting out there on the highway. "This'll be fine! This is good enough!"

"Thank you," Isolda said. "It was awfully nice of you to bring us. We appreciate it."

The man nodded to acknowledge her thanks. He was glad she wasn't a daughter of his going off up that dark dirt road with Longhair. He shook his head as he drove off. The guy hadn't even offered to carry the girl's suitcase. There she went, lugging it herself. Pretty little thing. Foreign, though. Had an accent. Deserved better than she was getting all the same.

The car was parked beside the two-story farmhouse. There were no lights on in the house.

"What the fuck!"

Rod stamped up the steps and across the porch and put down his overnight case and got out the door key. Then he tried the door. It wasn't locked. He flung it open, kicked his case inside and snapped on the light.

"Chris!" he yelled at the top of his lungs. He strode through the rooms, snapping on lights as he went. "Chris!" He yelled the name every time he got enough breath to yell it again. He ran up the stairs, still yelling it.

Isolda stood in the living room, bewildered, still

holding her suitcase. Who was Chris? He hadn't ever mentioned a Chris to her.

She heard the door slam upstairs. He was talking to somebody. She could hear his voice, but she couldn't hear what he was saying. She couldn't hear anything from whoever he was talking to. Chris. . . . A girl?

She heard the door slam again and heard him clomping toward the stairs and then down them.

When he came back into the living room, he was smiling. He'd put that smile on his face just outside the door, and she knew it. "Zonked," he said. "Man, he's out of it. He'll have to stay the night and sleep it off. I'll get him out of here tomorrow."

"Who?"

"Friend of mine. I've told you about him. Artist I know. Uses this place to paint during the week."

He had never mentioned a Chris to her or any of the rest of it. But she let it go. She didn't want to make him mad again.

"Hey, sugar! Relax! It's okay! It's okay!" He took her suitcase out of her hand and dropped it on the floor.

"I'm relaxed. I know it's okay." She smiled at him.

He put his arm across her shoulders and pulled her along with him toward the back of the house. "That snot-nose at the airport didn't recognize me. Did you notice that? Chris ain't the one that's out of it! *He* is!" He led her to the kitchen and sat her down in a chair at a round table covered with an oilcloth in a garish design of yellow flowers. "What'll it be? You want coke or grass?" As he spoke, he got a large bottle of red Chianti out of a cabinet and put it on the table. He uncorked it, got two glasses and poured them full.

Isolda watched him. He had fascinated her from the first, and still did. She loved his crazy looks. He was tall and skinny. His bones looked as if they would clack when he walked. All his joints gave the illusion of bending the wrong way or both ways. His mouth was big and loose-lipped, his nose hooked; his black eyes were small and narrow, his cheeks sunken under prominent cheekbones. His dark hair was long in back and short around the crown and on the top. It stuck up in spikes.

He was never altogether still. If he were standing still, he swung his arms, snapped his fingers, twisted his shoulders in disco motion. He looked and acted like the rock star he was.

Her life had changed drastically in the months she'd known him. How many now? Seven? She was in a haze so much of the time that there were a lot of things she couldn't remember. But it had been March when she met him. It was after a concert he'd given. She'd been invited to the bash afterward. She'd been surprised when he singled her out. She wouldn't have thought she'd be his type. She hadn't been then. But he had changed that. That was why her life was so drastically changed. She didn't live her life now. She lived his, his schedule, which reversed day and night. Anyone else would be thinking now of a steak supper and bed. Not Rod. If they ate at all, they'd have scrambled eggs after the sun had come up.

He was laying out the coke stuff, elbows flapping while his hands stayed steady, humming, singing snatches of songs, feet moving to the disco beat in his head. "Here's for starters! Breathe in, baby!" He snapped a popper under her nose. She had the sensation of flying up out of her chair and rising toward the ceiling. Poppers always did that to her. But it lasted only a few seconds. Then her heart would start beating as if it were going to come right out of her chest. She laughed and took a gulp of wine. "Atta baby! Atta baby!"

He ran into the living room and put his latest album on the record player and ran back, dancing.

The volume was loud enough to lift the house off the ground. "Dance with me, baby! Dance!" He was singing to the tune on the record. He pulled her up out of the chair with one hand, drinking wine with the other. "Dance with me, baby!" He'd sniffed several poppers. He was saving the coke. When he got a mellow on with wine, he started coming down, and that was when he wanted coke. He always laid it out for when he would be ready for it.

Around midnight, it couldn't have been much later than that, Isolda thought—but she couldn't be sure, there wasn't a clock in the kitchen—he flagged out. "Hell, I'm busted on my feet. I'm dyin' on my feet." He looked as if he were. His eyes were almost closed; his mouth was slack; his body sagged. "I'm goin' to bed." He stumbled out of the kitchen and through the living room toward the stairs. Isolda followed him. She picked up his overnight case and her suitcase and trailed him up the stairs.

He fell on the bed in his clothes. He flopped over on his back, already asleep . . . or passed out, breathing heavily, mouth open. Isolda was scared. Could poppers and coke . . . ? Could you OD on poppers and coke? She wasn't high. She hadn't had anything but poppers and the gulps of wine she needed afterward to make her heart slow down. She hovered over him until his breathing became normal.

She got herself undressed and got in bed on the other side, herself under the covers, he on top of them. He'd get cold. It was cold at night in the mountains. She got up and found a blanket in the closet to cover him with.

There were no clothes in the closet. She went to the bureau. There was nothing in the bureau drawers. She went into the bathroom and looked in the medicine cabinet. Nothing of his, only things put there for the convenience of guests. She went back into the bedroom and looked around. This wasn't his room. This was a guest room. He hadn't taken her to his room because *Chris* was sleeping in it!

She stood staring at his sleeping form. She wasn't surprised that he hadn't made love to her. He didn't very often. He had the reputation of being a girl eater, but he wasn't. He always had a girl. There had been a string of them before her, but sex wasn't important to him—at least not sex with her.

She tried to keep what was pounding at her brain from coming into it. That wasn't true! That *couldn't* be true!

Then who is this Chris? the part of her brain that wouldn't be blanked kept asking. *What is this Chris to him? What are they to each other?*

Chris stopped at the open bedroom door. He was slight, willowy, smaller altogether than Rod. He smiled. A mocking, openly malevolent smile, Isolda thought. His hair was blond, his eyes blue . . . or he looked as if he'd have blue eyes, watery blue. She couldn't see the color; they were too slitted. He looked from her to Rod, still sleeping. Isolda quivered with embarrassment, unable to look away from the mocking smile and his eyes that went from her under the covers to Rod on top of them, only half covered by the blanket she'd put over him.

"Don't mind me," he said. "Don't pay any attention to me. I'm just going to the bathroom." He held out a corner of the big towel he had wrapped around him. He was naked under it. *Showing her that he was the one who belonged there, that she was the intruder in the house.* "Let him sleep," he said, eyes going to Rod's leg hanging off the edge of the bed with the pants he still had on twisted around it, hiked up, showing most of his bare hairy calf. "He doesn't like anybody to wake him up. Get dressed, and come downstairs. I'll make breakfast for us. He never wants breakfast." *Didn't wait for an answer, acted as if he'd given a command, went on down the hall.*

Isolda got up and went into the guest bathroom. When she was dressed, she went down to the kitchen.

Chris had already cleaned up the mess she and Rod had left. He was dressed in jeans frayed at the edge of the bell-bottoms. A shirt was half tucked in, half not, *on purpose.* He was barefoot, standing at the stove, frying bacon. *Right at home in the kitchen.* His hair was wet, uncombed . . . *on purpose. He lived here; he could go around here any way he wanted to.*

"Batter cakes and bacon," he said. "Does that suit you . . . ? What's your name?" *Showing her that Rod had never mentioned her.*

"Isolda," she said. "What's yours?" *Showing him that Rod had never mentioned him to her, lying.*

His eyes opened wide, pretending surprise that she would have to ask. "Why, I'm Chris."

Table all set with linen place mats and napkins. Fresh flowers in a vase, cut from the garden that morning. He had set up the kitchen before he'd come to the bedroom door, had run around indoors and outdoors naked. *He could do that at his own place, no neighbors around, house back off the road.*

She finished everything on her plate. She was starved. She hadn't eaten since noon the day before.

"What do you think of my batter cakes? I'm a good cook. Rod can't be bothered cooking."

"They were good," she said. She'd said very little to him. She couldn't think of anything to say.

"They'll hit you pretty soon."

That was the reason. He didn't say much that you could answer.

"Grass," he said, "cooked with grass. I'm thinking of writing my own Alice B. Toklas cookbook."

She was feeling light-headed. Her body was heavy, weighted against the chair she was sitting in, but her head was floating somewhere off her shoulders.

"You should have told me before I ate them."

He smiled that slitted-eyed, mocking smile. "Specialty of the house," he said.

She was beginning to feel sick. "I'm going back to bed."

"I'll clean up. I always do. Rod can't be bothered with cleaning up. If you've got to nap, sleep on the couch in the living room. You'll wake Rod up if you go back upstairs."

She had trouble getting to the living room and to the couch. He didn't offer to help her, just stood leaning against the table, smiling, watching her stumble out of the kitchen.

He had eaten the same thing she had, she kept telling herself. There wasn't anything wrong with it. It had hit her because she was so hungry. Her stomach had been empty. She'd eaten too fast. She'd be all right after she slept awhile. *Sleep on the couch in the living room. Mocking, knowing smile.* She couldn't have gotten up the stairs to the bedroom if she'd tried, and he knew it.

It was late afternoon when she came out of it. She couldn't believe she had slept the whole day through, but it was dusky outside, the room half dark and full of shadows.

When Rod disappeared, as he had with her this weekend, when his manager and press agent and all the other hangers-on were going crazy trying to find him, this was where he came, got away from all of them, drove out to Westchester by himself and took the charter plane, didn't use his own.

The pilot had looked surprised to see her. She had noticed it at the time. She had felt proud. This was the first time Rod had taken a girl with him when he went off to get away from the clutter of people always around him. If he'd been in the habit of taking a girl, the pilot wouldn't have been surprised.

"A passenger?" the pilot had asked.

"Yeah. Why? That up your charge?"

"No. One or four, no difference. Just mentioned it."

"Just fly this crate. That's what I'm payin' you for."

He hadn't had to tell the pilot where he wanted to go. The pilot knew. And he knew who was always there in the car to meet him. No wonder he'd been surprised to see her. No wonder there'd been that raised-eyebrow "so this is how you get your kicks" look on his face when he'd watched Rod helping her out of the plane before he took off back to New York.

She could hear them in the kitchen, Rod and Chris. Talking, Rod's voice low, tone soothing, the way he talked to her sometimes. Chris anwering, voice low, high-pitched, laughing low, sounding pleased. She couldn't make out what they were saying.

Everything was moving in slow motion except time. It had gotten dark in the little time she'd been awake.

Didn't Rod wonder why she was still sleeping? Whether she was awake yet? Why she didn't come into the kitchen? She got to her feet, head dizzy, mind hazy, body heavy. She got through the dark room without bumping into anything. She got to the door of the kitchen. Rod's back was to her. He was sitting in a chair pulled out from the table. Chris was sitting on his lap.

Chris saw her. He looked straight through her. No mocking smile, no indication whatever that he saw her. He bent his head close to Rod's, whispered in his ear, laughed. *Showing her that this was the way things were in this house; Rod had brought her on a whim; it had been a mistake; he didn't want her; he wanted it the way he had it now, he and Chris.* Isolda felt debased. Why hadn't Rod kept his secret? Why had he taken this chance and let her find it out?

There were two large Chianti bottles on the table, one empty, one almost empty. Popper shells were scattered on the floor. The coke had been set out. Part of it had been used. Rod had been awake and down in the kitchen with Chris a long time, maybe all after-noon.

Rod stood up and dumped Chris off his lap. He laughed when Chris fell on his bony rump on the floor. He turned around as if he knew she was stand-ing behind him in the door. His eyes looked as if they were spinning around in his head. He couldn't focus them on her. His loose lips made a sloppy smile. "C'mon in. Where you been? Got a party goin' here." He swayed as he moved around the chair, holding onto the back of it. "Party goin' here. You come up here to party-poop or party?" He came toward her on un-steady feet, reached a hand out and pulled her to him, braced himself with an arm over her shoulders.

The music blasted on in the quiet house loud enough to rock it on its foundations. Chris had turned it on. He came back in, dancing. He pulled on Rod's arm, dancing, trying to get Rod to dance with him. Rod pushed him away and stumbled with Isolda to the chair where he'd been sitting, pushed her down on it, patted her head, put his face down to hers. "Thought you were going to sleep all weekend. Thought I'd lost my good company girl." He pulled a chair close to hers and sat down in it. He pushed a popper under her nose, but she pulled her head back. His face contorted in anger. Then he laughed. He put his hand on the back of her head and held it still while he snapped the popper under her nose, almost ramming it up it. "Ain't that better? Ain't that bet-ter?" He laughed again, pushed a half-empty glass of wine toward her. She had to drink it; her heart was pounding this time before the popper wore off.

Chris had slumped into a chair opposite them. His face was sullen. He wouldn't look at either of them.

"You goin' to stay around here, Chris-baby, you goin' to have to join the party," Rod said. "Ain't that like I told you?" He leaned his face back to Isolda's. "Goin' to have a different kind of party." He winked at her, looked at Chris and laughed at him. Isolda tried to pull away, but he held her where she was, her face close to his, laughing at her now. He was enjoying himself. He liked sneering at Chris, making him cringe; he liked what he was doing to both of them. "Old Chris wants to hang around, so-o-o-o, goin' to have a different kind of party."

Isolda froze. Fear was on her like a cold, wet glove.

Rod took his arm from around her and poked her on the arm. "Goin' to have a three-way shtick tonight, baby." He looked across at Chris. Isolda could see the hard look he was giving Chris. Even in profile his face showed what he was thinking, the mood he was in. His eyes almost turned corners on his head, they were so wide, and his mouth was as wide proportionately. Isolda had never realized that about his eyes before. They were beginning to look like animal eyes, curving around the sides of his face.

He was somebody she didn't know. She'd been with him every night for six months or more, except for the weekends he had been out of town and the times he'd flown off somewhere to give a concert or to keep a recording date on the Coast or in Nashville, and she didn't know him.

She was in a strange country among strange people. But she had felt so secure, because of Helen O'Neil, like a mother to her. And because of Rod, because of having been singled out by such a famous person. She had loved everything about him, his crazy looks, his fame, the places they went and the things they did, the adulation of the crowds for him (herself on his arm or his arm around her shoulders while he accepted the adulation—she knew why now; he needed her or someone like her to help hide his secret), but she had never loved him. There was Bjorn at home, waiting. Patient, loving, understanding Bjorn. "Go," he had said when she had had the chance to go to London. She and another girl in Stockholm had been chosen to play small parts in a film being made there. "Stay," he had written when she had written him that she had the chance to do some modeling for a fashion magazine. "Go," he had told her again when she made a flying trip home to tell her parents and him that she had a chance to model for the greatest model agency in the world, Models, Incorporated, of the United States. "You will go," Bjorn had said. "I will finish my schooling. You will come back, and I will be here. If we do it so, you will not have regrets after we marry."

"You trust me, Bjorn? You know I will come back? I'm afraid."

"I trust you."

"Oh . . . !" She had clung to him. "If only you could come with me!"

"In my heart I will be with you."

"And I will be with you!"

He had caressed her cheek with his hand. "Go. Do it. You want to. It's natural that you would. Meanwhile, I'll study. I'll finish my studies. Then we'll marry. You will be ready, and I will be ready."

"I'll miss you!"

He smiled at her, teasing, the cleft in his chin deepening. "You had better!"

She had cried then. "I'm not going! I can't leave you for so long! I'm not going!"

"But you *are* going. I insist that you go. I would feel responsible if you missed such an opportunity. Also, sweet Isolda, later you might begin to resent me."

"Never! I wouldn't!"

"We won't take the chance. After all, we have the rest of our lives that we will live together."

"You love me, Bjorn?" Somehow she felt anxious.

"I love you."

"You trust me?" She had already asked him that, she knew.

"I trust you to come back to me the same Isolda who
is leaving me."

"I will! I will!"

"If you cannot, don't come back." He had kissed
her. "You see how much I trust you? I can say that to
you because I trust you, for I would take you back no
matter how you came back to me."

They spent the night in the kitchen, inhaling poppers, sniffing coke, drinking wine, smoking grass.
Isolda had gotten high on the first few poppers and
the wine she drank after them. She had known she was
getting high, but it didn't matter. Nothing mattered;
she didn't have a care in the world. She sniffed coke
when Rod did. Why, it was great! It was fantastic! She
was going to take enough to make up for all the times
she'd refused it before! Her body was as light as a
feather; she was filled with a good feeling for everybody, so much good feeling she couldn't contain it.
She had to be on her feet dancing, by herself, head
thrown back, eyes closed, totally within herself but
responding with wilder movements when Rod stamped
his feet and clapped. "Atta baby! Atta baby! Striptease,
baby! Striptease! Take it off! Take it off!" He started
dancing with her, unbuttoning her shirt, unzipping
her jeans, helping her get them off. That was what she
wanted, freedom, from clothes, from everything that
restricted and inhibited her. She danced with wild
abandon. Rod was grinding his body in front of her,
naked now, too. The music blasted; she wanted it to
blast louder; she wanted to be lost in it; it was glorious! The kitchen and everything in it were in sharp
outline one moment and soft and fuzzy the next.
Beautiful! Everything was beautiful! Chris was naked
now, all of them dancing. Chris's body was pale and
hairless; Rod's dark-toned and covered with black hair.
Beautiful! Beautiful! Three happy, beautiful, dancing
people in a happy, beautiful world!

* * *

The sky was streaked with light. The three of them were in the bedroom. Isolda was coming down. She'd been sick twice, barely making it to the bathroom to throw up in the john. She was cold and sick and frightened. Goose pimples covered her skin. Her nipples were hard and puckered, from the cold. Rod's penis was limp, and so was Chris's. Rod was still high. Chris was all the way down. He had wilted, was almost out on his feet.

"Get that dick of yours up and get on that girl and make her squeal!" Rod ordered. He had gotten a walking stick from somewhere. He had a straight chair in front of him, standing on one foot, the other foot on the seat of the cane-bottomed chair like an animal trainer with a whip, one elbow resting on the knee crooked over the seat of the chair. He reached out with the walking stick and touched Chris's limp penis. Chris shrank away.

"Use your tricks!" Rod ordered Isolda. "Get it up for him!"

Chris shrank farther away. He would have run out the door if Rod hadn't been in front of it. Isolda saw the glances he sneaked toward the door. She was sneaking them herself.

"You hear me?" Rod screamed. He looked like a madman.

"I can't," Isolda said. "I'm sick. I—"

"How many times you think I'm goin' to keep telling you?"

"I can't. . . ."

"You can't do anything but puke!" He threw the walking stick. It hit the lamp on the bureau, crashing it to the floor. He didn't see it or hear it. "I've got to do it all! The two of you ain't worth shit! But I'll get you goin'!" He came toward her.

"Get away from me! Don't touch me!"

He stopped, stood laughing, sneering at her. "First

time I've heard that." Sneering at Chris: "She wants you, Chrissie-boy."

"I don't! I don't!"

Rod stood with his hands on his hips. His penis was in full erection; he pushed his pelvis forward, making it jut out in front of him. He looked from it to Isolda and then Chris. "On your face, Chris!"

Chris cowered away from him. Rod grabbed him and flung him around and pushed him to the wall. He rammed his penis into his anus. He was so much taller than Chris that he lifted him up on the balls of his feet with every thrust. Chris screamed out every time his body was punched against the wall. Isolda felt cold chills running over her. She thought she could feel Chris's pain herself. Chris was scrabbling at the wall with his fingernails. Isolda could hear them scraping, tearing the wallpaper. He was crying aloud, screaming. The louder he screamed, the harder Rod lunged. Suddenly Chris's body convulsed. "Ah-h-h-h!" he screamed. The wallpaper was wet with his ejaculation.

Rod laughed and thrust again and then withdrew his penis. It was still engorged. He took his hands off Chris and let him slide to the floor. His chest was heaving with his hard breathing. He turned to Isolda. "You were thinking he didn't like that?" he sneered. He pointed at the dark, wet splotch on the wall. "What's that if he didn't like it?" He laughed again and lunged at her, grabbing for her arm. "Your turn, baby."

She dodged his grabbing hand, darted past him and ran out the door. She ran down the hall and down the stairs. As she ran to the front door, she heard him laughing. She knew he was standing at the top of the stairs, watching her run naked out the door, still laughing. The laughter followed her all the way across the front yard and to the dirt road.

* * *

Isolda huddled on the floor in the back of the car.
She'd gotten almost all the way to the highway before
she realized that she couldn't run out onto the high-
way naked. She had sunk down on the dirt of the road.
She was too exhausted, too overcome even to cry.
Tears rolled out of her eyes, but she wasn't crying.

Rod was a sadist. That was the only explanation for
the way he had acted. A sadist, maybe, a maso-sadist.
She shook as if she were in the throes of ague.

She felt the sun on her back. She dragged herself
up and walked in the weeds off the side of the dirt
road back to the house. When she saw the car, she
crawled into the back seat, then slid off the seat onto
the floor. She'd be out of sight there.

She went to sleep or passed out. The next thing she
knew Chris was shaking her shoulder. He was dressed.
His clothes were fresh. His hair was combed. He
looked smug and sure of himself, the way he had
looked the first time she saw him.

"Rod said for you to come in the house," he said.

"Bring me my clothes. Please bring me my clothes."

His eyes slitted. He didn't try to hide the venom in
them. "I'm not your go-boy."

She got up on her knees. "Please, Chris. I can't go
back in there. *Please.*"

He leaned toward her. "You fucked up," he said.
"You fucked up in the first place by coming here."

"I didn't know about you! He never told me! I
wouldn't have come if I'd known!"

"You'd have come. It would have been something
else to go back home and brag to *Bjorn* about."

"Bjorn? How do you know about Bjorn?"

The mocking, ugly smile came on his face. "You
know how."

"I *don't!* Who told you about him? I never even told
Rod!"

"Never told him? You couldn't shut up about *Bjorn*
last night. You were even calling Rod *Bjorn!* You

know how many times you blew Rod, showing us how you do it to *Bjorn?*"

"No! I wouldn't have done that!"

"You *did* do it. Come in the house like Rod said. And don't make noise when you pass our room. Rod's sleeping in there. You've missed the plane today, but I'll drive you to the airport to catch the one tomorrow. You won't be going back with Rod. He's finished with you." He turned and walked off. Isolda stared after him as he crossed the yard and then the porch and disappeared into the house. She wanted to call him back and make him admit the lie he'd told. She hadn't done what he said! She *couldn't* have! She wouldn't have done that to Bjorn!

All the time she was trying to deny it, she knew that she had. Bjorn would hate her if he knew. He would despise her the way he despised whores. He would think she was no better than a whore.

She knew she had no choice but to go back in the house. She didn't know whether she could make it. She was sicker than she had ever been, soul-sick because of what she'd done.

When she got to the room, Rod's overnight case was gone. Her suitcase was where she had left it. The bed was a mess. She shuddered at the sight of it.

A bottle of wine was on the bureau. She knew that Chris had put it there. She stood in front of the bureau, staring at the bottle. Her heart was pounding as if she'd just inhaled a popper. Nausea was getting the best of her. She needed a drink. She poured a glassful and downed it. She'd feel better in a minute. The wine would stop her heart from pounding and quiet the nausea. She stood staring at the empty glass, waiting to feel better.

She woke up on the floor in front of the bureau. She was dressed. She didn't remember dressing. Her suitcase was packed and closed. She didn't remember doing it. Her head felt too heavy to try to hold up. She got herself to her feet, holding onto the side of the bureau. The bottle of wine was empty.

When she was on her feet, she felt light-headed, clear-headed. She looked around. It was morning. The clock on the bureau said nine o'clock. It was nine o'clock on Monday morning. She had a ten o'clock booking that she wasn't going to make. She'd better call the agency. All these things were very clear in her head. She went to the telephone at the end of the hall and dialed the number of the agency. She remembered to dial the area code first. "Millie . . . ? Is this Millie? . . . I'm glad it's you, Millie. Look, I won't be back in town until tomorrow. Get me off the hook with Helen, will you? Tell her we had trouble with the car or something and missed the plane. Cancel my bookings for today . . . What? Yes, I'll be there tomorrow. I promise." She knew she wasn't going to be when she said it.

There was a note pad on the telephone table. For messages, she told herself. She had a message to write. She didn't have any more trouble handling the pencil than she'd had talking to Millie. Her head was clear; her hands were steady. "When I come down this time," she wrote, "I'm coming down for good. I'm going to jump off the highest place I can find." That was very well put, it seemed to her.

She went down the stairs. Very quietly. She didn't want to wake up Rod and Chris. She didn't want to disturb them. She didn't want to disturb anybody. She just wanted to find a high place. She could feel herself floating down from it. When she woke up, which she always did when she dreamed she was falling, she would be home, in her bed at hime, smelling the sausage her mother was cooking for breakfast. She'd hear her mother humming as she worked. She'd lie in bed, not wanting to leave the warm comfort of the covers. She'd plan what she would wear that night, what she'd

be wearing when Bjorn came, something that he liked
especially.

She was smiling softly as she walked out of the
house. She didn't go toward the dirt road. She went
toward the woods on the other side of the house and
then toward a high hill to the back of it. She had
plenty of time to find a high place. Rod and Chris
wouldn't wake up until noon. By the time they woke
up she would be home. This was the only way she
could ever go home, back to her parents and back to
Bjorn.

NINETEEN

"You must have some kind of psychological quirk!" Zoe snapped. She marched across the room to the wall-length window on anger-stiffened legs, heels clicking sharply on the bare areas of the parquet floor. "It's one thing to parade yourself around naked in front of me, but it's something else to show yourself off to anybody who happens to look in the window!"

She let the blind down with a crash that sounded as if she had torn it out of its brackets. "There's a name for men who do that!"

Zoe didn't know why Tim's habit of walking around without any clothes on had set her off today. If they weren't going out—and they seldom did—he always got out of his clothes as soon as he got inside her apartment. She had always loved that in him—that when he was there he was so totally *there,* so completely at home with her, so giving of all of himself to her. Today the repetition of the same old habit—so much in its own way, but so little if that was as far as it was going—infuriated her.

"We're seventeen floors off the street, Zoe," Tim said, smiling at her—always his response to her irritation.

"There are people in those buildings across the street!" Zoe retorted, refusing to be softened by his smile.

"They can't see in here." He reached for her arm

as she clicked past him on her way to the bedroom to draw the blinds in there.

Zoe swished out of his reach and marched on. *"You* may not care if you make a spectacle of yourself, but *I* do! I have to live here!"

Tim followed her into the room and from window to window as she drew the blinds, trying to crash the smaller ones as hard as she had crashed the large one.

As the last blind went down, Zoe's fury dissipated. It was gone as suddenly as it had come, leaving her feeling inadequate and inept and foolish. All she got out of an outburst of temper with Tim was just that— an outburst of her temper, a venting of her spleen. Her fury wouldn't change a thing.

Tim sat down on the edge of the bed and pulled her between his legs and held her to him, his face against her breasts.

"You feel good," he said. He unbuttoned the top buttons of her blouse and nuzzled his nose against her skin. "You smell good." He ran his tongue up and down the valley between her breasts. "You taste good."

Zoe held herself stiff. "When is it going to be forever for us, Tim? How long are you going to keep making promises and then not keep your promises? If it's not ever going to be you and me, I want you to tell me now!" Her voice was shrill and becoming more shrill with every word. "I'm not going to listen to another lying excuse!"

Tim threw his arms around her and flung himself back on the bed, and her with him. "Zoe, honey! Zoe, honey!" He was swarming all over her, scrambling around, pulling her legs up on the bed. "What are you doing to me? Sweetheart. . . ." He kissed her over and over, her mouth, her eyes, her throat, her mouth again. "Don't do this to me, sweetheart. . . ." His hands were at her clothes, tearing at them, getting them off her. He was holding her body clamped to the bed with his. His lips were quivering, his face working. Tears were in his eyes, on his lashes. They streamed down his cheeks and made them wet and made her face wet where his touched hers. "Zoe, honey! Don't talk about cutting me off! Don't . . . !" He was on top of her, penetrating her. "Zoe, honey! Zoe, honey!" A hot gush from him flooded up in her. He sank down on her, the full weight of his body on her. He sobbed brokenly, his face buried in the pillow beside her head.

Zoe lay unmoving under Tim, feeling the weight of his body, listening to him cry, feeling the shuddering heaves of his breath. "Hold me, Zoe," he begged. "Put your arms around me." His arms were as tight around her as he could get them, locking her arms to her sides. She couldn't have held him if she'd tried. "Please, Zoe. Hold onto me. Hold onto me."

Finally, he fell asleep, and Zoe eased her body out from under his and got up from the bed. She stood looking down at him. *Hold onto me.* How many times had she heard it? How long was she going to go on doing it?

Zoe went into the bathroom and looked at herself in the full-length mirror on the door. She was a mess. Her face was as splotched with mascara as if she were the one who had cried. Lipstick was smeared around her mouth. Her hair stood out in spikes in spots and was matted to her forehead and the side of her face in others. It looked like she'd sweated through a bout of fever.

Hold onto me. How many did it take to keep him afloat? More than Helen. Maybe more than herself and Helen. How did she know there weren't others? All she had for it was his word.

Why did she think that if she got him to herself, she could keep him afloat alone? Why did she even want to if she could? What was she trying to prove? That she, by herself, was stronger than she and Helen combined? Or she and Helen and others combined?

Big deal. She didn't look her reflection in the eye. She turned away from the sight of herself.

She cleaned her face with cold cream and then scrubbed it with soap. She brushed her teeth. She douched. She showered and washed her hair in the shower, then dried herself and her hair and powdered herself. She sprayed her underarms with regular deodorant and her crotch with hygienic deodorant. She sprayed a mist of Joy in a wide swath up and down in the air and then walked through it and back again. She put a colorless lip salve on her mouth and brushed her hair. She slid her feet into marabou slides and went to the kitchen.

By the time Tim woke up and came to the kitchen the baked potatoes were almost done, the salad was made and the steaks were ready to go under the broiler . . . and Zoe was halfway through the pitcher of martinis she had made for him. She had decided to get drunk. She didn't seem to be getting there, the liquor wasn't affecting her the way she had thought it would, but had taken the edge off her feelings a little.

Tim stood in the door as if hesitant to come all the way into the kitchen. He had as woebegone a look on his face as Zoe had ever seen . . . even on him. His eyes had a shamed, begging look in them.

Zoe poured a martini and handed it to him. "Take this to the bathroom to drink while you clean yourself up," she said. "The steaks will be ready by the time you are."

Tim took the martini. "Do you want me to get dressed? Do I have to leave after dinner?"

"No," Zoe said, "you don't have to leave after dinner. We have a few days, don't we?" She looked down at her naked body. "You don't have to get dressed," she said.

Tim started toward the bathroom and then came back to the kitchen door. He was smiling.

"You scared me there for a minute when you got so

mad earlier," he said. "Boy, you really scared me.
You know that?" He smiled more widely and saluted
her with the martini and turned again and went to
the bathroom.

It was all over for him—their little trauma. All his
little wounds were healed.

Zoe didn't let herself get mad at him. It wasn't his
fault that he could be left untouched by something
that scarred her so deeply. It had to do with his genes,
and he had no control over that. She threw out the
dregs in the martini pitcher and made a fresh batch.

TWENTY

"You have Vina Delphi tomorrow?" Zoe asked. She laughed. "When you finish that sitting with her, you may be ready to start a list of Won't-Work-Fors."

"Why?" Serena asked. "She's a good photographer. I saw some of her work for Boltz Fifth Avenue when I went there for the fitting on the outfit we're going to shoot. I liked her stuff. I think she's good."

"She's in the *Social Register* and *Who's Who of American Women,* too."

"What's that got to do with it?"

"As much as her being a good photographer, when it comes to working for her."

"That doesn't make sense."

"After you finish working with her tomorrow, it'll make sense."

"Come on, Zoe. What are you talking about? Is she a lesbo? So what? If I can put up with Zali's dyke stylist, I can put up with anybody."

"You haven't heard about Vina and her poodle?"

"Oh, Christ! Come off it, Zoe! Everybody in this business isn't wacko!"

"That's right. Even Vina's not, if you like poodles."

"Look, Zoe, I'm not going to get myself frazzled over a *dog!*"

"Just keep your legs together and face front at all times, and you won't have a thing to get frazzled about."

* * *

Vina Delphi answered Serena's ring. She was holding a large black standard poodle by the collar.

"Hi, Serena. I'm Vina Delphi. I can't tell you how long I've been trying to get time on you! Why do you let your agency book you so far ahead with your oldies? You can't get new clients that way! Come in. . . ."

Serena was already in. Vina closed the door.

Vina Delphi was a short woman with straight red hair cut off like a paint brush below her ears. Her eyebrows and lashes were almost white, lighter than the freckles that blanketed her face. She wore Gucci loafers and Ralph Lauren trousers and matching sweater. The loafers were Minnie Mouse wide, and the Laurens swagged off her shoulders and hips as if she were determined they were to look like bargain basement. She opened a door on one side of the vestibule and pushed the poodle through it. "Stay, Marco! Stay!" she ordered. "Be a good boy, lover. Mummy has to work now." She closed the door and led Serena toward the stairs and up them. "The people from Boltz are already here," she said. "When you get into the outfit, come back down. I'm going to use my solarium for background as long as I get good light in there. Then I'll switch to the fireplace in the living room. Suze can style you while I'm setting up." She led the way into a bedroom. "That's what you're to wear," she said, indicating an ermine-collared green velvet evening wrap spread out on the bed.

"I had a fitting on it," Serena said.

"Do your eyes darker, and slant them," Vina said. "Lots of liner. And put your hair up. They told me at the agency that you can do it yourself. Not too genteel. The look is Edwardian." She took a pair of spiked-heel emerald green satin pumps out of the folds of tissue paper in a box. "These are the shoes you're to wear. The jewelry is downstairs. Come down when you're ready. Take your time. There's the bathroom." She pointed toward a door and left.

Serena got out of her clothes and put on the shoes. In case they were stiff, she wanted to work the stiffness out of them before the sitting started. She had on georgette and lace teddies, a garter belt and stockings, and the shoes.

She was standing in front of the basin in the bathroom putting her hair in a loose bun on the crown of her head, careful to let little tendrils fall around her face and at the nape of her neck. She had already put on longer false eyelashes, shadowed her lids with silver, laced green eye shadow and drawn heavily penciled lines on top and bottom lids, filling them in where they met at the outside corners of her eyes and extending them upward in a slant. She hadn't closed the bathroom door. The bedroom and bath were her dressing suite. The bedroom door was closed, or so she thought. In fact, she wasn't thinking about doors. She was intent on what she was doing.

Something cold and wet and hard jammed into the back of her knee. She was too startled to realize immediately what had happened. She just felt the strange sensation on the back of her knee and automatically reached toward it. As she did, something hard and hairy tried to push between her legs and push them apart.

Serena screamed and tried to turn and lost her balance. The huge dog was behind her, his head between her knees. She landed on the john seat, kicking out at the dog and screaming.

The dog was snapping his bared teeth at her and coming at her. He was drooling, wet drops sliding off his red stretched mouth and falling on the floor. Every time Serena screamed she kicked. And she was hitting the dog—in his face, in his throat, in his chest. He growled and slobbered and kept trying to push his muzzle between her legs.

She caught him squarely in the nose with a spiked heel. He backed off, but not far. He gave his head a shake and then grabbed the heel of the shoe in his mouth and jerked it off Serena's foot and dropped it on the floor and went for the other shoe. Serena kept kicking and screaming. She was panic-stricken. Why couldn't they hear her? Why didn't somebody come? She couldn't get out of the bathroom and run. The dog was between her and the door. Her screams became earsplitting shrieks.

"Macro! Macro! Naughty boy! What's lover done now?"

Vina Delphi ran to the door and grabbed the dog by the collar and pulled him backward out of the bathroom. He was still slobbering and still snapping his bared teeth at Serena.

"You'd have thought the devil himself was after you, Serena, for God's sake," Vina said. "You scared me out of my growth. Look what she scared us to death over!" she called out over her shoulder to two women who had come running into the bedroom after her. "It's just Macro. He got out of the room where I'd put him. He wouldn't hurt a fly! Come on, boy! Come on! I guess I'll have to put you on your chain." She was pulling the dog through the bedroom and through the door to the hall. "Naughty Macro! You're too big to be so playful. Didn't Mummy tell you to stay? You're going to have to go on your chain now. Can't have you scaring silly girls."

Serena was still sitting on the john. She was totally unnerved. She put her arm on the edge of the basin and put her head down on it. She felt as limp as spaghetti.

"Are you all right, Serena?" Martha Kyle, the art director from Boltz, asked. "Are you sure you're all right? He didn't bite you, did he?" She was worried about the store's being sued.

Serena shook her head no, her face still down on her arm.

"Look at this shoe," Suze, the stylist, said. "Just look at this! It's a good thing this isn't Serena's ankle."

The satin that covered the heel of the shoe was slashed, small, jagged strips of the emerald satin hanging loose.

"Oh, God, don't say that aloud!" Martha Kyle said, snatching the shoe from Suze. "Call the store," she said to her. "Have them send another pair. We can't use this."

"It won't show under the wrap," Suze said. "The wrap has a train. It's supposed to sweep the floor a full six inches."

"Call the store! I don't want the poses restricted. I may want the skirt lifted. I may want the same pose Serena did in that Bill Blass taffeta for *Milady*." She thrust the shoe back into Suze's hands and turned back to Serena. "Will you be able to work, Serena? I'm up against a deadline on this ad. We put off the shooting until the last minute in order to book you. There were a number of other girls I could have gotten sooner, even Shari Holliday. If you're not going to be able to work now. . . . Do you want some brandy? What would you like? Do you want some water or coffee . . . ? Do you want to lie down and rest a few minutes? You shouldn't have let the dog scare you like that. You heard Vina say he wouldn't hurt you. Are you feeling better now? How do you feel now. . . ?"

Serena knew that Martha Kyle was putting it up to her whether the sitting would go on as scheduled. And Martha Kyle clearly wanted it to go on. She was also making it clear that Serena was the one who was going to be blamed if it didn't. Nothing, and no one, took precedence over a deadline sitting. You could be dying of pneumonia; never mind, just cover up the fever flush on your face with makeup, and stand up there and pose. Three months from then you might be dead and in your casket, but that photograph of you would be leaping off the pages of the latest fashion magazines in living color, right on schedule.

Vina came back into the bedroom. "Okay, Serena, he's chained up now," she said. "Poor baby will just have to stay chained up until you leave I guess. . . . It's his size," she said airily to Martha Kyle. "He's just playful, but some people let his size scare them. He wouldn't hurt a fly!"

Serena got through the sitting somehow. When she got home she called Models, Incorporated, and told the girl who took her phone call to start a list of Won't-Work-Fors for her and put Vina Delphi at the top of it.

Millie, the woman who was head of booking, came on the phone. "What happened, Serena?" she asked.

"I can't stand Vina Delphi's looks," Serena said. "Albino eyebrows turn me off."

"Seriously, Serena. If something happened—and something must have—tell me. Vina Delphi books a lot of models out of here. We have a responsibility for them. We don't want to send models out . . ."

Serena didn't believe for a moment that the agency didn't already know about it. Zoe had told her it was common gossip about Vina and her lascivious poodle.

"If you won't buy albino eyebrows, how about freckles?" she said facetiously. "Freckles give me spots before my eyes." She hung up the phone.

TWENTY-ONE

The party was in celebration of Marvena Mallini's first book of nude male studies—*Man, Male and Beautiful*. The ground floor of the Mallinis' town house on East Sixty-ninth Street had been converted into a disco for the occasion. The bouncer from Pompeii Nights stood outside the double garage doors. He wore the identifying black suit, black shirt and black tie that he wore when on duty at the Pompeii Nights disco on West Fifty-second Street. The invited guests had their invitations scrutinized by him before the doors were parted slightly to allow them entrance. Would-be crashers were turned away with the same finesse with which undesirables were turned away from the disco.

Atri Strombolis, the owner of Pompeii Nights, was inside the large double doors. Most of the people invited were known to him. Most of them were habitués of his disco. He had been in many of their homes. He was enjoying a season's popularity with the in crowd. His reputed connection with the crime lords—it was said that his disco was backed by Mafia money—added a spicy attraction. He was tall and blond, a Greek Adonis, but there was a lidded-eyed mysteriousness about him. Anything could be believed, and he did nothing to discount the stories that circulated about him.

Atri Strombolis was a great admirer of Mallini and a greater admirer of Marvena Mallini. He had closed his disco for the evening, which was Monday, and for the weekend before, because of his admiration for the two. His lighting engineers had worked all weekend and Monday to set up a system of disco lights in Mallini's ground-floor studios. His $60,000-a-year DJ was in charge of the music. A control booth had been built for him. The music was a continuous pounding of the disco sound. The lights were a continuous frenetic flashing, sometimes in patterns, sometimes spasmodic, of purple, silver and red.

The disco scene was in the studios behind the reception room. The reception room had been turned into a bar and lounge.

Atri Strombolis had the honor that evening of acting as receiving host. When the garage doors slid open the eighteen inches necessary to give guests enough space to slither through, the disco sound flooded out from beyond the reception room and reverberated off the walls. Strombolis would inform them that Mr. Mallini was receiving in the salon. Laughing, bodies swaying to the music from the DJ's booth, loud at first and then receding in their ears, they'd troop up the stairs or into the elevator.

It was quieter on the upper floors. The music on the salon floor was from a string ensemble in the supper room. The salon itself was a tribute from Mallini to Marvena. He had had murals painted on the four walls. One long one was an avenue of umbrella pines; the other long one was an avenue of cypress. They were in relief against ancient stone walls and the blue and white of the Italian sky with the hills of Rome in the distance.

On the wall at one end of the room there was a depiction of the Fountain of the Rivers in the Piazza Navona. On the wall at the other end the mural was of the Villa Florenzo, the *palazzo* outside Rome where Marvena had been born and which was still her home there.

The small conical bulbs in the three great crystal

chandeliers suspended from the ceiling gave off a
purplish shadowy light that was reminiscent of the
purple twilights and nights of Italy. Cut flowers were
in profusion everywhere, in standing urns and in vases
and silver bowls. For the evening the floor had been
covered with a flooring of grass-green tile patterned
with gravel walks and stone promenades.

Until the salon became too crowded to be seen in
its full effect, the guests stopped in admiration on the
threshold. "It could be the Borghese." "Or Tivoli. . . ."

The anteroom and the supper room were lighted as
usual and decorated only with cut flowers in lavish
abundance. Small linen-draped tables for four and six
had been set up in the supper room, and places set. A
long buffet with hot and cold dishes was along one
wall, a butler in attendance. Two waitresses in ankle-
length peasant dresses and crisply starched white ap-
rons stood by, ready to serve. Supper would be in-
formal, couples and small groups drifting in when they
felt hungry.

Uniformed waiters moved through all the upstairs
rooms with glasses of bubbling champagne on silver
trays. A bar for those who preferred hard liquor or
mineral water had been set up in the pantry.

All the rooms and corridors and halls and hidden
crevices and corners on all the floors of the town house
—except the salon, the anteroom and the supper room
—were a monument to Marvena's book. Enlarged
photographs of nude men—some life-size—were everywhere: on the walls, on the stairwells, on doors, in
obscure corners. There was one on the wall of the small
study on the second floor that had been wired for light.
It was the only illumination in the room.

"Intime," Mallini had said to Serena when she told
him she had received the invitation. "Wear anything."
She interpreted that to mean that there would be several hundred people there and that they would be

wearing anything from a $6,000 Galanos to Punk Chic.

Serena was wearing a black satin, bias-cut, skimpy gown that she had found at Nellie's Attic on upper Madison Avenue. She had paid $500 for it. It had probably cost $50 when it was new in the thirties. She had a body stocking under it, but she looked as negligently naked as the dress had been designed to make the wearer look—Lombard or Harlow probably. It had been culled from the wardrobe warehouse of a West Coast movie studio. Her shoes were pointed-toe pumps—black satin with tarnished silver filigree buckles on the vamp—also found at Nellie's Attic. She wore a waist-length single strand of crystal beads and a shorter strand around her head clasped in the center of her forehead. The clasp was a large round cluster of crystals set in silver. Her wrap for the evening was a silver fox cape, lent for the occasion by Bettleheim, Haute Couture Furs. Her hair fell in loose waves from beneath the band of crystals. Her makeup shaded from palest nude to palest pink.

Stephen gasped when he saw her. The lustrous wild hair, the translucent skin, the wetly gleaming pink mouth took his breath away.

Then his attitude changed to one of possessive anger. There was too much of that translucent skin showing, and what wasn't showing was even more provocative under the shimmering, clinging, revealing satin.

"I'm not going out with you in that getup!" he announced suddenly and angrily. "It's indecent!"

"Come out of the Middle Ages, Stephen, or go back to Cambridge," Serena said. "I'm going to the party."

"That dress is an open invitation to every man who looks at you!"

Serena picked up the silver fox and tossed it around her shoulders. "I think it will be better if you don't come with me," she said. "You'll get in a fight with any man who shakes my hand."

She started toward the door. Stephen reached it before she did. He took her arm possessively. "You're not going without me!"

There were only Beautiful People at the party, the Glittering Ones—the Glitterati. The appellation might have been born that night. It was used the next day in all the columns.

All the columnists and reporters gave a rundown of the guests: nonpareils from the *Social Register;* celebrities from the entertainment and sports world, from the creative fields—writers, playwrights, photographers, sculptors, underground poets, interior decorators, fashion designers, artists and songwriters—movie moguls and industrial tycoons; publishers; political ins and cosmetics manufacturers; committed Internationals and the Petted Poor in season at the moment.

The reporter for an afternoon daily opened her column by asking whether anyone else could have gathered so many of the right people together in the right place at one time. The columnist for one of the tabloids sprinkled her article more liberally than usual with "Don't you love it?" "Can you stand it?" "Is there any other way?"

. . . Mallini, affectionately known as Tonio to his intimates, greeted each and every one of his guests. Did he have time for anything else? The cheeks he bussed belonged to His Excellency former Ambassador Clarence Rengler and his beautiful Mimi in from Washington, D.C., along with Patty and Clement Richards and Mr. and Mrs. Jonathan Baily, Jr.; Sybil Singlehurst, swathed in a purple silk sari from India, though she was in from her aerie on Fifth Avenue; Nadine and Lionel Battinger, who live in a medieval castle outside Rheims on the proceeds from the champagne; and the newly titled Lord and Lady Conthrethmere, who used to be plain Jean and

Vinnie Cantwell. They came from London. Also from London, Viscountess Beverly de Nimes and billionaire Jamie Lavino, who picked up his wife, Nicole, and her daughter, Monique, in Paris and found room in his Lear Jet for Bibi Borchas and Patrice d'Astolle, who happened to be in Paris at the time. Gordon Knightsplit and Tanqui were there, though not together, dears. Helen and Tim O'Neil made a foursome with Lorna Medkai and Arthur Hamlisch, and wouldn't you like to? Sallie Calisher was there; oh, my, was she there! Alphonse and Collie Vega came from Brazil, as did Mrs. Claud Gleinsten, who happened to be in Brazil at the time. Serena Carr, the supermodel, was dream material on the arm of Boston socialite Stephen Neilly. Alfred Finn was there with his divine Khalie. Dr. Peter Nash was there without his divine Bettina. Mr. and Mrs. Pierre-Angel Manton-Rivera came from Greece. Rovena Countess Bigornia from Rome. Linda and Layton Hyatt flew in from Houston. Count Rega del Vostas del Delgado from Madrid. International playboy the Marquis Sebastian de Bragante tore himself away from his favorite playpen, the bullpen (as in toros), to attend. The marquis is affectionately known as Tanno to his intimates. He was black satin from toe to tie. Talk about dream material! Olé! Joseph Allen, our leading light among the literary, rumpled in. He was rumpled frown from toe to tie. The Tiny Terror. . . . Well, I have to stop somewhere. Could you care? Of course, you could. But you get the picture, *n'est-ce pas?*

Marvena didn't make her appearance until all the guests had arrived. Mallini went to fetch her and brought her to the salon. Her appearance was greeted by a thunderous outburst of applause, led by Sybil Singlehurst, who raised her hands above her head and started to clap. Everyone followed suit. Shouts of "Bravo!" echoed from around the room. Marvena was at first startled and then smiled widely. Mallini stood beside her like a knight beside his queen. His pride in her and in the work for which she was being applauded was evident in his face.

They made a striking picture. Mallini was dressed in tightly wrapped white Indian pants and a pale blue Nehru jacket. Marvena wore bright spring green lamé gathered at every seam. It was slit in front from her knees to the floor and had a small train. The gown fitted her like the inverted sheath of a lily.

Marvena's ripe figure and thick reddish blond hair were set off perfectly by the green lamé. Her wide green eyes were the colors of emeralds. She could as easily look like a peasant as an empress, and sometimes she did. When she smiled, her full mouth, her healthy, prominent teeth, her frank and open stare, her abandonment made one think of a worker of the field with black rich soil on his hands. There was nothing of the peasant about her tonight. She looked magnificently regal. She accepted the congratulations with an exuberant lack of reserve. If what anyone said was flattery, any ill intent or facetiousness was lost on her. She took every word as being as honest as her honest efforts to earn it.

It was impossible not to like Marvena, and Mallini was counting heavily on that. There was more to be got out of the party that evening than the satisfaction of having hosted the season's most important gala. Mallini was aware of the shock that Marvena's book had caused in some circles. Its enormous success would take care of that. What the public would never know was Marvena's triumph, wrested from fear itself, the long effort to gain mastery over a symbol, to subdue a child's terror at last. Mallini was aware that the talk was that he had done the photography in Marvena's book . . . or had had a big hand in it. He was hoping to squelch that kind of talk by putting Marvena on exhibit together with her work.

Mallini's affection for Marvena was limitless; his jealousy of her success, nonexistent. She was the one person in the world that he could absolutely count on. It had been so from the time of their marriage. She trusted him and admired him, as an artist and as a man. She considered his form—while in miniature—perfect. He had been her first nude subject. Their marriage was solidly grounded in mutual love and respect. There had never been sex between them.

Serena saw Helen and Tim O'Neil when they first arrived. It was hard not to see Tim in any crowd. He was well short of six feet, but he stood with his neck stretched and his chin lifted to give him a panoramic aerial view of the action. He seemed on a sharp lookout for somebody who might need his always-available attention. No doubt about it, Serena thought, he was all PR. She had never been drawn to his type. He was chubby and pink-cheeked. It didn't take much imagination to picture the butterball he'd been as a kid. He had the amber-eyed, reddish blond coloring of a child's teddy bear and the same bland, round-faced look—even his features looked round. He didn't look like Zoe's type any more than he looked like hers. It was absolutely impossible for Serena to picture Zoe and Tim as a couple. And the more she saw of Tim O'Neil, the less she could understand how Zoe could be taken in by him. *No one* could feel like smiling *all the time*. He wore "good disposition" the way other people wore their clothes. She could hear him now laughing good-naturedly when someone asked him which of the photographs he had posed for and whose head had been spliced onto his body. Tim didn't have to answer. Helen answered for him, her hoarse laughter rising as she punched out the crucial words in her sentences. "*Tim* couldn't have posed for *any* of them! *His* equipment makes these fellows look like *midgets!*"

Serena lost all interest in Tim O'Neil when she saw who had come in with him and Helen—Arthur Hamlisch, with a dazzler on his arm. The dazzler was Lorna Medkai, the author of a new best seller, *The Myth of Phallicism,* the book that advocated taking the sexual initiative from men and giving it to women. Lorna Medkai was a strong believer in women's rights, but in that direction only. She refused to align herself with the outspoken feminists. She didn't think that women were stronger than men physically or intellectually, but she thought they understood sex better than men and were better, more accomplished lovers . . . or could be, if they would take the initiative.

No wonder Arthur Hamlisch was impervious to the models who surrounded him, Serena thought. He had Lorna Medkai to fill his bed. In addition to her bedroom know-how, Lorna Medkai had looks. She was a dead ringer for Elizabeth Taylor with all the right things about Jackie O thrown in. . . . Could she have been mistaken in thinking Hamlisch had more than a professional interest in Zoe? Serena wondered. She had been so sure. . . .

Serena wandered around in the crush, avoiding elbows and heels, smiling and moving on when someone tried to detain her. She couldn't find Zoe or Stephen. Probably Zoe had dragged Stephen down to the disco. And just as probably Sallie Calisher had followed.

Sallie Calisher, famous for wearing the first topless bikini in Southampton, was in eyelet chiffon, seethrough, top and bottom. The dark shadow of her pubic hair showed with every step she took. Stephen had stiffened at the sight of her and turned his face away.

He wasn't quick enough. She had spotted him. She flew across the room, nipples hardening as they bounced, and enveloped him in a smothering hug, body pressed to his, exclaiming, "Stevie Neilly! Look who's making the scene! Stevie Neilly! When was the last time I saw you? . . . Don't tell me! I remember! It was that summer you deserted me in St.-Tropez and went to . . . where was it? Wherever it was, you broke your leg! Deserved it, too,-for deserting me!"

Serena deliberately trained an eyebrow-lifted smirk on Stephen, but he wouldn't meet her eyes. Good old Back-Bay-Boston-Double-Standard Stephen. He'd always denied that side of him, and now he'd been caught. The Sallie Calishers of the world were his sometime playmates.

"Do you know Serena Carr?" he asked Sallie, stiffly trying to disentangle himself from her octopus clutch.

"Don't you look heaven!" Sallie tossed off in Serena's direction by way of acknowledgment of the introduction, not taking her eyes from Stephen. "Come to my place for breakfast afterward, Stevie. You owe it to me! Admit you do! I have oysters iced and waiting! Just the way you like them. Slimy-raw and oozy!" She turned a sloe-eyed, insinuating look on Serena. "What this boy can do with an oyster is absolutely immoral!"

"Can it, Sallie." Stephen managed to unglue her arms from around his neck. "Go find another lamp-post."

"Does that mean you'll come?"

"It means go find another lamppost."

Sallie gave Stephen a reproachful look and then brightened as she looked at Serena. "You make him come, Serena. He owes it to me for old times' sake. I'll send him back. Promise. Hardly scratched!"

"There are a hundred and forty-four places in this house where you can be out of people's sight, and there's something dirty going on in every one of them!" Helen whispered dramatically to Tim, eyes flashing from side to side as if expecting to spot more dirty doings.

Tim put his hands on her shoulders and bent his face to hers. "If you're going to keep sticking your nose in places where you've got no business to stick it, you've got to expect to smell a stink sometimes instead of roses," he said. He gave her a peck on the nose. "I'll get you a drink," he said.

"I don't want a drink! I'm worried about Tanqui. She'll be coming later. I never should have let Mallini invite her. This is a hell of a first impression for her to get of America at play!"

"I wouldn't worry about Tanqui's first impressions," Tim said. "She gives off a few herself. What you need is a real drink." Helen had been drinking tonic water with a lemon twist. Tim had had three scotches.

"You mean you're ready for another one. You're going to get yourself as sloshed as Peter Nash."

"Come on, sweetie. I thought you were going to relax tonight."

"Peter's trying to get in Marvena's pants! He won't score there, and God knows where he'll try next. He may go after Tanqui when she gets here."

Tim glanced around to see whether Helen might have been overheard. He hugged her to him and held her there. "Come on now, sweetie," he whispered. "Relax. Peter's not that far gone."

"I didn't see what I just saw then!"

The first time Serena ran into Gordon that evening he was talking to a man she didn't know. Gordon was dressed out of character in starched jeans, ruffled evening shirt and Greek waterfront sandals. The man with him wore a white suit, yellow silk shirt and white tie. He meant for his 1920s clothes to be noticed, and they were. He was as tall as Gordon, but he was not as sleek. He stood in a slouch. It would have looked like an attitude on Gordon. On him it looked like a slouch.

"Serena-luv," Gordon said, "Peter Nash."

The name came as a jolt to Serena. Of all the people in the room this man was the last one she would have picked out as the eminent Dr. Nash. Peter Nash was a top-notch plastic surgeon. His clientele was strictly top-echelon, the rich and the famous. He'd done more than a few of the people at the party, male and female.

His handclasp was limp, and he seemed rather drunk. Serena wondered whether he had surgery scheduled for the next morning. His words were slurred. His black patent-leather hair had lost its careful comb. Even his pencil-thin mustache looked out of line. Nash was married to Bettina Clark, a beautiful woman, but cold, it was said. He played the field hot and heavy—with Bettina's blessing, it was also said. His charm escaped Serena. He looked as though he could use some of his plastic surgery himself. Some more, that was. He'd already had his face done twice. Friends kidded him about his do-it-yourself kit.

The moment Marvena appeared in the room, Peter Nash ambled over to her. He hovered close to her, eyes trained on her, giving her the total concentration of a drunk. When she and Mallini moved on to greet another group, he moved with them. Serena couldn't figure out what was going on. Was Peter Nash trying to get it on with Marvena? It was a generally accepted fact that Marvena was a lesbian. Peter Nash must be even drunker than he looked.

"I won't keep you away from the party long," Peter said to Marvena when they reached her studio, "but we'll have to take care of this now or it will be two months. . . ."

"I didn't want to make you be a doctor tonight when you came for a party," Marvena said in her huskily lilting, accented voice. "I shouldn't have mentioned Tommy's problem. You're too generous with yourself, Peter."

Peter smiled down at her. "Don't look so apologetic, Marvena." He was standing as straight as an arrow. There was nothing drunk about him. The slackness had left his features. Even his clothes didn't seem as wilted. He reached out and pushed the door. Marvena caught it before it closed fully.

"You'd put us in the dark," she said, and flicked on the lights. She went to the counter and put a negative in the viewing frame. "There," she said. "That's what has him so worried. You see . . . ?"

The negative showed the body of a male from shoulder line to crotch. Marvena indicated a bulbous roll of flesh that marred the sleek lines of the otherwise youthful abdomen. "He can't get rid of it. He's . . ."

Peter put his arm over Marvena's shoulder and leaned toward the negative.

"He's tried everything," Marvena said, "diet, exercise. . . ."

Peter's hand caressed Marvena's upper arm. She ducked out from under his arm and removed the negative from the frame. "The only thing left for him to try is surgery," Marvena said, "but he's worried about the scar." Peter reached for her, but she moved away and put the negative in a drawer. "He wants also to know whether the surgery will be a onetime thing. He thinks he can't bring himself to do it more than once . . . let himself be cut. . . ."

Marvena's tone of voice hadn't changed at all. She was ignoring Peter's overtures. And Peter didn't like it. "I don't do that kind of work, Marvena. You know that I send all my bodywork to be done in Japan."

Marvena stood up from the drawer, looked at him and smiled. "But I'm not asking you to do it, Peter. I'm asking your professional opinion about the possibilities of the success of the surgery and the—"

"My best opinions come to me in bed," Peter said.

"Ah, Peter. Always you must joke."

He closed in on her, turned her around and put his

arms around her. One hand went down and tried to push between her legs. The other went up to cover a breast. "Quit playing dumb with me, Marvena."

Marvena took both his hands and pulled them away from her. She stepped away from him, still holding his hands, and then dropped them and turned around to face him.

"We'll talk about Tommy some other time," she said. "I've been too long from the party."

Marvena turned to leave the room. Peter grabbed her arm. "Isn't Tommy worth bargaining for?" he asked. "He's one of your protégés, isn't he? I'll make a bargain with you. You give me half an hour in bed, and I'll give him half an hour in my office. I'll make the time for him."

"We'll talk about Tommy some other time," Marvena repeated.

Peter's eyes narrowed. There was anger in them and something of threat. "How long are you going to keep putting me off?"

Marvena smiled and shook her head. "Peter. . . ."

"How long have I been waiting? Six years? About that. How long do you think I'm going to keep on waiting?"

Marvena shook her head again, still smiling.

"One day you'll owe me one," Peter said. "When you do, you know my price."

The smile faded from Marvena's face. "You say crazy things, Peter."

Peter let go of Marvena's arm. He ran his hand over his hair, then patted it down. He adjusted his tie. "Just hope I haven't changed my mind when you get ready to bargain," he said.

"You're queer for touch!" Zoe spit out, pushing Tim away from her. "You haven't had your hands off Helen since you got here! What are you after, tactile sex?"

Tim's round face took on a puzzled, hurt look. "Don't give me trouble, Zodie," he said, as if pleading for kindness. "Helen is giving me enough. I can't hold her down tonight. She's on a real tear."

"She's always on a real tear, to hear you tell it!"

"Not so loud." Tim looked anxious, then smiled, an intimate, personal smile, just for Zoe. "We'll straighten this out later. I'm pretty sure I'll be able to see you later tonight. The mood Helen's in, she won't stay much longer. After I take her home, I'll come to your place instead of coming back here—" He broke off suddenly. His smile widened, became his world-embracing smile. "Perfect timing, Hamlisch!" he said heartily. "Take care of Zoe, would you? I have to get back to Helen with a drink."

"Has the bar upstairs run dry?" Hamlisch asked dryly. "I was wondering what brought you down here." He took Zoe's arm. "Let's dance," he said.

Zoe looked from one man to the other, mouth tight, eyes blazing. She jerked her arm away from Hamlisch, whirled around and stamped off back inside the disco.

One section of Marvena's book might have been pages from an artist's or sculptor's sketchbook. It contained details of a male figure—a forearm, a hand, the buttocks, the neck, an ankle, full arm, full leg, the torso—all the various parts and combinations of parts, from all angles—and then the final full figure. The man who had posed for the photographs was Manolo Bestima.

Manolo arrived in an impeccable black velvet suit by Hardy Amies. He was a perfect portrayal of the Regency look in the high-buttoned, wide-lapelled jacket flared at the longish bottom. The thin-line trousers were also slightly flared at the bottom. His shirtfront and cuffs were ruffled. His patent-leather dancing pumps were bowed with grosgrain ribbon. His face was framed in a thick mass of black curls, but

there was nothing handsome about his face. His shaggy
black eyebrows almost met in the middle. His strong
nose was broken; his teeth were crowded and crooked
in his mouth. He had the face and body of a roust-
about and the manner of a dilettante. He was an expensive pleasure for the women who could afford him.

Manolo didn't arrive at the party with one of his
patronesses. He brought a date of his own choice—
Tanqui.

Tanqui was the black model who had created a
sensation in Paris two years before. She had started
her career as a mannequin for Naguyu, the Japanese
designer whose emergence on the fashion scene had
been as startling as hers. Every house of haute couture
in Europe had tried to lure her away from him, but
she had refused all offers until Helen O'Neil had convinced her to opt for photography and abandon the
runway.

Tanqui was six feet tall and made taller by her
hair, which she skinned up to the top of her head in
a thick slick bun or let spring from a band in electric
confusion. She was as sleek as a cheetah. Her long legs
seemed to extend forever. Her features were small;
her forehead was high and sloping. Her eyes had an
Oriental slant. Her small, full mouth was disdainful,
painted a deep magenta. Her cat-long nails were lacquered with magenta. Her eyes were shadowed with
kohl and bone dust. Her skin was a deep velvet brown,
difficult to photograph in color, almost impossible in
black and white, but any photographer extant would
have been willing to put his favorite camera up for
ransom for the chance to try.

She had chosen Punk Chic for the party. Naguyu
had designed an outfit for her and air-expressed it to
her. A gold safety pin was in one pierced ear, an old-
fashioned hairpin in the other. She wore a hip-length
white angora sweater. There was a large hole that
exposed her right shoulder and extended down her

front almost to the nipple of her breast. There the hole was secured with a padlock. The left elbow was patched with chamois. The sweater was belted in at the waist with a nailhead-studded black leather belt. A motorcycle helmet hung from it, center front. She wore an ankle-length black crepe skirt, gored, out at the seams in places, finished off at the hemline with shiny black feathers, some of them molted. She was barefoot. Both ankles were encased in tiers of elephant-hair bracelets, some so wide they fell down over her insteps. Her hair was in an elevated bun spiked with eight-inch copper stickpins.

Manolo and Tanqui spent most of the evening on the dance floor in the disco after an obligatory round of introductions upstairs. Mallini had asked Manolo not to arrive before twelve o'clock. He was the star of the book and deserved his share of the limelight. Mallini hadn't wanted Marvena to share the limelight until the party was well on its way.

A heavy breath on Serena's shoulder sent a shiver down her back. She knew it was Gordon Knightsplit before he spoke or she looked around.

"Send Stephen off with Sallie when you're ready to leave," he said. "Why spoil the best hours of the night with an amateur? Come home with me."

He wasn't smiling, and Serena wasn't smiling when she answered him.

"You never quit trying, do you?" she said. She didn't try to keep scorn out of her voice. "That ego of yours really sucks!"

Gordon's face, his whole body, froze. His eyes became as steely and as deadly as knives. He turned on his heel and walked away from her.

"I'm not suggesting that you do an exposé, Ms. Singlehurst," Hiram Barnstaple said. "I'm interested in a serious, in-depth treatment. You have to agree with me that you owe it to American fashion to leave a memorial."

"Every issue of *Milady* for the past thirty-three years is a memorial to me," Sybil Singlehurst answered.

Sybil was holding court in the small study lit by the framed nude. She always held court. She never circulated. Everyone came to her.

Hiram Barnstaple was an editor turned publisher. A few years before he had left one of the major publishing houses to form his own house. His dream had been to publish only works of literary value. He had quarreled with his partner, who wanted to get out of the red by publishing commercial blockbusters. They had not been able to come to terms, and Hiram had had to separate himself from his dream. He was attached to another major house now, but publishing under his own imprint. He had published Marvena's book of nudes. He was trying to persuade Sybil to write the story of her climb to the top in the field of fashion, which would also be the story of the rise of American fashion to a place of eminence.

"The book will be written," Hiram said. "There's talk of it going around. I'm surprised you haven't been approached by somebody wanting to do your official biography."

"I've been approached by several writers."

He smiled. "Your tone of voice tells me you turned them all down. You were probably right to do so. . . . What I have in mind is your life story written by you. Your own voice, your terminology, your speech idioms would have a strong impact, would give the book immediacy. You could write in whatever form you'd be most comfortable with—memoirs, a diary, a chronological narrative. The point of emphasis, however, must be you, your life. People want to read about a human being, someone they can hope to emulate, perhaps identify with, even envy. They want to know about a person's beginnings, his hopes, his ambitions, the stumbling blocks that threatened the final success. When you get to your professional years, you will be telling the story of fashion and fashion publication, but the emphasis must always be on you, the human being at the center."

"I am not a writer, Mr. Barnstaple."

She had put up a barrier. Hiram Barnstaple sensed it. Something he had said had hit a wrong chord. She hadn't been receptive from the first, and she was less so now. At what point had he lost her? *A person's beginnings. . . . The stumbling blocks that threatened. . . .* Was there something in Sybil Singlehurst's life that she didn't want known? He could almost begin to believe there was. But the woman was the most successful person in her field. She held a unique position, was a legend. That was undeniable fact. Nothing from her past could destroy that.

"Would you collaborate with somebody, Ms. Singlehurst? I don't mean an anonymous ghostwriter. I mean a recognized literary figure, someone of the caliber of Joseph Allen, say, or . . ."

"Joseph Allen . . . ?"

"He's here tonight. Let me introduce you to him."

"I know Mr. Allen."

"If you know his work, you know that while he's primarily a fiction writer, he's a thoroughly capable reporter, a highly skilled portrayer of the American scene." He watched her closely when he continued. "As I said, people want to know everything about their heroes and heroines these days. They want to feel they know them personally when they finish reading the book. They want in on the secrets, the person's likes and dislikes, the mistakes he's made that make him human, the eccentricities that set him apart. Allen's very good at that. People come alive on his pages."

"Mr. Allen has a work in progress, I understand."

Was she beginning to come around? That was a temporizing statement.

"We could fit our schedule to his," he said. His intuition told him the discussion should stop on that note. "I shouldn't take up any more of your time tonight, Ms. Singlehurst. Let me call you tomorrow. I'd like to make an appointment to meet with you in my office. I want to talk to you about the financial terms I can offer, the ideas I have for promoting the book. I'd like you to have a full picture of what I have in mind while you're making your decision."

"Perhaps I've already made my decision, Mr. Barnstaple."

"I hope not. I'm afraid I would be disappointed. I hope you will hold off making a decision until we've talked further. May I call you tomorrow?"

She shook her head as if she were going to say no. But then she shrugged. "If you wish," she said.

"Do you like the party? How do you think it's coming off?" Mallini asked Gordon. He wasn't really asking a question. His face was eager but shining with pleasure. He expected praise and congratulations on his party for Marvena.

"Sweet . . ." Gordon said. "It's a sweet little gathering." He looked down at Mallini's chest. "You look sweet in your little Nehru jacket." His voice was condescending, his face a supercilious sneer.

The beaming pride and happiness left Mallini's face. He shrank into himself, surprised and hurt by Gordon's attitude. "What's the matter, Gordon?"

"Disco dippos in the basement, people popping in the pantry, sniffing in the dressing rooms, jerking off in the bathrooms. . . ."

"Who made you mad?"

"If it was a circus you had in mind. . . ."

Mallini's lips quivered, but he got control of them. His eyes were bright with tears, but he blinked them away. "Don't try to ruin Marvena's—"

"Marvena's marvelous."

"Don't you ruin Marvena's party!" Mallini couldn't stand up to Gordon on his own account, but he could for Marvena.

Gordon's eyes lost the vague, bored look that had come into them with his description of the party. They became hard and angry. "The next time you have somebody you want me to give up an evening to meet . . ."

Mallini went cold. It was that bitch Serena Carr again. He wished he'd never seen her. He wished he'd never brought her within a thousand miles of Gordon. She'd caused him nothing but trouble. He couldn't count the number of times he'd had to put up with Gordon's bad temper because of her. Why couldn't she come down off her high horse just once? She guarded that cunt of hers as if it were Tutankhamen's treasure. . . . And what had got into Gordon to keep after somebody he couldn't get? My God, he'd scored every other time. So what if he didn't for once? He'd introduced him to half a dozen girls since he'd introduced him to Serena Carr. Why wouldn't he go after one of them?

"That bitch isn't worth your time, Gordon," he said. "But if you want to set her back on her heels a little, we will. If she wants to give trouble, we'll give *her* trouble. I'll kill all my bookings with her. I'll—"

Gordon gave him a push. It was more like a disdainful flick of his finger against Mallini's chest. "You'll keep out of this," he said. His tone of voice was more withering than the disdainful flick.

Mallini couldn't stand being physically pushed and shoved. A finger on him not in friendship or love, and he felt pushed and shoved. "You keep me in the middle of it! You get mad at her, and you take it out on me!"

"Bear up, sonny," Gordon sneered. "Bear up."

"She means more to you than I do!" Mallini could have bitten his tongue off for saying that, but it was out before he realized it was coming out. Gordon wouldn't take that kind of nagging, and Mallini knew it. It put Gordon off as nothing else would.

Gordon reacted as Mallini had known he would. He withdrew. He spoke to the air above Mallini's head. "I don't think I'll stick around for the little boy's contentious female bit," he said.

"Gordon, I didn't mean that. It just popped out. I'm nervous tonight. I . . ."

Gordon laughed. The laugh was ugly, a worse slap in the face than the shove had been.

"Laugh!" Mallini screeched. "You're not the only one laughing! You can bet *she's* laughing at you behind your back!"

Gordon gave Mallini a withering look and turned on his heel.

"You'll be sorry!" Mallini screeched, his voice shriller than before. "You'll be sorry!" he screamed again at Gordon's disappearing back.

The crowd began to thin out at three. At four o'clock the Mallinis and Sybil Singlehurst were sitting in the kitchen having eggs benedict and champagne.

"You were an angel, Sybil," Marvena said, "my really true angel to stay for all the party."

"I didn't show up just to give you a halfway endorsement," Sybil said. "I came to see all your demons laid to rest."

"We convinced them all, you think?"

"I don't think there's a doubter left in this bunch."

"It's funny, isn't it, how sometimes people would rather believe something not the truth—" Marvena broke off and put her hand over Mallini's. "You made it all come true," she said. She turned her head to Sybil. "I didn't want to have the party. I was afraid.

But Tonio believed always that it would work . . . would convince people my work really was *my* work. . . . And you think he was right?"

Sybil smiled and shook her head at Marvena. "What will it take to convince you?"

Marvena put her free hand over Sybil's. "I'm being greedy," she said. "When I have two such boosters, to ask for more is being greedy."

"You're not being greedy," Sybil said. "You want what it's your right to have . . . recognition for what you've done."

"As you have, and Tonio has," Marvena said.

"You have it now, too," Sybil said. "Hasn't she, Mallini? . . . Why are you so quiet, Mallini? Answer me. Marvena has recognition now, hasn't she? The thing now is not to lose the position she's gained. You and I could tell her about that. It's sometimes harder to keep it than it was to gain it."

"Not harder, just more nerve-racking," Mallini said. "We have more to lose than we had before we got where we are. It's a long fall from the top."

Marvena laughed, a delighted, full-hearted laugh. "We're not going to fall! Not one of us! Are we?"

She was surprised when neither laughed with her or agreed quickly with her. She looked from one to the other. Sybil looked thoughtful. Mallini smiled at her but said nothing. Marvena saw the hurt sadness behind his smile. It was because of Gordon, she knew. Something had happened between him and Gordon. Her fingers tightened on his hand. It was the only sympathy she could show . . . that she understood.

"Hiram Barnstaple wants me to do a book," Sybil said after a moment, "memoirs, or an autobiography . . . perhaps have somebody do an official biography. . . ."

"But that's marvelous!" Marvena said. "And you should! Don't you think she should, Tonio?"

"By all means! Of course!" Mallini tried to show enthusiasm.

"I don't know . . ." Sybil said. She was still thoughtful, deep in some private wonderings and speculations. "I don't know. . . ."

PART 3

TWENTY-TWO

Serena's father was uncomfortable in Serena's apartment and uncomfortable with Serena. He refused the drink she offered him and then changed his mind and said he'd have it. He sat on the sofa and changed to a chair and then went back to the sofa.

"It's more than a year, Serena," he said. "You've had the year you wanted. . . ."

"I'm not ready to come home for a visit, Daddy." Serena was more impatient than uncomfortable. She was as impatient with having been put back into a childhood role as anything else. She stumbled over the use of the childish term "Daddy."

"I'm not asking you to come now. If you would come for Christmas . . ." Wells said. "I don't think you realize how much that would mean to your mother and me, and to the rest of the family . . . your grandmothers. . . ."

"I'm sorry, Daddy. I'm just not ready."

Wells didn't know how far he ought to go in telling Serena about the condition of things at home, how necessary a reconciliation between her and her mother was. Serena's success was a continuing, festering sore in Ellie. The success was so blatant. Covers on magazines, pictures of Serena inside, her face appearing suddenly and unexpectedly on the television screen. It was a success that Ellie couldn't get away from. He had hoped that in time, Ellie would become reconciled, even proud of Serena. But she hadn't. She'd had a reaction that in the beginning had surprised him but that since had become a constant and increasing worry. Ellie was letting herself go. His bright, sparkling, always-on-the-go Ellie, who had always been the best-dressed, best-groomed woman in their crowd, had to be prompted to have her hair and nails done, had to be urged to shop for herself, had to be coaxed to go to parties. And she was drinking. She didn't try to hide it. "I'm on my third. You'll have to hurry if you want to catch up with me." That could happen any time of the day. She was gaining weight. Or her weight was shifting. She was getting heavy in the trunk and skinny in the legs. She was getting the figure of a woman who had been on alcohol for years. She looked ten years older than she was.

Wells sighed. Serena also looked older than her age. Not ten years older, but she looked the twenty-five she had earlier claimed she felt. There was nothing of a twenty-one-year-old about her. He had failed both his women.

"I'm worried about your mother, Serena." Wells felt it was hitting below the belt to use that kind of pressure. Hitting Ellie below the belt. She'd consider it groveling, begging for sympathy, for pity. And she wouldn't want either.

Is she wandering again? Serena wanted to ask, but she didn't. "You're pretty hard up for something to worry about if you're worried about Mother," she said. "Worry *because* of her is one thing. Worry *about* her is something else."

Neither Wells nor Serena had forgotten the time he had slapped her because of a remark about Ellie. This time his response was not physical. "You've gotten hard, Serena," he said.

"You've had to be hard in your business from time to time, haven't you? You have to be hard if you're going to get to the top. You have to step on a few toes.

You have to pass a lot of people by. There's not room at the top for everybody."

"That's off the point. We're not talking about business. I'm trying to—"

"There's no use talking to me about coming home for a visit. I'm not going to."

"Why do you feel the need to work so hard, Serena? To work all the time? You haven't had a vacation that I know about since you started to work. You need a vacation."

"I'm strong for the work ethic."

The sound of a buzzer jarred into the silence that had fallen between Wells and Serena. Serena got up and went to answer it.

"It's a friend of mine, Zoe Bergson," she said when she came back. "She's coming up."

The woman who breezed into the room with a casual "Hi, Pops," dropped her large carpetbag purse on the floor with a thump and headed for the bar was like a brisk, chill sea wind to Wells. He stared, and knew that he was staring, and couldn't stop. In her narrow black wool dress and black lisle stockings and high-heeled T-strap shoes, she was unlike any woman he had ever seen. She was all thin bones and energy. With her tossed black curls and her breezy attitude, she was as invigorating as the crisp sea wind. She turned with a bottle of Perrier held up in her hand. "Everybody have everything they want?" she asked. The slanting sunlight caught her eyes. Wells had never seen truly violet eyes before. Zoe's were startling in their color. He had never seen light glint from eyes as it glinted from hers. He couldn't take his own from them.

He walked over to her and held out his glass. She poured Perrier on the dregs of his scotch and plumped a couple of ice cubes in the glass. "God, it's a day out there!" she said. Her face was bright with laughter, belying the annoyance in her voice. Wells felt up-lifted, buoyed by her vivacity. He felt a smile rising in him, laughter crowding back of it. He wanted to laugh with her. He was intensely aware of the long shanks of her legs, the push of her breasts against the black wool, the long, vulnerable line of her pale, bare throat. He felt stirrings in him that he hadn't felt since he had first had them for Ellie when he was sixteen.

Wells turned abruptly and went to the window as if to look out at the view. He was afraid his face would redden, afraid his eyes would give him away. What would Serena think if she knew what he was feeling? What would the woman think? . . . She wouldn't think anything. It wouldn't touch her in any way. Relax. *No sweat,* he told himself.

Zoe crossed over and sat down on the sofa where Wells had been sitting earlier. "I'm baby-sitting you," she said to his back. "Did Serena tell you?"

Wells turned from the window. Zoe was smiling mischievously. Serena was looking efficient, business-like.

"I have a late booking," Serena said. "One of my steady clients wants to shoot a picture under a street-light at Second Avenue and Sixty-seventh Street, if you can believe it. We've been trying to do it for three nights, but it's rained or misted every night. It's sup-posed to be clear tonight."

The explanation was a little too long and a little too glib. Still, Wells felt he should make a mild pro-test. "I don't mind having late dinner," he said. "What time do you think you'll be finished?"

"God only knows. Ten o'clock. Twelve o'clock. Two o'clock. We'll be out there until we get the picture be-cause this is the last night I'm giving them on it."

She was dismissing him. She wasn't going to spend any more time with him. She had said what she had to say, and she didn't want to hear any more of what he

had to say. She wasn't even leaving the door open to
have breakfast with him in the morning before he flew
to Paris. If she worked until two o'clock, she couldn't
be expected to get up in time for seven o'clock breakfast. He had failed in his mission, but he didn't feel
the cut, the hurt he would have felt if Zoe Bergson
hadn't been there. He wasn't sorry that Serena had a
booking—if she really had one. If she didn't, he wasn't
sorry that she had made up a lie.

"It's quite different from Serena's place," Wells said.
He stood in the middle of Zoe's living room, looking
around him at the zebra hides on the floor, the tribal
masks on the walls, the Masai spears point upright like
cattails in an umbrella stand, the heavy bleached wood
chairs and loveseat with slung-hide seats and backs,
the raw-wool throws over them. "It looks like you,"
he said. "Serena's place could be anybody's. I don't
mean that it's not well done," he added quickly.

Zoe laughed. "Serena doesn't give anything away,"
she said.

Wells looked puzzled.

"Her personality," Zoe said. "Her inside self. She
keeps herself for herself. There aren't more than two
people in this world who really know Serena, and maybe not even two, because I'm not sure Stephen does."

"But you're sure you do?"

"Not all the time. But sometimes. But it doesn't
matter. I know as much as I need to."

"Do you think it's healthy for Serena to keep herself bottled up the way she does?"

"Bottled up? I didn't say anything about bottled
up." Zoe laughed again. "That girl can let 'er rip
when it suits her to. I mean she doesn't need identifying tags on things like her apartment or her clothes or
her hair comb that say, 'This is Serena.' She's too sure
of herself to need that. Besides, she's not interested in
things like apartments and clothes."

"What *is* she interested in?"

"Serena. Making a success of Serena."

"She has, hasn't she?"

"She's a phenomenal success. No doubt about it."

"Why can't she accept that she is? What is it she still wants? I'm dense, I admit it. Explain it to me."

Zoe put her hand on his arm. "You're not dense," she said. "Far, far, far from dense." Their eyes met. Wells looked quickly away. "Coffee or a drink?" Zoe asked lightly.

"Have you brandy?"

"The best."

"It's nice of you to let me keep you up talking about Serena. If I weren't so worried about her, I wouldn't. . . ."

Zoe was at the bar pouring a Rémy Martin for him. She turned her head to him, smiling. "I wasn't a minute too soon getting to her place, was I? Both of you really had the squirms."

"The squirms . . . ?" Wells smiled. "That's a pretty good description of the state I was in. But I didn't have the impression that Serena was anything other than impatient to get rid of me."

Zoe paused for a moment before she spoke, and then she said, "I haven't been exactly leveling with you. A few minutes ago, when I said Serena was a phenomenal success, I meant as a model. She's a downright failure as a person. She's not bottled up. The reason she doesn't show much is that there isn't anything inside her to show. She has no feelings. She won't let herself come alive."

Zoe was angry with Serena for the hurt she had caused Wells. He didn't deserve it.

"I thought you liked Serena."

"She's the best friend I've got in the world. . . . Now that's enough about Serena." She came to his chair and sat on the floor at his feet. "Let's talk about Wells."

"I'm afraid there's not much about Wells that's interesting."

She looked up at him. "I think there is."

Wells felt his hands begin to shake. He tightened his fingers on the glass. He tried to take his eyes from hers, but he couldn't. She smiled at him. He thought he'd never seen a sadder, sweeter smile. His heart twisted inside him.

"You and Serena cooked up this evening, didn't you? She didn't have a booking."

Zoe's eyes stayed on his. She lifted her face toward his. Wells felt his conscious will leaving him. He leaned forward and kissed her softly on the mouth; then he put his glass down and stood up and pulled her to her feet. His arms went around her. "Zoe. . . ." His voice was a whisper. He kissed her cheek. His arms tightened. "Zoe. . . ." He kissed her mouth. Her mouth was soft under his, her lips parted, taking his kiss, returning it. Her arms were soft, but they were tight around him. She didn't have to tell him that she needed his tenderness as much as he needed hers. He knew that she had a hurt as deep inside her as the hurt he had in him.

Still, the old constraints, the habit of all his life with Ellie came back. "I shouldn't be doing this, Zoe."

"Because you're Serena's father?"

"No. I don't see you as Serena's friend now. I see you as someone I—"

"I don't see you as anyone but Wells."

"Zoe, I've. . . . This may sound old-fashioned, but I've never been unfaithful to my wife. I've never wanted anyone else. And then, this afternoon, almost as soon as I met you . . . I was afraid you could see it in my face. . . . I . . ."

She took his face between her hands. "You wouldn't have done anything about it. It wouldn't have come to this except for me. You didn't start this. I did."

Her eyes on his were so soft, so full of feeling for him. He wanted to lose himself in them.

"Zoe, I don't want—"

"You don't have to say that you don't want to hurt me. I know you don't. Don't worry about me. I'll be all right afterward. Will you?"

"I don't think I care whether I will be or not. Right now I don't care about afterward."

When Wells made love to Zoe, it was quickly over for both of them. Later, when Zoe made love to him, it was longer, more of lovemaking. When she took him in her mouth to make him big again, he wasn't surprised or shocked. It was done with such love, such giving. He had never kissed a woman below the waist before. He kissed all of Zoe's sweet, responsive body. He held her in his arms the night through, smiling at the tickle of her hair against his nose, feeling the soft gusts of her breath on his chest. He had never had the release that he had that night with Zoe.

Zoe slept with a peacefulness that she hadn't felt since she was seven. She had been telling the truth when she said to Wells that she would be all right afterward, but she had thought she was lying. She had been afraid that because he was Serena's father, making love to him would raise the demon of her own father. But it hadn't. Wells hadn't brought the demon back. He had exorcized it.

"Come with me to Paris, Zoe."

They were sitting at the breakfast table. Zoe had made bacon and eggs and toast and coffee. They had drunk some coffee. Neither had touched the food. Zoe's hands were on the table, reaching toward Wells. He gripped each of her hands in one of his.

"Come with me to Paris. Please."

Zoe shook her head. In the sunlight the tears in her eyes deepened the purple of their color. Wells knew that he would never forget those eyes or the love for him that was in them. He knew it wasn't romantic love. He knew that she was as chained to somebody as he was chained to Ellie. But the love that they had given to each other and accepted from each other since their first kiss was the purest exchange of feeling that he had ever experienced.

"Please, Zoe."

Zoe shook her head again. She smiled at him. Her tears spilled over and ran down her cheeks. He gripped her hands harder. He didn't think he could turn them loose. He didn't know how he could walk away from her.

The shrill, strident ring of the phone made Wells jump.

"That will be Serena," Zoe said. "I'd better answer it. You can let yourself out, can't you?" She pulled her hands from his and stood up. "Thank you, Wells," she said, and then repeated it. "Thank you."

"Hello," Wells heard her say as he walked to the door. "Not at his hotel . . . ? He's probably on his way to the airport. . . . Don't worry about it. If you'd acted any other way, he'd have known it wasn't the real Serena. . . . Yes, we did. We had a . . . a good evening . . ." Wells stood outside the open door. "He's a great guy. You ought to get to know him sometime. Look, I've got to buzz off. Early booking. Talk to you later." Wells heard the phone click back in its cradle. "This fucking world shits!" he heard. "But mark one up for this kid!" Zoe was crying, punching her words out between sobs. "She had a good evening! The best shitty evening of her whole shitty life!" The bathroom door slammed. Wells closed the front door of Zoe's apartment and walked over and pushed the elevator button.

The lump in his throat felt as if it were choking him. His face was stiff. He was having to hold back tears. But as the elevator went down, he felt himself smiling at the operator's uniformed back. He was smiling at the picture of Zoe slamming doors, shouting "shitty." His memories of Zoe would always bring him a mixture of smiles and tears, he knew.

When he walked out into the early sunshine and hailed a cab to take him to the Pierre to pick up his luggage, he felt that he was seeing things clearly for the first time in his life. He kept the image of Zoe's face before him. He was trying to print it forever in his mind. He wanted to be able to call it up every time he needed to see it.

TWENTY-THREE

Marvena's scheme had not worked. The weekend at Quogue was a dismal failure. Gordon had accepted the invitation, but only because he would not offend her. He had not spent any time at all alone with Mallini.

Mallini got out of the car with the camera bag that had been on the back seat and unlocked the door of the house for Marvena. Gordon got out and went to the trunk of the car and opened it.

"Will you stay for supper, Gordon?" Marvena asked from the door. "I can have Cook broil chicken."

"No, thanks, luv. Would like to, but I have an . . . engagement."

Marvena saw Mallini's hand on the doorknob tremble and then grip the knob until the knuckles were white.

"Perhaps then you could come up to the darkroom and help me," she said to Mallini, "after you've got the things out of the car. I'm not too sure of myself with outdoor exposures." She was wondering now whether she shouldn't stay down with him until Gordon left.

"I'll be up," he said.

"You won't be long?" She didn't want him to be alone after Gordon left.

"No, I won't be long. Mix the solution in the proportions I told you. I'll be up by the time you're ready to start with the film."

He sounded like an old man to Marvena, an old, tired man. There was none of his sparkle in him. She blamed herself for the weekend she had put him through. She took the camera bag from him. She wanted to put her hand over his, to comfort him, to make him relax. But that was probably the worst thing she could do. Better to pretend that she had not noticed his reaction to Gordon's announcement that he had a date.

"I'm not going to start with the film until you come up," she said. "I don't trust myself with it."

"I'll be up," Mallini repeated.

"Ta-ta, Gordon," Marvena called as she went inside. "Night, luv."

Gordon had the suitcases out of the car and on the sidewalk. Mallini went inside the reception room and pressed the button that opened the garage doors. Gordon made two trips bringing in the bags. While he was depositing the second load at the door of the elevator, Mallini closed the garage doors.

Gordon started back toward the large double doors, then, seeing they were closed, turned toward the foyer to go out by the front door.

"I want to talk to you, Gordon."

"Sorry, old man. No time."

"Take the time!"

Gordon turned to Mallini. His eyebrows were raised in condescending amusement, his mouth curved at one corner in a supercilious sneer. "I beg your pardon?"

"I said *take the time!*"

Gordon's sneer became a mocking smile. "You've just had forty-eight hours of my time. And you still want more? Greedy, greedy." He turned back toward the foyer.

"If you walk out that door, you're going to be sorry," Mallini said. He was beyond anger, and Gordon knew it because his voice had not risen. It was tight, but it was still low and husky. He was not losing his control to an ineffectual eruption of anger. When he began to lose control, his voice started going up.

Gordon had hesitated, but the hesitation was all inward. It didn't show in the movement of his body. He continued toward the front door.

"I have some pictures of you that would make very interesting viewing for certain people we know," Mallini said. "I might be able to place them for publication. Nothing as respectable as *Playboy* would handle them, but there are *Driven Flesh* and other magazines of that caliber. . . ."

Rage and shock and hurt ripped through Gordon. He whirled around. "You goddamn bitch!" He lunged toward Mallini, fists knotted, arms striking out. "You goddamn shit!"

Mallini darted into the studio, laughing goadingly, tauntingly. Gordon was right behind him, still swinging. Mallini pushed the self-locking door shut, ducked around Gordon and ran behind a wooden ladder-back chair. He backed away, still laughing, and came up against a prop table—a trestlelike board on end frames. He started to duck under it, but he stopped short of going under and darted out a hand and grabbed a stiletto from among the things on top of the table. He turned back to the advancing Gordon, brandishing the stiletto.

"Come on! Come close enough! Come on!" Mallini screamed. He laughed maniacally. "Come on! I dare you! Come on!" He changed his hold on the stiletto. He held it with the point of the blade between his thumb and forefinger, hand drawn back, poised for the throw.

Gordon grabbed the chair and flung it at Mallini. At the same instant Mallini threw the stiletto in a short, sharp arch.

Neither had heard Marvena pounding on the locked door of the studio. The pounding was loud now in the silence that followed the crashing of the chair to the floor and the crashing of Gordon's body upon it.

"Gordon!" Mallini screamed, his voice a shrill of terror.

Gordon had gone down with the chair. He was slumped over it, propped up by the ladder back. Blood streamed in a rushing gush from his face.

"Open the door!" Marvena shouted, pounding as hard as she could on the door. "Mallini! Open the door! Tonio!"

"Gordon!" Mallini wasn't screaming now. He was on his knees beside Gordon, too scared to scream, too panic-stricken to cry. "Gordon. . . ." Gordon's face was covered with blood. It ran off his face and onto the chair and dripped to the floor through the rungs of the ladder back. Mallini was sure he was bleeding to death, might already have lost enough blood to kill him. His eyes were closed under the blood that covered them. Mallini was choking with the fear that he was already dead. "Gordon. . . ."

He almost jumped back when Gordon spoke. He pulled back the hand he had reached toward him.

"Open the door, you fool," Gordon said. "Let Marvena in. You've blinded me."

"Gordon . . ." Mallini whimpered.

"Open the door, you idiot! I've got to have help! What are you trying to do, finish me?"

Mallini scrambled to his feet and ran toward the door, crying aloud the while, looking back at Gordon, trying to get the key out of his pocket. Half his lifetime seemed to pass before Marvena was finally in the room.

"Oh, my God, Mallini!" Marvena ran to Gordon. "What have you two done? Oh, my God!"

"We need an ambulance!" Mallini was grabbing at Marvena's arm, screeching. "We've got to have an ambulance! Get an ambulance, Marvena!"

"No! No ambulance!" Gordon said. He tried to lift himself. "No ambulance!"

"Be still, Gordon," Marvena said. She leaned down

and put her hand against his shoulder to hold him down. "Keep still," she said gently. "You'll make yourself bleed more."

Gordon sagged back down. "No ambulance . . ." he muttered thickly.

"I'll call Peter Nash," Marvena said. "You lie still while I call Peter."

"Call Nine-eleven!" Mallini shrieked. "Call the emergency number! Call Nine-eleven!"

"No!" Marvena caught his arm and shook him. "Gordon's right. We can't afford to bring outsiders in. Do you want pictures in the papers? Do you want reporters coming here, asking questions?" She was running to the phone. "Get control of yourself! I'm going to call Peter Nash."

"Hurry!" Mallini had quit shrieking. He was begging. "Hurry, Marvena! Make him get right over here. Tell him Gordon's hurt bad. Tell him. . . ." He sank to his knees on the floor beside Gordon.

"Get away from me," Gordon said. "Get away from me."

TWENTY-FOUR

"Is he blind?" Mallini kept asking, plucking at Peter Nash's arm. "Is he blind?"

"The cut is not in the eye," Peter Nash said. He was squatting beside Gordon's prone body, which he had turned face up and straightened out. His medicine case was open beside him on the floor. A used disposable hypodermic needle lay beside it. Bloodied swabs were also on the floor.

"He said he was blind!" Mallini grabbed Peter's arm with both hands. "He said he was blind!"

"Marvena, do something with Mallini," Peter Nash said. "Get him out of here. Give him a drink. Do something to calm him down."

"Come, Tonio," Marvena said. "Come away. Peter can't do what he has to do with you so close."

Mallini backed away a little, but he wouldn't leave. He clung to Marvena, shivering, unable to take his eyes away from Gordon's face.

Peter had swabbed away the blood and cleaned the cut. The cut was a jagged-edged, gaping hole that slashed downward from Gordon's cheekbone to his jawbone on the left side of his face. There was also a deep cut on his eyebrow. The wounds looked as if they had been made by separate lunges of a blade held in a twisting, gouging hand.

"Threw the knife. . . ." Peter Nash sounded as if he were talking to himself. "I'm damned if I can see how a thrown knife could have done this."

"Mallini did not throw the stiletto," Marvena said. "Gordon stumbled and fell on it. He told me that. Gordon told me that."

"Mallini said he threw it."

"Tonio doesn't know what he's saying. Don't pay attention to what he says. You see for yourself the shape he's in. The shock has made him crazy."

Peter looked up at Marvena. His look was deliberate and unbelieving.

"You're saying this was an accident?"

"Yes, of course! Of course, an accident!"

"If it wasn't an accident, it will have to be reported to the police."

"Believe me, my God, Peter! How can I convince you to believe me? I swear it! Is that enough? I swear it!"

Peter's deliberate look stayed a moment longer on Marvena. Then he lookd around the studio. The only evidence of the fight between Mallini and Gordon was the overturned chair and the disarray of the things on the prop table.

Mallini started to speak. "Gordon was—"

Marvena cut him off. "He was horsing around, joking! He stumbled against the chair! He fell on the prop table where the stiletto was!"

Peter Nash wasn't convinced and showed that he wasn't. He looked at Marvena and then at the prop table and at the stiletto, which was still lying on the floor where it had fallen—a space of several feet. His eyes went back to Marvena. He shook his head.

"Take my word for it, Peter! Let my word for it be enough!"

Peter was a long moment answering. Then, "All right," he said, "I'll let your word be enough . . . Marvena." He smiled when he said her name.

Marvena felt cold ghost fingers crawling up her spine. There was meaning in Peter Nash's smile and in the way he had said her name.

"Why doesn't he wake up?" Mallini had come out of his shivering stupor and was back beside Gordon. "Why doesn't he open his eyes?" He was wringing his hands in his anguish. "Why aren't you doing something for him? Why all this talking? Do something! Do something!"

Peter stood up. "Is there a phone in here?"

Marvena got between him and the phone. "Who are you going to call?"

"I'm going to call the hospital, Marvena. I've stopped the bleeding and given him something to keep him quiet so he won't open the cuts more by talking or moving, but he's got to have attention I can't give him here."

"Not a public hospital!"

Peter smiled sardonically. "I don't work in public hospitals, Marvena."

"Can't you do whatever you have to do in your office?"

"If it were a matter of closing a clean wound, I could. But this isn't. Those wounds require surgery. They're going to require surgery more than once unless you want Gordon scarred for life."

Mallini howled as if he had been struck a death-blow. He jammed his knotted fists against his mouth. Tears gushed from his eyes.

Marvena flashed a look of hate at Peter Nash. "There was no need for you to say that!" She went to Mallini and put her arm around his waist. She put her free hand over his knotted fists, still jammed against his mouth. "It will be all right," she said to him. "Peter will make it all right. He won't let Gordon be scarred."

"The phone, Marvena," Peter said.

Marvena pointed to it on the wall.

"I'm not going to report this to the police," Peter said, his eyes on Marvena, "on your word that it was an accident. I'm going to call the Eye, Ear and Throat to tell them to be ready for me when I get there with him. I'll need an operating room. And they'll have to get a room ready for him. He'll have to stay there. And I have to have an ambulance to get him there." He spoke as if patiently outlining things he wanted her to be clear about.

"No ambulance!" Marvena said. "I don't want an ambulance coming here! Can't you take him in your car?"

Peter thought about it. "I could, I guess," he said slowly. He smiled at Marvena again.

Marvena held Mallini tighter and tried not to feel the cold ghost fingers on her spine. "Don't tell them who he is!"

"Half the patients in Eye, Ear and Throat are there under assumed names," Peter said.

Mallini wanted to go with Gordon, but Marvena and Peter were adamant. He could not go. He would be recognized, and if he were, Gordon's identity would be guessed. Gordon was not as well known a figure as Mallini, his face not as familiar. Swathed as he was, he would not be recognized. Mallini's presence would be a dead giveaway.

Marvena opened the double garage doors, and Peter drove his Mercedes inside and got Gordon onto the back seat.

"I'll be in touch in the morning," he said to Marvena.

Mallini had taken a St. Christopher medal from around his neck and had crawled into the back seat of the Mercedes.

"What are you doing, Mallini?" Peter snapped out angrily, patience with Mallini gone. Getting Gordon into the car hadn't been easy, and his position in the car wasn't the best. Peter was anxious to get him to the hospital. "You're holding things up! Come out of there!"

"I want him to wear this!" Mallini was trying to put the medal around Gordon's neck.

"You'll start the bleeding again!" Peter took Mallini by his waist and pulled at him.

Mallini grabbed Gordon's hand in both of his, struggling to keep from being pulled out of the car. He put the medal in Gordon's hand and closed his fingers around it. He kissed Gordon's hand and laid it gently on his chest.

Peter jerked back hard on Mallini, bracing himself against the car with his foot, hauled him out of the car and gave him a shove toward Marvena. She held him while Peter backed the car out and drove away.

Mallini cried brokenly in Marvena's arms.

"It will be all right," she said gently, trying to soothe him. "It will be all right. Gordon is in the best hands. Peter will take care of him."

She walked over to the wall, to the button that closed the doors, walking Mallini with her. Before she closed the doors, she stared out into the dark street that Peter's car had just left. She was thinking about what Peter had said the night of the party and what she could expect him to say when he called the next morning.

"It will be all right," she said, speaking to herself as much as to Mallini. "It will be all right." She hugged Mallini to her.

"I didn't mean to hurt him." Mallini sobbed. "Why couldn't it have been me it happened to? I didn't mean to hurt him, Marvena."

"I know you didn't. I know you wouldn't hurt Gordon."

"If he's scarred, Marvena. . . ."

"He won't be. I'll make sure that Peter doesn't let him be. You won't be able to know later that it happened."

"He'll hate me, Marvena. When he wakes up and realizes what's happened, he'll hate me."

"No, he won't. He loves you. You know he loves you."

"If he turns on me, I'll kill myself. If he's scarred. . . ."

"Mallini"—Marvena held him by his shoulders in front of her—"Gordon is not going to be scarred. And he's not going to turn on you. Have you ever had a fight that he didn't make up? No. Stop making worries for yourself."

"I don't trust Peter Nash! He's jealous of Gordon! He's jealous of his looks! He's jealous because he's English! He's jealous because women like him! He's—"

Marvena gave Mallini a little shake. "How can you be so mistrustful of him? Peter could be in trouble himself over this. Didn't you hear him say it should be reported to the police? He's the one who has gone against the law. He's the one—"

"I don't care! I don't trust him!"

"Trust me then. I'll see that Peter does the best job on Gordon he's ever done on anybody."

"You don't like him either! You know you don't! You never have!"

"He's the best plastic surgeon we know, Tonio. It's not important whether we like him or not. We have to have the best for Gordon."

TWENTY-FIVE

"When am I going to see you?" Peter asked.

Marvena had picked up the phone in her studio, knowing that it was Peter Nash. He called every morning shortly after nine, when he knew that she would be in her studio, and he called several times a day after that.

"When Mallini sees Gordon," Marvena said. It was her stock answer.

"Gordon refuses to see Mallini. You know that. I can't do anything about that. I can't tell the man what to do. . . . He'll see you. He wants to see you."

"I'll see him when Mallini sees him."

"Marvena, that's not my concern. I've done my part in this thing." His voice was edged. "I've gone out of my way, and you know how much."

"I don't know the results yet."

"I guarantee the results." His voice was more edged than before, dangerously so. "But the fact is that no matter what the results might be, I've kept my part of the bargain. If you're not willing to keep yours . . ."

"Are you thinking of threatening me, Peter?"

"What could I threaten you with? I'm more liable in this thing than you are. You know that as well as I do. You knew what kind of crack you were asking me to put my tail in when you asked me not to report Gordon's *accident* to the police. I covered up for Mallini. If it hadn't been for me, Mallini would be sweating out a jail sentence right now."

"Gordon would never bring charges again Mallini."

"He wouldn't have to. The state would if the state knew there had been an assault." That was a lie, but he was pretty sure Marvena didn't know that it was. He had no feelings of conscience about lying to her. She deserved to be lied to. She wasn't keeping her part of the bargain. It might not have been said in words, but he and Marvena had made a bargain the night Mallini slashed Gordon's face, and she knew it as well as he did.

"Do you want to come for dinner tonight?" she asked.

"No. I don't want to see you there."

"Where then?"

"Do you know the Sumatsu Inn?"

"Yes."

"I'll meet you there."

"When?"

"Tonight. Nine o'clock."

The Sumatsu Inn was about eighteen miles north of the city on the New York State Thruway. It was a secluded place, in the hills, well off the thruway. It was a lovely place. Marvena and Mallini had been there with Gordon several times for dinner. It was, naturally, a favorite place of Gordon's, as nearly authentically Japanese as anything in the States, he had assured Marvena and Mallini. Marvena drove up to it, trying to imagine Peter Nash in the setting. She couldn't.

The encounter got off to a bad start.

"This is a perfect little spot," Peter said. "Might have been made to my order for my convenience. It's not half an hour out of town, but so far it's not been discovered by the mob. It's only been operating since spring."

"I've been here often," Marvena said. "It's one of

Gordon's favorite places. I believe he helped choose the location."

Peter grimaced with irritation. "I thought I'd left Gordon at the hospital," he said. He was disgruntled and had been ever since Marvena had refused to greet him as if they were lovers when she arrived. "We'll be in a private dining room. Maybe that will be new to you."

"Yes, that will be new," Marvena said.

The private dining rooms were bed-sitting rooms, small separate suites built a distance from the main building. The place had been set up to cater to executives who were too busy to get away for a weekend or overnight or too horny to wait. Everything was low-key; respectable. The main building housed a small office, a lounge and bar, a dining room. When Marvena and Mallini and Gordon came, it was for the quiet Japanese atmosphere and for the food. The food was the best Japanese food around, except that from Gordon's own kitchen. They ate in the dining room in the main building. Except for a few Japanese families, they were always the only ones there.

"You know the layout, though," Peter said dryly.

"Yes, I know the layout. We used to come out sometimes when they were building."

"I'm sorry I made this my choice," Peter said. "There's a place on the palisades—"

"This place will do as well as any," Marvena said.

The evening deteriorated from that poor beginning.

Peter wanted to be the masterful wooer, and maybe he was with some, but Marvena found everything he said duller than what he had said last. He even seemed to find himself dull.

"We don't have anything rushing us," Peter said. "We have all night. I haven't got anything scheduled until eleven o'clock in the morning."

"My day always starts at nine, Peter," Marvena said.

Peter wandered around the room, pointing out various things to Marvena, things that she knew more about than he did. He insisted that she come to the sliding door which he'd opened onto the private terrace, to see the little artificial waterfall which was lit from above by little, flickering lights, dimly, so that it seemed to reflect soft starlight. It was lovely, picturesque and utterly lovely. Under other circumstances Marvena would have appreciated the serenity and beauty of the scene and of the night.

Marvena decided to take the lead. If she didn't, it could well be morning before her part of the bargain was fulfilled and she was free to leave.

"I can't stay the night, Peter," she said. She didn't add, *So let's get started on why we're here and get it over,* but the words were in the air.

Peter gulped down the drink he had in his hand and poured himself another.

"And I'm not hungry for dinner, Peter. I had dinner with Mallini at home before I left."

"First Gordon . . ." Peter muttered. "Now Mallini. . . ." He bolted down half the fresh drink. "Where'd you tell Mallini you were going?"

"Mallini never questions what I do."

"You didn't tell him you were coming here to meet me?"

"Mallini never questions me."

Peter Nash's eyes narrowed on Marvena. "You're putting me off. You know that? You're really beginning to put me off."

"I don't mean to put you off, Peter, but I haven't all the time you might wish I had. I will not stay the night, and I don't want to leave Mallini alone any longer than—"

"Cash-and-carry," Peter said. He was getting drunk. His words were slurred. "You're making this pretty goddamn cash-and-carry. You know what you're beginning to sound like? A whore. That's what you're beginning to sound like."

"Perhaps you're right," Marvena said. "I don't know. There aren't any whores among my acquaintances. I don't know what one sounds like."

"You're trying to make me turn off. I know what you're doing, acting so high and mighty. You think I don't know what you're doing? You're trying to make me turn off."

Marvena stood quietly before him. "Maybe, Peter, you would rather be turned off."

"Oh, no, you don't! You don't get off with that!" He put his drink down. The glass hit the tabletop so hard that part of the drink sloshed out, wetting his hand. He paid no attention. "You don't get off. No shit like that! You don't get off!" He grabbed Marvena and pulled her to him. He kissed her on the mouth, his own mouth hard, his teeth grinding against her lips. His hands scrabbled up and down her back, searching for zippers or buttons or whatever held her clothes on. She was wearing a pants suit and a silk blouse buttoned down the front. He slid one hand up under the jacket and caught the waistband of the pants in his hand. He jerked at the band. He would have ripped the pants off if the seams had given.

Marvena reached behind her and took hold of his wrist. "Let go, Peter. I'll undress. You get yourself undressed. That will be better." She kept her tone light. She didn't show the anger or disgust she felt.

Peter let her go. He stood swaying on his feet in front of her. "Do it then," he said. "Get undressed."

Marvena took off her jacket and put it on the chair where her purse was. She sat down on the chair and took off her shoes. She stood up, turned her back and took off the pants, then the blouse. She wasn't hurrying, and she wasn't making a show of it. She was simply undressing. She stripped off her pantyhose. She was naked. She turned to face him.

"But you've not undressed," she said.

Peter swayed on his feet. "You undress me," he said.

"If you like." Marvena started toward him. She had decided that the only way to handle him was to humor him as she would humor somebody she knew was mad.

"Wait a minute!" Peter backed off. "Wait a minute! I want to look at you."

Marvena stopped. She stood still before him.

Peter's body no longer swayed. His eyes were focused. He looked first at her crotch, at the dark honey red mass of pubic hair. His eyes moved up to her heavy breasts with their dark purplish red nipples. He was still looking at them, his eyes moving from one to the other when he spoke. "Do you shave your armpits? Raise your arms. Let me see."

Marvena wasn't easily shocked, but that shocked her. She could only think that Peter Nash, being a doctor, had undue concerns about hygiene.

"Why do you ask me such a question? Why would I not? Of course, I—"

"Raise your arms! Let me see!"

Marvena's inclination to refuse was so strong that she wanted to turn away from him and walk out of there, naked as she was. But that wouldn't end what she'd gotten herself into, and she didn't want Peter in a worse humor than he already was. She raised her arms. The idea nauseated her, but she raised them. She held both arms straight up above her head.

Peter looked from one armpit to the other. He laughed softly, chuckled. He moved toward her and rubbed his fingers over her armpits. He put his nose between her breasts, breathing heavily. Marvena could feel his intakes of breath as far down as the rise of her abdomen. She could feel the outgusts on her pubic hair.

"Nice," Peter said. "I like that. Nice."

Marvena's armpits were smooth. There was no stubble of beginning hair growth. She didn't shave her underarms. She had them waxed.

Peter slid his hands upward along Marvena's arms, so that her arms and his were straight above them. He gripped her wrists. He held her by both wrists and leaned his head down and licked one of her armpits. His tongue wasn't soft and wet. It was wet, but it was tense and greedy. He moved his face to the other armpit.

"I'm your slave," he said. "I have to do anything you tell me to do. Tell me what you want me to do. Tell me where you want me to lick you."

Marvena didn't want him to lick her anywhere. She wanted to be done with it and get out of there.

"Let me take your clothes off, Peter," she said.

" 'At's right," Peter said, his words slurred. "Clo'es off. 'At's right. Got to get clo'es off." He seemed about to sink to his knees on the floor before her, he was so spaghettilike on his feet. "Clo'es off. Then you'll be the bull dyke, and I'll be the lady dyke."

Marvena heard what he said, but she pretended she didn't. Peter was babbling, as drunk as he needed to be to do what he wanted to do. Whatever that was.

She got his jacket off him. She unbuckled his belt and got it off . . . his pants, while he stumbled and lurched . . . his shirt . . . his jockey shorts. He was finally naked. His penis was at half-mast.

Peter didn't seem disappointed with it. He swayed his hips, looking down at it. He made jerking motions and moved closer to Marvena and took one of her hands and put it on his penis. "See that old fellow there," he said. His words were so slurred that it came out, "Shee 'at ol' feller 'air. 'At ol' feller. . . ." He frowned, concentrating, trying to remember what it was he had wanted to say. He couldn't. He flipped one hand limply in the air and gave up. He leaned drunkenly toward Marvena and wrapped both arms around her. He was too drunk to stand. He stumbled forward, pushing Marvena backward. She tried to push him away, but he held on, and they both went down. She was prone on the floor, and he was on top of her. She spread her legs and waited for him to enter her.

But Peter didn't do anything. He lay flat on her for a while, and then he rolled off her and pulled her over on him. When he spoke, he sounded cold sober. "Do it to me, Marvena. Do to me what you do."

"What, Peter?"

"What you and your dyke friends do to each other! Do it to me!"

Marvena pushed herself off of him and sat up. "Peter. . . ."

"Don't tell me you don't know what to do! Every dyke knows what to do! I've hired them by the hundreds. Suck on my breasts! Suck on them! Give yourself an orgasm sucking on them! Make me come! Hurt me! Bite me while you're sucking! Do it! Be a lesbian on me!"

Marvena stared at him in revulsion. She almost never lost her temper, but now she lost it completely. She pinched both his nipples between her thumbs and forefingers and twisted as hard as she could twist. He screamed. She straddled him for a better grip and pinched harder, twisting her fingers savagely as if she would tear off his flesh . . . and she was furious enough to want to. Peter screamed and writhed and ejaculated. She felt the hot spew of his ejaculation against her back. He jerked beneath her, bellowing.

Finally, he was quiet, and his body still.

Then he started to cry. He lay spread out beneath her, arms flung out and legs spread, face up toward the ceiling, crying aloud.

Marvena got off him and stood looking down at him. She wanted to kick him, but she felt pity for him, too. He was really sick, the sickest kind of masochist. He craved both mental and physical abuse.

She went to the bathroom, got in the shower and scrubbed herself over and over, trying to feel clean. When she came back into the bedroom, Peter was lying as if sleeping on the futon that had been laid out while she was in the bathroom. There was a second futon laid out beside the one he was on.

Marvena went to the chair where her clothes were and dressed herself. She walked over to where Peter was pretending to sleep. She stood over him, looking down at him.

"You can't come except with a lesbian, can you, Peter?" He didn't answer, but she saw his eyelids tighten. "Don't worry, Peter. Your secret is as safe with me as mine is with you. . . . For your information, I'm not a lesbian. . . . Poor Peter."

She turned and walked out.

TWENTY-SIX

"I'm sick with worry about him, Sybil," Marvena said.

"Do you want me to see if I can talk sense to Gordon?" Sybil Singlehurst asked.

"It wouldn't do any good. Gordon freezes up at the mention of Mallini's name. He acts as if you hadn't spoken when you mention Tonio."

"Which is perfect proof that he's hearing you!" Sybil said. "Have you told him what his refusing to see Mallini is doing to Mallini?"

"Every time I see him I tell him. But he doesn't seem to care. Nothing touches him if it has to do with Tonio. He won't let it. He's built up a wall against it."

"Then Mallini is simply going to have to snap out of it!"

"He can't. That's what I'm trying to get you to understand. He can't!"

"He *can't* do anything for himself, and Gordon *won't* do anything for him. It's a fine pickle he's got himself into!"

"Please, Sybil. Tonio needs your sympathy during this bad time."

"This *bad time*, as you phrase it, has gone on long enough! He hasn't come through with a decent photograph in weeks! What do you think I've been, to put up with it this long, if not sympathetic?"

Tears came into Marvena's eyes. "I'm more worried about Tonio than about his work," she said. "His work will come back when he's all right again. His spirit is sick now. How can he be expected to work when his spirit is sick?" She barely whispered the next. "I'm afraid, Sybil. I'm afraid he may hurt himself."

"What?"

"I'm afraid he may hurt himself."

"*Kill* himself?"

Marvena shuddered. "Don't say it, Sybil. I don't believe in saying aloud some things. It might bring them on."

"Nonsense! You have to face up to things. You can't turn your back on them. How can you do anything about them if you pretend they aren't there?"

"I'm not pretending. I'm trying to do something. I want to get him away from here for a while, away from where Gordon is, so he won't keep hoping that Gordon will let him come to see him. If he were away somewhere. . . ."

"Take a vacation! Go to Marbella . . . or Ischia. There's the whole globe for you to choose from. Nothing keeps him here in New York!"

"He won't go on a vacation. I've tried to persuade him. He won't go."

Sybil Singlehurst's eyes narrowed and then relaxed. "I think I'm beginning to understand what this conversation is all about."

Marvena's eyelids fluttered. She looked frightened, but she kept her eyes on Sybil's. She didn't answer her.

"Do you realize the risk you're asking me to take?" Sybil asked. "Mallini's in the worst slump I've ever known him to be, and you want me to set up a location trip to get him out of New York . . . and not for a day or two days, or even a week . . . something more like a month or six weeks." Her eyes narrowed again. "That *is* what you want, isn't it?"

"Yes," Marvena whispered.

Sybil pushed herself up out of her chair and away from her desk, walked clop!clop!clop!, stamping, to the window and stared down sixteen floors to the street as if she were staring daggers into everybody on it.

Marvena knew the expression on Sybil's face from the look of her straight, tense back.

"Mallini has always done his greatest work for you, Sybil," she said softly. "Think of all—"

Sybil Singlehurst flashed her head around so fast her body was slow following it. "Don't tell me I *owe* Mallini! I don't *owe* Mallini!"

"I didn't mean to suggest—"

"I *owe* myself! I owe it to myself not to make mistakes! I owe it to myself not to make decisions that are based on anything except good solid business sense! I owe it to myself not to be swayed by any considerations except those that are in the best interests of myself as a professional and in the best interests of *Milady*!" She glared down at Marvena as if accusing her of thinking she might do otherwise.

Marvena stood up. She glared back at Singlehurst. "The best photographs that have ever been in *Milady* were Antonio Mallini's photographs! All of them! All of the best! And he is *still* Mallini!"

"He has not been photographing like Mallini lately!"

"But he *will!* Under other circumstances, he *will!*"

"Sit down, Marvena. I haven't got the time or the inclination to cater to an Italian temperament."

Marvena sank down on the edge of the chair seat and dropped her face in her hands and started to cry. She was crying with relief. What Sybil Singlehurst had just said meant that she was going to work something out. All her arguments had been with herself, not with Marvena.

TWENTY-SEVEN

"You better be in there with all you've got today, kid," Rhoda Elliston, the receptionist at the offices of *Milady*, said to Karen Vogel when she arrived that morning.

Rhoda, envious by nature, her envy in ratio with the importance of the person, would have liked to take Sybil Singlehurst down a peg or two—as she would have expressed it. Since she didn't dare, she used Karen Vogel as a surrogate. She sat back in her chair and watched for the effect of "kid" on Karen and also to see whether Karen knew what she was talking about, hoping she didn't. She couldn't stand Karen and her pushy self-importance. "Singlehurst is in high gear," she added.

Karen made a point of looking distracted by other enormously important things on her mind. "I got here as early as I could," she said. "I had to check out some accessories on my way in this morning." She rushed by Rhoda's desk, glancing at her watch. "Shit! Twenty of nine already! I promised Ms. Singlehurst I'd be here by eight-thirty latest!"

Rhoda made a face at Karen's departing back and grinned with malice. "Promised Ms. Singlehurst," she mimicked to herself. That was a lie. If Karen Vogel had known Sybil Singlehurst was going to be in by eight-thirty, she'd have broken her ass getting there by eight-twenty.

Karen hurried down the long corridor of offices.

Sybil Singlehurst's was the last one at the end, a large corner office. By the time Sybil arrived at it every morning—or any other time—she knew what her editorial staff was up to because the doors along the way were not closed. If one was, she rapped sharply on it once and opened it. The only time she allowed a door to be closed was when she was behind it.

Karen had a large room across the corridor from Singlehurst's, a combination dressing room, fitting room and general catchall room for things to be photographed. Most of the space left over was taken up by files of things Singlehurst wanted near at hand. Karen had a small desk in one corner. . . . None of all that mattered, not to Karen. It was across the corridor from Sybil Singlehurst's office. That was what counted.

Karen's lower intestine knotted up with sharp, demanding cramps. Shit! She had to go to the bathroom! That shit, Rhoda! It was her fault, throwing it at her that Singlehurst was already there and on a tear! Karen had to run back down the corridor and around a corner to the ladies' room.

Two editors came in while she was sitting on the john. She recognized them from their voices—Carole Plymouth, the beauty editor, and Virginia Orcutt, who did "Little Things Mean a Lot," the shopping column. Karen pulled her feet back so they couldn't see them in the space under the door. She knew they'd look around to see if anyone was in there—as they did because it was a minute or two before they said anything other than the generalities they'd come in saying.

Then they got down to what they'd come in the ladies' room to be alone to talk about.

"Singlehurst is in her element today, isn't she?" Carole said.

Virginia laughed. It was a tense, forced laugh. "I'll say! Two feet off the ground!"

"If not ten. And a greyhound would have a hard time keeping up with her!"

They both were nervous. It showed in their voices. When Singlehurst took off to a higher planet, everyone else had better do her damnedest to keep up with her. The whole floor got hyper. Karen could feel her insides tensing up even more. If this kept up, she'd spend the day in the bathroom. This kind of tension gave her the runs.

"Singlehurst gets more out of twenty-four hours a day than anybody I know," Virginia Orcutt said. "Even when she's sleeping, she's not wasting time. She's *using it, sleeping!*"

"You're right there. Sleeping is something Sybil *does*. It's not a state she's in."

They stopped talking while they went into cubicles. When they came out, Karen couldn't hear what they were saying because of the noise of the flushed toilets and the running water in the basins as they washed their hands. She gritted her teeth trying to hear through the racket. Suddenly it was quiet.

". . . up, do you think?" Virginia Orcutt was asking.

"Damned if I know," Carole answered. "All I know is that she wants Lauder's newest line early . . . like yesterday! She's known all along that Lauder was perfecting something new and was coming in a little late. Now she wants it early! Bliss, over at Lauder's lab, almost had a heart attack when I called him a few minutes ago. He's had Lauder on his back for months, and now he's got Singlehurst, too!"

"I thought the new line was ready."

"It is, except for one rejuvenating cream he's retesting for the umpteenth time. He's not satisfied the tint won't marble. I told him so what if it does? Just advertise that as the closely guarded secret that makes it work!"

They both laughed, a little shrilly, at Carole's feeble attempt at a joke.

"Is he going to be able to get it over here?" Virginia asked. "That's the question."

"He's praying. If the batch he's testing now comes out all right, he'll be able to. I told him to send me the rest of the line, and that later, but he said Lauder won't let him break the line. If he can't get the stuff over soon enough to suit Singlehurst, he's going to blame the packaging people."

"He won't get by with that. The packaging's been on ice for a couple of months at least. I've had empties photographed for my column."

"Does Bliss know that?"

"I don't know whether he knows the packaging's been photographed, but he ought to know it's wrapped up. He knows what a ball buster Remington is to get in there first."

"Remington likes to spring surprises. He'd be the last to let Bliss know. I'd better get back to my office and call him and give him the bad news."

The two left. Karen waited until she heard the click of the door before she came out of the cubicle.

Sybil Singlehurst was standing at the far end of the corridor when Karen came hurrying breathlessly back into it. She was standing, fists on hips, obviously holding herself still by main force and obviously impatient with Karen for holding her up. The corridor seemed three miles long to Karen. She walked as fast as she could without running. At the same time she was trying to look unhurried and unruffled because of the people inside all the open doors she was passing. She didn't want to look like a scared ninny to them.

"Schedule me with these!" Singlehurst said, and thrust a sheet of her memorandum paper under Karen's nose. "This afternoon, tomorrow and Thursday!"

Karen quickly scanned the list—Adolfo, Geoffrey Beene, Halston, Calvin Klein, Mary McFadden, Yves Saint Laurent, Lagerfeld.

"Get Galanos on the phone!" Singlehurst ordered, and turned toward her office.

"It's only six o'clock in California," Karen said, hoping that would get her off the hook a little about being late.

"Get him at his house!" Singlehurst snapped. She changed her mind about going into her office and marched up the corridor. "Carole!" she called out. "Plymouth! How are you coming on the Lauder line?"

Carole Plymouth came to the door of her office. "I've just spoken to Bliss at the lab again," she said. "Between eleven and twelve o'clock, he thinks."

"Thinks! Thinks isn't good enough! Get him back on the phone, and tell him I said I have a concrete promise from Lauder that I'll have the line this morning. That's *before* twelve! What about Revlon and Quant? You have them, don't you?"

"Yes, I—"

"Karen!" Singlehurst called over her shoulder. "Get Davenport Studio on the phone! Serena Carr's booked there for *Milady* today! She's to come here instead as soon as she shows up there! Davenport will have to use another model. Holliday! Tell him to use Holliday if he can get her! If not, hold the booking for Carr when she's finished here! Orcutt! How are you doing on the leather stuff . . . that new designer . . . what's his name? Clutch bags and shoulder straps! I want both! And cinch belts! Nothing under four inches wide! And the Morrow jewelry! Don't forget the Morrow jewelry! . . . Vogel! Haven't you got Galanos yet? Greene! Leslie! I want designers' sketches in my office in ten minutes! Vogel will tell you which ones! Vogel! I'll be in Plymouth's office when you get Galanos! . . . All right, Carole, let's see what Revlon and Quant have to show us!" She disappeared from the corridor into Carole Plymouth's office.

TWENTY-EIGHT

"You've done all this!" Marvena flung her arms wide to indicate the designers' clothes, the shoes and purses, the scarves and flings and jewelry, the cosmetics, the trunks open and ready to be packed. "You've gone to all this trouble! And now you want to throw it all to the winds!" She stood spread-armed, face amazed and incredulous, staring at Sybil Singlehurst.

"Nothing is going to be thrown to the winds," Sybil said. "The important thing, for everyone concerned, and especially for Mallini, is that the *best* come out of this."

"He won't work with Serena Carr! He *can't!*"

"At the moment he can't seem to work at all," Sybil said dryly.

"He won't go if she is the model!"

"I'm taking only one model, and that model will be Serena Carr."

"Why? *Why?* There are hundreds of models! There are dozens of great models! You could have your choice of any one of—"

"The best model for the kind of work I want to come out of this is Serena Carr. I didn't choose her from a number of possible candidates for the job. I had her in mind from the inception of the idea. But let me set you straight about something. You're mistaken if you think there are dozens of great models. There are not. There are, at any given time, two or three . . . if we're lucky, four or five great models. You should know that from Mallini."

"Sybil, about—"

"We are not arguing the point, Marvena."

Marvena's arms dropped. Her shoulders sagged. She looked at Singlehurst with hurt, accusing eyes. "And I thought you were doing this to help Mallini."

"I'm doing it because it is a totally new and totally *good* fashion approach for *Milady*. The timing happens to coincide with a time when a trip away from New York will be good for Mallini. I will grant that it was our talk about Mallini that started me thinking in this direction."

"He won't go now," Marvena said in a small, defeated voice.

"He will. He won't even give me a strong argument. You'll see." Sybil laid a hand on Marvena's arm, a rare thing for her to do; she seldom touched people. "You're being overprotective of Mallini," she said. "You're failing to see the whole picture. Mallini can't spend the rest of his life running away from everything that reminds him of Gordon. He has to learn to live with all of it."

"But she—"

"Most of all, *she!*"

Mallini gave no argument at all. He had sunk into a deep apathy. He went through the motions of what he had to do and did what he did mechanically well, but he showed no spark of enthusiasm or any feelings of any kind.

It was Serena who balked. When she was first approached about the trip, her answer was a flat no. Mallini hadn't booked her since Gordon Knightsplit's accident. Even before that Mallini had been cool toward her—since his party for Marvena, Serena realized when she thought about it. And she knew why. He was mad at her because she wouldn't play beddy-body with his pal. Well, fuck him! If she didn't count any more as a model to him than that, he wasn't going to count as a photographer to her!

Serena knew how big an opportunity she was turning down when she said no. It hadn't been given out as general knowledge, but those involved had been let in on the secret of just how big the photographic assignment was. A whole issue of *Milady* was to be photographed on location in Tangier, Casablanca, Marrakesh and other cities in Morocco. It would be the first time the entire editorial section of the magazine—or any fashion magazine—had been done by one photographer, using only one model.

"Mallini doesn't want me on that job!" Serena said to Zoe. "You know who wants me on that job? Well, Singlehurst does, of course, I wouldn't have been asked if she didn't, but I'm not talking about her. I'm talking about Marvena Mallini. Do you know what she had the gall to do? She had the unmitigated gall to call me up and tell me that I owe it to Mallini to go! Shit with that stuff!"

"Listen to the prima donna," Zoe drawled.

"I'm not being a prima donna! Why should I get myself stuck off in Morocco for two whole months with a photographer I don't want to work for?"

Zoe shrugged. "What's the big deal? What's two months out of your life? Do the guy a favor. He helped put you on the top, didn't he?"

"Are you saying you agree with Marvena? Are you saying you think I owe—"

"I'm saying what's the big deal?"

Serena let all her breath out in one heavy, exasperated gust. "Oh, Christ, Zoe! Now I don't know what to do! I thought you'd stick up for me!"

"I am sticking up for you. You're about to let your stupid pride do you out of the biggest modeling job that's come along in a decade. That's what I meant when I said prima donna. You're thinking to yourself you'll *show* Mallini. You want to give him tit for tat. That's just plain stupid. So he's stepped on your pride. So what? Eat a little humble pie. It's not poison. It won't kill you."

"Your talking like that is going to make me feel like the biggest shit on two feet if I don't go."

"Then go."

The group that flew to Lisbon—the first stop en route to Tangier—included Marvena, Mallini, Sybil Singlehurst, Serena, Mallini's assistant, Carmine, and Singlehurst's stylist, Karen.

TWENTY-NINE

El Minzah was a lovely hotel near the Place de France
in the center of Tangier that was the New City. Behind its enclosing white stucco walls, the hotel and
its gardens were an island of tranquility in the midst
of the bustling, crowded, hurrying, never still and
never quiet sea of the city.

The building was Moorish in style with tiled floors
and ornately carved wooden ceilings. The huge windows, wide patios and arches gave an openness to the
lobby and the reception rooms that was accentuated
by the potted plants and bubbling fountains. The
plants and flowering shrubs and trees of the gardens
were tropical and lush—the red-leafed bougainvillaea,
the jacaranda with their constantly dropping mauve
flowers, the pungently perfumy yellow mimosa, the
persistently sweet night-blossoming jasmine—the Musk
of the Night as the Arabs called it.

There was a continuous clicking and rattling of the
fronds of the date palms. When the east wind—the
sharqi—blew, the sound became clacking and thunderous.

The mingled scents of the flowers of the garden
made the very air heavy. There was a vigor, an alive-
ness, almost a sense-altering quality in the combination of scents. It was very different from the always
distinctive, separate odors of the streets—the ever-
pervading smell of dust, of spices, of human bodies

and human breath, of smoke, of overripe fruit and produce and of clogged and stagnant seawater.

Mallini spent the first two days scouting Tangier for locations. Carmine was with him, lugging a couple of cameras so they could view the sites through the lens. Sybil Singlehurst, with Karen in tow, scouted the shops and markets for local designs and crafts that she might want to use. Marvena spent the two days with friends who had a villa on Djebel Kebir.

Serena had declared that she was going to have two days of vacation. She liked to "walk a city," she said. She didn't feel she knew it until she had walked it. That was how she was going to spend her two free days before the work began.

The second day, when Serena arrived back at El Minzah in late afternoon, she was surprised to see Sybil Singlehurst and Joseph Allen, the writer, sitting in the bar talking. When they saw her, they waved her over. She excused herself almost as soon as she sat down. She wanted a shower and then a long warm soak in the tub.

About seven o'clock Joseph Allen called Serena and asked her to have dinner with him.

"Love to," she said. "What time and where?"

"Have you been to Hammadi's?"

"I haven't been anywhere," she said, and laughed. "Inside anywhere, that is, except this hotel. I've done nothing but traipse the streets. What was the place you mentioned? How do you spell it?"

He told her.

"I don't think I've seen it in my wanderings. Where is it?"

"It's in the Old City, the Casbah."

"Oh, well! No wonder I didn't see it. You'd have to have a dozen pairs of eyes in your head to take in everything there in one walking."

"I'll pick you up at eight."

"Pick me up? You're not staying here?"

"I'm at the Rif. Place on the beach."

"What's dress for dinner in this oasis?"

"Anything, as long as you don't show your legs."

Serena hung up the phone with a strange sort of deepwater feeling, not quite sure what she'd gotten herself into. What kind of man was Joseph Allen? It was hard to tell at parties—which was the only place she had ever seen him until today—because he was always surrounded. In their one-to-one on the phone he had sounded brusque, impatient, certainly not companionable . . . not even in a good mood. He'd made it sound like a chore. Why had he bothered calling at all? she wondered. What the hell, she told herself, she'd at least see some of the nightlife of Tangier.

She had an hour, so she made a leisurely job of putting on her makeup and brushing out her hair. Strange about Joseph Allen. She could almost feel him in the room with her, watching what she was doing . . . and disapproving of all of it. She shrugged off the feeling. She didn't have to please Joseph Allen.

She spent some time deciding what to wear. She put on wide-legged black silk evening pajamas, then decided there was too much bare skin showing at the top and took them off and put on a long batik skirt and a peasant blouse. She put on low-heeled sandals.

"Nice," Joseph Allen said when he saw her. He frowned when he said it.

In Hammadi's they sat on a small banquette on a raised platform enclosed by a waist-high wooden railing next to the carpeted center of the floor that served as a stage for the dancing boy.

The band, a quintet made up of two violins, a banjo, a set of small ceramic drums and an oud, sat on a raised railed platform similar to the one in which Serena and Joseph sat except that it was canopied in brilliant red and white satin. The musicians were bare-armed and turbaned, swathed in white, seated on pillows. The music was native, low and mournful. "*Haouzia,*" Joseph said.

"What?"

"The music. From Haouz, the plain beyond Marrakesh."

The restaurant was elaborately decorated with intricately carved panels and hanging tapestries and rugs. The corners of the doorways and open entrances were triangled with fringed embroidered heavy silk and velvet. The floors were covered with Oriental carpets. It was as plush as the Drap d'Or in Paris, which had been furnished and decorated with the red velvet and gold lamé trappings of a condemned whorehouse. The waiters wore gold turbans, colorful handworked waistcoats and the traditional wide pantaloons gathered at waist and calf.

Dinner started with a clear soup filled with leafy greens. Next there was shishkebab of lamb. After that there was bstila, a pastry cooked with pigeon meat. Mint tea was served, but Joseph had it taken away and sent out for a bottle of wine. It was a local wine since the importation of wine into the country was illegal. It was a red—Cabernet—and it was excellent. Small, very sweet, very spicy cookies were served for dessert.

Serena was enchanted and repelled by the dancing boy. His appearance was heralded by a dramatic increase in the tempo of the music. He slithered in with all the sensuousness of a snake, and the music slowed. He was dressed in a woman's caftan. An embroidered shawl was draped over his head and around his shoulders. A heavy woolen dark red cloth decorated with tassels was wrapped around him at the hips. How he could slither in all that was a mystery to Serena, but slither he did. She watched, fascinated. The tempo picked up, became faster and faster, and the twirls and whirls of the dancer became faster and more sensuous.

He was a beautiful boy with black curls and smoldering black eyes. There was delight in his eyes, and there was also danger. They were both a challenge and an invitation. His mouth was small and full and red, pursed slightly, smiling always, taunting and seductive.

He did not look at Serena at all. He played to Joseph, openly and determinedly. Joseph ignored him. When the dance was over, the dancing boy gave Joseph a look of pure malice, tossed his head proudly in angry disdain and scorn and stalked from the room.

"Do they always do that?" Serena asked.

"Do what?"

"Pick one man in the room and dance for him?"

Joseph shrugged.

The evening began to wear on Serena before they were halfway through dinner. Joseph Allen wasn't an easy person to be alone with. He was a tense, brooding man with streaks of gray in his black hair and a young but lined face. He was tall, with the slim but hard-muscled build that she associated with polo players. His heavy eyebrows lowered over brown, sullen eyes. She knew that he was thirty-four.

Joseph Allen was jaded, Serena decided, and lonely. He was not married now, but he had been married and had two children. He had few, if any, close friends and a number of declared enemies. He had stated for publication that he had no peers and therefore no real communication and exchange. The controlling thing about him was his enormous conceit, Serena decided.

After dinner Joseph took Serena to the Tangerinn, a crowded, noisy bar in the Hotel Muniria. There was a continuous blaring of music and dancing that overflowed the dance floor. Joseph hunched his shoulders against the noise of the music and didn't want to dance. Serena wondered why they'd come there.

"If there's anybody in town you know, you'll see them here if you stick around long enough," Joseph said, looking around, glowering.

"Is that why you came?"

"Not anybody I want to see."

"And this isn't a place you want to be. Why did you come? Because you thought I would like to?"

"Who knows?"

Serena felt like asking him what the hell his problem was. Trying to talk to him was like trying to net a wasp. Once you got the damn thing, you were in more danger from it than you had been when it was loose.

"Why don't we find a place that's quiet?" she asked. "If you don't want to dance, it's silly to try to talk over all this noise."

Joseph shrugged and ordered another round of drinks. Before the waiter brought them, he stood up abruptly. "Let's walk on the *plage*," he said. He put some money down on the table to pay for the drinks and took Serena's arm.

Serena considered telling him to take her back to her hotel . . . but not for long. She didn't want to go back to her hotel. Conceited, inconsiderate ass though he was, she wanted to stay with him.

When they crossed the wide avenue to the beach and walked onto the sifted sand, she stopped and took off her sandals. Joseph laughed and swung her to him and kissed her. "You get better all the time," he said. "Models ain't my bag, as a rule."

"I'm Serena Carr. I'm not *a model*. Modeling is something I do." She looked at him. Their faces were very close. He was still holding her tightly with one arm. "That's not how you feel about yourself, is it?" she asked, more wondering than pleased that she had hit upon a truth. "You're a writer first and then Joseph Allen. Is that right?"

He looked embarrassed. "Something like that," he said.

Serena smiled at him. "You know what?" she said. "You're getting better yourself."

When they came to the railroad track that ran along the *plage*, Joseph picked Serena up in his arms and carried her across them. "Splinters," he said. He didn't put her down until they were beyond the tracks and the line of cabanas and beach bars and were on the beach near the water. Then he held her hand. He didn't say anything, but the pressure of his hand on hers was firm.

They hadn't gone far along the beach when Joseph turned back toward the avenue. They were at the Rif.

Serena had a thought that she didn't like. She stopped and put her hand on Joseph's arm to stop him.

"Did Sybil Singlehurst sic you on me?" she asked.

Joseph gave her an impatient flick of angry eyes, throwing off what she'd asked as if it didn't merit answering.

"I mean it!" Serena persisted. "Did Sybil hint around . . . or just lay it out to you—which would be more like her—that it would be nice if you took me out, got me relaxed, took me to bed . . . ? She knows I'm uptight about working with Mallini, and that's one of her little gambits, I'm told, when she thinks it will help the cause."

Joseph snorted. "You think I'm available for stud service?"

"That doesn't answer my question."

"I've got a question of my own. Are you going to want to get up and go back to your hotel? Because I warn you right now that I'm not going to get up and take you back."

Serena took her hand off his arm and tried to pull her other hand from his, but he held on, his grip so tightened it was painful.

"You're straight out, aren't you?" she said.

Joseph grinned. "Sex makes me sleepy," he said. He released her hand and put his arms around her. "Doesn't it make you sleepy? Or are you one of those frigid dames who make a big show of getting sent to the moon while they're gritting their teeth waiting for it to be over?"

Serena stiffened. "Straight out doesn't nearly say it!"

He laughed and kissed her. She wouldn't respond.

"You'd better loosen up that spine, honey," he said, "or I'm going to think I hit on the truth."

"Are you daring me?" She was furious.

"Nope." His eyes were soft on hers, his breath warm on her face. "I'm wanting you," he said.

THIRTY

Birds were chirping. A cat—it sounded like an army of cats—was crying its whanging, nasal, unceasing whine somewhere below the open window, begging morsels of food or lamenting a morsel stolen by a cat even hungrier than it was. The fresh, crisp, scent-laden, dewy morning breeze fluttered the sheer curtains and floated into the room. It had gentled to a wafting wisp by the time it reached Serena and Joseph on the bed.

Joseph leaned up on one elbow and looked down at Serena. "If you play your cards right," he teased, "I may let you be Mrs. Allen Number Two."

She kept her tone as light as his. "And then ex-Mrs. Allen Number Two? Are you sure you can afford it? I've heard your divorce settlement and alimony add up to a million."

"Will have by the time I'm dead, I guess."

"You don't care?"

"Why should I, as long as the well doesn't run dry?"

A fleeting unhappiness crossed his face. Serena knew what had caused it. She lifted her head from the pillow and kissed him. His head went back down with hers, prolonging the kiss. He slid his arms under and around her, pulled her next to him and then moved himself on top of her. He continued to kiss her, gently, his mouth soft on hers. Sweet, was the way Serena described his lovemaking to herself. Sweet and loving, tender, giving. Being made love to by him was like being wrapped in a cocoon of love. It was the last thing she had expected.

He liked his loving "straight," he had said. He wanted to see her, to be able to look at her. The lights had stayed on until daylight came. He wanted to touch her with his hands. When he kissed her, he kissed her on her eyes, her face, her mouth, her throat and shoulders, her breasts. His head went no lower than her breasts. When he touched her clitoris, it was with his penis, not his hands. Serena had an orgasm twice before he entered her the first time. He wanted the feel of her hands on his body, but not on his penis. He wanted her kisses, but no lower than his shoulders. There was nothing priggish about it. There was no revulsion in his attitude or in his voice when he talked about it. The connections that felt best to him were those of penis and vagina and those of mouth and mouth. Those he didn't tire of, and he didn't see any point in waiting around to get to them. He was the best lover Serena had ever had. The strength of orgasm that he brought her to with his gentle, tender lovemaking, that became violent only when he was mounting to orgasm, was beyond any she had ever felt. She was nothing but sensation. She was totally out of control. When she came back to herself, it was as if she had been temporarily out of her mind . . . and she had been.

They had been awake most of the night. They had slept at most two hours. They made love, or they talked. Joseph did most of the talking. He, who had been taciturn and silent all the while they were among other people, became open, approachable, even candid after they were alone.

"You're good for me, Serena."

"I am?"

"Um-hum. In my sixth sense I must have known it, because when I called you to ask you to have dinner with me, I didn't know why the hell I was doing it."

"That's how you came off on the phone."

"I'm lucky you accepted."

"After I hung up, I wondered why I had."

Their conversation would slow and idle and slip into lovemaking or become silence shared. They skipped haphazardly from subject to subject, neither surprised at anything the other brought up, answering almost as if having anticipated the question. Serena had never felt more comfortable with anybody, except Zoe . . . but the comfort with each other that she and Zoe shared was not the easeful, relaxed comfort that she felt with Joseph.

"I don't want to get up," Serena said. "I don't want to have to work today."

"I don't want you to leave me. Don't."

"Stop time for me, Joseph. See that sun trying to come up? Don't let it clear the rooftops."

Joseph turned her face toward his and away from the window. "Done," he said. He kissed her eyes to close them. "Let's not stay in Tangier," he whispered. "Let's leave. Right now. This morning. I've always wanted to go to Afghanistan, the Khyber Pass. Let's go there."

"Oh, God, I'd like to do that."

"Then let's do it. You don't have to stay here. Let's do it."

"I can't."

"Sure you can."

"I can't leave them in the lurch . . . Singlehurst and Mallini. I can't just walk away from my obligations."

Joseph moved away a little and lay flat on his back, staring up at the ceiling. "I've walked away from mine, looks like," he said. There was bitterness in his voice. Serena knew what had put it there—the same thing that had caused the unhappiness in his face earlier.

Joseph had been paid half of a $600,000 advance for a book that he couldn't get started on. He was suffering from the first writer's block that had afflicted him in his lifelong writing career. He wasn't handling it because he didn't know how to. He didn't know what caused it. All he knew was that he couldn't write. It had been a year and a half, and his publishers were more than just a little itchy. They weren't on his neck because they couldn't afford to be; they had too much money invested in him. Pressure might make things worse, and it was too big a chance for them to take. They couldn't push. And Joseph could not tolerate the fact that he was being easefully handled. His publishers were keeping their itchiness to themselves and leaving him alone. But he knew they were feeling itchy. And he knew why they were leaving him alone. The whole thing was a convoluted intertwining of vicious circles.

There were several things on Joseph's mind, each of which could have caused the block. The most important, to him, was that his children were doing most of their growing up away from him. The most important, to his accountant, was the large amount that was going out every year in alimony—and that large amount looked in danger of being upped. The most important, to his lawyers, was that there was a complaint filed against him in Connecticut by his ex-wife. A complaint claiming assault and brought for good reason—assault. She'd provoked him into a physical fight, and he had come within an inch of choking her to death before he realized what he was doing and got control of himself. The most important, to his agent—who acted as his press agent as well as his literary agent—was that the story might hit the newspapers. They'd have a heyday with it. "Push sales, wouldn't it?" Joseph had growled. "What's your beef?"

There were pluses going for Joseph, but they weren't helping. *Death on the Sands,* his first novel, had been bought for a mini series on television. One of the book clubs was readying a reissue of his first three novels to be sold in a casing as a set. *Hell Street,* his last book, had been made into a movie and was grossing millions at box offices all over the United States and from foreign releases. Joseph got a percentage of every ticket purchased. He wasn't in trouble for money, much as his accountant bitched and tried to convince him that he was.

"I'm an ass, Serena."

"Don't expect me to deny it. Your saying that you are proves it."

"Thanks."

"You sound like a double ass when you put yourself down. If there's one thing that's fake about you, that's it. It's all put-on and show and a play for sympathy. You're the most conceited braggart in the world, and you know it."

"Thanks again."

"Hell, that's okay, Joseph."

He reached for her hand.

They lay without speaking, holding hands tightly. The sun rose above the horizon and topped the roofs and shone in the window.

"Shit!" Serena said. "Hell! . . . Say some words for me, Joseph."

"Cunt, fuck," Joseph said lazily. "Bastardshithead-assholemotherfucker."

He sat up in the bed, picked Serena up and turned her so that she was against him, their bodies touching from their hips to their mouths. He kissed her deeply and then took his mouth from hers and buried his face in her hair. "Thank God for you, Serena," he whispered. "I thank God for you."

Serena clung to Joseph. A lump tightened in her throat. Tears stung her eyes. "I remember that," she said. "I heard that on a late, late movie on television."

He put her away from him. "Get dressed," he said. "Get out there, and get that goddamn job done so we can get the hell out of here. Afghanistan calls."

"It'll have to still be calling two months from now if it's going to be answered," Serena said.

Joseph looked appalled. "That long? How many goddamn pictures do they need for that goddamn shit wiper?"

THIRTY-ONE

The group was on the wide and graceful Avenue Menendez y Pelayo, on the block between Rue Sidi Bouarrakia and Rue San Francisco. The avenue was on an elevation. On the bay side, where they were to work, was the cemetery. There were no buildings to block the view downward. There were only the tall umbrella pines in the cemetery to frame the city scenes that extended from the point of the elongated triangle of the cemetery—the Grand Socco, the wall of the Old City, the Petit Socco, the Grand Mosque and, beyond, the bay.

The air was clear, visibility unlimited. As he shot down from the eminence of the avenue, Mallini's background, from any angle, was breathtaking: the green serenity of the cemetery; the muted dark colors of the low roofs of the buildings and stalls of the Grand Socco, the big market; the gray-white of the ancient wall; the crowded, stacked whitewashed stucco houses and shops behind it threaded with narrow dark trees and alleys; the shadowed Petit Socco, the little market; the sparkling blue and red and white and green tiles of the minaret of the Grand Mosque and the deep blue purple-shadowed water of the bay.

It was fairly quiet on the avenue. There was vehicular traffic in the street—automobiles, buses, drays and carts—and there were some few pedestrians on the sidewalks, but the jarring clamor of business—much of which was done out in the open on the streets—was far below. Avenue Menendez y Pelayo was removed from the mainstream.

The shots they were going to do would be ambience shots for the opening page of the editorial section of *Milady*. Serena would be wearing the fashions and accessories and jewelry that would be shown in detail on the following pages.

The layout called for a montage of pictures with various backgrounds depicting different aspects of Moroccan life: desert, oases, black tents in the desert; souks; the harsh black risings of the Atlas Mountains; caravans; djellaba-clad men and women hurrying about their business; country women of the Djebli tribe in their red-and-white striped robes and wide-brimmed straw hats on which they could carry a half dozen or more potted plants or a whole carcass of a slaughtered lamb; scenes in the Casbahs of Tangier and Casablanca; the rose-red walls and buildings of Marrakesh.

Mallini had scorned the concept, saying that he wasn't there to do a travelogue. Instead, he would do photographs of the different outfits against variations of one background.

Singlehurst didn't give him an argument. She wasn't altogether in favor of the change he insisted on making, but she was more interested in getting Mallini back in harness than in agreeing on backgrounds. Later she could pull whatever photographs she wanted from the mass of all that would be made all over Morocco to montage for the opening page. She might even prefer Mallini's concept after she saw what he did with it once they were back in New York.

Serena's first outfit was a Halston, a rust-colored Ultrasuede wrap dress, very simple in line. It was accessorized with shoes by Valentino—rust suede high-heeled pumps—jewelry by David Webb—a large gold pen set with diamonds and emeralds placed high on the shoulder. Her makeup was by Lauder—from the new line that had so nearly caused a flack.

Mallini and Carmine were at the camera. Single-hurst and Marvena were standing nearby. Serena and Karen were a little apart, at a wooden bench where the things Karen might need were laid out—brush and comb, makeup, a mirror, pins. Serena was ready.

Serena and Mallini had been cordial to each other throughout the flight over and during the times they had been together since. A stranger would not have known that there was any tension between them.

"I'm set," Mallini called out, turning his head in Serena's general direction.

"Coming," she answered.

He turned and watched her walk over to the camera.

"What I want is just that ease," he said. "Just that ease you were walking with. I don't want anything posed. I don't want anything static."

Serena's spine stiffened at the insult. *Posed! Static!* Was that what he was afraid he would get from her? She was never posed or static! She was completely at ease in front of the camera! He knew it! Better than anybody! He was being deliberately insulting!

"Let's see you, Serena," Sybil Singlehurst said.

Serena turned to face her.

"It's right. It's absolutely right," Sybil said. "The color is magnificent for you. Isn't it, Marvena?"

"And so beautiful against Mallini's background," Marvena said. "It's going to be a beautiful picture, a really—"

"Let's work," Mallini said, cutting off the conversation.

Serena turned back to the camera.

And she froze.

"Hold it!" Mallini said. He snapped the picture.

Serena couldn't believe Mallini had taken the picture. She hadn't been ready, and he knew it. She was nowhere near the mood she needed. "I wasn't ready, Mallini," she said.

"I don't want you *ready*," Mallini said. "I'm using a fast lens. Just move . . . turn. I'll catch what I want."

Serena's spine stiffened again. He had made "ready" sound as if it were the same as "posed" and "static." She felt like a piece of cardboard. Her face felt like a mask. But she began to work. She moved, and she turned. She gave Mallini pose after pose—profile, half profile, three-quarters, face and figure. She felt like a mechanical doll, but Mallini snapped everything she did. He continued shooting through several rolls of film, calling no stop. They were working in total silence.

All of a sudden Sybil Singlehurst strode up from behind Mallini, where she had been standing for the last half of the session, and placed herself squarely between Serena and the camera. She was furious. Her mouth was drawn into a dangerous line.

"We're not in Miami Beach photographing Carrie Foy's cruise line!" she barked at Mallini.

Mallini gave Singlehurst a blank look.

"Standing there, clicking that camera, doesn't make pictures!" Singlehurst said. "You haven't made a picture yet that I can use!"

"I'm the one in back of the camera, Sybil," Mallini said. "I know what I'm getting."

"You're not getting anything!" She snapped her head around toward Serena. "And you're not giving him anything! You two act like two people who've never met!"

Mallini moved indolently from behind the camera. "Do you want to take the pictures?" he asked Singlehurst.

"Don't get smart-ass with me, Mallini!"

"Sybil. . . ." Marvena tried to intervene.

"Don't interrupt, Marvena! I've got a job to get done here, and it's not getting done!" Sybil was not keeping her voice down. "These two may think they're fooling me with all this pretense of working, but they're not! I never saw two people more completely out of sync! I know what they're capable of doing! I know what they can give me if they try! And I'm not settling for less! Is that understood by both of you?" She flashed furious eyes from Serena to Mallini.

"I can't give you anything if you don't get out from in front of the camera," Mallini said. If Singlehurst's tirade had had any effect on him, he didn't show it.

"Perhaps if you and I left them, Sybil . . ." Marvena said.

Singlehurst ignored her. "I want to change the outfit, Karen!" she said. "Put Serena in the Chloe. It's chiffon. It will have some movement even if she doesn't!"

Serena and Karen went across the avenue to the apartment of an official of the airline that had flown them from New York, which they were using for changing. They had brought a number of outfits there from the hotel. When they came back, Serena was wearing a calf-length, full-skirted chiffon print. It was in muted pastels, and it was a very soft, very feminine dress. Serena felt more fluid and relaxed in it . . . or she tried to tell herself she did.

But she froze again the minute she was back in front of the camera. Mallini was just as frozen on his side of it. Or he was oblivious, unseeing and uncaring. He snapped away, anything Serena did, just as he had before.

Singlehurst watched. She was not quite as long this time as she had been the time before. After about fifteen minutes her patience gave out. "That's it!" she said. "That's enough! I've had all of this I want! This is nothing but a waste of time! Get the stuff together, Karen! We're going back to the hotel!" She strode angrily to the hired limousine, wrenched open the door before the chauffeur could get to it, flung herself inside and sat set-faced, staring out the opposite window.

Mallini, without a word or any sign of what he was feeling, turned and walked off in the direction away from El Minzah, leaving the cameras and other equipment for Carmine to handle.

"Mallini!" Marvena called, running to catch up with him.

He stopped, but he didn't look at her. He put his hand on her arm. "Let me be by myself for a while," he said. "I'll be all right. Let me be by myself." He squeezed her arm gently, then took his hand away and walked on.

Marvena stood desolate, staring at Mallini's back. It wasn't straight and proud and beautiful now. His head wasn't high. He looked small and forlorn. Tears sprang up in her eyes. Her heart hurt. What had she done to him now? Why did everything she tried to do for him turn out so badly?

And things were going to get worse. The knowledge was like a premonition. Every intuition in Marvena told her that things were going to get worse for Mallini.

Serena didn't go back to the hotel with the others either. She walked down to the walls of the Old City and climbed one of the ramparts and stood looking out at the water.

She couldn't sort her feelings. She didn't know whether she was angry with Singlehurst, irritated with Mallini, disappointed in herself or what. After a while she realized she wasn't feeling anything. She felt numb. She knew that by the time she arrived back at the hotel Singlehurst might have everything packed and ready to go back to New York, but she couldn't even seem to feel anything about that.

The street boys had spotted her. They moved in. They came singly and in pairs and groups, touting wares, touting services. Serena brushed them all aside, sometimes having to remove clinging fingers. She left the rampart and walked to the Rif.

Joseph wasn't there. She had missed him by not more than five minutes, the concierge told her.

THIRTY-TWO

"Christ, Sybil," Joseph said. "Is that what you got me over here for? So you could sit there and snort at me? Relax. So you had a bad morning. Tough tits. There'll be other mornings." He leaned toward her. "You didn't give my girl a hard time, did you?"

"Your girl . . . ? What are you talking about?"

"Serena didn't mention me to you?"

"No."

"Then forget I opened my yap."

"I never forget anything!"

"Give yourself a new experience . . . forgetting what I said." He leaned closer. "I'm serious. You queer me with Serena, and I'll write a book all right, but it won't be the book you have in mind." He tapped her hand with one finger, hard. "I mean that, Sybil-baby. Until Serena says something, I haven't opened my trap. And *don't* you forget that."

"So that's where you were last night. Out with Serena. I tried to call you."

"I was *out*. Period."

"I didn't know you even knew the girl, any more than to say hello to."

"I don't."

Sybil studied him for a long moment. "Then it shouldn't bother you," she said, "if I tell you that Serena could be in trouble."

"Any trouble you could give her isn't the kind that would bother me."

"Serena is very serious about her career, her professional life. Whether it bothered you or not, it could be climactic for her."

"Anyone doing a job ought to be serious about it," Joseph said. He leaned back in his chair, pretending a casualness he didn't feel.

"I've got four trunkfuls of top-secret fashions from eight designers," Sybil said. "I've got the top photographer in the business. And the top model in the business. And they're working like they're photographing the fall and winter Sears, Roebuck catalog at Meeker's ranch in Tucson! Have you any idea what that means?"

She stopped, but Joseph didn't say anything.

"I thought I'd see fireworks! I thought they'd show some guts! But they *died!* What burned me, Allen, what really burned me—"

Joseph wrinkled an eyebrow at her. "You mean what really pissed you off."

She ignored the interruption. "Was that they tried to fool me!"

"Sybil," Joseph said, "it would take the rarest kind of idiot to think he could fool you. And I don't think you associate with idiots, rare or common."

She ignored that also. "I've got to find some way to get them back together. They're the best model-photographer team I've ever worked with, and I've worked with them all."

Sybil's mood changed. She studied the empty air in front of her as if trying to evoke the physical evidence of the intangible she was talking about. "This is one of my precepts, Allen. Rapport between model and photographer is the basic, bedrock essential for the kinds of photographs that appear in the editorial pages of *Milady* and *Vogue* and *Harper's*. . . . I will tell you frankly that when I feel it will be beneficial, I'm not above phomoting an affair between a model and a photographer."

Joseph was taking a personal interest now in what she was saying.

"Serena Carr and Mallini have rapport," Sybil was going on. "It's still there. They've closed each other out. They've got to be brought up short, knocked out of themselves. . . ."

"Looks like you've got a problem," Joseph said.

"To the contrary." Sybil spoke slowly and clearly, meaning Joseph Allen to hear every word so he could repeat it to Serena. "I don't have a problem. I have an aggravation. Mallini and Serena have a problem. This could be the beginning of the end for both of them."

Strange little chills over Joseph's skin made him twitch in his chair. He was at sharp odds with himself. He wouldn't care if Serena's modeling career were suddenly ended. But he didn't want Serena hurt, didn't want her disappointed in herself. He knew what it felt like to run up against the tape and to find that it was a strong, taut, unbreakable, cold, wet rope instead of the light thread that was supposed to snap for the winner.

"Can't be all that bad, Sybil," he said. "I mean, this is the first time it's happened." He wasn't at all sure of what he was talking about. He had no familiarity with the traumas that could beset the fashion world.

"I've always been able to handle Mallini," Singlehurst said. "But Serena. . . . If this keeps up, if we go back to New York without this job done, Serena can kiss her editorial career good-bye."

Sybil drew herself up straight, from her bony buttocks to the top of her head, and faced Joseph squarely. "That's the way it is," she said.

Joseph's face had gone white. "You'd do that to her?" He stood up. "You're the goddamnedest bitch ever born!" He was speaking through clenched teeth. "Where is Serena? Where is she?"

Sybil breathed out the stiffness in her spine. "Probably at your hotel, looking for you," she said. Her voice was as relaxed as her body was now.

She watched Joseph ram his way between the tables toward the door. She was fully satisfied with her interview with him. If he could get Serena Carr feeling for him anything near what he felt for her, Serena Carr would soon be ablaze before the camera.

Now what was she going to do about Mallini?

THIRTY-THREE

Mallini didn't know why he was so taken with the boy. But he was, and had been since the boy had first approached him on the street in Tangier. Perhaps it was the shyness about him—something that was missing in the other street boys. All the others had been brazen, their eyes knowing, even intimidating. They were street-wise and men-wise and old and cunning in the knowledge, some by the age of ten.

But Azziz had approached him almost timidly, eyes lowered, face abashed.

"American?"

"Yes, I'm American."

"First time you come Tangier?"

"Yes."

"You stay with Azziz." He looked fully at Mallini then and smiled shyly. "Other boys not bother you, you stay with Azziz."

It had turned out to be true. The hovering street boys, always ready to pounce, held back. Mallini soon realized that Azziz's posture by his side, his complacent strut, his proprietary air was what held them back. It was the code of the streets. Azziz had marked him as his property. His approach had been a piece of acting. But Mallini smiled when that thought came to him. He was more pleased with Azziz than offended by him.

Mallini looked at Azziz now at the wheel of the limousine. The boy was sitting forward on the seat, hunched lovingly over the wheel, both hands on the top of it, his face straight ahead, eyes on the road they were traveling. Mallini didn't think he had ever seen such sheer joy in a face. Azziz's eyes, intent as they were, were fairly shooting sparks. His lips were pressed together in concentration, but every now and then, when he shot a quick look toward Mallini, they parted in a happy smile to show a flash of white teeth.

When Azziz had suggested, soon after they met, that they drive the "big Mercedes car" to Marrakesh, Mallini knew that he had been staked out. But that only amused him, as everything about Azziz did. On impulse, he agreed. He'd had a few misgivings after they started, but they all were gone now, wiped out by the joy on Azziz's face.

"Best hotel in Marrakesh Mamounia," Azziz said as they were entering the city. "People all time talk about Mamounia."

"Find out where it is," Mallini said. "That's where we'll stay."

Azziz stayed in the car, and Mallini went inside the hotel to register.

"I'd like accommodations for my driver and myself," he said to the clerk.

The desk clerk's face became a perfect blank. "I'm sorry, sir, your driver will have to find his own lodgings."

"What?"

"I'm sorry, sir. We cannot accommodate your driver here."

"Why not?"

Mallini felt his face getting red. Other hotel employees and a few guests in the lobby were turning to stare. Eyebrows were being raised. He was embarrassed, but he was also angry.

"Those are the rules, sir. No exceptions."

The hell with the rules, Mallini thought, he'd take a room for himself and sneak Azziz in later.

"I'd like a large room," he said. Then he added nonchalantly, "With a view."

The desk clerk almost permitted himself a smile. Several around did smile. They all knew what Mallini was thinking. That sort of thing was dealt with every day. Something in Mallini told him this, but he quashed the little presentiment that he felt and signed the register.

"My luggage will arrive later," he said. He fancied that the smiles deepened. The hell with them. Maybe he wouldn't come back there. Maybe he and Azziz would spend the night in one of the baths.

When he got back out to the car, Azziz said, "Everything go fine okay?"

"Everything went just fine."

"We drive around Marrakesh now," Azziz said. He was grinning and eager, twitching to get started. Mallini knew he couldn't wait to drive the "big Mercedes car" all over Marrakesh, even in the dark, showing it off and showing himself off driving it. Mallini smiled and got in beside him.

"Do you know anything about the baths here?" Mallini asked.

Azziz was a moment answering, his attention on maneuvering the car along the crowded street. And when he dd answer, it was with an unmistakable lack of enthusiasm. "Baths . . . ? No. Not me. First time I been Marrakesh."

"You could find out about them, couldn't you?"

"We got hotel room, no? Every room got bathroom. Big fine bathroom." He gave Mallini a cocky look. "I get me in. You tell me room number. I get me in."

Mallini wasn't going to be put off. Azziz obviously wanted to stay in the big, fine hotel, so he could boast about it later to his comrades, no doubt, but

Mallini wasn't even sure he was going back there, and besides, he wanted to visit a bath. There wasn't a story told about Morocco that didn't include a reference to the famous—or infamous—baths.

"We came to Marrakesh because you wanted to," he said. "Now we're going to visit a bath because I want to."

"Maybe take a chance," Azziz said.

"What do you mean, take a chance? You're in them all the time in Tangier, aren't you?"

"Tangier. . . . But Marrakesh. . . . Maybe take—" Mallini cut him off. "Stop the car, Azziz!"

Azziz gave Mallini a startled look. Mallini made his face stern. He gestured toward an opening among the parked cars large enough to take the limousine. Azziz pulled the car into it and stopped. Mallini reached over, turned off the ignition, took the key out and put it in his pocket.

"I'll stay here," Mallini said. "You nose around and find out about the baths." When Azziz hesitated, he said, "Go ahead. It'll be all right. Marrakesh is no different from Tangier. You'll see. Besides, I'm not going to let anything happen to you."

"You got plenty money?"

"Don't you worry about that. You just go find us the best bath in Marrakesh."

Azziz smiled suddenly and hopped out of the car. He leaned back down to the open window after he closed the door. "Back in two shakes," he said, grinning, holding up two fingers, proud to show he could speak "American."

It was awhile before Azziz came back to the car. The traffic and the crowds had thinned. It was late.

"Better we walk," Azziz said. "Leave car here."

They walked a short way down the wide street and then through a maze of side streets and alleys, but

Azziz led the way as if he knew exactly where he was going and the shortest way to get there. It was an instinct, Mallini decided, that sense of direction.

The large wooden door in the high wall was not locked. Azziz glanced around on all sides before he pushed it open enough to allow Mallini and then himself to get through. Mallini slipped through the opening and found himself facing another door.

"Ten dirham," Azziz whispered. He hung back when Mallini approached the second door. Mallini looked around at him. "You go," Azziz said, keeping his voice low. "First you go."

Mallini pushed open the door and went inside, leaving the door open. The small room that he entered was empty except for an old man huddled in his djellaba seated on a stool. He got up and stood beside the stool when Mallini came in, but he didn't come toward him or speak. He held his hands clasped together in front of him. Mallini walked over to him and held out a ten-dirham note. He knew that he was bribing the man. The going price at the baths was nearer one dirham than ten. The old man took the dirham note but made no move to step aside. He was standing directly in front of the door to the bath itself. He secreted the money somewhere in the folds of his robe. His eyes went to Azziz, hanging back at the door. Then he looked at Mallini and held out his hand. Mallini shrugged off his annoyance with the old man, pulled out another ten-dirham note and gave it to him. It was either that or not get in and lose the other ten in the bargain.

The old man moved aside and deliberately turned his back. He deliberately didn't see it when Azziz followed Mallini into the bath.

Mallini knew that it was illegal for a foreigner to go to the baths with a Moroccan, but it was a law so openly flouted that he hadn't thought there would be any pretense that it existed. It seemed right, though, fitting, that he had had to bribe their way in once they were in the bath itself. Every sound and smell in the place reeked of intrigue. There was little that could be seen, and that only dimly.

The bath was one common room. It was almost unlit, and it was filled with steam. There was evidently good hot water and plenty of it. It was grotty, the floor underfoot wet. Mallini could make out rows of arches and shadowy forms of men. There were stalls for showers, spigots and buckets for those who wanted to scrub.

Azziz led Mallini to a corner of the room. The floor there was slightly elevated and not wet. Built into the back of one of the wide arch supports was a shelf for clothes and personal effects. Azziz undressed, but only down to his shorts. When Mallini started to pull his shorts off, Azziz stopped him. "Not yet," he whispered, and led the way back around to one of the shower stalls. Mallini's eyes were more accustomed to the lack of light and the haze of the steam now, and he could see that all the men in the bath who could be seen were wearing jockey shorts. He remembered then that he had heard that Moroccan men never got naked in front of each other. He had heard, too, that they never gave head. He wondered if that was also true.

Mallini felt a thrill run all over his body when Azziz turned the warm water on him. "More hot?" Azziz asked. "You want more hot?"

Mallini scarcely heard him. But his other four senses were bursting with sensation: the smell of men's freshly cleaned bodies, the male smell, the pungent smell of lovemaking, it was there, it was going on, he smelled it all around him; the feel of his body bared to the warm haze of steam to the warm water sluicing over him, to the touch of Azziz's slithery, wet body every now and then, of his engorged penis throbbing and pushing against the tight confines of his wet shorts;

the taste of the place, as strong in his mouth and down into his throat as the smell was strong in his nostrils; the dim, provocative sights of Azziz moving about beside him, his body wet and glistening, seen only in its parts as he turned about under the water, soaping himself, rinsing himself, a slim forearm, a lifted thigh, a curve of white-sheathed buttock, and all the other men in the distances of the room, more tantalizing in their wet and closely clinging shorts than they would have been fully naked; the sounds that came to his ears, the splash and spatter of water, the muted sounds of movement and the hushed gasps that could only be lovemaking. . . .

"Now!" Mallini whispered insistently to Azziz. "Now!"

Azziz laughed softly, took Mallini's hand and led him back to the corner where their clothes were.

Neither Mallini nor Azziz was aware that the place had been cleared. There hadn't been any talking among the men in the bath so there was not that to miss. And they hadn't noticed that the muted movements and hushed gasps had stopped. The sounds of water running and splashing had continued. Spigots and showers had been left on. Mallini and Azziz were not aware of anything except each other until the beam of an oversized flashlight blinded them. They thrust each other apart and scrambled to their feet.

Mallini stood shocked and outraged, trying to see beyond the glare of the light that was beaming mercilessly straight in his face. He could feel Azziz moving jerkily around behind him. "Your clothes!" Azziz hissed in a whisper. "Put on your—"

"Call in the gendarmes!" a terse voice behind the light barked. "We're going to make an arrest here!" Someone could be heard walking away, shoes thumping squishily on the wet floor, the thumping as purposeful as the terse voice had been.

The policemen must have been waiting just outside because the man who had gone for them returned immediately with two men in the gray and black uniforms of the Moroccan gendarmerie. They went straight to Mallini and Azziz and grabbed them by their arms, pinioning them behind them. Azziz had managed to get his trousers on. Mallini was stark naked.

The man with the flashlight had stepped back, and Mallini could see a little better now. The two men who had come in first were in plain clothes. Mallini felt the first shock of fear. The secret police! This was no routine raid if that Gestapo-style force had been called in. Had the old man tipped them off? That wasn't likely. He'd be cutting off his main source of income if word got around that he was working with the authorities.

"You, sir . . . *Américain*," the plainclothesman who was holding the flashlight said, "will find it convenient to leave Marrakesh! Pronto!"

Mallini had never been ordered out of a place in his life. The offense to his pride almost got the best of him, but he held himself back from showing anger. "What about the boy?" he asked.

"He is not your concern!" The man gestured toward the policeman holding Azziz and then toward the door. The policeman started hauling Azziz away. Azziz was too frightened to try to hold back or make a protest, but Mallini lost all control and all regard for the consequences. His body made a violent heave and twist, and he was out of the grasp of the policeman holding him. He flew at the one herding Azziz. He made a flying leap and grabbed the policeman around the neck with both arms, his knees in his back, jerking his head up and back with both forearms locked under his chin. Another policeman ran up and grabbed him, trying to pull him off, but he couldn't break Mallini's hold. The two plainclothesmen got into it. It took all three to pry Mallini loose from the policeman.

Azziz was cringing and whimpering. The plainclothesmen and the policemen were cursing and shouting, calling Mallini crazy, loco. Mallini was screaming. "What do you want?" He struggled to free himself, screaming all the while. "What do you want? If it's money you want, I'll pay you! Let him go! I'll pay you!"

The plainclothesman who was obviously in charge had gotten out of the fracas and stepped aside. He had dropped the flashlight. He stooped and picked it up and then stood to his full height, anger and outraged dignity in every inch of him. He was not accustomed to being reduced to scuffling. "The boy comes with us," he said. "As for you, you leave Marrakesh. Get his clothes on him!" he ordered the two still holding him.

The policeman holding Azziz started again toward the door, and Mallini went wild again. He couldn't use his hands, so he kicked. He kicked and swung his body from side to side, kicking the policeman and the plainclothesman, trying to knee them in the groin. He got away from them and made a stumbling run after Azziz. He was at him and pulling at him before he was grabbed again.

"He's loco! The man's crazy!"

"Get his clothes on him! He'll go in the street naked! Get him decent!"

Mallini suddenly quit struggling. "Let me go with him! Take me, too!"

All the others, even Azziz, gaped at him. One of the policemen made finger circles in the air by his head.

"Let me go with him," Mallini pleaded. "I'll put my clothes on. I won't give you any more trouble, if you'll take me where you're taking him."

"We can't turn him loose," the man in charge said. "He's not accountable. He could do anything." He shot a look of disgust at Mallini and gestured shortly with his thumb toward his clothes.

Mallini got himself dressed as hurriedly as he could, fumbling in his haste, his head swinging back and forth as he tried to watch the policeman holding Azziz and tried to see what he was doing at the same time. When he was dressed, he snatched up Azziz's shirt and shoes and ran to him. "Let him put these on! These are his! Let him put them on!"

The plainclothesman shot him another look of disgust, but he nodded to the policeman to let Azziz put on his shirt and shoes. "No trouble!" he said to Mallini. "You give more trouble, you don't go with the boy!"

Mallini gave no more trouble. It would be all right, he assured himself, when he got to somebody in authority that he could talk to. He wasn't going to let them put Azziz in jail. He kept remembering Azziz in the bath—his lithe, young, strong-muscled body that had brought the growing, mounting tension in his own body that should have come to eruption. Neither of them had finished. . . .

THIRTY-FOUR

Joseph and Serena were awakened by the insistent ring of the telephone. Joseph picked it up.

"You and Serena get over here!" Sybil Singlehurst exploded in his ear. "Mallini is missing!"

"Hold on, Sybil," Joseph said. "Hold on. You're in Tangier, remember? Mallini's not missing. He's having himself a night with the boys. Go back to bed. He'll turn up."

"He will *not* turn up! I tell you he's missing! I've had Carmine out half the night with one of the street boys who knows every place in the city. He is *not* in Tangier!"

"That boy isn't going to look in the right places. You think he's crazy? He's onto a good thing. The longer he strings out the search, the more he gets paid. You've got a lot to learn about—"

"Carmine and that boy have been to every dive, every den, every bath, to every hashish peddler. . . ."

"Everywhere but where that boy thinks they might find Mallini."

"Don't keep giving me arguments!" Singlehurst screamed. Serena could hear her as well as if she were holding the phone instead of Joseph. "Get over here! If you know so much about street boys, get over here and make this one talk! Marvena's hysterical! She thinks Mallini's lying dead in an alley somewhere with his throat slashed."

"Okay, Sybil. Okay, okay. Take it easy. We'll come

over. Goddamn waste of time. Guarantee you one
thing, Mallini's in better shape right now than you
are. Christ!" He hung up the phone.

Joseph didn't have to do more than take one look
at the Arab boy to know he was telling the truth—he
didn't know where Mallini was. He'd seen him, yes.
He knew who they were talking about. The American
had been with his friend Azziz about . . . well, he
wasn't sure . . . about noontime, he thought. He wasn't
in Tangier now, his friend Azziz wasn't.

"Where would he have gone?" Joseph demanded.
He knew only a few words of Arabic and the regional
French. "Where does his family live? Would he have
taken the American home with him?"

The boy trembled. His mouth twitched. He was
afraid of Joseph. He had been enjoying the game up
to now—his star role in it. Now he just wanted to get
the money promised him and get out of there.

"His family live in the *carj dgdid,* the New Quarter," the boy said. "He's not there, Azziz. Not home.
Not in Tangier."

"*Where* then?"

"Me no know."

"You keep stalling me, you're going to get belted
around! You'd better come up with something!"

The boy kept looking at Carmine as if expecting
protection from him, or hoping for it. He edged
toward him. If he could have, he'd have gotten behind
him.

Carmine raised his hands, palms toward the boy.
He wasn't going to help him. He was ready to kill
him. He was dead for sleep. The boy had been dragging him around on a wild-goose chase all night.

The boy's eyes skittered everywhere around the
room. He looked everywhere except at Joseph. "Azziz
all time talking about Marrakesh," he said. "Want

to go Marrakesh. No money to go. He can't go. No money."

"Marrakesh is six hundred kilometers from here! You'd better come up with something better than Marrakesh! It's over twenty hours on the train!"

"Drive a car," the boy said. "Ten hours . . . maybe eight. . . . Drive fast. Azziz drive fast."

"Your friend Azziz can drive a car?"

The boy nodded emphatically. "Yes. Best thing he like. Drive a car. Cock'a walk, him, driving car."

"He was driving a car when you saw him with the American?" Joseph wasn't guessing. He had seen naked envy in the boy's eyes.

The boy nodded even more emphatically. "Big car. Mercedes car."

"That's the limousine!" Sybil Singlehurst said. "Call the garage, Carmine! Find out if Mallini took the car! Find out what time the driver left there with it!"

"No driver," the boy said. "Azziz drive."

"Call the garage, Carmine!"

"You think Azziz drove that car to Marrakesh?" Joseph asked the boy.

"Man say yes, okay, him drive Marrakesh."

Carmine had called. He put the phone down. "Mallini took the car just after the driver put us off here and got back to the garage," he said.

"That's it then," Joseph said. "Marrakesh. These boys can be pretty persuasive when they want something."

"Oh, my Go-o-dd!" Singlehurst seemed ready to tear out her hair. She stamped off a few clopping steps in her agitation and then whirled back around. "What does he expect us to do? Sit here and twiddle our thumbs till he takes it in his head to come back?"

"I'm going to Marrakesh," Marvena said.

"Don't be a fool!" Sybil snapped. "We don't know for a fact that he's there!"

"Man say yes, okay, Azziz drive Marrakesh," the boy repeated.

Joseph went to the phone.

"Whom are you going to call?" Singlehurst rapped out sharply. "Whom are you calling?"

"The police inspector in Marrakesh," Joseph said.

"I don't want the police involved!"

"I'm not going to involve the police. I'm calling for information. I'm going to find out whether Mallini is there. That's the way it's done here. You want to know something, you call the police."

"All right, all right!" Sybil threw her hands out. "Call!"

Joseph's conversation with the police inspector was short. "He's there," he said. "Pay that boy whatever you promised him, and get him out of here."

"He's all right?" Marvena asked anxiously. "Mallini's all right?"

Joseph didn't answer until the boy had left. "They're holding him," he said.

"What are you talking about?" Singlehurst shouted.

Marvena's face had gone stark white. "Who's holding him? The police . . . ?" She ran to Joseph and grabbed his arm. "The police are holding Mallini? For what? Where? In jail? The police have Mallini in jail?"

"Calm down, Marvena!" Singlehurst ordered. "Going out of your head isn't going to help!"

"He's not under arrest," Joseph said. "But if you want him out of there, we'll have to go get him. . . . Bring plenty of cash," he said to Sybil.

THIRTY-FIVE

It was near sundown when they arrived in Marrakesh. A soft mauve light was settling over the rose-red walls of the city and its buildings. The ancient Koutoubia rose in sharp outline against the Atlas Mountains beyond.

They had seen nothing of the country except what they could see from the highway as they hurtled along, or crept along, depending upon whether the road ahead was empty or overrun by an ambling small herd of goats or taken up by overladen donkeys prodded now and then by the long sticks their owners carried. The road was theirs, too. They didn't pull off to the side to give automobiles and trucks space to pass. Half the trip, it seemed to Serena, was made to the raucous sound of blaring horns.

Joseph and Serena were sitting in the front seat of the Mercedes—this one not a limousine. Singlehurst and Marvena were sitting in the back. Carmine and Karen had been left in Tangier. They would pack the clothes and other trappings and the cameras and camera equipment and fly down when Singlehurst called them to come. The four were driving down because the flights out of Tangier were not scheduled daily, were not direct to Marrakesh and would not have put them in Marrakesh until the following day.

Marvena could in no way be persuaded to wait, and Singlehurst did not want to waste a day. Joseph felt the sooner Mallini was safely back in the fold, the better, but he was being casual, even offhand, about the whole thing to try to make the others less anxious.

Joseph hadn't wanted to come. He had wanted Serena to stay in Tangier with him while the others went.

"I can arrange everything from here," he had said. "With one more phone call I can arrange everything."

"In any case," Sybil answered, "I will have to insist that Serena come."

"Serena is committed to you for the work she's agreed to do. That's all. Her personal life is her own. She doesn't have to trot around after you like a kid after its nanny."

"It would be foolish for me to be in Marrakesh and not photograph there, wouldn't it?" Singlehurst said.

When it was put to him that way, Joseph had no choice but to go to Marrakesh if he wanted to stay with Serena.

On their route they passed Asilah, where, if they had been touring, they could have seen the still-intact ramparts of an ancient fortified Portuguese warehouse; Lixus, which in former times had been a Roman supply station and where the indispensable spice garum was produced; Larache, resting place and refuge of bygone Turkish pirates; Souk el Arba du Rharb, which was the end of the main stem of the route south from Tangier and where one took either the inland route to the makhzens, the imperial cities of Fez and Meknès, or the coastal route to Rabat, premier imperial city because it was the capital, a former *ribat* or fortified monastery; and Casablanca, a modern commercial metropolis, the second largest in Africa and a far cry from the mysterious and exotic Casablanca of movie fame.

Before leaving Casablanca and the coastal route to turn inland and south for the long half of the drive to Marrakesh, they had lunch at Hotel el Mansour.

It was an excellent meal, which none of them could really appreciate. Joseph insisted on the long stop and insisted that they all eat. None of them had had anything except coffee all day. He chose the restaurant and did the ordering. For all of them he ordered harira, a rich soup, and the bstila that Serena had had before, the pigeon-meat pastry that required the pounding, then baking of dozens of different layers of thin, flaky dough. He ordered a different main course for each: souajen, a fragrant stew which could be made from meat or chicken, he chose lamb; hout, a redolent fish stew; djaja mahamara, chicken stuffed with almonds, semolina and raisins; and mchoui, fragrant pit-roasted mutton. For dessert, kab el ghzal, almond pastries.

It was midafternoon by the time they left Casablanca. The sun became relentless. They had left any breeze from the sea. The sameness of earth color became oppressive. The land became flat with little relief from the flatness for seemingly endless stretches.

Before, they had passed almost unbroken successions of roadside souks selling rugs, leather goods—wallets, handbags, hand-embroidered leather slippers—copper kettles, pots and braziers, silver jewelry inlaid with semiprecious stones, silk and cotton caftans, woven mats, amber beads, fruit and other produce. They had passed single stalls selling chickens only, selling fruit and produce only. Single boys and sometimes girls stood along the road holding out a single orange or maybe two. A lone man would offer a tethered goat.

Now the roadside souks became less frequent, the single stalls nonexistent. The frequency of single boys and girls and ancient men lessened. There was something new. Every now and then they would pass a lone man selling water from a dented and rusted bucket. They passed more people walking now. People with large bundles of dried, leafless limbs on their heads, sometimes a man prodding a donkey so laden with the awkwardly bundled sticks that only his legs were visible, looking like sticks themselves.

"What do they do with them?" Serena asked. "Are they for firewood or what, those sticks?"

"They use them in building," Joseph said. "Make the framework for the adobe."

Serena looked anxiously at Joseph. He sounded a little as he had the first night, taciturn, clipping his sentences.

Joseph felt her glance. He reached for her hand and drove with one hand on the steering wheel and one hand holding hers.

"Do you want me to drive awhile? Are you tired?" Serena asked. "You must be."

He smiled at her and squeezed her hand, shook his head no.

There was a sweetness in the air, and a heavy dustiness. The very rolling weight of the cars and trucks on the paved road seemed to agitate the dry earth beyond and send up clouds of dust that drifted over the highway.

Everything was built of earth—the isolated small houses, the enclosing walls of the rich men's houses set up on little eminences in the distance and the walls of their palaces inside their walls. The earth and everything that rose from it seemed the same. There was much that was beautiful around them, but they were more receptive to the things that were congenial to their depressed mood and tended to deepen it. No one had done much talking. Sybil and Marvena had been more silent than not all morning since they had left Tangier and were altogether silent now.

"This is one of the best highway systems in the world," Joseph said. "Every major city in Morocco is connected by it."

It was one ribbon of road, a two-way highway.

"Humph!" Singlehurst said from the back seat.

Joseph smiled to himself. At least she had answered. "It was laid out and built by the government, and it's maintained by the government," he said. "You won't find the highway anywhere in the country any worse than what you've seen."

"It's not exactly a parkway," Serena said.

"It's exactly what's needed here. That's what makes it one of the best systems in the world. Meets the requirements."

"What I require is to get to Marrakesh," Singlehurst said. "And I'd feel surer I was going to get there if I had a driver with two hands on the wheel."

Joseph cocked up his head and caught Sybil's eyes in the rearview mirror. "Do you hear bat wings, Serena?" he asked, grinning at Sybil in the mirror.

Serena laughed and moved closer to Joseph and put her hand on his thigh.

"Drive with both hands if it makes her feel better," she said, whispering the words and keeping her face forward so Sybil wouldn't see her whispering. "Everyone's on edge. Why make it worse?"

Joseph shifted his position on the seat, pushing himself against the back of it to loosen the tightness of the crotch of his pants. "You sit over there in your corner," he said, "or you're going to bring this little cavalcade to a halt."

Serena blushed and snatched her hand away from his thigh and moved back to where she had been. He squeezed her hand hard, let it go and put both hands on the wheel.

The commissariat was in the Djemaa el Fna, the huge marketplace that was the rumbling, restless heart of Marrakesh, one of the most famous squares in the world. From the outside the commissariat could have been any kind of building. It looked the same as all the others behind its rose-red pisé walls. The gate was open, making it a little different. Most gates and entrances were kept closed. Inside the gate there was a small garden. The walks were paved with red and green tiles in symmetric design. There were green and red tile designs set in the walls. On each side of the walkway to the door there was a date palm tree. Dahlias bloomed in profusion around the base of the trees. There was no one in the little garden. It was serene and peaceful, restful after the crush of the square. It looked like anything except the courtyard of a police station.

The *inspecteur de Bureau de Police* was a most gentlemanly man who spoke softly accented perfect French. He was light brown-skinned with a small, precisely trimmed black mustache, dressed in an expensive Western-style business suit. He very politely, very solicitously but very firmly refused to talk to anybody except Joseph. He was distressed by the presence of the ladies, and his distress was evident. He greeted them, but he talked to Joseph. The *mesdames* should be taken to a hotel. He would recommend the Hotel Mamounia. They would find it comfortable; perhaps they had heard of it; it was famous worldwide. Very comfortable indeed, and not far, on the Avenue Bab Djedid. He would telephone and secure accommodations for the *mesdames*. They could rest there from their long journey, have a leisurely dinner; they would find the food irresistible. Tomorrow they could enjoy the pool. . . .

"Tomorrow?" Marvena burst out. *"Demain? Non! Non, non!"* She threw out a rapid fire of French, demanding to see Mallini then! That moment!

The inspector looked even more distressed. He set his mouth in a thin line and became silent. He was not going any further with anything until he and Joseph could talk man to man. This was men's business.

Joseph took Marvena by both elbows and propelled

her out into the courtyard and toward the gate. Single-hurst and Serena followed.

Joseph was angry now. He paid no attention to Marvena's protests or her struggles to free herself. He had wanted to leave the women at the hotel in the first place. Now he was going to have an indignant, irritated man to deal with.

When they went through the gate and toward the car, they saw another car parked behind it.

"The car, Sybil! There's the car!" Marvena cried out. "He *is* here! Mallini *is* here! There's the car!"

It was the Mercedes limousine, parked in back of the smaller Mercedes they had driven down—the big black car with the thin red stripe beneath its windows, the curtained wraparound rear window, the vinyl top, the license plate with "Tangier" painted on it. No one was in the car.

"Does that mean they're going to let Mallini go?" Marvena clutched at Joseph. "Is that why they put the car there? Because they're going to let him go?"

"I didn't drive all the way here to turn around and leave without him," Joseph said. He opened the door of the smaller car, made Marvena get in and then handed Singlehurst in. He gave the keys to Serena. "You drive, hon." He crooked a finger at a group of boys clustered a few feet away. The boys didn't want to come any closer to the gate of the commissariat, but one of the larger boys took a few tentative steps toward Joseph.

Joseph held out some coins. "The Mamounia," he said. "You know it?"

The boy nodded eagerly but came no closer.

"Show the ladies the way," Joseph said. He tossed the coins. There were four. The boy caught them all one by one in a sweeping circle of his hands as if he were performing a juggling act. Not one hit the ground.

* * *

Half an hour later Mallini and Marvena and the Arab boy Azziz were in the limousine on the way back to Tangier. Mallini wouldn't stay any longer in Marrakesh than it took him to drive out of there—or took Azziz to drive out of there. Sybil and Serena and Joseph were going to stay the night and fly back the next day.

"Mallini's little adventure was pretty expensive," Joseph said to Singlehurst. "It cost three thousand dollars to spring him. Fifty for the boy."

"As far as I'm concerned, the boy could have stayed there!" Sybil snapped. "I lay this whole thing to him! He's to blame! Not Mallini!"

"Mallini didn't see it quite that way."

Joseph kept grinning as if enjoying a secret joke.

"Nothing about this is funny!" Singlehurst said angrily.

"Mallini's performance was."

There was a short silence. Then Sybil said, "I'd like to know a little about 'Mallini's performance.' "

"It was short but effective," Joseph said. "When he found out I had arranged for his release but not the release of the boy, he flew into me, ready to kill me. I never saw so many arms and legs on one man in my life." He laughed. "I mean, he wanted that boy out of there, and he wasn't leaving without him."

Singlehurst was silent. Then, with a smile, she stirred herself. "You two get out," she said. "I need a good night's rest. You do, too, Serena. We have a load of work ahead of us when we get back to Tangier."

Singlehurst ushered Joseph and Serena out the door. She was still smiling when she closed it.

She wouldn't have to do anything about Mallini. If the boy Azziz kept Mallini on a cloud, and Joseph Allen kept Serena on a cloud, her two stars would glow again.

* * *

The next morning about ten o'clock Mallini called Sybil.

"Don't get on that noon plane! I'm coming back to Marrakesh! I'm going to photograph in Marrakesh!"

Singlehurst was not surprised by the call. Had she stayed in her room expecting it?

Mallini was bubbling like a fountain. He'd telephoned a friend in New York, a designer who had a house in Marrakesh. They would live in his house while they were there. He had seen too many backgrounds he wanted to photograph in Marrakesh to be worried about idiot police. Singlehurst was to stay put. He and Marvena and Carmine and Karen—and Azziz; he had hired him as second assistant—would be down kit and caboodle with all the stuff the next day. He'd chartered a plane to fly them directly there.

Singlehurst wanted to assure herself that Mallini wasn't on an emotional high that he could fall down from any moment. "How's Marvena?" she asked. "Did she survive that twenty-four hours of driving? I've been worried about her." She could gauge the situation better if she knew what state Marvena's emotions were in.

"I'm fine!" Marvena said. She was on the connecting phone in the other room of the suite. "I slept like a baby all the way back to Tangier." She knew what Sybil was worried about. "We're *all* fine," she said. "We couldn't be better if we tried to be." She gave the final assurance. "What do you think of Mallini's new assistant? Carmine has been working with him all morning. He says he learns faster than anybody he's ever taught before."

"He'll free Carmine to do some darkroom work," Mallini said. "I'm going to rig up a darkroom in one of the bathrooms in the house. I want to be able to see black-and-whites as we go along."

"It all sounds good," Singlehurst said. Then: "Let me talk to Karen. I want to talk to her about packing the things. Do you have your list of the inventory, Marvena?"

"Yes, I have it. I'll make sure everything is packed," Marvena said. "Well, I'll go call Karen to the phone. Ta-ta." Her phone clicked off.

There was a moment of quiet. Singlehurst waited.

"How is Serena?" Mallini asked.

That was what Singlehurst had wanted to hear. "She's fine," she said. "As ready for work as you are. I'm looking at her now through my window. She's ?² the pool in a string bikini. Joseph Allen is holding the other men at bay."

Mallini laughed, a free, ringing, no-cares laugh.

"Get yourself down here, Mallini! We're going to turn out an issue of *Milady* that's going to knock the other magazines back on their heels!"

"Yes, sir, she's my baby. . . . No, sir, I don't mean maybe . . ." Joseph crooned softly. He was lying on his back, his front exposed to the sun. His hand reached out and touched Serena. His fingers spider-sneaked over the naked flesh of her waist.

Suddenly he turned over flat on his stomach.

Serena laughed. "I saw!" she whispered happily. "I saw!" She turned over on her stomach and threw her arm over Joseph. "Was that for me? If it wasn't for me, you're dead!"

"You're the goddamnedest witch I ever knew," Joseph muttered.

"Was it for me, or wasn't it?"

"Let me get it down so we can get away from this goddamn pool and I'll show you!"

Serena laughed again. "Never mind," she said with pretended indifference. "I've already come. I don't need anything more from you. Just seeing you pop up like that made me come." She hummed aloud a musical phrase from an old television show she'd watched as a child. *Dragnet,* she thought it was. "Dum-de-dum-dum. . . ."

"I swear to God, Serena. . . ."

"That's from Tchaikovsky," Serena said. She didn't know whether it was or not. "That's where they got it. Tchaikovsky's Fifth. Dum-de-dum-dum. . . ." She giggled.

"I swear you'd deserve it if I took you right here!"

"Go ahead!"

"You're going to drive me out of my skull! Where's the towel? Goddamn it, where's the goddamn towel?"

Serena got up, picking up the towel with her. She sashayed off, tossing the towel back behind her. Joseph grabbed it and held it in front of him, shielding his distended penis.

"You wait up for me!" he yelled.

Serena pivoted around, her eyes as wide as she could open them. "Were you addressin' me, suh?"

"I goddamn hell was!" Joseph stumbled over the dragging end of the towel. He almost lost his balance and then regained it. "I goddamn hell am!"

"Oh, my! Ah reckon then Ah bettah wait up an' listen to what y'all have to say," Serena said in an exaggerated southern accent, still giggling. "What did y'all want, suh?"

Joseph walked up to her. "You," he said. He stood over her, his eyes burning into hers. "You."

Serena went limp in every muscle and sinew and bone. She wasn't sure she wasn't going to collapse on the tile. The tone of his voice could do that to her. Certain expressions on his face could do it.

She reached toward Joseph. He took her arm in a tight grip. They stood locked in an embrace of eyes, neither aware of anybody around them nor of where they were.

The first letter Zoe received from Serena was a shock. If it hadn't been in Serena's handwriting, she wouldn't have believed Serena had written it. "You'll never believe who's over here. No less than our main claim to literary fame—'our' meaning the good old USA. *Joseph Allen!* Guess who he took to dinner the first night she saw him! No more guesses! *Me!* How about them apples? Guess what else! He ain't all bad! That's a word of Joseph's—ain't. He's so . . . I don't know what! He's so *himself* when he says words like that. He is so *himself* all the time! I've never known anybody before who was such a *total person!* He's certainly an addition to this group! He's going to be with us. He's doing Singlehurst's biography, so he'll be around, tra-la! Well, enough of these carryings-on. And don't get ideas. Serena still has her two little heads on her two little shoulders."

Not a word about Mallini and how the work was going. Not a word about any of the others. Zoe had to look at the postmark to find out where in Morocco Serena was when she wrote the letter.

This was what she had wanted for Serena, but Zoe was worried. Joseph Allen? Women he had dropped were scattered over two continents.

THIRTY-SIX

Serena, Mallini and Singlehurst worked with a harmony beyond any they had ever had before. They were a team of one, or they worked as if they were. Nothing went wrong. Not even a piece of equipment failed or malfunctioned. The backup cameras were never used.

They lived in Marrakesh and made working trips to the Dadès Gorges, Ouarzazate, Tafraout and Essaouira.

Joseph was a member of the group, and he was working. He rented a portable typewriter and carried it around wherever they went. He worked every single morning, Saturdays and Sundays included, just as the rest of the gang did. He wrote out what he and Singlehurst had talked about during their last conversation; he had already completed a rough outline of how the biography would be set up.

None of them realized, until it was almost over, how fast the time had flown. The only proof of the passage of time was the mass of finished work that had been done. It was a shock when they realized that it was over, and the time had come to go home.

"We're not going to do the opening page wrap-up in Tangier," Singlehurst said. "We've peaked. Do you agree, Mallini?"

"We'll go back to the original concept for the opening page," Mallini said. "I couldn't get anything better out of Tangier than what I've already got from here."

"That's what I thought."

Mallini's mood had plummeted. He was going to have to leave Azziz in Tangier. He talked of getting him to the States, but it would take time. It wasn't that easy to arrange, and it couldn't be arranged before the group had to return to New York, and their return, especially Mallini's, couldn't be delayed. All his work was still on undeveloped film, except for the black-and-whites Carmine had developed. And they had been developed only for guidance. Few black-and-whites would make it to the magazine.

The delay in getting Azziz to the States—he wanted desperately to go—was not what bothered Mallini the most. The boy wasn't going to transplant well. Azziz was insistent that he would be gloriously happy in New York City. Mallini knew that he would not. In time he would miss, and want, his familiar surroundings, the numerous family members that he had such close ties to. He would be homesick and miserable.

Mallini brooded. His mood grew blacker by the hour. And Marvena began again to be anxious about him.

On the last morning in Marrakesh Serena woke up with the realization that she and Joseph were going to have to make a decision. They were going to stay together, or they weren't. The fear that they might not made her actually sick to her stomach.

All day she waited for him to say something, but he went about as if it were a day like any other. The longer the day went on, the more fearful she became. Had it been nothing more than a "shipboard romance" for Joseph?

In late afternoon, when they were taking a walk in the garden, she said, "Things will be different when we get home, Joseph."

"Damn right they will. They'll be better."

"How can they be better? You're not in New York much of the time."

"So what? You'll be where I am."

"How can I? My work's in New York."

"To hell with your work."

She was startled. She stopped and stared at him. "What if I said that to you?"

He frowned, looking puzzled. Then he grinned. "You're not comparing writing to modeling, are you?"

Serena stiffened with offended pride. "What's wrong with modeling?"

"Nothing. I'm not putting modeling down. But it's not as if it were a lifetime proposition. You'll just be quitting a little sooner than you might have. That's all."

"And what if I don't want to quit?"

Joseph frowned again. "You wouldn't give up modeling to be with me?"

Serena's thinking went haywire. She thought he was looking for a way out.

"Would you give up writing to be with me?"

Joseph shook his head, baffled. "Honey, you're off the wall."

She lost all reason. "If you were looking for an excuse, you've got it!"

"What the hell are you talking about?"

"I'm not going to give up *my* life! *My* work!"

"Yoo-hoo! Yoo-hoo!"

Karen Vogel had come partway across the garden toward them. She stopped when she saw they'd heard her.

"Champagne supper's ready! Celebration time! Everyone's waiting for you!"

"Coming, Karen!" Serena called out. Without another word to Joseph she turned and walked away from him to the house.

*   *   *

She could feel Joseph's eyes on her all through the celebration supper. They never left her. She didn't dare look at him. If she did, she would collapse in on herself like a punctured balloon.

She laughed at everything anybody said, laughed more gaily than anybody else. She had to keep it up, she told herself, someone had to be the life of the party.

She stood up. "I'd like to propose a toast!" She lifted her champagne glass. "To Sybil Singlehurst! This has been the most fantastic location trip of my entire modeling career! And it was Sybil Singlehurst who made it fantastic!"

She ignored the glances exchanged as everyone except Singlehurst lifted their glasses and drank. She was aware of Joseph's dipping his glass toward Singlehurst and taking a sip. She could feel his eyes on her over the rim of the glass.

Other toasts were proposed. "Hear! Hear!" she sang out after each, laughing more gaily with each "hear, hear." Tears stung the backs of her eyes. She was running straight off a cliff and knew she was and couldn't stop. And Joseph was doing nothing to stop her.

As soon as they left the table, she moved a little apart from the group. "I'm exhausted!" she said, laughing as she said it. "It has been a *fantastic* evening, but I am *exhausted!* I don't want to see a *soul* until it's time to get on that homeward-bound plane tomorrow!" She swept out of the room without a glance at anybody, especially Joseph. She was tossing the gauntlet, she told herself. That last remark had been meant for Joseph, and he knew it.

But he didn't pick up the gauntlet. He didn't come to her room. It was the first night since they had known each other that they hadn't slept together.

At two o'clock she couldn't stand it any longer. She went to Joseph's room.

The door was open. Joseph wasn't there.

She stood in the empty night-lit room, feeling herself grow as cold as the lifeless, dead-feeling, vacant spaces around her. No room had ever felt so empty. Joseph's rented typewriter sat, dimly outlined in the pale light, stark and deserted on its table before the window, no paper in it, no loose sheets of scribbled notes around it. Nothing said to her as plainly as that abandoned typewriter that Joseph wasn't there.

She went to his bed and sat down on the edge. The covers were turned down, as the maid had left them. He hadn't been in the bed. He hadn't rumpled the covers. Usually he rumpled them, or they both did, for the sake of appearances, so not to embarrass the maid. The Western permissiveness toward sex wasn't acceptable here. Sometimes they had slept in Joseph's bed when making love wouldn't wait. Then she was the one who had to get up before the household servants were about and go to her own room. Her hands were wet, clutching Joseph's bedcovers, thinking about the times that had happened.

None of Joseph's things were around. She knew that without getting up to look. He must have packed and left as soon as he came to his room after she had come upstairs. He had been packing, just down the hall from her, while she stood, numb and miserable, staring out her window, waiting for him to come to her.

She was still sitting on the edge of Joseph's bed when dawn came. She got up and went back to her own room. There was an envelope on the floor just inside the door. She hadn't seen it there when she had left her room earlier. But it had been there. She knew it had. Joseph had slid it under the door while she stood staring out the window at the garden where the quarrel had taken place. If she had heard some sound. . . . If she had turned in time and seen. . . .

There were only a few words, scrawled in Joseph's unruly handwriting: "If you ever kick the Serena habit, let me know."

It wasn't even signed.

THIRTY-SEVEN

They came down at Kennedy through a haze of smog. The big plane lumbered awkwardly as it made its approach to the landing strip assigned to it. It was too big to handle the lower atmosphere comfortably.

Serena dreaded the touchdown. Things had been in suspension as long as they had been aloft.

Zoe was at the airport. Serena was surprised to see her beyond the customs barrier. Her welcoming smile was thin, barely a smile. A dread came over Serena. Something bad had happened.

Getting through customs took an interminable time, but finally, she was with Zoe. "What's happened?"

"Wait till we get in the taxi."

"Your mother is dead, Serena."

Serena gaped at Zoe in unbelieving shock.

"I didn't know any way to tell you except straight out."

Serena still gaped, unable to speak.

"I know this has come at a bad time for you. You're going to have regrets about not having gone home for a visit. But you were planning on going for Christmas. Keep remembering that."

A long time of silence passed. They were on the FDR Drive when Serena broke the silence.

"How did she die?"

"It was an accident. She drowned."

"Where?"

"In the pool."

"At home? The pool at home?"

That was the question Zoe had dreaded most. "Yes."

"She was an excellent swimmer! She was an excellent diver and an excellent swimmer!"

"Serena. . . ."

"She didn't drown by accident!"

"Leave it alone, Serena."

Serena paid no attention to the warning, if she heard it. "When did it happen?"

"It happened yesterday. The funeral is tomorrow. They're waiting to give you time to get home. I was going to send you a cable to come home, but when I called Singlehurst's secretary to find out where to send it, she told me you were scheduled in today. . . . Wells thought it would be easier for you if I were the one who told you."

"Give me the details, Zoe."

"There aren't many details," Zoe said. "Wells arrived home from a trip yesterday and found her floating in the pool, face-down. She had been dead about an hour, the coroner said."

Ellie walked quietly about her sitting room, thinking, going over in her mind the things she had done, the preparations she had made, making sure that she had not forgotten anything. She didn't want to leave any loose ends. Several times she passed the bar that she had bought for the room two years before. She glanced at it each time, but she didn't stop and make herself a drink.

She sat down at her desk and read her will again, making sure again that she hadn't forgotten anybody. She folded the will and put it back in the drawer. Then she looked over the lists. She had made lists of all her personal possessions that were not included in the will, parceling everything out, some things to people, some to charities. She folded the lists and put them under the will.

She left her sitting room and went to her mirrored dressing room. She watched herself undress in the mirrors, looking at her too-thin legs, her bloated chest and waist and abdomen. She looked at her face. It was a surprise to her every time she saw it. Her face hadn't changed. It wasn't bloated. Her eyes weren't puffy; there weren't bags under them. That was all that would be seen in her casket—her face.

She put on a bathing suit. It was one of the new one-piece suits. She had been glad when they came back in fashion. Bikinis weren't for her anymore, but even if they had been, this wasn't an occasion for a bikini.

She started out of the dressing room, but then she turned around and went back in. She had almost forgotten something important. She took a large towel out of the closet and went in the bathroom and took a bottle of suntan lotion from the cabinet. She went into her bedroom and got a pair of sunglasses and a book.

She wanted a drink. She craved one. But she walked through her sitting room without even glancing at the bar. She didn't want any liquor in her body. It would be in the coroner's report. She didn't want people thinking she had gotten drunk and fallen in the pool and been too drunk to save herself.

None of the servants saw her go out of the house. It was the time of afternoon when they had finished all the rooms of the house and were either in their own rooms or somewhere about the kitchen. The timing had been fortunate. Wells was due back in an hour or so. He'd scheduled his flight into Atlanta for three o'clock.

She walked along the path under the arbor, not hurrying, but not hanging back either. She wasn't afraid. She just wanted to do it absolutely right. She had set it up pretty well, she thought. She had mentioned stomach cramps and leg cramps to Wells for the past few weeks. He would tell people that she had been complaining about them.

She was rid of both Wells and Serena now. Wells had someone. She knew about the secret telephone calls, the many trips to New York. Wells was no good at intrigue.

Wells had said that Serena was head over heels about the writer Joseph Allen. From what she had read about him he seemed to have a strong character, even a domineering one. That was good for Serena. It would take somebody that strong to handle her. Stephen Neilly had never been a match for her.

Ellie came out from under the arbor and walked across the lawn to the pool. It was a hot, sunny fall day. That was fortunate, too. No one would find it strange that she had decided to take a swim. She was known to swim as late as October.

She put her things down beside the pool, dived in and swam across and back. The water was a little chilly. She didn't mind. She got out and dried herself. She wanted the towel to be wet as if she had been in and out of the pool several times. She opened the book and laid it pages-down, as if she had been reading and were keeping her place. She opened the bottle of suntan lotion, rubbed some on herself and left the top off the bottle when she finished. Then she dived back into the pool.

She took a strong inhale of water as she went down head first. She knew she was going to have to fight her strong instinct for survival. But she could master it. She'd always gotten what she wanted if she wanted it badly enough.

The water seemed to explode in her head. She felt her arms and legs clawing through the water, trying to take her to the surface. She opened her mouth and felt the rush of water down her throat. She felt a crushing weight in her chest, a desperate sucking for air in her windpipe. Then she felt her arms and legs relax, felt the explosion in her head ease. The desperation for air was still there, but the weight had lifted from her chest. The water felt soft around her. Conscious thought was leaving her. She was only feeling now, and that feeling was one of satisfaction. She had done it.

"Will you come to Atlanta with me, Zoe?"

"I'm sorry, Serena. I can't."

Serena didn't turn to look at Zoe. She was staring out the window. The lights of the city were glimmering faintly. They were faded-looking and bleary through the dusk and the smog. The driver would be coming soon to drive her to LaGuardia, where one of her father's planes was waiting to fly her to Atlanta.

"Daddy had been away on a trip, you said. A trip where? Here?"

"Yes," Zoe said. She hesitated before speaking, she couldn't help it, but she said the word firmly.

"You saw him while he was here?"

"Yes."

"And times before that?"

"Yes."

Both were silent for a moment. Then Serena said, "If Mother knew about you and Daddy, it might have been something she had been waiting for. I think it was." She turned around to face Zoe. "I want you to believe that. I'm not lying to try to make you feel better. Mother didn't do things halfway. All the little details had to be taken care of. All the strings neatly tied. . . . Daddy was just a worrisome little detail in her life."

PART 4

THIRTY-EIGHT

"It's really great having you back, Serena," Zoe said. "I've been so lonesome with Wells and you both out of the country." Serena wasn't being very talkative. Zoe chattered on. "But that was the best thing you and Wells could have done, go away for a while."

"Of course it was," Serena said briskly. "It got all of us over the hump."

They were in Zoe's living room. Zoe was sprawled on one of the low-slung hide chairs; Serena was tense and uneasy in the other. Zoe pretended she didn't notice Serena's uneasiness or her obviously put-on attitude. It was a cover-up. Serena was trying to hide how miserable she was. "How was Japan?" she asked.

"Like Gordon Knightsplit's apartment."

Zoe laughed. "And China?"

"Big."

Zoe laughed again. "I don't think you quite got out of those countries what the travel folders promise."

"I got out of them what I wanted to get."

Zoe didn't look at Serena. She kept her eyes on her fingers, which she was lazily lacing and unlacing. She knew Serena had meant to sound breezy. But she had sounded hard. "I know that girl I hear talking," she said. "That's the Serena Carr I used to know."

"You don't sound like you're all that happy about it."

"Oh, I might make a few little changes around the edges if I could. I think I'd tuck back in some of what caused those vibes I used to get from your letters from Morocco."

"Do me a favor and forget Morocco!"

"Forget it? After the great work that came out of that trip? Did you see the November issue of *Milady* in Hong Kong? I remember that's where you and Wells were when it came out."

"Yes, I saw it! You couldn't get away from it! It was all over the place!"

"Made quite a splash here, too. They say it'll make history in the fashion publishing business."

"Good for Singlehurst!"

Zoe waited a minute before speaking again. Then she said quietly, "Wells wrote in several of his letters that you never mentioned Joseph Allen." She saw Serena pale, but she went on. "He didn't say he was, but he was worried about you. . . . What happened between you and Joseph Allen?"

"What happened?" Serena tried to sound flip. "Nothing happened. It flared up, and then it died out. That's all."

"Just like that?"

"Why not? Didn't something like that happen between you and Tim?"

Zoe knew what Serena was doing—trying to go on the offensive. "No," she said, "I fell in love with Wells and broke off with Tim. . . . I answered your question. Are you going to answer mine?"

"I've already answered it. It flared up; it died out."

Zoe looked at Serena until she made Serena look at her. "I got your last letter two days after you were back in the States from Morocco," she said. "It was dated the day before you left Marrakesh. That letter was all *Joseph Allen, Joseph Allen,* just like all the rest of your letters had been. I don't buy your answer."

Serena's face looked like gray paper. Her eyes had sunk back in her head. Zoe was almost sorry she had brought up Joseph Allen. But she couldn't see Serena as miserable as she was and not do something to try to help.

"He walked out on me," Serena said in a cracked whisper.

Zoe leaned toward her. "Oh, Serena. . . . Oh, I'm so sorry. . . ."

Serena pushed herself up out of her chair. "Don't sympathize with me! I couldn't stand it! I acted like an ass! I don't blame him for walking out!"

Zoe stood up. Serena's eyes had a wild look in them. She looked as if she were going to run out of the room, just start running and never stop. "Maybe it's not for good. Maybe—"

"Oh, it's for good! He's not off somewhere nursing a snit! He's been very decent. He sent me a telegram of sympathy when he heard about Mother. But he's finished with me!"

"Sit back down, Serena," Zoe said gently.

Serena was still wild-eyed. But she went back to the chair and sat down.

Zoe pulled her own chair up close to Serena's and sat down. "Tell me what happened, Serena.'"

"I can't, Zoe. I can't talk about it." Tears rolled down her face. It was the first time Zoe had ever seen her cry. "I . . . We quarreled. I . . ."

She told it all, in stops and starts, tearing the words out of herself. When she finished, she opened her purse and took a folded, worn-out-looking piece of paper from a zipped compartment and handed it to Zoe. "That was on the floor inside the door when I went back to my room."

Zoe looked from the note to Serena and back to the note, relief on her face, her violet eyes lighting up. "All you have to do is get in touch with him! All you have to do—"

"It's too late." Serena's eyes were dull, her voice lifeless. "Haven't you been reading the papers? He's back with his wife."

THIRTY-NINE

The music had a triumphant, martial air. When it became muted suddenly, the chatter and laughter of the glittering crowd in the banquet room became muted also. People looked expectantly toward the red-carpeted dais in front of the orchestra.

Alexander Stone, the publisher of *Milady*, was standing at the microphone.

"Ladies and gentlemen, if I could have your attention, please. . . ."

The music stopped altogether. The room became silent.

"I want to thank you all for being with us this evening to share with us our pleasure in marking the fiftieth anniversary of the publication of *Milady*—"

A spontaneous burst of applause stopped him. He smiled, inclined his head several times in acknowledgment, then held up his hands to stop the applause.

"As you have seen from the replicas of former mastheads of *Milady* and from the credits on the photographs on exhibit, a great number of people, over the years, have contributed toward the success of *Milady*. But no one has made a greater contribution, if indeed *as great* a contribution as our present editor-in-chief, Sybil Singlehurst."

A tumultuous roar of applause went up. Alexander Stone left the dais and disappeared in the crowd for a moment. When he appeared again, he was leading Sybil to the dais. The applause became even more tumultuous. Alexander Stone held up his hands again to stop it.

"I am not going to ask Ms. Singlehurst to make a speech." He smiled. "That is not what she does best." The crowd responded with laughter. "I would like to call to the microphone now someone whom many of you know personally and all of you know by reputation, the curator of the Museum of Contemporary Art who offered the use of the museum for this great occasion and who is our host tonight, Walter Jawolski."

Applause, but not the thunderous ovation that had greeted Sybil Singlehurst's appearance.

Walter Jawolski acknowledged the introduction. "Thank you, Alex," he said, and turned to the assembled guests. "I am not going to make a speech either," he said. "I thought you would like to know that first." Laughter from the crowd. "But I am going to make an announcement. I have been authorized by the United Association of Museums to take this most appropriate time to announce the creation by the association of a new post. I take it upon myself to say that that post would not have come into existence if the person qualified to fill it had not come along first. The post is that of fashion consultant to the association. The person qualified to fill it is Sybil Singlehurst. Ladies and gentlemen, it is my great pleasure to be able to say that Ms. Singlehrust has accepted the post. I want to take this opportunity to express my sincere congratulations to her. She has earned a signal honor, one of the highest honors ever achieved in the field of fashion publishing. I look forward to a long and rewarding . . ."

The rest of Walter Jawolski's remark was drowned out by the deafening ovation for Sybil Singlehurst.

"Speech! Speech!" was demanded from all around the room. The two men stepped aside and left Sybil alone at the microphone.

The crowd quieted. Sybil's small, dramatic figure, clothed in royal purple, commanded silence.

"I will not make a speech," Sybil said. She looked out over the crowd. "But I have an announcement to make, too." She paused, looked out over the crowd again. There were several ambitious editors out there, from *Milady* and from other fashion magazines as well. "The announcement that I wish to make is that while I have accepted the post of fashion consultant to the United Association of Museums and feel greatly honored that the position was offered to me and intend to honor that position by fulfilling it to the best of my abilities—she paused again—"I am *not* retiring from my position as editor-in-chief of *Milady*."

Alexander Stone led the thundering applause that greeted Sybil's announcement. Sybil could imagine that the ambitious editors were less enthusiastic in their applause than the rest of the crowd. She smiled and stepped down from the dais.

The preparations for the fifty-year retrospective celebrating the fiftieth anniversary of *Milady* had taken weeks. The arduous preparations had paid off. There had never before been such a collection of notables of fashion from all over the world. Designers, publishers, editors, photographers, celebrated wearers of fashion—socialites, film stars and stage personalities—came from New York and other leading American cities, from London, Paris, Madrid, Rome, Milan, Tokyo, Athens and Moscow. The furor in the press began days before the exhibit opened and continued for days after. The event received worldwide attention.

It had been estimated that the galleries devoted to the blowups of selected photographs and representative replicas of mastheads from fifty years of monthly issues of *Milady* could comfortably accommodate 600 people. It seemed they all arrived at the same time, along with a crowd of more than 2,000 onlookers. The crush of people extended from the doors of the museum to the street and down the length of the city block. People who had never stood in line before in their lives waited for as long as two hours to get in. Photographers and reporters mingled with the waiting guests, interviewing, taking photographs. "My God, what a bonanza!' one reporter exulted. "I've never seen anything like this! I can't interview one person without having to turn my back on somebody else I want to interview!"

Those gathered in the banquet room began to disperse when Sybil left the room. Mallini looked around for an escape. He was tense and nervous and wanted to get away from the cluttering people and the never-letting-up need to respond to praise and compliments. He was also hurt and disappointed. The one person he had hoped to see at the exhibit hadn't come.

He went into Walter Jawolski's private office. He had been there only a moment when he knew that someone was in the room with him. He turned around. Gordon was standing inside the door.

Mallini almost reeled. He felt his face go white. His skin was ice-cold. He had hoped against hope that he would see Gordon but he hadn't been prepared for it.

They stared at each other, neither moving nor speaking. Then Gordon walked slowly over to Mallini.

"Where's your little friend?" Gordon asked. "The Arab boy you finally got over to the States. Azziz. . . . That's his name, isn't it? Pretty name. I understood you kept him with you all the time."

Mallini could barely speak. "It didn't work out with Azziz," he finally managed. "I sent him back to Tangier."

"Too bad."

"I didn't expect it would work out."

Neither was looking at the other now. Each was careful to keep his tone of voice cordial but not eager, as he might with somebody he didn't know very well.

"Congratulations," Gordon said. "Your photographs in the exhibit are some of the best."

"Have you seen the whole exhibit?"

Their eyes met.

There was a photograph on exhibit that showed Serena's face and throat and part of one shoulder emerging from folds of deep brown velvet. She was wearing a wide gold neckplate. It was a blowup of the first cover that Mallini had made of Serena for *Milady*. Out of all the photographs he had made for *Milady* over the years, it was the one he had proposed first for the exhibit. The small white placard beneath it had two lines of print: "Jewelry by Gordon Knightsplit." "Photograph by Antonio Mallini."

Gordon's voice was low. Mallini could barely hear him. "I saw the picture, Tonio."

Tears stung Mallini's eyes at the sound of Gordon's voice calling him Tonio. "I was afraid you wouldn't get to see it. I thought you hadn't come."

"I didn't plan to. I sent regrets. But then. . . . Well, I'm here."

Both made little gestures. Neither knew what to say.

"How have you been, Gordon?"

"So-so. . . . So-so. . . ."

"You look . . ."

Gordon smiled slightly. "Like myself?"

Mallini trembled, remembering that night of horror when he had wrecked his life, reliving the sight of Gordon, lying bleeding over the back of the chair and then being carried away so white and still. "Yes. Like yourself."

"Miracle man, Nash."

Mallini moved closer to him. "There's a scar under your eyebrow. It's not very noticeable. I didn't see it until now. He ought to have gotten rid of it."

"Rather distinguishing, I think."

Gordon smiled a little more broadly. Mallini tried to smile back. "Marvena's having a few people in for supper," he said. "She always likes to have one or two people in after parties, you know. Will you come? She'd like you to come."

"I'd rather have supper at my place. What time do you think you could get away"

Mallini had to blink back tears. "I can get away by three."

Gordon smiled into Mallini's shining, grateful eyes. It would be fun to be with Tonio again. Maybe he'd make him pay for that scar. On the other hand, maybe he wouldn't. "Three then," he said.

Serena hadn't wanted to come to the exhibit, but she had been obliged to. The issue of *Milady* that had been photographed in Morocco had three photographs on view. And there were other landmark pictures of her included. She and Khalie King had the largest representation of all the models used by *Milady* over the past fifty years.

She arrived with Wells and Zoe. She hadn't wanted an escort. She had stopped seeing Stephen. She seldom went out on a date. She stayed close to Wells and Zoe all through the evening.

"There's that familiar combination," Zoe said, pointing out Helen and Tim O'Neil and Hamlisch.

"Where's the great Lorna, I wonder?" Serena said.

Zoe laughed. "She's in Australia, I believe, researching sex among the aborigines. Hamlisch isn't missing her. He's got all the company he wants."

Serena was making every effort to get out of herself and into at least a pretense of a party spirit. "Did I ever tell you I used to think he was in love with you?"

"He's never been in love with anything except preserving Models, Incorporated, intact. But Hamlisch is okay."

"*Now* he's okay. There was a time when you didn't

think he was. Can I take him off my shit list now?"

"Sure. He's been off mine ever since I met Wells."

Serena felt someone's eyes on her from across the room. She clutched Wells's arm.

"What's the matter, Serena?" Wells turned to her, immediately concerned. "Is something wrong? You don't feel well?"

Serena couldn't look at him and couldn't look across the room. "I'm all right. I think I'd like a drink. Let's find the bar and get a drink."

"You stay here. I'll get you a drink. You stay with her, Zoe."

"I'll go with you," Zoe said. When Wells started to protest, she took his arm and squeezed it as a signal to him. "I'll *go with you*, Wells." She had seen Joseph Allen start across the room toward them. She pulled at Wells's arm to hurry him.

Serena stared after them with stricken eyes. She couldn't make herself move to follow them. She hadn't looked in Joseph's direction but she felt him coming toward her. She turned and ran blindly out of the room.

It was cold in the long corridor that she found herself in. She shivered with the cold but was grateful for the shock of it against her burning face and body. She breathed in the cold air, leaning against the wall for support.

"Hello, Serena."

Her whole body reacted to the sound of his voice. She felt as she had so many times before when certain of his tones of voice made her unsure she could support herself. She was afraid to look at him. She turned her back, still leaning against the wall, shivering uncontrollably.

Joseph took off his jacket and put it over Serena's shoulders.

"Go away," she begged. "Please go away."

Joseph's hands were on her shoulders, over the

jacket. He tightened them. She felt them as if they were on her naked flesh.

"I can't," Joseph said. "I was able to do it once. But I can't do it again."

She jerked away from him and flung herself around. "What are you trying to do to me? I know you're back with your wife! Everyone knows you're back with her! It was in all the papers! It's common knowledge!"

Joseph stood with his hands at his sides until she stopped the tirade. Then he said in a quiet, firm voice, "I'm not *back* with anybody. I'm not *with* anybody. I haven't been with anybody since I was with you."

"Don't lie to me! I don't want to hear your lies!"

"Sara and I took the children on vacation together. The papers blew it up into a reconciliation. . . . I haven't changed, Serena."

Serena stared at him, tears gathering in her eyes. She felt her breath leaving her, her body going weak.

She swayed toward him. "Oh, Joseph. . . ."

His arms went around her. She cried against him, heartbroken, body-racking sobs. He held her close, his arms tight around her, kissing her hair, her forehead.

Finally, she stopped crying and was quiet. "I died that night in Marrakesh, Joseph."

"So did I, baby." Joseph's voice was choked.

Her face was still buried against him. "I'd give up anything for you, Joseph."

"You won't have to give up anything. We'll work something out. . . . Look at me, Serena."

She lifted her face to his. Joseph couldn't say what he had intended to say. He couldn't speak. His mouth went down on hers. They clung to each other straining their bodies together, sharing a deeper, more binding kiss than any they had ever shared before.

Wells looked around the room, the worry on his face deepening. "Where is she? Where could she have gone?"

Zoe had looked around the room, too, but she had been looking for Joseph. She took the drink that Wells had brought for Serena and put it on the tray of a passing waiter. "She doesn't need that now," she said.

Wells looked puzzled.

Zoe smiled at him. "And she doesn't need us. Let's go home, Wells."

Dell Bestsellers

- ☐ **RANDOM WINDS** by Belva Plain $3.50 (17158-X)
- ☐ **MEN IN LOVE** by Nancy Friday $3.50 (15404-9)
- ☐ **JAILBIRD** by Kurt Vonnegut $3.25 (15447-2)
- ☐ **LOVE: Poems** by Danielle Steel $2.50 (15377-8)
- ☐ **SHOGUN** by James Clavell $3.50 (17800-2)
- ☐ **WILL** by G. Gordon Liddy $3.50 (09666-9)
- ☐ **THE ESTABLISHMENT** by Howard Fast........$3.25 (12296-1)
- ☐ **LIGHT OF LOVE** by Barbara Cartland $2.50 (15402-2)
- ☐ **SERPENTINE** by Thomas Thompson $3.50 (17611-5)
- ☐ **MY MOTHER/MY SELF** by Nancy Friday $3.25 (15663-7)
- ☐ **EVERGREEN** by Belva Plain $3.50 (13278-9)
- ☐ **THE WINDSOR STORY**
  by J. Bryan III & Charles J.V. Murphy $3.75 (19346-X)
- ☐ **THE PROUD HUNTER** by Marianne Harvey ..$3.25 (17098-2)
- ☐ **HIT ME WITH A RAINBOW**
  by James Kirkwood $3.25 (13622-9)
- ☐ **MIDNIGHT MOVIES** by David Kaufelt $2.75 (15728-5)
- ☐ **THE DEBRIEFING** by Robert Litell $2.75 (01873-5)
- ☐ **SHAMAN'S DAUGHTER** by Nan Salerno
  & Rosamond Vanderburgh $3.25 (17863-0)
- ☐ **WOMAN OF TEXAS** by R.T. Stevens $2.95 (19555-1)
- ☐ **DEVIL'S LOVE** by Lane Harris $2.95 (11915-4)